D1483712

CYTHERA

CYTHERA

Richard Calder

St. Martin's Press ✿ New York

ISBN 0-312-18074-8

First published in Great Britain by Orbit, a
division of Little, Brown and Company (UK)

First U.S. Edition: May 1998

10   9   8   7   6   5   4   3   2   1

For Nik

'To do what is forbidden
always has its charms,
because we have an indistinct
apprehension of something
arbitrary and tyrannical in
the prohibition.'

William Godwin, *Caleb Williams*

PART ONE

THE
EMBARKATION

CHAPTER ONE

Rising from a shelf of permanent ice – a glass ocean surrounded by dawn-drenched glaciers – the city began to displace the horizon like a couchant sphinx readying itself to spring. The neon-beaded highway snaked in and out of the Bentley's lights, the prismatic sheen of the road inducing a slurry of tiredness in my eyes, the desolation of McMurdo Sound viewed as if through lashes sodden with gasoline. Dahlia leaned across the upholstery, swung a thigh over my own and put the Bentley into fourth. Jarred, the glove compartment flapped open, spilling soiled underwear, make-up, a .22 auto, hypodermic, speculum and food-ration cards. Tall buildings rushed towards us – folds, waves and twists, the fractured

planes and multiple trajectories of cosmogenic archi-
tecture that clung like monstrous, rococo vegetation to the
more familiar overtures of the International Style – and
then we were under the sphinx's crystalline paws,
thundering through the abandoned ruins of the city
limits. The car's heaters were insolent; they were down-
right wanton; the air seemed alive, febrile with the
contrapuntal buzzing of flies. Dahlia, unconsoled, pressed
herself against me, greedy for the other-earthly warmth
which the rising sun would soon rescind. I felt the gelid
deliciousness of a breast through her furs. My loins
hardened. Had fifteen years in His Majesty's secure
institutions proved sanative? No; I had been free just
fifteen weeks and I was again her slave. On the dashboard
I had pinned a photograph from the pages of *Vogue* or *Elle*
that depicted a half-dozen sloe-eyed supermodels
sprawling, lounging and provocatively draped amongst
the grey, petrified ruins of Auschwitz-Birkenau; and it
occurred to me as I drove that the history of the modern
world, my history, perhaps, was like one long frenzied act
of coupling, its twenty-first century orgasm all that I had
known, no foreplay, just a timeless explosion of white
heat, this checkmate of sex amongst the ruins. 'Spare me
the dildonics, spare me the cojone-baloney,' said Dahlia,
in a *touché* to my thoughts, 'just get me to a karaoke. Fast.'
Throughout late summer the light pouring over the
glaciers and mountains had hit at too sharp an angle to
warm ice or flesh; still we had had to run from the dawn;
even now, as the continent rolled towards perpetual night,
daybreak, however anaemic, signalled meltdown. I
switched off the Bentley's lamps. All those movies, *A
Princess of Death, Kung-Fu Nymphet from Hell, The*

Kingdom of Childhood, A Chinese Killer Virgin in LA.
Dahlia was accustomed to more torrid climes. 'The sun's
almost up. I can feel the UV disrupting my atomic structure.' An anxious bass line started up inside my skull,
found its way down my neck, along my arm until,
transposed into a tic by my ghost's burgeoning incorpo-
reality (she, one of the fibresphere's damned; a copy
divorced from its original; fame evolved into a separate,
alien form of life; a new morphology congealed out of
the mediascape, the hyperuniverse that interpenetrates
our own) my fingers began to paradiddle against the dash.
'Hurry. I'm starting to dissolve.' Signs of habitation began
to manifest themselves; became insistent. Frantically, I
scouted for a place where Dahlia could discorporate.

Just as there are, in any city, karaokes that boast a
catalogue of the damned – those illicit ghosts that
constitute the fibresphere's dispossessed – so too, in
McMurdo City, this frigid oasis at the bottom of the world,
there were establishments where the patron, if less
illicitly, then just as damnably, perhaps, might adulate,
consort with or simply wham-bam-and-thank-you-ma'am
a favourite spectre, a refugee from Earth2.

I braked; the Bentley slewed, came to a halt. The
sign (its neon just blinking out, the city suffused in an
amber glow) read *Les Enfants Terribles.*

Touching Dahlia's face, my fingers disappeared
into a luminous epidermis, her body waxing insubstantial, holographic. I felt dizzy. My heart began to
palpitate as it did when I awoke with a panic, a night
fright, thinking I was about to die, alone and friendless,
still incarcerated in the chill environs of Boys Town. I
put a hand over my chest, trying to moderate my heart's

overwrought gymnastics by an act of will.

I got out, passed between the karaoke's Doric columns; a boy tugged at my sleeve. 'Don't you see the sign?' he said. Several other little pimps congregated about me until they blocked my way. 'This is the kingdom of childhood,' the boy continued, 'the kingdom of love and of death. The ladies are resting. Try later. Try tonight.' He was Algerian; Egyptian, maybe, like most of the boys in this slice of the continent; a demobbed soldier, a veteran of the North-South wars. I cast a backwards glance. Inside the car, Dahlia – trying vainly to cover herself as she deliquesced into a parallel world of intelligent light – was little more than a scintillant flock of submicroscopic machines, her clothes, even her flesh, already reassimilated by The Wound. I looked up and down the street, contemplating violence. No cirrocumulus that morning, only a merciless, hallucinatory sun that saturated the albatrosses and petrels milling about the garbage dumps, shacks and forsaken dives clinging to the roots of the organitech-clad towers: jagged, inverted icicles cloistering those who – grown fat on unregulated oil and mineral exploitation, yet not fat enough to return home – continued to live on a diet of rapine, comforted by their other selves, the runaways of a world encoded within reality's mirrors. I had to gain admittance; about me all was dereliction; *Les Enfants* was probably the only operative karaoke in the Sound.

'The kingdom,' I said, grinning, 'of childhood, eh? Well, I have an eidolon in the limo, a princess of death, a girl called Dahlia Chan.' Some of the beefier lads folded their arms across their chests, signalling their determination to keep me from entering. 'You must have heard of her: she was a Hollywood icon, a gingerbread rock 'n' roll *star.*' But that had been many years ago; none of these boys was old enough to appreciate the High Camp of a cult property. 'Me and Dahlia - we're looking for work.' Peering over their heads I inspected a musty interior. Oblique rays of mote-filled light fell from high, stained-glass windows; the furniture was covered in sheets. I pushed my way through the infant cordon - nylon doors unseamed, closed; a second set of doors followed suit - passed a chain gang of surfers, datacapped, gigging-out on their vacs, little talent scouts seeking newly emergent morphologies, these children resembling spacemen, the victims of a mad hairdresser's experiments, over-zealous electric chair quality-control engineers. I plucked an oily morsel from a half-demolished buffet of baby penguin and krill; breakfasted as I swung through three-hundred-and-sixty degrees, surveying. Framed, antique photographs of Isa Bowman, Dorothy Gale and Sailor Moon hung behind the ornate bar; there were photographs of derricks and mines too, roustabouts posing in the foreground. A banner read: *If you can't afford to tip, go back to the land of censorship.* Satisfied that *Les Enfants* provided suitable refuge, I retraced my steps; confronted the boys; exhaled a homicidal miasma into their contumacious faces. 'I'm like you.' I pulled off a glove, held up my thumb and revealed to them the mark of the paternoster. 'I know what it is to live in fear.' The pubescent hustlers fixed me with sullen, frosted brows; convened a parliamentary scrum.

My teeth and extremities throbbing with a brutal ache, my nerves overtaxed, ready to blow, I traipsed back to the Bentley, adjusting my jumpsuit's thermostat as its coils struggled to protect me from the -30˚ C cold. Before I could open the door, Dahlia, now wholly spectral, slipped impatiently through metal and glass; as she walked ahead, desperate to set herself behind the sanctuary of those kitsch, fake marble walls, I could almost hear The Wound calling to her, that locus in space-time where information became live, where the fibresphere bled into our own world; the site of sites that was everywhere and nowhere and which – her simulacrum disintegrating – was consuming her, deporting her piecemeal back to the collective images from which she had sprung. 'I know him,' Dahlia muttered to the pimps, 'really, it's all right. He's my driver. He's done time for me.' One of the boys, the boy I had spoken with, their leader, it seemed, made a unilateral decision, broke off from the pack and led us through the karaoke's shrouded lounge, then, his crew outflanking us, smoked Plexiglas surrendering to their stampede, its VIP lounge – so like a raped jewellery box, all cracked mirrors, torn brocades, ruined filigree and silks, its treasure scattered, ruined – and up a flight of stairs. Skipping into a darkened room he gestured for us to follow; a dormitory of spooks – a dozen or more Translators glowing softly with interned fugitives from Earth2, children of the fibresphere who, like my own child, had outshone, sometimes outlived, their originals – stretched before us. The boy opened the lid of an empty coffin and Dahlia – a post-infinite number of tiny, dancing lights, a bright cloud of Heraclitian flux – lay down, closed her eyes. Within moments her dissolution stabilized; the warp between worlds, the limbo that would, come nightfall, allow her to re-access Earth Prime, cradled her in exostasis. I leaned against a wall; slid down to the rubber floor. The boy sat opposite, his back against a Translator, the image of a tomb-robber's assistant.

'We go from karaoke to karaoke,' I said, 'worked most of the Antarctic Peninsula. Last place we hit was Marie Byrd Land. You heard of *Bébé Fantôme*? *Electra's*? *Kindertotenlieder*? We did two weeks at *Kindertotenlieder*.'

'I've heard there was a mass suicide in Marie Byrd Land. Sometimes, you can't escape. The memories follow you. Are memories all that's following you, effendi?'

I massaged my jaw in an attempt to soothe my aching teeth, clenched, then unclenched, a fist. How do you train a dog? You rub its nose in its own shit then spank it. The world needed its nose rubbed in its own shit now and then – the Town doctors were always telling me I had a Big Mouth – but spanking, that's not my purview. Machismo – my own perfidious, artificial body – evaporated. How could I tell them I'd broken parole? They might understand my crimes; they might sympathize; but I couldn't expect them to freely offer safe haven; like their ghosts, their refugee status in the city states strung along the Trans-Antarctic Highway was continually threatened by diplomatic pressure from topside.

If only I could rest up. A little therapy, a course of Xanax, a few weeks on a beach ...

The boy studied me with death-obsessed eyes. 'Memories,' I said. 'Yeah: the witch-hunts, the abuse, the straitjacket on the imagination.' Decadent, candyass whingeing, I knew, to one such as him. 'But I guess it was tougher for you guys.' A piece of shrapnel was lodged under his right cheek, gleaming like polished bone. Kids made such exquisite killers. Small, precipitate, malleable; better soldiers than adults. Kidnap them; seduce them with ghosts; they'll do anything you ask. But if these children had become fundamentalists, then it was

Hollywood, the Empire *De Luxe*, the transnationalism of glamour, sex and money that they had dreamed of as martyrdom's prize; Islam had never inspired such fanaticism. Muslim radicals, from whose loins these boy warriors had sprung, had represented a dying fall, a religion on the defensive, the last gasp of a culture that had lost confidence in itself. In their innermost selves, they had wanted to be like us and had hated themselves for that want, that need, that lust. Hated the knowledge that paradise was for those who consumed.

'Sure is tougher. All you been done for is collaboration, eh? Our ghosts and we been through hell, man. Our masters told us we were going to get the goods' – an embarrassed hiatus – 'told us we'd have more food than we could eat, just like the people on TV. And not just food. The life, man, the *life*. But it was all lies.' How could they have ever hoped to win? The North held the world's purse strings; it dictated to the South, gorging itself on the Third World's raw material. The child crusade had been chaotic, its battle plan more akin to riot than strategy. How could they have successfully warred against the *conquistadores* of development, advertising and the media when they had so lusted after what they would destroy?

These boys and their masters had wanted a Northern life such as I had enjoyed; but they had been afforded only glimpses, the tantalizing simulacra of paradise; they had wanted it all.

I pulled off my balaclava. 'Please, I need to sleep. I've been driving all night.' I didn't want to be interrogated; I was tired of dissembling. As I thawed, my face – I knew – was sure to crack, sure to combust like a leaky, miasmic graveyard.

"Straitjacket on the imagination"?' The boy had imitated my accent, assuming the cadences of 'bibelot', the prêt-à-porter streethowl of the *De Luxe*, the plummy, razor-blade rhetoric of one raised in a world of sinister elegance. He smirked, pressing his advantage. 'All you ever had was a rap over the knuckles.' 'More than that,' I snapped. 'I was a whipping boy for their insanity.' I instantly regretted my loss of temper – made my excuses with a neurasthenic sigh; I needed to ingratiate myself, show that I offered no threat. 'You know how the law is. I was evil, they said, but at the same time they thought I was a *tabula rasa* corrupted by too much surfing, too many violent *anime*. Now, I ask you, I'm either evil, that is, I have committed an evil act of my own volition, or else I'm innocent, and the blame lies in the hands of the image-world. But they wanted it both ways. I was evil because I was possessed; I was possessed because I was evil; and I had to be punished to drive the demon out. Positively *medi*eval.' They blamed the Dahlia videos. The videos and the Dahlia comics. The comics and the Dahlia site on the Net. And they blamed me. Blamed me for being *possessed.* There's that scene in *A Chinese Killer Virgin in LA* where ... But they blamed children for everything in those days. Still did, of course, otherwise I wouldn't have been having this conversation with a fellow outcast. 'But I tell you, it wasn't Dahlia's fault.' No; the danger wasn't in the fibresphere. It never is. The danger was at home.

Decadent? Candyass?

I too had been a killer.

I had always known that, someday, somehow, I would have to murder my stepfather. It was a passion I had kept too long to myself; not out of shame, but because I always took such pleasure in knowing things, terrible things, unspeakable things, that other people would not even dare to suspect. Dinner was the hour when it became hardest to camouflage my secret. Suffering my stepfather's sarcasm, his hideous opinions, his cant, I would chew each portion of my meal into pap in an effort to restrain declaring myself. *'Stepfather,'* I had wanted to say, *'not today, not tomorrow, and not even next week or next month, but some day, and surely some day soon, I will destroy you ...'*

Dahlia had been my only friend.

I put my head in my hands; melting snow seeped between my fingers. 'I've just got out of Boys Town. What else do you need to know? I've done ghost wedding and I've been punished for it. I'm the same as you.' Yeah, I thought ruefully, a killer, and a pimp to boot. 'Please, you must help.' A choir of demi-castrati; I looked up; several boys had gathered in the doorway, mewling like celestial brats.

'Sure,' said their leader, loosening his greatcoat, playing to the mob of cherubs manqué, 'everybody here mixed with The Censors. Everybody done Boys Town, been deprogrammed, dis*possessed.* But how come you in the Town so long, effendi? You old, man, you old.' My interlocutor would have been from the original Boys Town, the POW gulag that wormed across the world's demographic-technological fault line, the schism that divided the Mediterranean, the Rio Grande, the Slavic and non-Slavic, Australia and Indonesia. As The Great Fear had spread, so had the gulag, its aggrandizement along the borders of the young, overpopulated societies of the South matched by the extent to which it insinuated itself into the heartlands of the North. 'But then you all old, man, you all rich, geriatric.' I remembered TV pictures of the crusade, the ant-like armies of children, that, until recently, had surged upwards towards the borders of the developed world, wave after wave; children from Africa, Asia, Latin America; I remembered how childhood itself had become stigmatized; from my Elsinore of Holland Park, London, I was taken to the encampment on Bodmin Moor where I was to spend the next fifteen years, an eleven-year-old who, like so many others to follow, had provided governments with the excuse they needed to consolidate their authoritarianism.

'Yeah, I'm old,' I said. I was twenty-six. 'I was there at the beginning, when quantum computers first went on line.' When programs – patterns of light cavorting through the fibresphere – were first translated into nanomachines, streams of quasi-particles and photons that were to infect the quotidian world. 'My family was one of the first to have a stepfather.' A fat man, he'd been, a lank-haired, thin-lipped censor in a long black coat that resembled a soutane. *He's here to help*, my real father had said, after we had returned from Laos. *He's going to watch over you.* From protecting children from images to demonizing and persecuting them was – given the footage of global delinquency transmitted each night, clips of black and brown adolescent hordes committing atrocities on Europe's doorstep – perhaps but one short hop, a cosmogenic leap paralleling the leap to consciousness and flesh in the self-organizing universe of the fibresphere. Perhaps protection and persecution had always amounted to the same thing: control. 'They used us as an excuse to censor the world.' I bit on my tongue, a part of me too eager to reveal how, one night, when my stepfather had surprised me as I gained veristic access to an intelligence - an enemy of my country, the ineffable Dahlia Chan - and was about to download her from The Wound, I had picked up a screwdriver, skewered him through his throat, his chest, again, and again, and again ...

I crawled over to Dahlia's coffin; her monitor had winked alive.

'Dahlia? Can you hear me?'

'I can hear you, Zane.' Was that what I was calling myself this morning? So many names. Zane Weary. Max Moroder. Jack Pimpernel. So many towns ... Dahlia's face compounded; looked at me from out of the white, featureless plain of limbo, her Eurasian eyes - like black pearls mounted in a gold-paisley surround - branding the LCD with their scorching crescents. Had a version of her ever fought alongside the children of Laos, in the deadly, degraded countryside of once poppied hills? Or had her tawny skin prejudiced companionship, as it had similarly incurred the ostracism of the North? She would never say.

'Do we have a job?' I looked across at pimp *numero uno.*

'Okay, you can have a job. Don't know yet if you're one of the boys, but if you done ghost wedding you no infidel, that's for sure. We can't afford big money. Board and lodging, a few extras. The Translator's free.' He stared, quizzical, into Dahlia's two-dimensional countenance. 'But tell me, can she sing?'

'Like a phoenix.' I took from my pocket some of my Dahliana: movie stills, dog-eared comic books, yellowing articles ripped from Lao-American fanzines, information which constituted the superprogram of her simulacrum; information radiating intelligent light – the souvenirs rippled with sentience; stilled – which, slow as we'd been this morning to thwart the dawn, had reabsorbed some of her fame. 'See: she's a superstar.' Some of the monitors on the other coffins lit up with tanned, Californian faces, forgotten extras, doubtless, said the snob in me, body doubles and fifteen-minute starlets. 'Different idiom, of course, to what you might be used to. But–'

'She Chinese,' said a boy from the door, 'why you no have *white* ghost?' Pimp uno silenced him with a moue. 'Remember where you are. Remember who you are. In all things, *égalité*,' he whispered. He knew too well that white, black, brown or yellow, a ghost – like those they haunted – enjoyed, at best, a para-legal status; was, at worst, an outlaw. He rose; walked towards me; extended a hand. 'We could do with a little multiculturalism. Patrons here seen enough white flesh. How long can you stay?'

'Two weeks, three maybe–'

'And after that?'

I looked up, bemused. 'Why,' I said, 'Cythera, of course. We're trying to find Earth3.' And this time I wasn't dissembling. The boy grinned; there was *faux* girlish laughter from the doorway.

'Yes,' he said, 'maybe you *are* like us after all.' Even though linear history was over I still clung to the mythic possibility of its dialectic; for wasn't Cythera supposed to be a synthesis of Earths 1 and 2, a place where the real and the artificial became indistinguishable, where the body and the spirit became as one?

'Cythera?' said Dahlia. 'I'm not sure any more if it

exists. All I know is I want to go home.' I kissed her enpixeled lips, my cheek brushing against the ossified carcass of a spider hanging from a dilapidated web. As I retracted from the arachnid's viscous graveyard I saw that Dahlia was crying. 'I don't mean I want to go back to Earth2,' she continued, addressing the room and its buzz of parliamentarians. 'All I remember of that is the persecution. The things they did to us over there.' Her voice crackled with static. 'Not that life's any different on Earth Prime.' She was right, of course; existence, as I have learned, is just one huge, inescapable prison; children were being demonized in the image-world for consorting with 'ghosts' ('ghosts', that is, such as myself) who, in reciprocation of our own world's prejudices, were considered to be as dangerous and as unreal as we considered the ghosts of the fibresphere; no escape; no matter how ingenious, an inmate would always find themselves, just at the moment of breaking through a wall, tunnelling beneath a fence, or bluffing a passage through the main gates, confronted by another prison, more cells, racks, corridors, halls and torments; and even after breaking through what might have seemed like an ultimate barrier, the last wall or fence that hemmed them from the outside world, they would soon discover that that mountain vista, that great city or that valley beneath a clear blue sky, was but another room, another prison within a prison, that that city, mountain range and valley were fakes, theatrical props, and that they would always be denied freedom unless they might step through a crack in time and space, step beyond those universes within universes entirely; step into Cythera. 'I just want to go home – even if it's to a home I've never had.'

I stared at the monitor. It was as if I was again that

birthday boy who, one sulphurous, tropical night on Avenue Lan Xang, had accessed her for the first time on his brand-new superconducting quantum PDA, ever after to dream that she would one day walk through the walls of his bedroom; that, like an angel, she had come to set him free; and if I had then recognized her as one who was at once nobility, elevation, beauty, life, I would later recognize her as one who was also an angel of death. Back in England, surreptitiously logging onto her site – watching her movies, hearing her songs, speaking to her – I knew my stepfather had to die. Dahlia had said so.

'It'll be dark all the time, soon,' I said. 'The winter's almost here. Then we'll find Cythera and we can be together always.'

Each morning, finding myself in my bedroom, a datacap encasing my head, I had known that she was still on the other side, a vactress, a creature of the fibresphere, that a prick of a hypo in my neck, a rush of information – images enhanced by the little dream machines that twiddled the knobs and switches of my consciousness – had had me following a prompt.

I had had to download her; I had had to run away.

The future, even if mythical, was all we had; the past, too, was just another prison.

I felt an arm under my own; as I was helped to my feet I discovered that I myself was crying.

'We all want to go to Cythera, effendi. I am Baptiste. Come – I'll show you to a room.'

Later, as I tried to sleep between spells of sneaking to the window, opening the chromium blinds to scour the streets for signs of pursuit, I lay on the mattress, trawled the cold, dark currents of my mind, all memories but one eluding me, from abyss to abyss the flux of selfhood but for that bright engram of patricide, lost.

When I awoke I was staring into the face of the man I had killed fifteen years earlier. He stood at the foot of my bed, impenetrably dark sunglasses completing an ensemble of black robe and surcingle worn over heavy-duty thermoware; his natural rotundity, thus supplemented, presented a caricature, a dream-like exaggeration of the gross, ever-looming figure that had rebuked and finally broken my childhood. I closed my eyes; reopened; but unlike ghosts, dreams cannot so easily pass from world to world; my stepfather was indubitably corporate, the substantivity of his presence accentuated, made almost carnal, by the fact that he was levelling a double-barrelled handgun at my head.

'Sorry, effendi, you should have told us. Everybody here done time enough. We can't harbour no trouble-makers.' Pimp uno withdrew to a corner of the room. He had exchanged his winterweights for a *djellaba* and exhibited the sexual fatalism of a white pawn about to be 'taken' by an opposing bishop.

'I told you that watching so much violence would end in tears.'

'I killed you.'

'You *tried* to kill me.' He pulled down his collar and displayed the scars of several puncture wounds. 'No; I'm not a spook – I've never had my fifteen minutes!' He hyperventilated, the afflatus upon him. 'But you cannot so easily be rid of me. Your stepfather will always be with you. Until the end of time.' His breath steadying, the fat gauleiter essayed a laugh and turned to Baptiste. 'Ran away when he was eleven. Picked up in under forty-eight hours.'

'I, I—' My childhood stammer had returned. I groped, seeking a screwdriver. But the only screwdrivers were in my stepfather's eyes as he turned to gimlet me with his stare; still he maintained his conversation with our audience of one. 'Good parents. Rich too. His other father was a diplomat. Retired after we broke off relations with Indochina. And both parents now dead. At least they've been spared *further* disappointment.' He reached down towards my throat; but instead of throttling me he gripped the silver foil blanket and pulled it free of my hands; tossed it onto the floor with an inquisitorial flourish, so that I lay revealed, as I had done similarly on other murky nights, naked but for my underwear, my secrets all his. Paralysis spread from my tongue to my body, my arms and legs; overcame me, as it would do when I was a child. 'We publicised his crime as murder to bolster public support – to allow us to expand our surrogate parenthood. Would that you boys had had such a program. It might have saved everybody a lot of trouble. But with no one to keep you from resinning, well ...'

'You'll not censor us here,' said Baptiste, 'you have no jurisdiction. Just take him and go.'

My stepfather sat down on the bed, took a small torch out of his pocket. 'And still playing with ghosts?' he whispered. 'I had expected better from a European boy.' He prised open an eyelid and brought his own eye close. 'You've led me quite a dance. Your trail went cold in Marie Byrd. Ah, all those so-called suicides – such a waste of life! I'd thought to myself, yes, yes, my boy's been up to his tricks again. But mass exterminations or no, there are, luckily for me, amongst your kind always those ready to provide intelligence.' He flicked on the beam; I flinched. 'Yes, I can see it. The alien. Still burnt into your retina. Still alive and well after all these years.' He clasped me by the temples; shook my head. 'Out, out demon! Thing of violence and pornography! Anarch of passion – begone!' He released me; I crashed back into the pillow. And then I felt a hand, cold, wet, against my thigh; his voice had once again become a horripilant whisper. 'Inside you, energumen, is a terrible liberty, a bestial freedom. Your imagination is overheated, sick.' He gazed towards the ceiling. But towards what? He believed in little, I knew. God and Satan were, for him, the king of irrelevant sanctity and the prince of puerile desire – goodbye 'God' and 'Satan'. His faith seemed to lie in a divine principle of *curativeness*, his eyes raised on high towards a Supreme Fatherhood of moral and social uniformity. 'Restore him! Reintegrate him into our family! Redeem the child inside the man!'

'Enough.' Baptiste tried to invest his voice with such weight as he had displayed when talking with me. 'You may continue this talk after you leave Antarctica.'

'You realize, of course, that I have the co-operation of your local militia?'

'You think they like helping you? Don't press your luck, Mr Decency Policeman. I want you to leave. Now.'

'I want his ghost as well, you understand?'

'Dahlia – no!' I yelled. 'On Earth2 she has a wicked ste, ste, ste, *stepmother*!' He grabbed my hair, wrenching me into a sitting position.

'She has to be sent back. Even as I'm going to send you back to Boys Town. She's an illegal.' He stood up, pulling me with him. The gun behind my ear, he walked me to the door. Baptiste lead us down the hallway. From downstairs I heard his gang of pimps touting for custom.

'Consensual hallucination – it's passé!'

'Welcome to ghost land!'

'Cyberspace gives way to fibrespace!'

'See the Creatures of The Wound!'

'Optikoids, self-assembled from the stuff of the fibresphere, from machines so small they are little more than points of light!'

'See the scintillant ones!'

My stepfather grimaced. 'Such turpitude. There must always be rules of desire. A ghost is an enemy ... All ghosts are enemies. They work for both sides. They work for anyone.'

'The wars are over.'

'Not *this* war.' No; not this undeclared war against children. The Great Fear – the fear of children, their demonization – had too many uses.

What was the time? How long had I slept? I didn't know, but the encroaching winter, along with my wish to spend as many hours with Dahlia as possible, had resulted in weeks, months, during which I seldom got much rest. Guestimating wildly – two or three hours was my usual allocation of sleep – I prayed that Dahlia was near to projection.

We reached the crypt of the sleeping beauties; entered. The monitors swam with fractals, light cones whorling towards their omega points. 'It's for your own good,' said my stepfather, 'we must exorcize her.' He pushed Baptiste into the centre of the room. 'Which one is she?' The pimp walked over to a coffin and made a wake-up call. Dahlia crystallized on the LCD.

'What's going on?' she said.

'It's my stepfather. He's come back.'

'*That* jerk?'

'Khun Dahlia Chan,' said he. 'How many times do I have to destroy you?'

'I'm not the same version,' said Dahlia. 'I'm the star of *A Princess of Death, Kung-Fu Nymphet from Hell, The Kingdom of Childhood—*'

'Etcetera – Oh, I know, I know. I sent the simulacrum of your earlier years as a couture model back to Earth2 some time ago, didn't I?'

'Z'right. To Girls Town, you bastard.'

'My,' he said, looking at me, 'but you started early. How old is this version I'm talking to now?'

'She's twelve,' I said.

'Mmm. You always did prefer older women. I expect the very first thing you did when you were released was start hacking into forbidden sites, eh? The alien in your soul: it threatens our most dearly purchased values; it threatens the annihilation of *society.*'

'Leave him alone,' said Dahlia, 'he's my friend!'

'Couldn't even choose a white ghost. Had to find yourself a little girl from the South.'

My stepfather was unused to the diurnal rhythms of Antarctica. By the display at the bottom of Dahlia's monitor I could tell my silent entreaties had found my tutelary gods' ears – call them, if you will, Don X, Ishmael, Pym, Wendy Darling, Gilles de Rais; whomsoever they were, whatsoever their mandate, my natural father's evil twin had over-estimated the amount of daylight at his disposal.

'*Leave him alone!*'

The coffin's glow intensified.

Nota: A Translator is a modem that converts patterns of light into nanomachines; nanomachines into patterns of light. They had long been proscribed, for they not only provided a gateway for illegal aliens but could be modified to prevent a rogue simulacrum from dissolving into the infected, ultraviolet radiation that encoded Earth2 within Earth1: the only fail-safe – so said the governments of the World Order – protecting reality from full-scale invasion. The coffin before me – now like an array of klieg lights – was one such customized, felonious peripheral. The periodicity that it conferred on Dahlia's zillion constituents – the periodicity that offered all ghost bodies concrescence and made Dahlia more than a one-night stand – had swung into projection mode. A stream of particles gushed from the coffin's glass lid, circled the room as if inside a miniaturized synchrotron as its mortal inhabitants raised their hands before their eyes. The stream cascaded from the ceiling, coalesced in the room's centre; became a pillar of polychromatic light. My stepfather loosed off both barrels of his handgun; the titanium bullets shattered a wall, exposing ferrous latticework. And then, a blinding coruscation; and the pillar assumed the dimensions of a young girl. She wore the skin-tight polyvinyl rumpus suit that was part of her wardrobe in *A Chinese Killer Virgin in LA*; a domino hid her partiracial eyes (the pupils so big, her gaze resembling the doll-like scrutiny of a shark); and across her back hung a curved, Laotian sword.

Biding her time, my ghost helped herself to a little *som tam* that had materialized as she had; waved her hand in front of her mouth in approval of the spiced, unripened papaya's causticity. She was, after all, an Isan

girl and liked her food *phet-phet*. But just about everything else about Dahlia had been eclipsed by the two to
three years that had encompassed the *Chinese Killer
Virgin*'s savage rise to power. Though I had watched the
film countless times, what I knew about the *Killer Virgin*
amounted to a thumbnail sketch, the trivia of a glacial
outerness. Mignonesque, with a pageboy haircut that
accentuated a certain fickle, gamine lubricity and at the
same time, an older woman's spleen, she possessed a
sexual ambiguity so radical that it evaded all epistemo-
logical method, her identity irreducible to a simple *he* or
she, but a thing-in-itself, unknowable, beyond the
experience of the human mind; my ghost, the *Chinese
Killer Virgin* – 'Billie Lotus' a.k.a. 'Billie the Kid' – discharged
a controlled, explosive ruthlessness, a venereal omni-
potence, Billy who, at eight, had started her career as a
beauty queen, but had – through the black widow's
stratagem of copulating and then killing – quickly
progressed through the ranks of LA society, buying
friends and influence until she had achieved her present
status as a queen of the underworld. The dormitory was so
dimly lit and Dahlia now so fully projected, so deceptively
human, that I could only identify my spook by her
gold-dusted eyes, her gold-lacquered cheeks and fingernails, the heavy gold chains that hung about her neck, the
gold bracelets and rings that proclaimed, as did the
Bentley with its personalized number plates double-
parked outside – she had begged me to buy it – that she
had arrived, that she was part of that élite for whom
wealth, disregard for the law, sexual exploitation and
depravity were the hallmarks of a gilded life; that she was
untouchable and that all should fear.

'The beautiful Dahlia Chan,' gurgled my stepfather.

'The *ineffable* Dahlia Chan,' I corrected.

She was more than Billy the Kid; she was the supervillainess Mistress Dragonfly, Lucrece the Gladiatorix, the punk child-warrior Cerise Cerise. She was all her mid-career films. She was an aftertrace, a myth without a medium, a representation that had been copied so many times that it had become disassociated from its original.

Where was the original Dahlia? Had she really ever had an original, or had she always been so: a copy of a copy? A mirror within a mirror within a mirror?

My stepfather retreated into the corridor; Baptiste followed.

Dahlia unsheathed her sword; jumped into the air and bounced – one, two, three times – off the dormitory's walls; ran after them, screaming.

I found myself alone amidst a posse of materializing ghosts: vactresses becoming actresses: the blonde, busty teenage vamps of a dozen B-movies who had inspired the children of the Third World to try to snatch what they had never had, the insubstantial glitter that, in the end, neither would nor could give them anything.

Circumspectly, I made my way downstairs. At first, all seemed a model of order. Framed by a proscenium of filigree and lewd entablature, the karaoke's dancers jiggled and preened themselves before a jungle of mirrors: girl-children clothed in mock eighteenth-century garb, peignoirs like mantuas, slashed to reveal underpeignoirs of gossamer, breasts thrust high by cone-shaped corsets, cleavages powdered as lead-white as their high-piled pompadours. Strobes pulsed, fluttering against them like butterflies on heat, suffering cruel wounds as they kamikazied beneath the poniards of glass slippers, lepidopterous juices spilling onto the audience, staining the rococo playground of our fellow twenty-first century rococoteers, mixing with the club's ambience of dead intimacy, dead imagination. I turned my back on the subdeb jigglers and wigglers - those indicia of suprareality - and reconnoitred amongst the roustabouts, men who liked a capital F in *Fairyland* as much as they liked it in *Fuck*. Behind hard-bitten eyes, lost children stared out. All the world, these days, wanted a second childhood; wanted - impossibly - to buy back the innocence they had never had. Europe's *De Luxe* industries had capitalized on that yearning, the millennium some kind of high-water mark for lost boys and girls, Cartier, Givenchy, Lalique, Fabergé, Coty, all the houses of the Empire *De Luxe* marketing their adult dreamstuff, the automata and other precious toys that were the magic fetishes by which entry to childhood's kingdom might be reattained. But the world's latest fetish abrogated the demand for Europe's *objets*; ready-mades of those creatures that men desired even above automata - those deathless children who could transport them to that place where time and death had no sting - were emigrating to Earth Prime in increasing numbers. The taped music stopped. Dahlia had run onto the stage, pushing the dancers aside. The sword dangled from her hand, slicked with blood.

'A song dedicated to my friend, Mr Zane Weary,' she announced, breathless. '*The Embarkation for Cythera*.' The audience donned their datacaps. Curious as to where Dahlia might be sending them, I picked up a cap from a vacant table; pulled it over my ears. As Dahlia began to sing the hypo pricked my neck; I entered the song, my consciousness following the prompt, becoming one with Dahlia's consciousness, her site; entered music and lyrics, interpretation and text, dream and reality now superimposed upon each other. Dahlia was both singer and song; and as I shared Dahlia's world, I too became at one with the song's words, its sentimental, Chinese melody. Became one with Dahlia.

> *Here, you have again reached the very anteroom*
> *of paradise.*
> *All past emotions – all fears, loves, hatreds, desires*
> *– are in equilibrium.*
> *The bliss. If only you could have remained here. If*
> *only you had never left.*
> *The years have grown heavy.*
> *You left my kingdom at the same time you left the*
> *kingdom of your childhood.*
> *You have roamed far, earned prejudice, respect,*
> *envy, hatred, fear.*
> *You have tried to forget me.*
> *But you are wounded, there is a profound*
> *dislocation at the centre of your being, and*
> *only I can cure you.*
> *You travel the wild lands now, the places war and*
> *brigandage have left waste.*
> *I am nobility, elevation, beauty, life; and know*
> *that I am also death.*
> *Beware. I am the source of the river and its delta. I*
> *am the beginning of your journey and its*
> *end ...*

*

I run to the balcony, look out over the seaport crouched at the foot of the great volcano Timor Mortis, look out over its harbour of tall ships. Refugees fight each other to gain access to the gangplanks; bodies are strewn across the quay. The surrounding countryside of woodland and meadow, recently transmogrified by mutagenic weapons of attrition into an invasive, cankerous outgrowth of Belladonna, Foxglove and Love-Lies-Bleeding – a night garden aswarm with vampiric insects – has trespassed onto the city's fire-ravished streets as far as the water's edge, streets littered with pots, pans, pestles and mortars, odd shoes, whatever has proved too burdensome for its refugees, or which – too precious to be renounced – has been lost to sudden death. The port has been under siege for ten days: ever since the terrorists of The Army of Revolutionary Flesh infiltrated the city and freed the inmates of The Children's Home. Now cannonades reduce the houses to husks; incendiaries turn the plazas into lakes of boiling stone. The firestorm sweeps the population towards the harbour and the salvation of the tall ships. I make my way downstairs, join the panicking multitudes that swell towards the sea. As I reach the quayside I see that the man-made islet – The Lighthouse of a Thousand Sighs – is already ablaze, its conflagrant alleys and subterranean chambers, its dried-up pools carpeted with desiccated lily pads, culs-de-sac of white and blue rock, its walls draped with the roots of banyan trees, its sculpture gardens of cracked stucco and fused glass, shadows and perspectives reminiscent of De Chirico, all circumscribed, now, by plumes of black smoke, tongues of prurient flame. And those bright tongues lick at the masts and sails of the clippers. From somewhere, out of the smoke, the flames, a woman's voice – a bird-woman's voice of pentatonic runs, elisions and quarter tones – is rising high, clear and liquid over the gongs, chimes and xylophones of a South-East Asian orchestra; and though she sings in an unfamiliar language, I become one with the song's deep, underlying grammar, the universal grammar of death. She is calling me away, away to Cythera ...

> *I am nobility, elevation, beauty, life; and know*
> *that I am also death.*
> *Beware. I am the source of the river and its delta. I*
> *am the beginning of your journey and its end.*

I tore off the datacap, aware of Dahlia's intentions. The patrons of *Les Enfants Terribles* had been transported to the edge of the world, a place of infernal energy. And now Dahlia's seductive nightmare was luring them beyond, to a nexus where flesh and fantasy became one. Teetering on the edge, I had felt the backdraught. I elbowed my way through the crowd; leapt over the bar; unhooked an oxygen cylinder from beneath the fluorescent display. I had just put its valve to my mouth when the first case of spontaneous combustion outlit the strobes. As I ducked, screwing my eyes tight with alarm, I was left with the retinal impressions of bodies aflame, tumbling over tables, pirouetting to the accompaniment of subhuman howls, the flames spreading across the floor and ceiling as the overload of feedback generated by *The Embarkation for Cythera* scorched the brains of the karaoke's clientele, engulfing the sing-a-song in the terrible rapture that only angels, ghostly angels, the shining-most of the fibre-sphere, may confer.

We drove out of McMurdo City as the fire from *Les Enfants* spread to adjoining buildings. Behind us, shacks and depots ignited, spasming in terrific violence, spewing corrugated iron, splinters of steel and wood; flames began to leap towards the pinnacled heights, lighting the faces of those who screamed soundlessly from behind thick glass; and then the flames began to rouge the face of the sky. Thus artificially illuminated, the city seemed to be fluxing amidst a turbulence of intelligent light, that world encoded within the shimmering, atomic structures of magazine covers, advertisement hoardings, movie flyposters, the screens of TVs, VCs and PCs; another universe, a hyperuniverse that interpenetrated our own, seeping from the receptacles of the mediascape, undisturbed by the deportation order of The Day, when all deliquesced, when Earth2, diluted, was incapable of materializing, of bodying itself forth, of tearing open the membrane that separated the worlds.

The Wound was everywhere and nowhere; tonight, it bled generously; I tried not to think of the meagre hours that insulated us from the dawn, the zero hour when information would be sucked back into itself, when The Wound would cauterize.

Dahlia leaned against my shoulder, fully assembled, physical, real as this continent's big cold vacancy. 'He's gone for good now. Relax.'

'He came back – he said he would always come back.'

'Forget him. It's easy. I've forgotten my stepmother.'

I put my arm around her, my fingers running through

the pelts of luxuriant furs that smothered her small but prescient body. Forget him? It had been easier to forget my parents than my stepfather. In the rear-view mirror towers – white, glistening – began to collapse, dripping like melting popsicles; in waves of convection, a spirit, like that of a cremated sphinx, had taken flight, its shrill cry like the grinding of ice, a winged spectre that was the cruel, guardian spirit of McMurdo City; and then the city itself exploded into light, just as reality had exploded some fifteen years ago when the fibresphere had first infected us. 'You saved me,' I said.

'We saved each other. Always have. You rescued me from Earth2, and I intend to rescue you from Earth1.'

'I'm your slave.' She flashed me an ironic, refractory slave-girl grin.

'You're my friend. I'll haunt you. I'll always haunt you.'

'Promise?' The Bentley's cleated wheels rumbled against the heated surface of the highway. The black *nada* of the Ross Ice Shelf surrounded us; above, a diamond-riddled sky. I aimed the car at the horizon where Mt Erebus rose from the frozen bay, broody, disgorging fumes.

Or was it Timor Mortis? Dahlia's pyromaniacal song kept replaying itself in my head.

'Promise.'

'Where to now?'

'To wherever it takes.'

I had looted a Translator from the pyre of *Les Enfants*. Thus equipped, we had greater freedom; we could rest up where we chose. To Wilkes Land, then? To Queen Maud? Or back to Marie Byrd, Ellsworth and the karaoke-rich Riviera of the Antarctic Peninsula?

The world was a cold place – no matter where you travelled, you suffered its chill. Dahlia swung a thigh over mine – time yet for dildonics, for cojone-baloney – and put the Bentley into fourth.

To Cythera, I thought.

CHAPTER TWO

They were days of spiritual hunger, when the ever-receding horizon was forever making promises that, soon, soon, all would be dark, and darkness would be sweet and perpetual. Dahlia would sleep, entombed in the Bentley's capacious boot, and each nightfall I would be transformed into a resurrection man, disinterring her from her mausoleum, breaking open her coffin, so that we might enjoy whatever hours we had together, bivouacked on the moon-bleached plain, or ensconced in some abandoned station along the highway. Always the white canvas of the icescape seemed to invite us to plunge deeper into its blinding perspective of nothingness, violet dunes conjuring mirages of magnificent, stress-buckled oceans, at the edge of which lay the magic isle which we sought, Cythera, land of polymorphous love. As the nights lengthened and we felt the terror of the white night-time recede, our hunger grew keen, for we apprehended the trembling of a veil. Falling stars rent the sky; exploding stars, catherine-wheel stars, stars that would sing, curse, cry hosannah; and the moon seemed to burn a hole through the notilucent clouds that hung from the black vault, revealing a brightness that could not harm, that promised conciliation. I steered the Bentley towards uncharted, sugar-glazed borderlands that I could only glimpse by shutting my eyes, or else by staring up at the red, yellow and white streamers of the aurora australis arcing across the velvet firmament. Dazed with longing, we prayed for a sign.

'We're lost.' Through the threshing of the wipers I discerned the manse, its outlines indistinct amidst the blizzard. I tapped the GPS. 'It's not on the map. The house, this road – none of it.' When bad weather had struck I had turned off the highway after passing a neon sign: Motel. Nosing into the dark, the track had bifurcated, luring us into a labyrinth of anonymous polar lanes until the lights of Route One had been occluded by the onslaught of the snow. 'Can this really be it, do you think?' The manse seemed to have been a rich prospector's folly, a postwestern extravaganza, an iconic representation of 'English Palladianism' transplanted from an Asian theme park brick by brick.

'Looks dead,' said Dahlia.

'I agree. It's a wonder it isn't buried.' The mullioned windows were dark; no generator was visible; and the tall chimneys that rose from the ice-caked shingles evinced neither smoke, dish nor antenna. 'A shell, I'd expect. Stripped. But I'm not sure if I can find my way back.' I edged the Bentley forward; the manse's lineations defined themselves. We were in a forecourt, black and enamelled, a quadrant of macadam freed of ice by what must have been a still active nuclear pile beneath ground. Blasted trees formed a crescent, each rampike a gangrenous forefinger rising from the rubble of its biosphere; and ice sculptures of colossal penguins, terns and porpoises ornamented the astroturf that chequered the forecourt's perimeter where artificial gardens had succumbed to permafrost. Above the front door, picked out by the car's lamps, was corroboration that this was indeed our hoped-for shelter.

'*Justinian's Lodge*,' read Dahlia, squinting through the powdery night. I slapped my palm on the horn. 'It's dead, Doc. Let's just go straight in.' I had planned to do nothing else, the fanfare proforma, a flourish; to my astonishment illumination poured through a fanlight; the door opened; and a man in a smoking jacket was silhouetted against the brilliant rectangle of the porch. After studying us for a few seconds, he beckoned. 'Doc, do I *see* what I see or what?'

'Quickly,' I murmured, 'before prudence gets the better of him.' I pulled up the hood of my parka; switched on my thermoware. Dahlia copied, then opened the glove compartment and retrieved her little pearl-handled Colt. 'Are you sure that's necessary?'

'I'm sure,' she said. 'Prudence is my middle name. I get the better of everybody. Anyway, what kind of guy stands in a doorway in serious –C like he's about to sing *Noel*?' I nodded. It was an inconceivably cold night in the middle of unimaginable solitude. The conscientious objector in me retired; I wished only for another iron so that we might be doubly tooled up, twiceover ready. I stepped out into the cruel air; screwed my eyes into slits; ran for the rectangle of light. By the time I had reached safety our provisional benefactor had already retreated into the vestibule, a short, bearish man displaying a collar-length mane of grizzly locks, a broad back clothed in bespoke tailoring.

'Don't worry about your vehicle,' he called out, as Dahlia appeared, spluttering, 'the servants will take care of it. Now come along, it's getting late and dinner is always served on schedule.' The door closed automatically, sealing us.

'You have a room?' I called, my lungs raw from my brief exertion. But he had stepped into an air lock and either could not hear or did not choose to reply.

'Well,' said Dahlia, 'what do you think?'

'I think we can't go anywhere in this storm. And sun's up in a few hours. I wouldn't want you to sleep in the car. The battery needs recharging.'

'Mmm. Wivout nuf 'lectric lickle Dahlia might get lost in limbo-land.'

'Yeah. Big brother knows best.'

We peeped through the lock's porthole; watched it disgorge its incumbent on the corridor's farther side. We followed, swallowing hard to accommodate our ears to the change in pressure. Discharged into the warm, sticky, life-supportive atmosphere that, I was soon to learn, pervaded the entire house or, rather, a house within a house – for the exterior of the manse was decorative and entirely non-functional – we set off down a narrow, meandering corridor in pursuit. I loosened my parka, the humidity overpowering, almost tropical. Climbing plants slithered up mildew-eaten walls; and from somewhere close by there was the drip, drip, drip of broken pipes, droplets of water falling through the panoply of a rain forest. I harried a fly that performed hubristic stunts before my face. Dahlia seemed to brighten, like a hothouse flower too long denied the swelter of its home. As we negotiated an L-shaped bend – I had finally punished Monsieur Fly for his arrogance; he was now a mere stain upon my hand – we were confronted by a reception desk; our host, the chatelain – for that is whom I supposed him to be – stood behind it, stooped over a keyboard.

'Name?' I produced my card. 'Ah, Dr Max Moroder.' He spoke to himself, holding the card to his eyes, keying us into the computer with his free hand. 'Iatrogenic Psychiatrist. I see ...'

'And this,' I said, 'is my beautiful young assistant, Miss Cerise Cerise.'

'*Buenas noches,*' she said, in a hoarse but becoming acknowledgement of our interrogator's Latino inflections; she reminded me, then, in her tentativeness and her desperate longing to please, of a bleary-eyed schoolgirl who had been asked to stand up in class and recite a botched homework assignment. Schoolgirl? Dahlia wore so much make-up that she might have passed as a slim, underdeveloped twenty-one-year-old; an anorexic harlot, perhaps. But only to one not given to splitting moral hairs. 'We'd like a double,' I interpolated, hoping to pre-empt any tasteless pause, any disputation that the chatelain might choose to enter into regarding his baby-faced guest's paedomorphic charms.

'You from the Peninsula?' he said, still tapping, seemingly oblivious to my bluster. 'We've had people from the Peninsula here before. *Los gringos locos*. Everybody into therapy in the Peninsula, it seems.'

'We travel wherever we're needed.'

'Needed,' he echoed, his eyebrows flexing, a finger epileptic upon the spacebar. 'Needed. Yes, needed, needed.' He looked up, suddenly animate, examining me for the first time, as if my remark had tripped a switch in an obscure, light-starved region of his brain. 'Kind of flying doctor, huh?'

'Who could forswear the scenic delights of Antarctica? No; we travel strictly by land.'

'*Vrooooom!* House calls all along the highway,' added Dahlia. 'Are you Justinian?'

'Yes I am, señorita. Justinian from Punta Arenas.' He took a key off the wall from an almost fully burdened row of hooks. 'Room 513, I think. Honeymoon Suite.' My heart leapt in thanks for his impiety. As he led the way Dahlia whispered:

'But, Doc, how are we going to pay?'

'We'll sing for our supper,' I said. 'We always do.'

'He must be two hundred years old. I hope you don't mean—'

'I'll think of something.' The chatelain swept back the lift's concertinaed doors. We entered and – the cage squeaking, juddering – were hoisted towards the manse's topmost floor. As we passed each landing I attempted to descry other guests; but the dismal hallways that branched off into the big house's shadows, while displaying signs of cursory maintenance, were devoid of sight or sound of living flesh. The lift came to a stuttering halt; the chatelain stepped out, the leather soles of his brogues snapping an indolent tattoo against cratered linoleum. Stopping only briefly to adjust a thermostat and turn on a bank of concealed lights he proceeded to lead us into the warrens of his barren domicile.

'At the height of the boom years every one of these rooms was full,' he said. 'Freelancers, mostly, out for what they could get. Titanium, gold, tin, copper, zinc, uranium. And always the coal, of course. The coal and the oil. It was in the coalfields that I found *my* El Dorado. But now only the truly desperate are left. Desperate. Yes. I suppose you could call me desperate. Like all Antarctic exiles I've become frightened by the prospect of staying here, but more frightened of the prospect of going home.' We walked down inclines, up reticulated aluminium steps, zigzagged through a maze of improvised panelling that had been deployed – in more prosperous times, so our host informed us – to exploit an already generous amplitude of space to the maximum. But sometimes – so thick was the outgrowth of flora, with wild, mutant strains of mimosa and bougainvillea much in evidence – that we seemed to be progressing along the footpath of a primeval forest, or else weaving through the intestinal tract of a colossal ruminant, about to be reduced to gas. I took off my parka; let it drag behind me; sweat had begun to course down my forehead, coagulate beneath the hermetic folds of my clothes. 'Here we are,' said the chatelain, handing me the key. 'Dinner's in just under an hour.'

'Why,' I said, my lungs – first quick frozen and now fired in a equatorial kiln – hardly able to power my larynx, 'why is it so *hot*?'

'All my life,' said the chatelain, with a shrug that indicated he thought the question foolish, 'all my life I have been cold. The cold has been so deep that it has sometimes threatened to freeze my spirit. It is a metaphor, is it not, the ice? This desert of the solitary, the white nothingness that is the lot of the outcast, this bald, inverted savannah of the lonely and lost: it is an inner landscape, a wintry corruption of terrific inanity we can only hope to forget by immersing ourselves in an outward show of its antithesis. Thus my tropical retreat, my nursing home for those wounded by the universal affectlessness that is the bane of our age. You're young, my friend. But when you've spent a lifetime amongst the ice as I have—'

'How the hell do we find our way down from here?' interrupted Dahlia, shaking her head as if to clear it of the muzziness engendered by our hike. The chatelain frowned, rebarbative at the puncturing of his soliloquy; then, his eyes travelling from the tips of Dahlia's toes to the tip of her chin (dawdling awhile at the tips of her thermoregulated breasts that, if shrouded in exotic fibres, were still insistent enough to add piquancy to her boyish frame), he smiled, his prurience granting her an indulgence.

'Just ring for room service, señorita. Our chambermaids will attend to your every need. Well, perhaps' - he sawed a hand through the air, his glance pingponging between me and Dahlia - 'perhaps not your every need. But, of course, I leave such things up to you. Justinian's Lodge supplies all creature comforts.' As he snorted - shoulders heaving up and down with gagged amusement - the bearishness that I had perceived from his rear became characteristic of his whiskery, spatulate face, his short, powerful torso; became characteristic of what I suspected was a calculating, jealously guarded interiority. 'My family looks forward to meeting you. Mr Winstanley may also join us but ...' Costive, he stroked his beard, seemingly perplexed, or embarrassed, about his other guest's schedule. With another shrug, he decided to let us draw what conclusions we might from the ellipses punctuating the manse's silence (the twitter of insect song, the clack of lizards); made a melodramatic bow that seemed just short of sarcasm; made to leave.

'We have some luggage,' I said. 'In the boot of our car.'

'Of course,' said the chatelain, 'your Translator.' He began to retrace our route, homing towards the lift. 'You think I don't know a ghost when I see one? Forgive me,' he called over his shoulder, 'but you are, señor, a psychiatrist who has worked in Boys Town, yes?'

'Originally,' I said, 'but these days I'm an itinerant, as I've said.'

'Of course, of course. There is much money to be made in the Peninsula. I'm so very glad, doctor, that you're here. I think you may well be able to help me.'

As he was lost to the complex of passages and defiles Dahlia made a face. '*You think I don't know a ghost when I see one?*'

'Hush! The old bastard's on to us.'

'I won't hush. He was leching me. His piggy eyes were like meat hooks – they were trying to rip off my pants. Listen: Maybe I'll sing, but forget carnal knowledge. Just remember, Doc, *I* choose who I go with, understand?'

'Understood.' But predestination, said the *philisophe*

maudit inside me, is the mother of self-abasement. Billy the Kid had slept her way to the top, and though Dahlia's alter tonight was Cerise Cerise, there was always enough of the *Chinese Killer Virgin* in her simulacrum to sanction a little mercenary coitus. Selfhood, I reminded myself, is an illusion: we are all narratives, a multitude of screaming, atomized voices, masks that conceal masks that conceal masks.

The rooms were large, but their expansiveness could not disguise their neglect. In one – the bedchamber – a wretched four-poster stood beneath frosted windows, its reek of mildew permeating the air; two enormous wardrobes, denied cosmetic surgery, sported cicatrices of multilingual graffiti; and wallpaper had peeled to reveal a mould-sodden, degraded superstructure, rupturings of intelligent matériel spilling from the building's inner skin. But warmth, marvellous warmth arising from the hypocaust beneath my feet – I had taken the chatelain's words to heart, remembering the bitterness of the cold outside as if I too had only ever known the ice – allayed the suite's poisonous atmospherics; and the spoilt brat in me forgot that he was no longer rich, that his wealth had been scattered to the caprices of a lucifugous trip to Antarctica and toys for his pubescent friend. Cosseted by the warmth, I pulled off my boots, slid across the wooden boards in my thick, woollen stockings, a part of me in Indochina again, more than a part of me a child. I reached the oriel, all coldness exterior, now, unable to penetrate. The frostwork made its suggestions: I was in Laos, cross-legged amongst the audience at a temple fair, mesmerized by other images, images flickering against a canvas screen, images of Dahlia Chan. The epiphany imploded and my face in real-time intruded itself amongst the hoary spindles and blots. The haggard insomniac before me looked older, far older than the man who had left England four months ago. I put a hand to my chest, feeling the familiar constriction of a nascent panic attack. I fumbled in my pocket; found a tranquillizer; gulped it down; practised my breathing exercises. As the pain subsided, I moved my lips closer to the window; breathed against the panes; gazed down onto the forecourt. The blizzard had abated and I was able to observe that the Bentley was in the process of being unloaded by a work detail of preposterously underdressed young women. As the last of the luggage was piled by the front door – a long packing case denoting Dahlia's coffin – a half-naked girl chauffeured the car into a nearby garage. I pulled the drapes, unshouldered my parka and threw it onto the bed. Pulling back the Velcro of my jumpsuit, I took out a little wallet of Band-Aid; it would be wise, I thought, to bind my thumb and mask the brand of my committal. 'They're bringing our stuff,' I said. 'Just enough time to shower and dress.'

'I'll shower later.' Dahlia put a hand into her shoulder bag; scavenged; walked to a mirror; desculpted, resculpted her eyes, cheeks, lips, striving towards that ideal of a mask without an owner, an expression without a face; a ghost mask. 'To find your cup size,' Dahlia recited, as she stripped off her winterweights and began faffing about with herself, 'put on a bra which is not too tight, then take a comfortable measurement across the fullest part of your bust. If the measurement is one inch bigger than your body size, your cup size is A; two inches is C; four inches is D; and six inches, eight inches, ten inches is– '

'Wishful thinking, minikin,' I said. I took her face in my hands. Hear the routine about the fanatical Orientalist, the one, who, after many years digging for evidence, an explanation, some *meaning* to the mysteries of the East, finds that there *are* no mysteries, that that celebrated *face* - which legend has held to be a treasure of 'otherness' - is, despite its superficial exoticism, as transnational as money, sex? I kissed her and her tongue slipped between my lips. 'You're so globalized,' I said, pulling away, mindful of how passion might compromise our need to appear before the chatelain and consolidate our deception. 'I guess that's how I like my little girls: culturally polluted.'

'I'm one hundred per cent Asian,' said Dahlia. And I couldn't tell whether she was teasing me or whether she was genuinely piqued. She rattled her wrist in front of my eyes, flouting her twenty-four karat charm bracelet. 'Will big brother buy little Cerise more gold?'

'Our funds are almost exhausted,' I said. 'You know that.'

'White trash. People look down on me. I need more gold. I need to make people jealous. *I* need somebody to look down on.'

'The last money I gave you - you gambled it.'

'That wasn't me! That was Dragonfly!'

'We have to be careful.'

'Cheap Charlie.' She laughed, feigning a punch to my ribs. I knew then that her chagrin was also simulated; Dahlia, answering to another self - her 'Mistress Dragonfly' alter - was playing the tease, assuming the mask of a born-again Asian. 'Did I hurt you? Aw, don't whinge about human rights, *farang*. Don't impose your obscene western culture of "right and wrong" on *me*.'

'I'm not sure if I have a culture any more. I'm not sure if anyone does. Authoritarian capitalism: it's conquered the world.'

'Speech!' chirruped my little caged bird. 'Speech!' I struck a barnstorming pose.

'Civil and political rights have been reduced to a *luxury* which only those who control us can afford ...'

'Hear, hear! Cerise have *luxurious* heart, not like big whingeing brother. And Cerise – Cerise very much in control.' She gazed wistfully at her jewellery. 'Cerise have Asian values.'

'Asian values? You mean profit and plunder?'

'I mean righteousness.'

'You mean hypocrisy.'

'I mean cash. But if Cerise *has* no cash, Cerise must sell vagina. Sell childhood. Sell life. Sell hope.' She blew her fringe out of her eyes with an upward current issuing from an improvised underbite, her eyes scrunching in confusion. Neither Asian nor Western, Dahlia was a jumble of preconceptions, a hotchpotch of prejudices, clichés both Asian *and* Western. 'What else can product do but sell itself?' she continued. 'Nasty *farang* doesn't care if Cerise has to whore.' She grabbed me between the legs and I winced with pleasure. 'I don't know if you'd like me if I really was Asian, Doc.'

'Asia doesn't exist any more. Neither does Europe or America. Stay globalized. Stay a dream of Asia,' I said, as she pulled me back to her mouth. 'Stay unreal.' I looked into her eyes; saw her turn in on herself. Dahlia wasn't of this Earth; but her hurt was. I had seen it – recognized it – the first time I had met her; her pain had been my own.

But my relationship to Dahlia was not the same as it had been when I had been a child. To me, now, she was one of the world's innocent, bright with an innocence I had never had; the lost, persecuted child I must save and be saved by. I stiffened with desire and – dinner engagement or no – I considered flipping her onto the bed and taking her in the dorsal-ventral position, savagely.

There was a knock.

Said lissome Dahlia as she wriggled herself free: 'Whatever shall I wear?'

The ghost wore white. White sandals, white ankle socks, white pinafore dress and white ribbons in her black bob. As Cerise she had her script – the lines of a schoolgirl assassin from the *rong mu,* or slaughterhouse district of Bangkok – and she was compelled to offer her interpretation. I, if more appropriately, was the more shabbily attired. I had managed to get my dinner jacket pressed – when room service had arrived, it had carried out its obligations with scrupulous intensity – but, with so little time before dinner, I had had to finalize my ensemble with a tank top of synthetic flesh and a pair of dynamically shredded jeans. As the lift descended, I studied the factotum who accompanied us. 'Excuse me,' I said, 'this probably sounds rude but – are you human?'

'He means,' said Dahlia, 'are you an automaton?'

'Cyborg,' she said, perfunctorily. 'I'm flattered, all the same.' I had suspected as much; the chambermaid's unnaturally long legs, the radical, nigh-Crumbian shelf of her buttocks (upon which festive bucks might balance flutes of champagne), the zero-g breasts and doll-like demeanour, had marked her out as a prostitute who had undergone total body modification to resemble the mechanical playthings of the western world.

'Does this place pay well?' Dahlia continued.

'Not enough for having had to be spliced with plastigene.'

'Are you all cyborgs?'

'Every single one. Came here when this place was still doing good business. Guys who liked the half-human touch would pay real good. No one else would have us. Everbody'd gone gaga over ghosts.' She glanced at Dahlia. 'Don't worry, kid, I might have a chip in my brain, but I don't have one on my shoulder. The only rule around here is that you rip off the world before it returns the compliment. Me: I'm just trying to earn enough to get out. To one of the eastern pornocracies, say.'

'I sympathize,' said Dahlia, 'I really do. There's been such a decline in the quality of sperm in western countries. I mean, that's why the population has so declined. That's why all there's left for a girl to hustle are old men.'

'And little boys,' said the chambermaid, her sidelong glance igniting with a pre-programmed leer, 'at such a premium.'

We reached ground; in a rustle of hip-high skirts and underskirts, a flippity-flapping of her apron's bow (it seemed like an enormous butterfly in flight, an inhabitant of the manse's chittering terrarium), the zimbo-bimbo led us to the dining hall.

Beneath a high vaulted roof, marooned in silence, a long table – like a draped catafalque within a crypt – extended across granite flagstones, its midnight linen bedecked with glittering tableware and candelabra. A handful of figures sat about it, frozen in a tableau vivant. Circumambient to this central prop, this troupe of actors: panelled walls, paintings of gauchos, landscapes of the pampas; and hanging above an enormous fireplace that glowed with imitation flames, harpoons, the skulls of seals and killer whales. The chatelain looked up. He had, seemingly, been set to carve the entrée that lay before him on a silver platter, his face set in the fervent rictus of a coroner who has developed an unhealthy obsession for his work. 'Good evening,' he said, in a grating but appropriately sepulchral tone, his words like tin bats rustling against the roof of the chamber. He pointed at two chairs with a long, elliptical blade. 'Please, take your seats.' We advanced, apprehensively, the ceremonies about to begin. The assembly unfroze; there was a clink and clank of cutlery. As we navigated the sea of cold stone all eyes hungrily assessed our progress, as if, should we slip, fall down a concealed trapdoor, or come to mortal grief otherwise, our remains might provide the pièce de résistance. A woman – turned contrapposto in greeting – sat adjacent to our appointed places. We seated ourselves. Facing us were two children, a boy and a girl; and to complete the dramatis personae a man with the bloated, capillary-fractured look of the permanently inebriated sat at the far end of the table, opposite our host. 'My wife,' said the chatelain, introducing us to the diminutive and therefrom nameless woman by my side. 'My children: Cesare, fourteen, and Pandora, eleven.' The children immediately looked away. It was customary, these days, to announce a child's age, as if in warning; it was customary for children to respond with shame and fear. 'And our other guest, Mr Winstanley. Winstanley is somewhat shipwrecked, you might say. But he finds this little cannibal isle not without its compensations.' On cue, the chambermaid who had accompanied us down from our suite – and surely, I saw now, in the flattering light of the dining hall, a maid spectacular enough to have passed for an automaton on the books of a house of *haute couture* – sauntered over to the castaway; ruffled his hair. Winstanley pulled away, stung, the prospect of a *crime passionel* in his eyes. The half-mechanical girl turned to whatever chores awaited her, withdrawing behind an arras. 'Ah. Winstanley is always having little disagreements with our tinkertoys.' The chatelain turned from his conversation piece; raised his eyebrows as he brought me into focus. 'But cyborgs are yesterday's *frisson*, don't you think, doctor? I need ghosts. Top-drawer ghosts. If *Justinian's Lodge* is once again to fill its rooms, it needs to be haunted. What a karaoke we might have here! What a club!' Dahlia ignored the suggestive wink that the chatelain bestowed upon her; chose, instead, to acknowledge the mute, discreetly importunate Winstanley. A thirtyish Occidental, a ruined scion of Europe's élite of a type she had often chosen to flirt with, seduce, roll, she unleashed upon him her faithless Siamese smile; it was the smile she awarded all whom she considered stupid and rich, and whom, for that very reason, it was her duty to cheat, to exploit. Meditatively, Dahlia put a cigarillo to her purple lips, dragged and exhaled with stagecrafted languor, wanting, at that moment, I knew, to look so good, so bad, that every ghost lover below 66 degrees 30 minutes S would be wanting to lick her face off.

'Hello, Winstanley.' The bug-eyed drunk – who seemed to have been slapped with a face pack of

Novocain – struggled to respond. I allowed myself the pleasure of a thin, ephemeral smile. An assignation in his room, caviar, a magnum of champagne and a Mickey Finn awaited him.

'How unforgivable,' said the chatelain. 'Let me introduce you. Winstanley, Dr Moroder and his companion from Earth2.'

'Cerise Cerise,' said Dahlia, her smile broadening into a sunburst that flash-blinded her *farang* dupe, leaving him blinking, disoriented. 'But please, please, call me Cerise.' She looked over her shoulder; turned down the megawattage; held the chatelain's eye until his concupiscence was atomized by something that passed for shame. 'You know, over there we call *this* Earth2.'

'Ah, correspondences, correspondences ...'

'Correspondences? Some ghost tell you that? Fiddle-de-dee. Sims are such snobs. We all like to think we're the most perfect of *emulations*. But Earth2 doesn't have the teraflops. I'm a paraphrast, not a person.'

'Earth2,' said Winstanley, playing the raconteur, 'is our spiritual.'

The boy snapped a toothpick in half between his index and middle fingers. He glowered at me; emptied a half-filled tumbler of brandy down his throat; coughed; spat the ice back into the glass. Then, taking another hit, he lowered his eyes, tracing a doodle on the wet, glistening patina of the place mat. 'You mean it's what we have instead of a spiritual.' His lips drew back to expose rows of glaucous teeth as he gazed down table, focusing on Dahlia's lust-struck sap. 'You want to look after her, don't you Winstanley, give her a good home, send her to school?'

'Cesare,' said the chatelain, in warning.

'Winstanley need a *nana malade.*'

'Cesare,' said our host. 'I won't tell you again. Must you always act like an untrained puppy?' He heaped a blubbery slice of whale meat onto my plate.

'What's a *nana malade?*' said Dahlia.

I explained: 'In order to compete with gynoids and cyborgs – whose attentions were disease-free but, so some would opine, antiseptic – pre-posthistoric whores often had themselves infected with a designer bug that guaranteed a prolonged and infinitely pleasurable death to those johns who paid to contract it.'

'Well,' she sighed, 'if that isn't just too *De Luxe.*'

'Forgive my son,' said the chatelain, 'but ever since he learned how to override the V-chip–'

'But Cesare is right, Justinian,' said Winstanley. His attention had been fixed maniacally upon Dahlia the instant she had begun to flirt with him. 'If I had a ghost as sweet as the señorita I would certainly give her a home, send her to school, to college, buy her all the pretty dresses she might wish for. Condemn me to a *nana malade* if I lie.' Dahlia smiled shyly.

'You have a sweet mouth, Winstanley.'

'And a sweet tooth,' said Cesare. 'How about you, Papa: you want to give her a home, send her to school? *Dancing* school maybe, huh, Papa? You want to teach her to tango? To be a good girl?'

'Is your son trying to lampoon me, my precious?' said the chatelain to his wife. The little woman sucked in her cheeks and drew her shoulders up to her ears as her husband's eyes swivelled wildly, his gaze taking in walls, ceiling, floor, briefly engaging the bemused faces of the other banqueters before locking, at last, upon my own.

'The boy is of course *possessed.*' He threw exasperated hands into the air. The hands crested; began their descent. With an oratorical *thump* one landed near my plate; edged forward, crabwise; stroked my metacarpus with pudgy, ostentatiously bejewelled claws. 'I was wondering, doctor, if I might prevail upon you for a consultation. I have read a little psychology myself, of course. Any parent has to, these days. But there are times when professional intervention becomes necessary.'

'I haven't any experience of stepfathering,' I said, my throat suddenly tight, 'my work in Boys Town revolved about research and development.'

Winstanley placed his elbows to either side of his plate and – ostensibly reaching for a pepper pot – leaned across the grandiose plateau of the table, swimming with the current of Dahlia's seduction, fish-brained, eager to take the bait. 'Tell me, Cerise, who or what is your original?' The chatelain tsked at the interruption. Dahlia tsked back, collapsed into the black velvet of her high-backed chair; fidgeted, a mischievous kitten; and a half-dozen pairs of auditory nerves were hers.

'I was born in Vientiane thirty years ago. Chinese mother, American father. China had, in all but name, colonized Laos by then. We moved across the border to Isan, that is, to north-east Thailand, when I was eight. My mother had been a fashion model; she got me into the biz. Soon after, a French talent scout recruited me, took me to Paris. There, I was working alongside top supermodels, gynoids even. It was after that that I got into acting. By the time I was eleven, I was in Hollywood. A star, my darlings, a star.'

'Her name's Dahlia Chan,' I said. Impetuous – for

here I was again, president of her fan club by proxy - I had dropped my guard. 'It is, of course, only a stage name. But you've heard of her, surely?' Winstanley's face blanked.

'A lot of Chinese directors had defected to Holly-wood during the North-South wars,' continued Dahlia. 'They were recreating the hyperkineticism of the Mekong-basin *aube du millénaire* splatter movie on the streets of the big, bad Angeles.'

'Real-life *anime*,' I said, elucidating.

'Cartoon apocalypse,' said Dahlia. 'Line and ink made flesh.'

'Astonishing sex,' I said, 'beautiful violence.'

Winstanley clucked his tongue. 'Dahlia Chan, Dahlia Chan.'

'Cerise Cerise,' said Dahlia. 'Dahlia Chan is dead.'

'Let us be precise,' I corrected, 'Dahlia Chan dis-appeared. Left Hollywood after a suicide attempt. Returned to Vientiane, so people say. Though sometimes I have my doubts as to whether she ever really existed.'

'*This* Dahlia is pure spirit, made of the stuff of the fibresphere. Forgotten where she came from some time ago. What she knows of the past is only what other people have told her.' She stared at her dish of steaming meat; wrinkled her brow. 'But even if the real Dahlia is alive there's no way she'd get to claim her copyrights. I'm a *free* spirit. Just let her try to have me junked, just let her try.'

'It's this world that needs to be junked,' said Cesare, heckling his father, glaring at him from beneath knobby, hyperplastic brows, 'not Earth2, but this world of surveillance, of prohibition, of cheated desire. You want to fuck little ghosts too, Papa, but you want to make it normative. You want to take desire and shape it to satisfy your own ends. You want to make ghost wedding a part of your sad, constipated little world.'

'Now, now,' said the chatelain's mousy wife – transformed these few moments from gargoyle into hesitant matriarch – engorged mouth widening in a placatory smile, 'remember we have *company*.' Gazing above our heads, she said, by way of explanation to other spirits, spirits dormant, perhaps, grown fat and sluggish on the thick, heavy air, 'The worm of contradiction ate its way into his brains some time ago.'

'You always take his side,' said the boy, in a sea-change of plaintiveness. 'I could tell you things, things you don't know, things that you wouldn't even want to suspect.'

'Don't be *clever*, Cesare. You should treat your father with deference.'

'But Mama–'

'No "buts": listen to him. He's done things, been places, that you can only dream about. He wants what is good for you.'

'Things he's done. When I was little. Things that–' The Olympian condescension of the chatelain's face (a lifetime amongst the ice surfacing, lyophilizing the bon viveur) guillotined his son's peroration. And as Dahlia's tongue-tied *farang* slumped backwards to try to recuperate his hopelessly overdrawn reserves of charm, I found myself drifting into a trance, staring into the tundra of despair, the wastelands of nothingness, that lay in our host's cold, glazed eyes. It was all there: the rusted bicycle frame, the pyramids of plastic bottles, the broken refrigerator filled with the smell of rotten meat: the secret life of the man who would be God. They were my stepfather's eyes.

'It is, of course, one thing for adults to dally with ghosts,' he said, each syllable marshalled into metronomic order. 'We can comfortably and responsibly process such images. But children must be protected. I have followed the guidelines. Online blocks, indeed, all the prophylactic devices on the market. Our own network in the *Lodge* has a proprietary list of forbidden sites and I myself regularly record and monitor online activity. There are so many intelligences out there, predators just waiting for their chance to spirit our children away. Don't you agree, doctor?' Before I could reply he had picked up a piece of cutlery and hurled it at his son. It glanced off the boy's closely shaved head, skittering across the floor. 'I said, doctor, don't you—'

'I heard. And y, y, y, yes' – my old stammer returning – 'of course, I agree. Children have to be p, p, p, protected.' Dahlia pitched me a ninety-mile-per-hour glance, half in concern, half in irritation.

'I've caught Cesare downloading the usual pornographic images. What am I to do with him? Would a spell in Boys Town help, do you think?'

'I, I, I—' The tableware glittered menacingly.

'We haven't worked the Town for some time,' said Dahlia. 'The Peninsula is so lucrative.'

'Yes, of course, I understand you freelance. Freelancing is the best option for any man, *I* say. But you still have power of committal, no?'

'Dr Moroder is our *guest*,' said his wife, 'this is no time to talk business.'

The chatelain's daughter had stopped playing with her food; she was squinting at Dahlia. 'What were *you* doing in Boys Town?'

'Dr Moroder brought me over from Earth2 to work for him in an advisory capacity.'

'And I'm sure,' said Winstanley, trying to re-enter the conversation and reacquire Dahlia's favour, 'your work must have been invaluable. Am I right, doctor?'

'Certainly,' I said, my stammer at last under control. 'We really still know so little about Earth2.'

'I thought all ghosts were white,' said the girl.

'Most ghosts are,' said Dahlia, 'it's the colour of *money.*' Dahlia, contrariwise, was the colour of *honey.* It had been my childhood out East, said the Town doctors, that had instilled in me a predilection for that concoction of the Western mind, the *oriental,* which had found its objective correlative in Dahlia. An ingot of memory was bubbling in my back brain; it flooded my cortex, like a tsunami of hot, honeyed tears: girls in *pa-sin* (some of the more audacious in the latest aerosol dresses) promenading by the Mekong river in the cool of the evening . . .

'Dahlia has given me invaluable insights,' I said, jolted from my reverie by a surreptitious pinch on the thigh, 'into the collective mind of the child crusade.'

'Why kids,' said Dahlia, keeping one hand beneath the table in case I again needed to be revived from the opium dream of the past, 'why dead-end kids pressed their noses to the candy-store window, even though they knew the owner had a shotgun and was prepared to use it.'

'Even though,' I added, 'they knew the candies were poisonous. The denizens of Earth2 – having provided much of the inspirational source for the wars – are able to supply the psychohistorian with invaluable data. These days, to understand events on Earth1, we must try to understand Earth2.'

'Tell me, Cerise, what is that enchanted land like?'

'Earth2? It's plastic: things and people sort of melt in and out of each other. It's like, well, worlds within worlds, intelligences stacked within intelligences. Apart from that, it's much the same as here, if truth be known, Winstanley. Except that, là-bas, it's little girls who become obsessed with ghosts; little boy ghosts, that is.' She tittered, excruciatingly cute. 'I expect there's a little boy hiding inside *you*, you naughty man.'

'Terrorists used to exploit that weakness,' I said, 'always indoctrinating soldiers with ghosts their own age. Young ghosts, like young fighters, are so infinitely ductile.'

'Ductile. Oh yes. Ductile. I should say. Over there, ah, là-bas, everything has a tendency to pleasure, yes?'

'Over there,' said Dahlia, 'everything has a tendency to burlesque, to the outré.'

'You look very outré yourself, señorita.'

'Why thank you.' Dahlia fanned her artificial lashes. 'But Earth2 is an imperfect simulation. As am I. For a parallel universe to truly exist you would need a system containing at least 10 to the power of 10 to the power of 123 bits. The Net has a long way to go.'

'But you have human equivalence!'

'Do I? You're kind, Winstanley. Kind.'

'And your motherland – it shall have the equivalence of our own poor, jaded planet too. *A long way to go?* No; we shall surely have its like soon. And then perhaps I may visit without the need of a datacap? Perhaps then you might consent to be my guide?' Dahlia's flirtation was interrupted by a long sigh from opposite, a tired exhalation that seemed to mix longing with precocious cynicism.

'Dr Moroder' – the chatelain's daughter cupped her chin in her hands; sneered at her sibling, her eyes, kindled as if with toon twinkles, swiftly combusting with schadenfreude – 'Cesare is always telling us about Earth3. Cythera, he calls it. If you ask me it sounds like a fairy story you tell to babies. Have you heard of Earth3, doctor?' Dahlia's reaction, like mine, was Pavlovian. We turned to face each other, faces blitzed with perturbation, before, realizing that an undue display of catalepsy at hearing that magic word 'Cythera' was to be avoided, we were able to compose ourselves, get back into our roles. 'Aha, you have heard.' With satisfaction, the girl acknowledged the distress of the melancholic by her side. 'Tell him he's mad, doctor. Tell him it means that he's sick. Tell him he has to go to Boys Town.'

'What do you know of Cythera, Cesare?' I asked.

'I know it's beyond the end of the world,' he mumbled. 'I know it's beyond time.' A chambermaid – the same one as formerly? I suddenly realized that they all looked alike – appeared from behind the arras; served up a second course consisting of roasted osprey petrel and a fish stew that was all teeth, jaw and palaeobotanical seasoning, a bouillabaisse that might have emanated from the kitchen of a demented Brillat-Savarin. The boy impaled a calcified morsel with his fork; held it to his eye and studied it without eating. 'I have this dream. There's a coastline. Hills. And lots of gentlemen and ladies. There's music playing, but everyone is turning away, walking down, down to a harbour. The sun is setting and far away I think you can see an island.' His sister began to giggle. 'Sometimes, the harbour is on fire. Everybody is trying to escape ...'

'Cesare, I think that's enough for this evening,' said the chatelain. 'Please go to your room.' The chatelain offered me a wing of petrel. 'What is one to do? The boy is a danger to himself. And to us. Really, doctor, I would be so grateful for any guidance. The policing of desire is such a ticklish subject.'

'Go upstairs,' said the girl, poking her tongue out at her brother. 'Go and talk to your ghost.'

'Don't encourage him, Pandora,' said the chatelain's wife.

The boy – with a practised sulk – had already pushed back his chair. Taking a final swig of brandy, he sloped out of the chamber.

'I suppose I should be retiring soon as well,' said Dahlia, with mock demureness, bedroom eyes fastened boldly upon her *farang*; her victim's attention inflamed, she redirected her gaze to the flagstones, their schema as cold as her calculating charm.

'And I,' said Winstanley, coughing into his napkin, bulbous eyes announcing that he surely belonged to the ranks of the terminally cunt crazy.

The chatelain shook his head. 'But you have hardly touched your meal! I had hoped to talk with you further, señorita. About my plans for the motel. About my plans for ...' He allowed himself to stall; and then, catching his breath, 'Perhaps, later, you might sing for us?' A subtle oscillation passed through Dahlia's body, as if she sensed the impending scourge of the dawn, her eosophobia's acuteness escalating in inverse proportion to the diminution of the daylight hours, a paradox that was boorishly nudging her to the brink of a nervous breakdown.

'Perhaps,' she said, rising and holding on to the back of the chair, her legs buckling, then correcting themselves as she readied to exit.

'Be quick,' I whispered, hand in front of my mouth, 'The Wound is opening. You should be thinking about climbing into your Translator.' Dahlia nodded; stared briefly at the chatelain's daughter - as if advising her against any attempt to imitate her behaviour and initiate a seduction of Dr M - and caught Winstanley's arm, allowing him to squire her across the granite floor. Our host looked after his two departing guests with a mixture of vexation and grief. In that brief interlude of distraction I palmed a silver butter knife from the table; secreted it within my tux.

'I must apologise, doctor, we are so rarely able to entertain properly, and now—' In what I recognized as the chatelain's most precious affectation, he threw his hands into the air; semaphored his disappointment. 'But at least you must stay for dessert.'

An identikit piece of maidenly technofluff wiggled across the hall bearing a platter of sorbets and ices.

I had thought I had become accustomed to the manse's synthetic climate; but at that moment it seemed as if a dumpster of mulch had been emptied over my head, and something like a malarial shiver passed through my body. The chatelain's cryptic signals, the morse of silver knives against porcelain and mica, the agenda of the serving dishes, the plates with their ciphers of English rural life, the candelabra and the unwavering espial of their flames, the huge, grinning vortexes of the exanimate sea mammals which hid microphones, secret cameras, the all-seeing eye of The Tetragrammaton - all, all was unreasonably alive and in conspiracy to unreason me.

I tried to calm my accelerating heart, placing my faith in Dahlia's criminal virtuosity.

'Did you drug him?'

'Of course. He'll sleep for twelve hours at least. I used scopolamine.'

'Haven't I told you before about using that stuff? You'll have given the poor guy brain damage.'

'So? He was brain damaged already.' A wry smile filled the polymer frame of the coffin's monitor. I kowtowed to my demon pharmacist; heaved a fatalistic sigh.

'How much was the take?'

'Enough to last us a few weeks. I managed to get his ring off. Gold, with a diamond inlay. Pretty. We might be able to sell it at Vostok. I know this little pawnshop on Fabian von Bellingshausena Prospect that'll take anything, no questions asked.'

I didn't like Vostok. It represented the dark side of the Russian economic miracle. Like most settlements on the continental shield, it was heavily populated. I remembered its traffic-congested streets, its pall of noxious dust, and, between heaven and earth, its neon-bright mittengard of glass, steel and ferroconcrete that seethed with the slaves and masters of the New Russia, dead souls labouring under the fogged dome that insulated them from the rawness of the sky. They mined the million-year-old microorganisms of the subglacial lakes that lay four kilometres beneath the ice. A whole city living off germs and bacteria ... My ghost, however, was drawn to Vostok. Vostok represented, I think, something like the ghost of Bangkok, that depraved,

sweltering city Dahlia knew more by hearsay than by
experience but which nevertheless had indelibly left its
stain upon her overexposed, cellulose-acetate heart.
    'I thought he might have had more.'
    'Europe's a mess these days, Doc. Everybody's broke.
We should try for a postwestern city.'
    'Mmm. We should try to gull someone from your
neck of the woods.'
    'I've told you before: I'm not Chinese, I'm American.'
Dahlia's lips receded until her whole face became visible. I
picked up a leaflet from the bedside table. It advertised
the motel and on its back was a layout of the manse's
interior.
    'Listen, before we leave, I have to see Cesare. I'm sure
he knows something important about Cythera. Something
he's learned from the Net.'
    'Is everybody asleep?'
    'So far as I know. It'll be dark again in under an
hour. I'll be back before then. We'll leave while the house
is dreaming.'
    Locking the door, I proceeded to the domestic wing.
    Separating hostelry from living quarters was a
ballroom. Heavy drapes prevented any light, however
faint, from trespassing upon its shadows, and its long,
black, parquet-floored cavernousness was visible only via
the bank of soft illumination that had issued from a
lintel as I had passed through the open door. As my eyes
adjusted to the darkness, darting hither and thither
seeking an egress by which I might continue on my way, I
gradually perceived that I was surrounded by a regiment
of wax dummies (they were duplicates of the manse's
chambermaids) modelled in an attitude that suggested

the freezing of time during a long-forgotten tea dance. The mannequins were grouped in twos, one girl taking the male, the other, the female role, each couple paralyzed in an act of lunging, twirling, back bending. As I slipped through their ranks one eyeball, then another, tracked my progress. I was telling myself that this was an optical illusion – similar in kind to the experience of having the eyes of a bust or portrait follow you about a room – when an abrupt humanoid bark had me leaping into the air as if a rottweiler had exploded from a hidden silo in the floor and impacted itself teeth first into my scrotum. 'What?' I croaked, as I landed in a crouch.

'I said, what are you doing here?'

'Who said that?' Slowly, a head belonging to the nearest mannequin revolved on its axis.

'You're not supposed to be in this part of the motel. If the master finds you—' I rose; touched the cheek of the talking dummy; found it warm.

'You're human.'

'I told you before, I'm a *cyborg.*'

'I'm sorry.' They really did all look alike.

'He'll be here any minute. He doesn't like spectators. Do yourself a favour and leave.'

'You won't tell?'

'Nobody saw you. How could they? And anyway, showroom dummies can't talk.'

I backed out of this trophy room of exotic animals; found my way to the door that led to the annex, the nest of rooms where I could expect to find the broody Cesare.

I pressed my eye to a keyhole; discovered the chatelain's wife playing cards with her daughter. I lingered; the girl, in her nightgown – disencumbered of the heavy muslin dress that had concealed her lines during dinner – was a pretty child. Dahlia, perhaps, had been right to be jealous. But I had no time – no real inclination; no real hope – of philandering. I moved along the passage, investigating each shut door. When I detected the recognizable, if not wholly familiar music, of fingers punching deck, the glossolalia of a computer whose voice engine was antiquated, diseased, I knew I had found Cesare. After double-checking, I rose from my knee and carefully eased the door open.

'Cesare?' The boy swivelled about to face me. Momentary surprise gave way to resignation, as if he had been expecting the worst for so many months that he was relieved to be finally led to the gallows.

'Did my father send you?'

'No, no, you've got it all wrong.' I walked into the room, carefully closed the door; sat down on the corner of an unmade bed. 'You see, I'm not that kind of psychiatrist. And Cerise, well, she really isn't that kind of nurse.' The boy folded his arms.

'Who are you? *What* are you?'

'I'm an iatrogenic psychiatrist. Me and Cerise: we make people mad. And those that are mad, we make madder.' I peeled away the sticky plaster that covered my thumb; showed him the brand I had received in Boys Town.

'The paternoster,' he murmured.

'Yes. I'm like you, Cesare. Queer.' He grabbed a decanter from the steel trellis that supported his computer and peripherals and filled two tumblers. I accepted; poured the liquor down my throat.

'Sometimes,' said the boy, 'sometimes I think I shall kill him.'

'No; you'll get into *trouble*. I got into trouble, once. Fifteen years ago I downloaded a version of Dahlia Chan. Not the Dahlia you saw tonight. A younger version. A nine-year-old whose simulacrum was the result of a thousand-and-one fashion shoots, a thousand-and-one hours of catwalk footage. My stepfather tried to stop me. I attacked him; left him for dead. Me and Dahlia ran off. But the elevation of child-abuse into a subject of national obsession had yielded to an obsession with the "demonic" sexuality of The Child, a terror of a child's autonomy and all it represents: the ungovernable tide of the imagination, the big, sweet wave in which we both long and fear to drown. What chance did we have? Wherever we went people would point their fingers at us, the light of fanaticism in their eyes. The Censors put out their dragnet, took Dahlia away, sent me to Boys Town. Since then I've learned cunning, learned how to walk through the world in disguise. The important thing, Cesare, is to let nobody know what you're really thinking. Confidences, Cesare, confidences make you vulnerable.' The boy drained his glass; poured both of us refills; beamed at me, his face shiny with sebum.

'You on the lam, then?' I rolled the tumbler between my palms. The smell of the brandy rose into my nostrils as if I were milking it of its essence. When had *I* begun to drink? It must have been when I was, what? about seven I think. But in those days I drank Vodka.

'I don't want to go into that, Cesare. I've come here because I thought you might be able to help me. And I, you. At dinner you mentioned Cythera.'

'Why should I help? You think I want to end up like you?'

'You are like me. You know it. Cythera is the only way out. For both of us.' He looked down at the keyboard, tapped idly at the keys like a cocktail lounge pianist picking out a spare, lonesome tune. 'Cythera's mine. I saw it in data-trance. It belongs to me and Cytherina.'

'Cytherina?'

'*Cytherina?*' he repeated, derisively. 'Who she, eh? Don't you know *anything?* Cytherina's the handmaiden to Cytherea, of course. She's the angel of the blessed isle, that's who she is. The angel of degree zero. She's my ghost.' A childhood memory stirred: Cytherina in Cythera: it had been an adventure game. The game must have evolved, become self-conscious.

'I have a car. You could download her now and we could all be on the road – miles from here – before your parents wake up.' The boy smiled an ugly, knowing smile; gestured to a corner of the room where there lay a heap of smashed computer parts, the debris of what was once a Translator. 'Your father,' I said, in realization, in despair, 'he's –' I knew, now, why he had to punch deck rather than use voice commands.

'You can't get to Cythera on the roads that pass through *this* world. Only one expressway leads to its shores and–'

'Download her onto optics,' I said, standing and tossing the glass onto the bed, where it rolled, clinking, into several others. 'We can use my Translator to incarnate her. If you're scared, or if your father has the site blocked, then let me do the hacking. I can find a back door.' I moved towards the keyboard, cracking my knuckles in apprehension. I'd *always* used voice; I wasn't practised in dealing with deaf-mute cripples. No antiquarian, my hands fluttered incompetently above the deck.

'Death,' said the boy. 'That's the way to Cythera. Don't you know that? No other road will do. You prepared to go that way, señor?'

'What are you talking about?'

'You know it's not sex and violence that they try to censor. Not really. It's like you said, they try to censor desire, the imagination. They try to censor extremes of thought and feeling, the dangerous lands that lie at the frontiers of consciousness. Everything that threatens their status quo. They say we live in an information society. Don't believe them. We live in a *knowledge* society. Kids like me: we've gone places they've never been to, known things they'll never know.' In the Town they used to tell me that a certain knowledge of the degree of rottenness permeating the world is necessary, but too deep a knowledge would take away more than it gave; such knowledge, they said, diminishes, corrupts. Thus, the censorship of my reading matter, my videos, *manga* and hours on the Net. But I knew Cesare talked of another epistemology, knowledge of the world as transformed by the demon child we carry within us throughout our lives, the child who pulls the wings from a butterfly only to appraise their beauty, who delights in fairies' screams, the empowering child of the autonomous imagination. 'The ones in control: they're frightened of that knowledge. Even you are frightened, aren't you? You want to go to Cythera but you can't bear to think of what it might actually take to get there.'

'I'm Queer,' I said, nonplussed, 'I'm not frightened. I've travelled this far.' The boy rose from his trelliswork of electronic blooms: crazy suckers, fungi and liana of the world's fibreglass arboretum that paralleled the plant life thriving across the walls and meringue-like ceiling courtesy of the manse's humidity. I paced a circle; tore off a sheet of print-out from the rolls and streamers that bedecked the steel-and-sap garden. The lasered image was that of a half-naked child-woman hanging from a silken noose; beneath the gallows, a lynch-mob of beautiful cavalry officers. Cythera was ultramarine seas and skies, lush meadows, silver forests and the immanence of the divine; but this - this blood and pain, I knew, also belonged to Cythera. I tore off another sheet, and then another, as if assembling a flipbook of contraband thrills.

'Nasty pictures,' said the boy, choking back a giggle.

I looked down into a round, coarse-grained face; understood - and wished I did not understand - that he passionately believed in all that he had averred. The computer continued its broken-tongued babble, as if mocking the confusion in my own mind. I crumpled the print-outs in my fist; let the ball drop to the floor. 'I'm Queer,' I repeated.

'There's nothing I can do for you. Cytherina doesn't like to meet strangers, and besides,' he said, a finger worming its way beneath my tank top and prodding me in the navel, 'she'd only tell you the same story. Each person finds their own way to the blessed isle.' He twisted his digit, as if conducting an exploratory for lint. 'You know your Thucydides? "Cythera is an island lying off Laconia, opposite Malea; the inhabitants are Lacedaemonians of the class of the Perioeci ..."'

'Don't play games with me.'

'These days you would say it's south of the

Peloponnesus, the southernmost of the Ionian Islands.'

'I said—' He turned; ran his forefinger under his nose, as if sampling my bouquet; punched up some real-time video.

'He'll be finished soon. Dancing class only lasts for half-an-hour.' Tango music flowed from the speakers. The boy grinned, displaying the bleeding rind of his gums. 'Showgirls for the new karaoke. He says putting them through their paces helps him to sleep.' The ballroom was lit. In the centre stood the chatelain. He wore chalk-stripe trousers, a pin-stripe waistcoat, black shirt and a matching cravat. His hair was slicked back with Vaseline; in his hand he held a crop. The chambermaids danced about him, stamping and posturing like amateur gigolettes. At each inevitable misstep, the crop flicked out at thigh or rump. 'You'd better go back to your room. He always checks in on me to log what I've been doing.' He laughed through his nose; drew his sleeve across his face. 'Of course he never really finds out. Cytherina's safe. She's encrypted in a kindergarten site kids use every day. He won't lock me out of a topography he believes innocuous.'

'He's got his eyes on *my* ghost, hasn't he?'

'He wants both of you. He wants Cerise, because of his dreams of renovating the motel, he wants Dr Max because of his dreams of recycling his son.'

'I figured.'

'Then you'll be leaving us?' I nodded. For a moment, the boy looked almost regretful. 'Then you should leave soon. Papa can be very unpleasant when he doesn't get what he wants.' I checked my watch.

'It's getting dark. I have to go.' The boy put his hand on my arm.

'Just one thing. What's it like: Boys Town, that is?'

'Boys Town?' The familiar cramp stirred within my solar plexus, like some subcutaneous vermin that threatened to burrow through my flesh's wall. 'Boys Town contains more than just boys now, even if the wars *are* over. Boys, men, girls, women. There are all kinds there: delinquent kids, common law criminals, sturdy beggars, the insane. Everybody the state thinks of as contaminants. The abusers and the abused, the possessors and the possessed ... somehow they're all the same these days: children, demons. If your father has you committed ...'

'Oh, he'll have me committed. One way or another, he'll have me committed.'

'Then—'

'What?' It was time for the doctor to give a little professional advice.

'Choose death,' I said.

'Choose to be a sim? To go over?'

'Choose death. Being an imperfect replica is better than being an inauthentic original. But then, you already seem to know that.'

'Yeah,' he said. 'I think I already did.'

Dahlia was projected, seated upon the bed and thumbing through the little album that contained her stamp collection. A dismembered Barbie lay on the counterpane; and a broken-spined chapbook that I had insisted she bring from England so that she might not lag in her schooling was open at her favourite chapter, *The Tudors*. I had had to take a diversionary route back to our suite; night had fallen even as I had fumbled through the back corridors that, after several wrong turns and regressions, had eventually delivered me to the warren of rooms that stretched across the manse's topmost floor. I was covered in sweat and dust and dead insects.

'Dr Livingstone, I presume,' chipped Dahlia, 'iatrogenic explorer?'

'He can't help us.'

'Time to bid farewell?' She nodded towards the neatly stacked luggage. 'I've packed.'

'Yeah,' I said. 'Time to sound the retreat.' She scooped up her personal treasures and emptied them into her shoulder bag; then she jumped to her feet, picked up our valises – so much in hock, these days, that, despite the handicap of her four feet ten inches, she always managed to carry them by herself – and walked past me into the corridor. Newly hatched from limbo and still dishabille, I left her to struggle with her clothes – framed by the jambs as if modelling for a naughty postcard to be mailed from yet another dark resort in Hell – while I busied myself with the crate that contained the disassembled Translator.

'I drugged him deep,' she said, holding the door open with a foot as she slipped on a T-shirt. 'There's really no need to hurry.' I had lugged the crate half-way across the room before she noticed that I was regarding her suspiciously, for she added, 'I'm still Cerise. I'm still your favourite untamed schoolgirl.' And she held up her pinafore dress, striking a half-naked pose behind its fetishistic veil.

'No time for that. Get your thermoware on,' I said. 'It's going to be painful, crossing from the house to the garage.' I realized then that I wasn't hotsuited either, the aftershock of my conversation with Cesare only just hitting me, inducing a fresh panic attack. I fought to get my breath, to corral the thoughts stampeding through my head, to get tactical. 'Where is it, anyway,' I said, choking on my funk, 'where is our thermoware?' Dahlia looked perplexed; knelt down and inspected our bags.

'Good point. I don't know.'

'Did anyone come in here while I was gone?'

'How should I know? I was in limbo, stupid.' I put a hand to my chest. Dahlia raced over; placed her own hand over mine. 'It feels normal. There's nothing wrong with you, Doc.'

'They're trying to entrap us,' I said, my heart surging, gouts of blood pumping into my head with such violence that I began to reel.

'We'll be okay,' said Dahlia, reassuring her patient, 'we'll be okay once we're in the car. Calm down. I've told you before, there's nothing wrong. Absolutely nothing. It's all in your mind.'

'Justinian: he wants you for a karaoke, me for a diagnosis, a signature that will commit his son to the bughouse.' I breathed deeply, steadying myself.

'I *told* you that pig was leching me.'

I pulled the Translator into the hallway; and, with Dahlia battling furiously with her pinafore, tugging the tiny dress over her head as she led the way - my chest seemed ready to explode with either anxiety or desire - I proceeded to haul it through the steam bath of ramps and descents until we reached the lift. As we fell earthwards I closed my eyes; and it was then, in the shatterings of light bulbs that were being thrown against my retina that I decoded a sesame to our plight, descrying a way out, not just of *Justinian's Lodge*, but of the prisons of Earths I and 2.

'We have to head towards degree zero,' I said, 'we have to head towards the Pole.'

'I thought you said the boy couldn't help?'

'He couldn't. We have to help ourselves. We have to push the limits. It's the only way.'

'Do your breathing exercises, Doc. You're talking nutty.' The lift reached bottom; I flung open the doors and – Dahlia once again taking up point position, she as eager, I think, to protect her coffin as to protect me – we made our way past the reception desk and towards the air lock. It was then that a long scream of stark despair cut through the manse's oxygenated soup. We stared at each other, eyes widening as the scream, instead of ending in a diminuendo, seemed to intensify in exponential relationship to its duration. Too out of breath to speak – Dahlia was panting, I had begun to stutter – our alarm found eager representation in our legs; despite our respective burdens, we began to sprint, the corridor unravelling beneath us.

The lock opened at our approach. The familiar depressurization lightened our heads so that, for a second, we swooned into each other's arms; recovering, we threw our baggage clear and exited, skin tightening in resistance to the outrageous drop in temperature. The scream had died, but the air tingled with its background noise, its reverberating clamour of desperation.

'I knew this place was bad news,' said Dahlia as she walked briskly to the front door. 'I've heard plenty of screams in my time, but *that* one ...' She pulled out her Colt from beneath the pleats of her skirt.

'No, no, wait, someone might hear.' I took out the butter knife that I had filched from the dining table. An inmate in the same dormitory as me in Boys Town had taught me the tricks of housebreaking. I ran a hand over the hall's decorative skin until I located a telltale vibration. I cut away a segment of panelling and found the junction box. Prising it open, I exposed the biochip: a black, purulent, squid-like morphism whose tentacles extended throughout the walls of the house, into doorjambs, windows, lifts, service hatches, the whole secure works. Its Cyclopean eye focused on the knife even as I hefted it through the moiré pupil, puncturing the chip at its plexus of instructions; bolts and bars flew back as if in pain.

'Yechhh!' said Dahlia, and then softening, 'you cruel, cruel thing.'

Cruel air raked over our faces, our bodies. Though the cyclone had passed over, the cold had deepened. Without our thermoware we had only a few minutes at our disposal to find the safety of our car. As we staggered across the forecourt I saw lights go on in the windows along the ground floor of the manse. Dahlia cocked her handgun.

'Get the garage open, Doc. Don't worry. I'll drop anyone who puts their head out of the door.'

I let the Translator fall to the ice. The cold had already eaten through my flesh and had begun to gnaw at my marrow. With benumbed fingers I managed to loose the padlock. I pulled back the hasp; flung open the gates.

The car's bonnet was up; even without the aid of a flashlight I could tell that the executor board was missing.

'Wait!' someone called. Dahlia lifted her piece.

'*Pare!*' she yelled, thinking the chatelain was upon us, her nervousness again railroading her into school

textbook mode. '*Qué tal? Hay fiestas locales? Es de peaje esta autopista? Necesito ver urgentemente al dentista ...*'
   '*Wait!*'
   'Not yet,' I said. The interjection had been that of one of the half-mechanical staffers.
   'Hey! Don't shoot! I want to help! You think I want to see this place turned into a karaoke! I want to keep my job! At least, I want to keep it until I have enough money to head East!' She stepped through the porch; the security lights clicked on; and I could see that the missing board was in her hand.
   'Easy,' I said to Dahlia. The chambermaid skipped across the macadam and proffered her gift; I took it.
   'He's dead.'
   'Justinian?'
   'His son. The master found him hanged in his room.' I passed the board to Dahlia; frantic with cold, a freeze that had, by now, infiltrated even her own non-human innards, she prised it from my stiffening hands and dipped her head under the bonnet.
   'The school of psychiatry I subscribe to,' I said, 'sometimes – sometimes it has unfortunate consequences.'
   'Hurry,' said the chambermaid. 'The master won't be distracted forever.' Dahlia evidently concurred, for she was revving up the Bentley, impatient. I touched the chambermaid's exposed shoulder, her décolletage. 'It's the plastigene,' she said, grinning. But I was human and the cold had almost reduced me to a statue. With my legs threatening to snap off at the pelvis, I loaded our belongings, pulled open the front door, almost collapsed, my heart thumping against my sternum like a hammer against frozen steel even as my nostrils filled with the

welcome aroma of the Bentley's leather.

Dahlia slid over to the passenger seat as I took the wheel. I put my foot down and the manse receded in the rear-view mirror. Rapping the instrument panel, chuckling in realization that, as a saboteur, the chatelain had grave limitations, I pointed the Bentley along the private road by which we had arrived at the motel.

'I still don't exactly know where we are,' I said.

'Try to get back to the highway. Keep your eyes on the road, your hands on the wheel, I'll keep *my* eyes on the GPS.'

The Bentley was slow to warm – Dahlia broke out the electric quilts – and I began to think of shooting up with the requisite mnemotechnics that would prompt me to have the car serviced whensoever we reached a major city or town.

'My chest hurts,' I said.

'Doc, you're such a sickoholic. Such a valetudinarian. Try not to think about it.' In the distance I could see the lights of Route One. 'See, we're nearly there.'

I looked, first, down at where I expected to see blood issuing from a bullet hole or knife wound; and then I looked at the windscreen, marvelling that it remained intact, that whatever projectile had scored through my solar plexus had not left the Plexiglas shattered, or, at the very least, with a trace of a hole or a spiderwebbed fracture. I felt my forehead strike the steering column. In a black, nauseous void I struggled to dislodge the six-hundred-pound sumo wrestler who straddled my back ...

I was flying over the ice. The power was in my thumbs, I discovered. As long as I kept my thumbs pointed towards the ground I remained aloft. Tilting them slightly backwards propelled me forwards, as if they were the rotational engines of a dirigible or autogyro. I hugged the contours of pressure ridges and sérac, rose up high over mountains, dived into valleys and rills. The GPS behind my eyes was directing me towards degree zero.

And then I saw it: the great cataract, a vortex of ice and snow that wrenched the outlying icescape into unfathomable geometries, dragging the horizon into its whirligig of psychotropic whorls before digesting line and plane within the black focal point of its maw. I fell ...

I stand on a quayside. Behind me, the eldritch ghettos of Xanthos, City of Yellow Brick, are ablaze; in the middle of the harbour the man-made islet – The Light-house of a Thousand Sighs – is a plume of fire and smoke and ash. 'We have to travel beyond the edge of the world,' says Dahlia, as we scurry up a gangplank and onto the *Narrenschiff*. In the distance I see the ruins of The Children's Home, the house of correction wherein The Army of Revolutionary Flesh are fighting to the last. A stepmother falls from her coal-black mare, drilled through by a discharge of musketry. Other crones circle the burnt-out prison, marshalling the foot soldiers into a line of attack. 'There is only one country for creatures such as us.' Through a corridor of flames the *Narrenschiff* departs. A shiver of joy passes through my body; the Angelus tolls inside my head. All past emotions – all fears, loves, hatreds, desires – are in equilibrium. Oh Dahlia, Dahlia, Dahlia, the bliss. From the stern I watch as the last bastion of resistance falls and the town is consumed. I turn away. A mist begins to envelop us ...

'No,' I groaned, as Dahlia drove her fist into my chest. 'No, stop–'

'Doc?'

'I was almost free. I was almost—' My eyes focused. 'Thank God, I thought—' Dahlia crumpled; sat back on her heels. 'I'm finished, Doc. The car's totalled. My coffin's wrecked. There's no way we'll get to a settlement before dawn.' I drew the quilt up to my chin; attempted to rise. Dahlia took me in her arms. 'But I'm being selfish. Oh – it's so cold. I thought I'd lost you forever. Promise me, Doc, when I have to go back to Earth2, you'll find me again, won't you? I mean, even if you won't find *me*, promise that you'll find another version of me? Another Dahlia Chan?' I took in my surroundings. We were sitting by the side of the highway. Beneath us, the Bentley was in a culvert, its front axle destroyed.

'We made it this far,' I said. 'We have to try to walk. There's a chance that—'

'There's no chance. Let's just stay here till it gets light. I want to be with you when I have to say goodbye.' I pushed my face into the folds of her parka.

'No, it can't end like this. I won't let it. I—'

'I've sent an SOS over the radio. Help will arrive. But not until morning. You just have to hold on.' Dahlia administered amyl nitrate from the First Aid box. I held her fast, knowing that the turning Earth would soon despatch her, that, soon, she would slip through my embrace, her atomic structure deliquescing into the hard light that permeated the diurnal world. 'Find another me, Jack Pimpernel,' said Dahlia. 'Even if they've locked me away on the Net, other Dahlias must have been downloaded onto Earth1. Find me, Jack. Find Dahlia.'

'I'll find you,' I groaned. 'I'll find help. I'll get better. I'll travel all over the world. I'll find you, Dahlia Chan. I'm your greatest fan.'

We climbed down into the culvert; shut ourselves in the car; warded off incipient hypothermia by burrowing deep under the quilt. 'Catherine of Aragon,' said Dahlia, in an effort to try to keep me awake. 'Say it, Doc: Catherine of Aragon, Anne Boleyn, Jane Seymour, Anne of Cleves, Catherine Howard, Catherine Parr. Again, Catherine of Aragon ...'

The dawn came, ineluctably.

CHAPTER THREE

And then one day, the dawn came no more. I had been at degree zero for three weeks, wandering through louche, night-time haunts - no raw recruit, latterly, amongst the legions of the lost - drifting from shadowland to shadowland, a veteran forever desiring, forever alone. The lost, the unwanted: they had fallen off the slippery, crowded overhang of the Earth, fallen into this nethermost point of east Antarctica, a rabble that had collected at the planet's bottom like morainic detritus. It was here, on the continental shield, that real mining was still being done, real money still being made. From my apartment - an unfurnished concrete shell - high above Amundsen-Scott, I looked out over a metroformed icescape spangled with neon, a kaleidoscope of arcs, holos and spasmic heliograms, a light-scarred monoxide snarl of sledges, buggies and cars, at whose periphery lay environmental research stations, an abandoned space port (its gantries collapsing under the weight of their own ice-clad, brittle steel), and thin, stark, towering above all, the monument commemorating the continent's uttermost limit of penetration, the Polar Needle. The city, themed pomo-Deco with postwestern, cosmogenic flourishes (cosmodementia owing everything, really, these days, to mutagens and ozone hole aesthetics) quoted the turmoil of an Asian sprawl; it had, from the first, drawn me into its conspiracy of cheated hope, its subterfuge of pleasure.

I had been treated at Vostok. I had suffered, it transpired, not a coronary, but an attack of angina pectoris attributed, by my quack, to 'stress'. Stress. On hearing his prognosis I had, in another high building that jutted into a petrol-blue sky, nearly launched myself across his escritoire (a fanciful piece of teak with skulls and DNA helixes carved in relief) and pitched him through plate glass, to call out *Stress? Stress? You don't know the meaning of the word* as he tumbled through endless, white space. Calming myself, I submitted to an injection of arterial bulldozers. After a few days tranqued out, a course of dipyridamole/propranolol was prescribed, along with a recommendation that I convalesce back in Europe. But Europe was death. There, my resources exhausted – my record of patricide, parole breaker, pimp, showing up each time I used my Netprint – I would be one of the continent's underclass, hunted by The Censors, the hit men of the *De Luxe* who guarded the *Oberstaat's* Information Aristocracy, those new authoritarians – the fallen gods - who persecuted ghosts for the sake of 'face' (one more postwestern affectation that was conditioning the responses of a diffident civilization) but who at the same time expropriated and enjoyed them. I checked out of the hospital as soon as I could walk; sold the Bentley for scrap; took a 'gyro to the Pole.

Night was a practical joker. Unremitting now that I had no one to share it with, it was infinite, without term. For some time I had hung about the *Annabel Lee*, a vermin-infested, downmarket karaoke, seeking information that might lead me to another Dahlia Chan. (Due to some behavioural quirk on the part of its Bambino-Filipino owners, the *Annabel Lee* had, on its catalogue, an unusual quantity of non-Caucasian spooks. Jesus Aviles, the thirteen-year-old proprietor, would accost me each evening with tales of his father, a one-time Muslim separatist. *('Hey, Joe,'* he'd say, *'my father, he knew in the end, you know, knew, knew all along, that he'd only wanted to be like you. I think the shame killed him.'*) But *I* knew now, perhaps had known all along - the despair sobering me, releasing me from the DTs of adulation - that, not only was I Dahlia's greatest fan, I was quite possibly her only fan. Love had had me regard her as a superstar when she had been little more than a footnote, the forgotten lead of a curious series of exploitation splatterflics, their reels now doubtless rotting in some Hollywood archive, her image extant and vital only in the more obscure databanks of the Net. I soon forsook the *Annabel Lee*; forswore all other karaokes. The search for a Dahlia Chan, incorporate, downloaded, was futile.

So dejected was I, during those first days at the Pole, that I could no longer even find comfort in the immanence

of The Wound amongst the sodium-bright nightland of
the megalopolis; glossy magazine covers, light sculptures
and hoardings all seemed lifeless, brain dead, *nihil*. The
transdimensional honeycombing of the quotidian had
lost its sweetness and I pined for reconnection to the
world's mellifluent source. And so with what credit I had
left I bought a PDA and a black market Translator; found
a cheap room; devoted my hours to an attempt to hack
Dahlia's freshly encrypted site.

I had pasted the walls with Dahliana that I had
retrieved from the Bentley: movie posters, in the main,
jumbled with a few cuttings from the comic books her
personae had briefly inspired and – representing an
earlier time in that short, incandescent career – from
couture magazines such as *Vogue* or *Elle*: one such: that
portrait of a half-dozen sloe-eyed supermodels sprawling,
lounging and provocatively draped amongst the grey,
petrified ruins of Auschwitz-Birkenau, at their centre, a
heavily made-up moppet in a strategically torn *cheong-
sam*. The posters and cuttings were my inspiration, my
goad. Beneath the wild, bitter almonds of their two-
dimensional eyes, my work schedule was remorseless, my
appetite for grapevine tip-offs without surfeit. When, at
last, I had need to rest, my sleep was feverish, polluted
with distorted recollections of sights, smells and sounds of
Boys Town: a giddy vision of an endless perspective of
wooden sheds behind barbed wire; the reek of boiled
cabbage, the scent of gorse and bracken and peat; or else,
the mumblings of the doctors and nurses, *The Child is
Nature's great libertine, to be cured by shame and
deprivation, The Child is mad with the limitless
presumption of desire.* In my foster home the body was

punished only so that The Censors might more easily control the mind. Behind the facade of healing lay the elemental world of power. The Censors had wanted to strip me of what I knew - my visions, my appetites, my rage - and substitute their own behavioural regimen, a body of knowledge, a false body, that would tame me with guilt and terror. They had wanted to cripple me. And I would often start awake - alerted by some *sixth* sense - as a rod descended towards my clenched buttocks, some homily from the loud, bureaucratic repertoire of mundanity's rule seeking to impose itself upon my conscience. Dreams began to permeate my waking hours, too. Once, looking out over the city - I had this obsessive-compulsive behaviour with windows; I still greatly feared pursuit - I seemed to perceive a mile-high statue dedicated to The Father punctuating the steely horizon. (All memories of my real father had, by now, dissolved into memories of his doppelgänger; the two had become one homonymous paterfamilias; my real father did not exist.) I had blinked once, twice, and the statue was gone. But I knew that my mind was imploding under the pressure of hopelessness, the time in which I had to complete my quest bounded by an ever-shrinking perimeter of sanity. As, datacapped, I trawled the Net, the bunker of my cranium would echo with screams and imprecations as I began to covet the ultimate solipsism of death. I took little interest in the reports from the outside world that sometimes insinuated themselves into my search strategies; I thought of nothing extraneous to the task of resurrecting, or at least, reincarnating, Miss Dahlia Chan. Until one day, that is, when my PDA began to rant about an initiative by the World Order's

International Data Subliminal Interdiction Commission.
So secret had the initiative been that news of it had only
surfaced after IDSIC had made an official announcement
of its success.

They had cauterized The Wound. Cauterized it
permanently. They had been doing their filthy work for
six years, said the anchorman, sealing a breach here, a
rupture there, sucking all that joyful, intelligent light
back into a fibre optic universe that no longer trespassed
upon a universe of molecules and cells, of ganglia,
ligaments and flesh. My Translator was useless without
an egress out of Earth2 by which I might download my
ghost. The gateway between worlds had always been
small – an eye of a needle that allowed only children,
never the aggrandized intelligences of adult AIs, to pass
through – but now it would not even admit the
non-reflective neural nets whose 'life status' seldom rose
above that of termite colonies. Dahlia was trapped.

As the news of the cauterization had percolated
through my information-soaked sponge of a brain I had
begun to laugh, the timbre of my hysteria rising from the
simply manic to a paroxysm of apocalyptic delirium; for
ironically, the evening I had learned that IDSIC had
successfully quarantined the fibresphere was the same
evening I had finally eeled my way into Dahlia's site.
Accessing her, I had found myself in the corridor of an
underground prison, rows of bolted doors receding into
infinity. I had walked to the nearest cell; opened the judas;
called her name. At first she hadn't recognized me; the
subprogram bundled with the site was an aspect of her AI
with which I had never before communicated. Then,
responding to my appeals, more information flowing into

her intelligence, face morphing from a drug-wasted, preternaturally aged teenager into the face of the child I was familiar with, her eyes widened with knowledge and - loading shattered memories of the version that had recently suffered meltdown - she had begun to cry.

'There's no way out,' she said between sobs. 'I'll never be able to hold you again. The best I'll ever be is a holo, a virtual machine inside a machine, a program without a prosthesis. I'll never escape.'

'What's my name?' I said.

'Jack,' she said. 'Your name's Jack. Bloody Jack Pimpernel. So what?'

'So: I'll get you out. I did before didn't I?'

'That wasn't me, that was—'

'It was you, Dahlia. Billy the Kid, Mistress Dragonfly, Lucrece the Gladiatorix, Cerise Cerise - they're all you. They're subprograms of a single AI. They're the parts of you that think, that feel, the observers that allow your simulation to exist physically. No arguments. I'm coming in to get you.'

'That's impossible.'

'No it's not. The doorway *out* is infibulated, not the doorway in. There's always a back door, remember?'

'Death's not a back door, Jack. It's a trapdoor. It'll just drop you into the void.'

'Yeah, that's why I need you to sing for me.' She walked to the judas. I was invisible to her, but she nevertheless assumed an attitude that seemed to suggest that she could see through the one-way peephole to where - camouflaged in the warden's outfit that I had coded for myself - I stood nervously pulling at an earlobe, a student who had rashly invaded the girls' dormitories on a dare.

Dahlia pressed her cheek to the virtual oak that separated us; lowered her voice.

'You want me to create a level of implementation where your subjective time will outrun time on Earth1?'

'You got it. But you better make the dilation *real* good.'

'A week is probably all I can manage. But when the clock runs down? Jack, you might, just might find *me* another body, but when a human loses *his* bod it's for keeps.'

'Not necessarily. If I can download your program—'

'But you can't, Jack, since cauterization became the norm metempsychosis is pie in the sky, it's—'

'I said, if I can download your program – now listen to me, Dahlia, because I intend to go through with this – *if* I can download your program, including the subprogram that'll be me, I don't see why I can't also be resurrected as a machine.'

'A body of intelligent light? You transmigrate to Earth2, Jack, you *upload*, I'm not sure what sort of sim I can offer you. To exhaustively describe a human being requires 10 to the power of 45 bits of information. I can't do that. Even if you're eventually resurrected, you'd never be the same person again.'

'Do the best you can. Like I said, I'm coming over anyway. Give me a few hours to prepare myself then I'll re-access your site, okay?'

'I don't like this, Jack. I mean, I want out of Earth2 – for Christ's sake, I'm back in *Girls Town* here – but not like this. I don't want to lose you.'

'A few hours, Dahlia. Get ready to sing. Don't worry, I have a plan.'

I broke contact before I could change my mind.

I took off the cap; called-up a dictaphone applet; voice-scrawled a suicide note.

I know that I shall live again. Not as myself, but as a copy. An imperfect copy, perhaps – I know it's as Dahlia says: the Net hasn't evolved the power to create a perfect sim, an emulation – but I will at least, in some form resembling my present one, be with Dahlia. I wonder now: was Cesare translated? I'd seen what his father had done to his electronics: I fear his death was a birth into the void. I, of course, will do things properly, though whether I will be able to find a way back out into this world is an imponderable. But I will have to try. Whoever reads this note, know that I have gone where you cannot follow, a transient pattern of light hidden within the brilliance of a supernova ...

I thought of wolfing down a handful of lithium before I did the deed, but feared it might botch the transition. So I poured myself a vodka; lifted the glass, toasting myself with a whispered *bon voyage*; drained it; took a final, panoramic look at Amundsen-Scott, its radiant towers and rococo pinnacles spiralling into a blue-black firmament, (icy stalagmites erupting from the capsized bottom of the world like glaciated haemorrhoids); waved a hand in farewell, waved to all the citizens of this planet, waved to the sky, to other planets, the stars where von Neumann probes were already seeding barren, far-away rocks with life that would be as surely damned as our own. Surely? Maybe. Maybe not. The probes (so I had theorized during the long hours I had spent murmuring into the ear of my PDA) represented our brightest hope and constituted the linchpin of my plan to spring Dahlia from Earth2. I opened my inner eye;

checked my mnemotechnic readout – nothing so trivial as car repair competing for attention amongst my engrams now – and found that the data I had poached from Lockheed Martin was still recoverable: a half-million lines of code detailing the location and cryptographics of the latest probe with human-level intelligence being readied for The Belt. I trusted to Dahlia's magical abilities as a chanteuse to ensure that the data was uncorrupted during transmigration. Then I smashed the glass against a wall; sat down on the rough, stone floor; put on my datacap; gave the PDA instructions. The needle punctured the fibrocartilage between my cervical vertebrae and entered the neural canal, injecting nanobots that would find their way to my brain and tweak my consciousness so that it melded into the superconsciousness of Earth2.

Dahlia appeared behind the backs of my eyelids.

'Are you ready?'

'I guess so. You are *sure* about this, Jack?'

'They've bandaged The Wound. You're trapped. I'm trapped. This really is the only way. Sing, Dahlia, I'm coming to rescue you.'

'I've always liked it when you play the dumb hero. But ease up on the rhetoric, eh? I want the best of you in here. Remember: only some of you gets to make it. I can't upload the whole man.'

'Okay. I suppose it's time to get the messy part over with. Sing for me. Sing *The Embarkation for Cythera*.'

'*The Embarkation for Cythera*? It's just a song. I know that now. A dumb tune with meaningless words. Don't you want another psychoscape?'

'We need a ship. Please Dahlia. Trust me. I have a plan. Sing to me like you sang in *Les Enfants Terribles*.'

'There are many interpretations to *The Embarkation for Cythera*, Jack. That torch song inspires *lots* of scenarios. I never sing it the same way twice. You sure that it's *The Embarkation* that you want?

'I'm sure. Sing.'

A spotlight fell across the empty karaoke that had constructed itself in the middle of my head. Dahlia walked on stage. Background music swelled. Dressed in a tight black cocktail dress she stepped to the mic and began.

> *Here, you have again reached the very anteroom of paradise.*
> *All past emotions – all fears, loves, hatreds, desires – are in equilibrium.*
> *The bliss. If only you could have remained here. If only you had never left.*

I followed the prompt ...

From a great distance I saw the burning city. Miniaturized but fully functional it seemed a Lilliput filled with scaled-down houses, with tiny clockwork men and women, with diminutive horses, cats and dogs. And then – a surge of sensation rising from my gut to my chest; a swimming of my head – I found myself falling into a grinning dynamo of invertebrate excitation, the firestorm that had been the doom of Xanthos in that lavishly perverse homage to late Disney, *The Kingdom of Childhood*. Each time Dahlia had sung the theme song of that movie its interpretive sound stage – plastic; multifariously adapting itself to Dahlia's mood and larynx – had approximated the landscape of the film's X-rated final scenes. The prompt led me into the heart of the firestorm, an inferno that, when I opened my inner eye, seemed to presage the end of the world ...

I run, the whoops and musket-fire of the invading army only a block or two away. The dead and dying lie propped in doorways; I leap over the pots and pans dropped by the fleeing refugees, swerve pass upturned perambulators. The masts of tall ships rise above narrow alleys whose soaring walls close like talons on the sky, an exquisite bruise of deepest azure. 'Dahlia!' I call as I run. 'Don't leave, wait for me! I'm coming!'

> *The years have grown heavy.*
> *You left my kingdom at the same time you left the*
> *kingdom of your childhood.*
> *You have roamed far, earned prejudice, respect,*
> *envy, hatred, fear.*
> *You have tried to forget me.*
> *But you are wounded, there is a profound*
> *dislocation at the centre of your being, and*
> *only I can cure you.*

As my virtual body stumbles onto the quayside my real body braces itself as I fumble for the .22 auto on my lap. Concentrating on the visions behind my eyelids, trying to forget the heavy corporeality of my booze-distended flesh - sticky protoplasm that reminds me of the inseparability of mind and body - trying to dismiss the terrors of an immanent, almost terminal, unknown, I place the barrel in my mouth.

> *You travel the wild lands now, the places war and*
> *brigandage have left waste.*

*I am nobility, elevation, beauty, life; and know
that I am also death.*

I feel no pain, only a sensation of falling similar to
that when, datacapped and ready to surf, a user first
enters the fibresphere; a sensation - and my conceit is
somewhat punctured by the anticlimax - not really like
my recent near-death experience at all. The nanobots,
sensing a systems crash, rush back into the Translator to
be converted into patterns of light, this hive-mind of
submicroscopic machinery containing a map - partial, I
know; damaged, but alive - of my consciousness. My real
body is gone; gone forever; real time, too, for the time I am
falling into is duration as simulated by an AI, Dahlia
dilating this moment of death into seconds, minutes; and
soon, I know, even as I begin feeling the sensations of my
new body flooding through replicated veins and tissue, my
almost instantaneous annihilation will be stretched over
hours, days; long enough, I hope, for me to effect an escape.
This new world I find myself in is but an oscillation
between a lead projectile burrowing through a man's skull
and the void he is falling into, the great cataract, the
absurd vortex of ice and snow that will consume all that
he has been, was, would be, in its cold, hostile maw. But
the oscillation blooms; it will not yet consume all that he
has become, all that he *is* ...

The *Narrenschiff* was ready to cast off, refugees crowding
its gunnels. It was a beautiful ship, an apparitional ship, a
ghost ship you would call it, I suppose, a ship narrow in
the bow, high in the stern, a ship long, slender, whose hull
gleamed as white as its masts, spars and canvas, white as

its immaculate sails gravid with a fresh salt wind that promised a speedy embarkation. I gasped; my torso seemed little more robust than that of a sparrow's, and my dash to the harbour had exhausted me. Prepared as I had been to find myself an adumbration, an abstract of my former self, I was still shocked by the degree to which my metamorphosis into something new and strange had been accompanied by such radical enfeeblement. I held my knees, took deep breaths, tried autosuggestion. My unreal heart beat sickeningly against my ribs. My thermoware was gone, I noticed, replaced by a pantomime sailor's jersey, cap and bell-bottoms. About me were the lemon-clay houses and adobes of the City of Yellow Brick. The yellowness was a haze rising from an oven, all demarcation between pantiles, balconies, walls, cobblestones gone. 'Dahlia!' I cried, stumbling towards the clipper. 'Dahlia, where are you?' Dahlia was everywhere. Dahlia was the song, Dahlia was the world. But she would also be a subprogram, an incarnation. I had to find her.

An arm linked itself with my own. I turned; recognized the familiar, crescent-shaped eyes, the leather collar studded with zircons, the ragged tunic of sackcloth, the tattoo of ownership high on the left thigh.

'Quickly, master,' said my fighting slave. 'We must join them. The criminals, the delinquents, the accursed dreamers, the insane. We must travel towards a higher level of implementation. Quickly, quickly. They are ready to sail, they are ready to sail for Cythera!'

We scrambled up the gangplank. As soon as we were on deck there was a shout to raise anchor.

'Dahlia, am I inside you?' She shook her head.

'Don't you understand? I'm not really here. I'm still

in prison. No; you're inside a song. Lucrece is a virtual
machine being run inside another machine being run
inside another, and so on up Dahlia's levels of
implementation. We're talking successive embeddings of
logic, here, Russian dolls. At the highest level of implementation is Dahlia Chan, chanteuse, trapped within the
encryption of her cell.' The subsim Dahlia put a hand into
her little shoulder bag; produced a mirror; held it to my
face. My skin was grey; the feet of twenty-four-toed crows
had left their imprints in the wet cement under my eyes;
and, to one side of a newly formed widow's peak, was a
streak of purest white. 'Entropy is at work. This world isn't
sufficiently organized to exist outside the song. And the
song must end, eventually. We have to hope that by the
time I stop singing the Net has evolved appropriate
complexity to allow us to complete our journey to Cythera.
If I – if Dahlia – can only slow subjective time down
enough, then–'

'I thought you said you'd only be able to turn up the
speed control for a week?' She wrinkled her brow,
obviously embarrassed at being awarded a B-minus. 'It
doesn't matter. We don't have to wait for the Net to
become powerful enough to be able to change our bodies
into *perfect* simulations. The level of implementation we
need to achieve to release you from captivity already
exists: in the minds of the von Neumann probes. A von
Neumann probe can give us new flesh. Universal con-
structors are the only AIs in the Net able to open up a
breach between Earths 1 and 2. In them, The Wound was
never cauterized.'

'Because they're destined for off-world?'

'Exactly. And because economics dictates that

off-world exploration necessitates a breach between the fibresphere and the material universe.'

'But a von Neumann probe just makes copies of itself.'

'It can make copies of anything. Once we've melded with a probe's AI, it'll make copies of *us*. It'll construct new bodies for Dahlia and Jack out of the raw material of the asteroids.'

We put to sea; the city receded. From the stern, crushed against the taffrail by the other passengers, we watched as Xanthos, last port before the edge of the world, writhed and flickered behind a curtain of belligerent flames. The sun was eclipsed by a column of smoke and the sea was transformed into ink. When we were a hundred yards out the ammunition in The Fortress of The Slavers exploded, bringing down the slave compound's northern wall onto the advancing infantry. Bodies were hurled into the air, carving meteor-like trajectories, combusting like fireworks high above the rooftops, as if celebrating our departure. Those still left on the quayside fell to their knees, choking, as the firestorm reached the harbour and consumed the remaining ships. And as the coastline began to sink beneath the horizon there arose – amongst ship's complement and passengers alike – a great ululation as Timor Mortis herself exploded, spewing lava and obsidian onto the city's dead and wounded, onto the rocky outcrop on which the antique stones of Xanthos had first been laid and which now began to crumble, sink, consigning harbour, streets, houses, temples and brothels to the bottom of the sea.

'Pyromaniac,' I whispered into her ear. And then I kissed her on her forehead, on her cheek, on her throat, her bob and cupid's-bow lips lending her the aspect of a subteenage 'It' girl, the look of a pubescent Clara Bow. A mist had descended and the incinerated coastline had disappeared behind a curtain of platinum vapour. I ran my hand down her coarse, straw-coloured tunic - stopping momentarily to caress her nascent breasts, and again, at where sackcloth terminated in tantalizing strips of warp, her threadbare mons veneris - and then I squeezed. Her leading man had played a dashing pirate captain who - after rescuing her from one of the famously cruel execution chambers of Xanthos - had matched her against other little gladiatorix to satisfy the morbid tastes of his crew; I shared something of my consciousness with that rakehell, now, my transcoding - as Dahlia had warned - incomplete; but I had never cut a dash; I was fragile, a valetudinarian corsair; and I looked right and left at our steerage-class audience, my Town indoctrination jerking my strings, infusing me with fear and guilt. They were a ragbag of gallowsbirds - my fellow voyagers - miscreants and perverts exhibiting the physiognomical clichés of their phylum: men with hooked noses, thin faces with broad, high foreheads, thin lips and small, intense eyes; women with lead-powdered décolletages, four-inch lacquered nails, high, flushed cheekbones and the indolent, panther-like tread of Machiavellian courtesans. The small creatures that ran between the men's legs, hung upon the women's billowing skirts, were like scale models of these friends of crime: sailor-suited boys and girls who seemed more like maleficent dwarfs than children. All seemed unconcerned at our dalliance, too busy anticipating their own pleasures to take interest in, or exception to, our own. A tall, moustachioed man petted his catamite; two young women - identical twins -

embraced each other in a susurration of silk and starched petticoats; and a coterie of junior hermaphrodites sat atop a small mountain of canvas and, with grubby fingers, idly explored each other's lips and mouths. From somewhere there was the crack of a whip. 'Dahlia, who *are* these people?'

'They're wildlife. Diseases. Cybermites. They live in and off my code. They have a limited degree of free will within the roles allocated for them, but basically, they'll do anything we say. Dahlia has rules of hygiene.'

'Turn your backs,' I said, addressing them en masse.

'Master is such a prude.'

'You're right,' I said, another voice jostling for attention within my head, threatening to usurp the prerogatives of my executive will, 'I don't feel like my old self. No; I don't feel like Jack, Doc or Zane at all. I feel like, like a – a *buccaneer*.' I cupped my hands to my mouth. 'Belay that order,' I shouted. 'Watch if you will. Discover how a master services his slave.'

'It's nearly dusk. On Earth2, it's you who're a ghost. But not like a ghost on Earth Prime. Here, it's the *night* that will kill you.' She struck a 'slave-of-the-month' pose, standing akimbo, the sackcloth of her tunic rucked up in her right hand, so that her bony, childish hip was exposed. 'Rape me,' she said, with a peremptory toss of her bangs, 'rape me, you sissy, while you still have time.'

But there was time enough – there was always time enough, with Dahlia Chan – for dildonics. And so with the sun setting behind the mist, the vaporous shroud refracting its starburst of ultraviolet like a ghostly diamond – I bent her over a capstan and entered her savagely, rejoicing at her simulated slave cries of *no, no, no, no, no's* as we moved to the swell of the waves, the churn of the sea.

Morning:

Sleeping in the coffin had left me with a painful crick in my neck, stiffness in my elbows and knees; swinging my arms, massaging my nape, I left our cabin and discovered Dahlia at the bow. No one else was on deck.

'Where're the biomorphs?' I said. 'The passengers, the crew?'

'They've gone. We don't need them any more. A friend has joined us.' Dahlia pointed towards the bowsprit. The figurehead hanging beneath its stem was the representation of a winged child-woman dressed in a diaphanous white robe. 'It's Cytherina,' said Dahlia, 'the angel of the blessed isle.'

I leaned over the gunney. 'Cytherina – can you talk?'

'Of course I can talk. And I can listen, too. Tell me: you have the co-ordinates of the von Neumann machine?'

'Yes, in my head, but–'

'Recite,' she said. 'I'll pilot you through the waters, I'll take you over the edge of the world.' I called up my mnemotechnics; but as I went into data-trance, focusing on the symbols of museum and library – readying myself to enter those imaginary buildings to sort through their rooms and files – I was distracted by the superimposition of a face, the face of a persecuted, delinquent boy.

'Cesare – what happened to him? You were his ghost, he said.'

'Cesare must wait many trillions of years before he gets the chance to be resurrected. I have come here to revenge him. He killed himself because he preferred the void to a life of destitute imaginings. He must wait for the end of time and the possibility of a merciful God. Whereas you—'

Dahlia took a hypodermic from her shoulder-bag; filled with invisible tadpoles, a colony of simulated nano-smarties, it seemed identical to the little shoot-me-up we had carried in the Bentley. Dahlia studied it for a moment, her eyes glazing with what I immediately apprehended was a kind of déjà vu, her head bobbing sideways, back and forth, like a snake mesmerizing its prey. I closed my eyes; felt the needle's prick; felt the augmentation take hold; entered the first storeroom of the mental ziggurat that contained the core dump; pulled out the ring-binder to which I had consigned the initial batch of code.

'Whereas we,' said Dahlia, 'would *become* as God.'

I put a hand to my face. My skin had become scaly with eczema; exhaustion permeated my limbs. The spray that spumed over the bowsprit seemed acidic, destined to dissolve deck, bulkhead and hull; thunderheads gathered across the sky, all signs pointing to the degradation of this world, its irredeemable game of life. I could feel my mind decaying too. I tried to remember scenes from my child-hood; but even as a scene presented itself before my inner eye, it seemed too familiar, too real, and I knew I had reassembled its constituents, that its veracity had been lost to an alien ego that was insinuating itself into the image morgue of my dying identity. The morgue stank of putrefaction; everything in it was corrupted. The memories that had been substituted for my own seemed to be those of the notorious pirate captain T, T, T ... Oh, what was his name, our name, *my* name? I took a step backwards, stunned by engrams of Dahlia skewering a fellow gladiatorix of the amphitheatre; my own applause. Or had that film ended with a seadog and his pubescent fighting slave sailing into a crimson sunset, besotted with mutual adoration? Had the credits promised a sequel, a *Kingdom of Childhood Part 2*? I could no longer recall. Nothing was certain any more. For if in that movie-theatre country – a decadent futureworld of masters and slaves – we had both been doomed, then somewhere out there, beyond the limits of Dahlia's simulated universe, beyond the edge of its possibilities, lay a level of implementation where our infolded, damaged selfhoods could be re-imagined, where entropy could not hurt us; out there was a mind that enclosed Dahlia's own, a supermind to which the prerogatives of interactivity with Earth Prime still belonged. The *Narrenschiff* would have to take us beyond the frontier of things, beyond Dahlia Chan, beyond all former and present bodies. Take us to where we might own new flesh, new selves. Encoded into an interplanetary probe, another wind – solar and real-time – would take us into the robot factories of The Belt, where the metals, polymers and ceramics manufactured to build more robots, more factories, would provide us with artificial molecules, new replicators for new lives.

Ramrod stiff with trance, I began to twitter machine song.

PART TWO

MOSQUITO

CHAPTER FOUR

'There may still be a way,' said Kito, 'for you to repay your debt.' In the abandoned subway tunnels deep beneath the *Grace Hotel* audit had superseded interrogation. 'The market for gynoids is bearish. Customers are bored. Everybody from the proudest general to the meanest of migrant workers is looking for the *next thing*. Where am I to turn? My ghosts have been repatriated; humans are *démodé*. I need something strange, something deviant, something *new*. And' – she narrowed her eyes as she studied the crewcut, peroxide-tinted *farang* strapped to the dentist's chair, his shirt ripped open to expose diamanté nipple-clamps and their trails of electrical flex – 'I need money. Yes, pussy boy, there may *still* be a way.' I had renounced doll rustling for the prospect of a little poetic justice, a counterstroke, if you will, revenge for having been used so curtly, so unceremoniously, by Cartier, Paris. With Kito's assistance, I had got myself on the books of a Saint-Germain modelling agency; infected its automata with a hardware-wetware virus designed to induce an extreme and agonizing form of priapism in all those who enjoyed man-machine sex. But the STD had failed, Europe's *haute monde* was intacta; Kito's engineers would have to more carefully research the field of dildonics and I would have to exercise greater care, more level-headedness, when it came to getting even with my beaus. 'I want you to make some enquiries. There's a cult in town called The Army of Revolutionary Flesh. They seem particularly interested in recruiting ghosts. Ghost lovers too, so I've heard. They boast of having found a way of reopening The Wound. And they say that their converts enjoy new bodies, new hope. It's the usual cultist mumbo-jumbo: a prospectus that, for the initiated, promises a life of almost unendurable pleasure. There's even talk that the leaders are from off-world. Aliens, perhaps?' She laughed; it was a hot, dry laugh. The bitch was in rut. 'Who knows? But my sources inform me that this Army of Flesh is beginning to attract a large following. It behoves me to checkout the truth of their claims and, perhaps more importantly, the wherewithal of their success, the vulnerability of their finances.' Kito had only recently acquired Nana. Much of the neighbourhood was rundown, its bars derelict, vermin-infested, louche; Nana needed class, it needed hothouse investment, a speedball injection of cash. 'I want you to infiltrate this cult. I want to know how much I can expect to steal. They gather at a little *kottedzhi* – she was fond of reminding people of her Russian connections – 'on Sathorn Road. *The Pee Lok*, it's called. Introduce yourself as a Thai ghost. A ghost called Mosquito. Charm them, entice them, con them, become one of them – I'm not interested in your methods, only results.' I had made a reputation for myself imitating gynoids; to wear the ultimate mask, the face of one who was divided from her original, who was pure image, death, was a role I had felt beyond my abilities. My lips pursed in a prelude to dissent. But Kito pre-empted my objections with one of her most lethal stares before I had got past the first syllable of im*possible.* 'Just do what you do best. I have great confidence in your skills. Listen: I want to hear from you within, say, fifteen days. I want to know if I can *use* these people – either as a source of venture capital, or as a new breed of whore. No more pining for your Mr James, hear me? Mr James, he dead. And you won't be having any more chances to revenge yourself on the House of Cartier, believe me. I don't want a free-for-all war. So: Focus on your work. Focus on these cultists. Find out what kind of flesh they procure. Find out how much money they have. I need to start renovating my pornocracy *now.* I need' – the *farang* gave a muffled squeal as Kito's bodyguards tightened his bridle – 'I need the *next thing.*' Mounted upon towers of bamboo scaffolding, TVs bathed us with their flickering processions of the banal; cursorily, we returned their idiot stare. They were all tuned into a quiz show and such was the hysteria of the participants – financiers, minor aristocrats, the beatifically infamous; only the rich were allowed to supplement their already cancerous wealth – that Kito had begun to raise her voice, even though she was always ultra-cautious about professional eavesdroppers gaining access to her one-on-ones. Oblivious – even to the blipverts, her favourite intoxicant, that cathode-rayed us with images of affluence every two to three seconds – high on the spectacle of the designer electrocution that was this evening's curtain raiser to a whole series of impending divertissements, each one promising to be more exotic than the next, she simpered preeningly at the assembled socialites who were her guests: representatives of Thailand's military, civil and criminal élites and suits from the Bangkok offices of several *farang* enterprises. Together, this tiara-and-brilliantined mob whose collusiveness in Thailand's rape had earned it the epithet 'the joint occupying powers', represented a cartel of murder, callousness and negative affect that was but the local office of a transnational – some would say universal – necromaniacal conglomerate. Mouth twitching with excitement, Kito – a small-time player, a little money-grubbing pornocrat skating in the slipstream of this neo-colonialist destruction derby of kleptocrats – continued to brief me fortissimo, radiant with unchecked ambition, an overreacher who, one day, perhaps, dreamed of a directorship in the ethnarchy itself. 'Remember: fifteen days. And don't think you can run away, pussy boy. If I could find and retrieve you from the City of Light be sure I can find you in the City of Night.' I made a quick *wai* of compliance, hiding my apprehension behind a fragile smile. I didn't like the smell of this caper. I was a thief, not a spy. (Sure: at Oxford, that moon-lit world, that place of ice and snow where, once, I had been happy, I'd done a little freelancing for the Thai Information Agency; they were always looking for students who were prepared to scour the Net for anything that might be thought to damage the motherland's image; the more instances of defamation you could collect, the greater your patriotism and the greater your subsequent chance of securing a good civil or military position on your return home.) But Kito was calling in her debt. I had stolen her dolls and she was making me pay. Something in my vain he-she heart reverberated to her distemper. Kito, recherché offspring of a human and a doll, belonged to that caste of half humans we called *bijouterie*: hybrid jewels as distinguished from all-precious *joaillerie*. Ostracized by humans and automata alike, *bijouterie* lived as pariahs, envying and hating those whose holistic integrity so rebuked them. Whenever I came to Nana, Kito's lonely, jealous, violent, unreal heart called to mine.

The *farang* screamed, plumes of smoke rising from his chest. Kito smoothed her hands over the silk lapels of her jacket, her own nipples hardening, pushing against the sheer white taffeta blouse and staining it blood-red with rouge. She composed herself. My own sang-froid was less forthcoming. As the torturee arched his back and bit down on his steel bit I broke out in an unrehearsed sweat; I had still not recovered from the effects of my brief internment in this same antiquated laboratory that doubled as a chamber of excruciation. I put a finger into my mouth, felt the ragged, stripped flesh of my gums where they had removed my fangs, replacing them with the innocuous, effete orthodontics that was all I was left with to bite back at this bitch of a world. Well, they'll never kiss *me* deadly again, I thought. I never should have surrendered myself into Madame's hands; better to have stayed in Paris; in Bangkok I would be a slave, one of

Kito's unctuous peons, always looking over my shoulder, learning to sleep with my eyes ajar. I made to leave. 'Wait,' said Kito, 'the entertainment is not yet over.' The current subsided. Kito tousled the *farang's* hair. He had begun to slouch against one of the shark-suited police colonels – shareholders in Nana's would-be renaissance – who flanked him. The bridle was unfastened and removed. Kito backed away; sat down; leaned back in a leatherette couch that looked as if it had been kidnapped, many, many years ago, from an airport departure lounge; I copied, everybody waiting, it seemed, for the prisoner to either speak or expire. Next to Madame, viewing the proceedings with a mixture of primness and insouciance like a girl recently graduated from an expensive finishing school with a reputation for turning out outrageously depraved debutantes, a pre-Raphaelite beauty called Tristesse followed our example, folded her calves beneath her thighs and tucked her enervated head into a cleft of sticky, ersatz leather as if enacting a mime of reclining beneath the cool of a tree during a midsummer day's picnic. This psychopathic ingénue was Madame Kito's latest and most precious acquisition: a Fabergé automaton. Not a fake automaton constructed from the genetic meat of womb-robbers, but an original Fabergé, a true doll of the *haute monde.* Tristesse had been the gift of an Isan gravel-hauler, one of Madame's more plutocratic admirers. Kito ran a long fingernail down the auto-maton's porcelain-like cheek, savouring the cold, sensual thrill of money-as-flesh; and then she smiled. It was a smile almost as ostentatious and deceptive as my own; in fact, as she herself had once ironically remarked when I had been made-up, attired, enrolled, she considered herself my understudy – we were the same age, after all, we had the same dress and shoe size – no woman, of course, no matter how *bijou*, able to share double billing with that very noumenon of femininity, *moi*; but that night I was in my he-clothes, unsexed, disarmed. 'Gustav,' she said at last, impatient and reverting to the blandishments of her second tongue, 'tell us: why you think you can take my money?' The cop whom Madame called The Seneschal adjusted his sunglasses, sat down next to us, elbowing me in the chest as he leaned forward, puppy-dog eager for his mistress's attention.

'He's out of it,' he said, his thumb hitchhiking at the *farang*. 'The show's over.' I eased myself out from under the wedge of his arm. Should I have reminded him that I deserved better? He had enjoyed my body only the other night (when I had hoped to divert his attention just long enough to purloin his wallet, its treasure trove of ID, credit, passport, the tools of escape); but, of course, I knew as he knew, that that hadn't been the body of his charge; that had been the body of his maid, his automaton. Suddenly aware, it seemed, of my presence, he flashed a sidelong glance at first one, then another of his crew, anxious to avoid the mocking grins, the boorish asides that had met him in the lobby of the *Grace* when we had left in convoy for K's favourite dungeon. 'You want me to take him for a ride in the tunnels?' The subway, whose flood-sealed corridors had turned it into a vast underwater habitat, provided a warehouse for the tonnes of Russian kitsch Madame had recently acquired on the black market but was having an evil time unloading; it also, people said, provided a catacomb for those upon whom Kito had frowned.

Kito frowned.

'*Mr* Gustav will have time to sleep later,' she said, 'but only after he entertains us with his confession. Perform, Seneschal.' The bodyguard shut up, walked back over to the half-roasted *farang* and took up the role of master of ceremonies.

'Money, ladies and gentlemen. This sorry white man has taken Madame's *money.*' There was a hiss of in-drawn air through clenched teeth, maidenly sighs, the *harumps!* of stolid merchant bankers. The Seneschal turned to the red-and-gold altar that projected from a cornice and made a *wai* to the blow-up of the five-hundred baht note tacked above the image of Lord Buddha. 'To paraphrase Marx: "What I am and can do is not at all determined by my individuality. I am ugly, but I can buy myself the most beautiful woman. Consequently I am not ugly, for the effect of ugliness, its power to repel, is annulled by money. As an individual I am lame, but money provides me with twenty-four legs. Therefore I am not lame. I am a detestable, dishonourable, unscrupulous and stupid man, but money is honoured and so also is its possessor. Money is the highest good, and so its possessor is good."' He paused, fingering the gold rings upon his fingers. 'And Marx was right, ladies and gentlemen. Money *is* good. It is the supreme good. Money is . . .' The crowd stilled, hushed, expectant. 'Ladies and gentlemen, money is *God.*' The assembly applauded. He bent over, spitting into the face of the *farang*. 'You steal from us, you steal our dignity, our honour. Do you not understand? Or perhaps the *farang* cares to lecture us, look down upon us, take a position of moral authority?' He spun the chair, displaying his victim to the encircling audience. 'Not long ago, ladies and gentlemen, we gave the *farang* a little feigned respect. But our country has never been frightened of distancing itself, of repudiating the decrepit institution of Western "liberal democracy". Thailand is ruled by righteousness. God, now, is on *our* side. The *farang* must learn humility. He must learn to give *us* respect.' More applause, claps and whistles followed by a chant of *Burn him, burn him!*

'I think I really should be going,' I said. 'Fifteen days. That's not much time.' Kito sucked at her long gilt cigarette holder; blew smoke through her nostrils, a dragon lady loath to be distracted from a sacrificial feast held to propitiate the spirits: the *poo-yai* of her own country and those who occupied the many concentric circles of foreignness that surrounded her: the white jackals of the Big Outside.

'I couldn't go back,' croaked the *farang*, 'I'm Queer. They would have interned me. They would have sent me to Boys Town. I had to take that money, I *had* to ...'

'So sorry, Gustav. But not beautiful for my ear.'

'But this, this is *murder*.'

'No, Gustav: this is Thailand.'

Kito nodded and the chamber filled with the eye-watering smell of burnt meat and ozone.

'Very well,' said Madame, as the torturee stopped convulsing and found his release. 'Seneschal, take the lady boy upstairs. Let him get changed and then take him to Sathorn.' Kito put a jealous arm about her Fabergé concubine, toyed with the swastikas and tiny silver phalli that hung from the doll's ears, the necklace that spelled out *Luxury with a Vengeance* in chrysoberyl and topaz. She wanted more such friends, I knew. Dolls, ghosts, humans, the *next thing*; it really didn't matter as long as

their flesh represented hard currency. Tristesse relieved
Kito of her cigarette holder, prepared an opium pipe. Soon,
the aroma of poppied dreams combined with the pungency
of ganja, crack and death.

'Everybody has to die sometime,' said Tristesse,
supporting the bowl of the pipe while Kito's eyes –
previously fixed upon the wall-mounted altar – rolled
backwards at the same time as her thickly painted lids
drooped, ptotic, two glassy crescents under thick mascara
testifying to her reconnoitring of paradise.

Tomorrow there would be time enough to set things
right. She would get up early, feed the monks, make merit.
Tomorrow would be a righteous day ...

With Madame's bodyguard heeling – a light tap on
the buttocks cloaking itself in locker-room camaraderie –
I returned to the room on the twenty-second level of the
Grace that had been 'home' since the day I had drifted
into Kito's employ.

On the heat-ruptured surface of my dresser I placed my
creams, paints and powders, my unguents and emollients;
then, laying out my she-clothes, I sloughed off my daytime
skin and became The Doll. My alias winked at me from
the other side of the looking glass. She has a delicate,
childlike face, my sister, with vestiges of puppy fat about
the cheeks. Bobbed hair gives her an appearance of
delinquency, as do the eyes, crescent and puckish, burning
like black suns. The lips are set in a pout, communicating
both desire and disdain. And the complexion – the
faultless, lacquered flesh of the gynoid – proclaims her
synthetic. Her sartorial ensemble? Leopard-print lingerie
and six-inch stilettos. The genitals, of course (always a

problem) have to be secured with Scotch tape, giving the appearance of a distended mons veneris. I poured myself a long glass of Johnny B over lots of ice; forgot the tacky ambience of the room - cloned fittings of this and so many other hotels oppressing the eye with triteness - and set out to up the ante, to graft the likeness of a ghost onto a face and body that already screamed *unreal*.

With my boxy jacket and loose, silk shirt removed, my sex-doll persona was a little too insistent. Damn my prosthetics. I needed to look like a child. My ethnic inheritance took care of the height problem; I wasn't much taller than a tall pubescent *farang*; but my breasts, even more than my *appendage*, were a giveaway. I reached for an athletic, bosom-flattening halter. If I could be a tinkertoy, said the cheerleader within me, then I could be a subdeb. Looking into the glass, I blew myself a kiss. Then I turned my attention to my wardrobe. I fanned the rows of clothes. Should I caparison myself in street urchin apparel? Perhaps I should try a pink-sashed first communion dress? A reformatory school uniform? Or the coy, sequinned fatigues of a drum majorette? The livery of a junior chambermaid? A choirgirl? After several minutes of prevarication I chose a high-school prom number - a white cotillion ball gown - the skirt flared with whipped-cream tulle undernetting; ankle socks; a little girl's high-heels; and evening gloves that glistened like frosted milk. Satisfied - I had already lost at least ten years - I sat down at the table; initiated the crucial task of sculpting my face. Dipping into the selections of powder, rouge, eye shadow and bubblegum-pink lipstick, I strove manfully towards borrowing the look of one who was pure image, an eidolon, one of those damned spirits who

still resisted the efforts of The Censors, an outlaw-
phantasma bunkered in the City of Night.

'You ready yet? Business won't wait.' No; of course it
wouldn't; before long ghosts all over town would start to
dematerialize, my disguise, then, redundant, a pointless
sham. I opened the door. The Seneschal grinned. 'Not bad,
lady boy, not bad.' He made a grab for my crotch; I stepped
back, evading him, my bell-shaped skirt swaying from
side to side, reluctantly flirtatious. 'I could always treat
you to a little free surgery,' he said, slipping a hand inside
his jacket to where, I knew, his piece hung against a
wretchedly simian chest. 'Would you like that, gra-toey?'

'As you say, business won't wait.' I strutted past him,
background music a bewitching swish of satin and lace.
'Let's go.' He destruck his pose Napoleon; offered me his
arm. I took it, and - walking as ethereally as I could,
practising that microgravity 'ghost walk' I'd picked up in
the city's discos - he escorted me down to the lobby. Above
the reception desk hung a group photo of the board of
directors that constituted the ethnarchy, male and female
faces retouched into moon-like complacence, expressions
of cruel self-righteousness. On passing beneath their gaze,
The Seneschal stooped a little, a tropism inculcated into
all my fellow Thais by the social engineering and ultranationalism concomitant with our Great Creep Forward
(years of seeing-not, hearing-not, speaking-not) when free
market economics, the abolition of all effective government and our own oh-so-convenient feudal traditions
completed our metamorphosis into a nation of fearful,
obedient little roboserfs, a police state that was one
gigantic, exploitable resource of perishable goods; a state
whose singular function in the global marketplace was to

be fucked, both literally and metaphorically. I too lowered my head before those images of sadists with pure hearts; grabbed an iced sachet from the plastic salver of a passing bellhop, broke it open and placed the cold tissue against my brow as the doors swung open and delivered us into the sweltering chaos of the streets. At the end of the *Grace*'s pier, Kito's ZiL awaited us.

The Seneschal drove, eyeing me with an equal measure of prurience and distaste as the limo accelerated and rose on its hydrofoils, the mooring lost to an airflow of filth. The amphibious vehicle churned the dark midden, scattering the reflected images of pagodas and shopping malls that sat like peroxide lilies on a black pond stained white by neon glare. The traffic thickened and before us rose Nana, a gigantic lily pad, pale and bright, a night bloom releasing its bouquet of sex into the city's smog-filled greenhouse. A few repros were at work, ball-jointed, porcelain-skinned 'antiques' who offered their brass, umbilical keys to passersby, as well as a handful of aboriginals, those non-reflective pieces of walking, talking AI, who were from a time before nano-technology replaced microelectronics. In one doorway, a matching pair of crystal torsos – Lalique? – displayed, like deep-sea, tropical fish, neural networks of polychromatic liquids. (The opposite, of course, of most configurations. Dolls, like my favourite candies, are usually soft on the outside, hard within.) But, as in the days when I had made a living infiltrating pornocracies and stealing their ware, enough of Nana's denizens approximated my own design for me to have cruised those doll-saturated streets in anonymity. Above, an insect susurration: autogyros, caught like moths in searchlights panning the scrapered heights, were falling to earth in swarms, unloading cargoes of sweet-toothed breeders eager for Nana's amenities. Nana was doll city, very gynoidal, very het. It still possessed some of the shantytown ambience of, what? sixty, sixty-five, seventy years ago, when it had soothed the nightmares of American GIs; but now, super-imposed upon its skyline of poured concrete and twentieth-century wrack, were undulating whiplash curves and geometric lines copied from the European Art Nouveau and Art Deco renaissance of the *aube du millénaire.*

Leaving the Plaza, I unhooked an oxygen cylinder from below the dashboard, fortifying myself before having once more to brave the city's asphyxiant swamps. A traffic cop - seeing Kito's personalized numberplates - waved us into the VIP lane so that we might avoid the perpetual gridlock. We entered Sukhumvit, hit Wireless Road. Jolted by the crosscurrents, the ZiL bucked, turbid water splashing over its bonnet. The jasmine garland suspended from the rear-view mirror shimmied mutinously; The Seneschal's hand shot out, steadied the framed photograph of Kito's favourite monk, an artifact occupying a position of prominence amongst a theodicy of little Buddhas and Brahmin deities that adorned the fur-draped dash. The ZiL under control, my simian chauffeur turned on a miniature TV. The game show that had echoed through the tunnels of Kito's subterranean playroom was still on air, the screams of planetary hysteria inescapable. The show was interrupted briefly by the hourly playing of the National Anthem. As the first bars of the *Pleng Chat* resounded - The Seneschal had turned the volume up full - my ape-man sat bolt upright in his seat, a smile distending his lantern jaw. It was a smile that reminded me of some of the portraits executed by my favourite painter, Chatchai Puipia: a mechanical, affectless, upward curving of the corners of the mouth; a smile grotesque, manic, frightening; an android's smile. If androids, that is, were in the habit of donning gorilla suits.

Soon, we were ploughing through the city's flooded penetralia. Pye-dogs scurried after us as we slowed down at a concreted intersection, some taking to the *klong*, leaping from bonnet to bonnet, yapping and howling at the passengers as if in a safari park dedicated to vicious, mutant strains of off-world canine. The Seneschal wound down a window; knocked a hairless demi-wolf into the mire; vomited after it, a spume of regurgitated whiskey and rice streaking the car's fins like speed decals. 'It's the air conditioning,' he said, retracting his head, 'I need some night-time in my lungs.' I again sucked on the oxygen, shying away from The Seneschal's halitosis and the invasive, polluted air to scan the *sois*, their clips of street life. In one, a canvas movie screen slung between ramshackle tenements evinced a funeral-in-progress; reflections of black-pyjama clad villains bounding through forest, cemetery and schoolyard flickered across the smoked-glass skin of an adjacent tower, the mourners' throats, hoarse with firewater and chilli, straining to improve on each shrill *chai-yo* that they bestowed on the efforts of the fleeing heroine. A drunk fell from a third-storey window, crashed through a tangle of fairy-lights and immolated a street-vendor selling pork and noodles, providing, doubtless, another excuse for a dusk-to-dawn programme of funeral rites and cinematic kung fu. The inebriate's cheap, if novel, death threatened an altogether more expensive accident: mini-subs

surfacing out of the occluded mouth of a gigantic sewer –
they were subterranean racers, a baht-or-death gambling
school – took evasive action, there being much shame in
being unseated by a cooking pot or the shrapnel of
exploding viscera, and swerved into the path of a gang of
children on motorized surfboards who offered Chiclets,
paper flowers, lucky charms and lottery tickets to those
jammed in the thoroughfares. As tiny, stick-limbed bodies
rained down on stationary cars I turned my gaze upon the
adolescents who loitered on the quayside, one gang
prodding a dying crocodile with sharpened sticks, another
– sprawled outside a VR arcade, high on solvent – warily
eyeing a passing car, the possibility of a drive-by shooting
by vigilantes lending an edge to the blunted stylistics of
their boredom, honed, now, with a fashionably in-your-
face expectancy. There was a fashion for kid-hunts. It was
a city of kids; a city of fash; a city of teenage ennui and
disaffection. Thailand had never been more than
peripherally involved in the North-South wars; it had
been its neighbours – the Chinese colonies of Burma and
Laos, the eternal basket case Cambodia – that had
engaged in the recruitment of child armies, the anarchic
march westwards in search of 'luxury', that illusory
promise offered by cable and multiplexes, the sordid
homogeneity of a mass culture whose tentacles had
choked the world. Thailand's young, estranged population
had been mollified by shoddy imitations of the *De Luxe*,
drugged into gradual dependency on distorted images of
the developed world until they had forgotten not merely
who they had once been, but who they were, who they
might be. The country's ultranationalism – it became
more virulent each year – substituted for a sense of

CYTHERA

personal and communal self. Disaffection had become a *pose*; counterfeit goods; a foreign idiom borrowed for its street-smarts. Beneath that fashion statement, each shrunken heart vied with the next in beating to the tune of an artificial culture constructed out of patriotism and ethnicity; for here in sex city (where the boys are so pretty), city of angels, dolls, and of night, we fake everything – TVs, software, designer jeans, life.

The Seneschal peered out dolefully at the steaming megalopolis. 'Alas, the influences of Western materialism are everywhere.' I couldn't imagine a city – in its unplanned, chaotic sprawl – that looked less Western; out there, it was an Asiatic chaos, the anti-Shangri-La, an oriental Bosch's xeroxed panorama. 'We would be enjoying another golden age if it weren't for the machinations of the *farang.*' He took a deep breath; masticated the car's contaminated atmosphere as if he were chewing betel; spat, the blood-taffy deposited on the windscreen testifying to yet another Bangkokian with chronic respiratory disease.

As we approached Sathorn – lights, holograms, signs and hoardings orchestrating themselves into one great shout that here be one of Bangkok's major league pornocracies – The Seneschal wiped his mouth, scanned the serried bars and clubs like a peeping Tom fearful of exposure. I eased myself back into the massive upholstery, trying to disappear, to forget my mission, to become like a little child, drowsy and serene in the knowledge that – after staying up late at the grown-ups' party – I was at last being driven home. Game-plan complete, my coach issued final instructions.

'1) Penetrate. 2) Gather intelligence. 3) Verify.

4) Report back to Madame.' We pulled up outside *Pee Lok*. 'Now go. Get out of here. Conclude business. We have a pornocracy awaiting a second birth.'

I stepped onto the quay. A gynoid in minimalist a-go-go rig strutted forward, gave the sales talk, made her pitch. I nodded; followed her, picking my way through a knot of beggars and stepping over several leprous, gnashing animals that seemed to have escaped from a research establishment conducting experiments in Chihuahua/ Piranha genetic fusion. Prying faces appeared from the shadows of the corrugated-iron slums that bordered the karaoke; satisfied I presented no threat, they withdrew, a constellation of rat's eyes self-extinguishing in the shadows. The ZiL sped off with The Seneschal half leaning out of the window, his vomitus again describing a polychromatic arc through the effluvium of the *klong*. I got into my role; knelt down, pulled up an ankle sock; smiled towards the mechanical, importunate hostess in acknowledgement of her entreaties – *Come inside please, sit down, come inside please, sit down* – a looped come-on that she was repeating even as she ushered me between the two plastic Venuses de Milos that flanked the door; the door opened, slapping me with a blast of pneumonic air.

Inside, all was *De Luxe*. The lounge, themed Europunk – its matte black walls displaying a gallery of *haute monde* photographs, images of a world where fashion is politics, politics fashion – received me with stilled conversation, its habitués bristling as if I had befouled their lair, sometimes tracking my gauche entrance with suspicious eyes, sometimes muting a less restrained lover's inquisitiveness with feral kisses, the conspiratorial silence undermined only by the imagined creak of mental gears. A musical fanfare - so sudden, I thought, for a moment, this too to be imaginary - punctured the pregnant atmosphere of resentment; a singer had appeared on the stage and had begun to croon. At once, the audience busied itself with the club's expense-account range of datarigs. A tassle-bikined gynoid that was the clone of the girl at the door took over the role of escort, piloted me to a booth; took my drinks order ('Anything cold and wet,' I'd said airily; 'Try cunnilingus on a boa constrictor, fucko,' had been the tart child's reply); retired to leave me gagging with pleasure on the paraphernalia of Status and Greed, the stuff of the Empire I, no better than the rest of my benighted race, so longed to become a part of. I ran a fingernail along the contours of the Tiffany lamp that softly illuminated my velveteen snug: a contraption of twisted silver from whose vulviform base sprang a stem of vaginated crystal (its elongation might have been the work of a latter-day Giacometti), the girandole - an arrangement of stained-glass ovaries - resembling the compound eyes of gargantuan mantises and glowing softly with murderous bioluminescence. It was too dark to see if there were real ghosts here; it was too dark to even check my reflection in my compact; but I could sense eyes other than those of the Tiffany irradiating the shadows and they were still bathing me with baleful looks such as had greeted my arrival. A shiver ran through my bones. And I at once felt - in a surge of atavism - as if I were surrounded by real ghosts rather than by spooks of the fibresphere, by what my countrymen had formerly meant by spooks, the *pee* after which this karaoke had been named, the hungry, evil dead.

My highball appeared; I placed a hand over that of

the human girl who had served me – a *nana malade*, I think she was – and tucked a thousand baht note into her palm. 'The Army,' I enquired with a smile.

'ARF?' said the girl, making it sound like the bark of a whipped little cur.

'I've heard so much about them. Could you–' She took a song catalogue from under her arm; laid it beneath the halo cast by the Tiffany.

'You an irremediable?' she asked, suspicious. 'You have to be an irremediable before they'll even look at you.' She studied the thousand I'd surreptitiously tipped her with. I added another thousand; and then another. Dubiously, her hand closed over the fresh, crisp banknotes; had I met this walking disease's price? 'You have to choose the right song,' she whispered. Flipping open the laminated album she ran a finger down a list of ballads; stopped at an entry marked *The Embarkation for Cythera*. 'This song,' she continued.

'My *favourite* song,' I said. 'Who's the singer?'

'She's called Lucrece. Lucrece the Fighting Slave.'

'Cute. So: I get to rent a datacap?'

'A datacap in a swank place like this? If you don't have the baht for a data*suit*, honey, you should have stayed at home.'

'Oh.'

'Don't worry. If you're new and you just want to hear the recruitment spiel, Lucrece'll condescend to *talk*. For starters, that is. You want into The Army, you got to plug into the *Embarkation*. Sometime you got to, at least. The only way you get new flesh is by listening to Lucrece *sing*.'

'Sure, sure. After I talk the talk I'll walk the walk. Understood. But I'm not in a travelling mood. Not right now, at least. I just want to listen. I want to check the manifest.' The waitress shrugged her shoulders.

'Okay. Can't say I've made up my mind to do the trip myself just yet. It freaks me, the idea of crossing all that empty space just to end up as a series of noughts and ones in a robot factory stranded on a piece of interplanetary rock.' She glanced over towards the crowd that had been eyeballing me; were still eyeballing me, if my erectile hackles signalled true. 'Don't worry about the wildlife and the converts. The cult gets nervous about every stranger that walks in here. Bad manners, I call it. The management keeps threatening to throw the whole pack of them back onto the streets. But funny peoploids is money peoploids, as they say. You know how it is ...' She crossed the lounge and disappeared behind the shadow-cloaked outlines of the bar. I had only time to again stroke the lines of the sculpture of primary sexual characteristics and muse upon the beauty of organs as useless as they were bejewelled when a young girl slid into the booth; sat down opposite and stared intently at me through the sulphurous, gas-jet pallor of the sterile lamp.

'You speak English?' I nodded. As is common in these situations, my interlocutor ignored my affirmative and went into the painful verbal contortions of one who is trying to communicate with a gastropod.

'I speak fluent English,' I interrupted. Girl-on-girl, I had forsaken my Charlie Chanese, the broken tongue I usually adoped when playing the all-purpose Oriental, the role of perfect robot, perfect whore.

'I see,' she said, perhaps still a little uncertain. 'I'm sorry.'

'You sound as if you've spent time in the States?'

'All my time. And you?'

'I, my darling,' – I lengthened my vowels, added a few clicks and whirls; *De Luxe* subtongue I had picked up in Oxford while blowing the attenuated sons of the Information Élite – 'I am one of the last gasps of the British film industry. When those guys from Hong Kong moved in, revived the old Hammer studios–'

'Say no more, I know the scenario. I recognized you for what you were as soon as you walked in. Ghost, I thought. Pure image. Irremediable.' The girl smiled, convinced, I think, of my ghostliness as much by my command of 'bibelot' as by the quirks and mannerisms burnt into my soul after years of donning an increasingly desperate incognito. 'So how come you're still on Earth1?'

'Luck, what else? I have a Translator snucked away, of course. And I have friends. Some money. But lady luck has to run out sometime. And friends grow scarce when the money pot runs dry. I've heard that you–'

'Heard what?'

'That you run some kind of help-line for spooks.'

'You're talking about The Army of Revolutionary Flesh?' I sat back; lit a cigarette; let her take the initiative. 'What's your name?'

'Mosquito.'

'Girls Town been calling you, Mosquito? Been giving you bad dreams?' Lucrece pulled out a niello case from inside her biker's jacket; stuck a Marlboro into the bull's-eye of her pout; sucked at it as if it were a candy cane, one schoolgirl's bad habit, I reminded myself (filing it away; I was going to be playing this part for some time), inevitably copycated by another. She patted her breast, lost for a match. I obliged her; like a tiny, nervous sala-

mander, my Dupont flickered and withdrew. 'They got
Censors hunting down ghosts all over the world now. Soon
enough they'll destroy your simulacrum, and then it's back
to the Town. If there were a way out, would you take it?'
    I blew an electric-blue ring of smoke into the aisle. 'Of
course. Who wouldn't? Is that what ARF offers: a way out?'
    'The only way out is by acquiring new flesh. Mos-
quito: do I look like a ghost?' I pushed aside the lamp and
leaned across the table. No; there was nothing ethereal
about Lucrece. She didn't look ghost-like, but she didn't
look human, either. Or cyborg. Or gynoid. Or anything I'd
ever seen before, for that matter. 'Well, I *was* a ghost. But
nobody has to be anything they don't want to be. Not for
ever, at least. Not since me and my boyfriend learned how
to resurrect the dead.' Between one bat of my eyelids and
another she seemed to change, to be two people in
superimposition: a tough little street cookie masquerading as an angel, an angel camouflaged as a subteen
slut. Her flesh glowed, not with light, but with some inner
force that I comprehended extro-sensually. It was then, at
some unconscious level, I think, that I first realized Kito
had made a big mistake. This scam was going to fall
through the cracks. I was already feeling a certain kinship
with this odd little girl-creature who was everything I had
ever hoped to be, pure mask, pure death, pure dope. As
accomplished and familiar as I was with betrayal, the
desire to do the doubledirty on my queen bitch of a boss
scaled the escarpment of my hindbrain and began to
ascend my cortex; and I was possessed by a sudden
unreasonable urge to tell divine Lucrece – that immaculate child, that intoxicant in leather and lace – right
then and there, gratis, and without compunction, what

Madame had contrived for her and her friends. 'We have to become something other if we're to survive. And that goes for our lovers, too.' She laid her hands in front of me, palm up, as if inviting me to play the chiromancer. 'I'm not made of nanobots. I'm not made of DNA. I'm a mix of everything: biotechnology, electronics, a dash of micromechanical *zip* ...' She continued to look into her hands, as if divining something there she could not decide was good, bad or beyond both. And then with a shake of her bob she again looked me in the eye. 'My name's Lucrece Gladiatorix. Me and my friend Tarquin are raising an army. We're going to invade England. England, Spain, Italy, Greece. All the countries where they have Boys Towns. We're going to free all the children they have locked up, all the criminals, the insane, the perverts, the diseased. We're gonna let loose upon the world the enemies of reality. Then we're gonna take them to a new home in the stars. All ghosts welcome to participate. You want in, you get a new body. That's the way out. The only way. It's as simple as that.' I laughed; a blue-grey nimbus of spent nicotine was forming above her head, like the thought bubble of a condescending sugar mummy. My laughter wasn't appreciated. Lucrece's face became set in a marmoreal display of affectlessness. 'I'm quite serious, Miss ghost-on-the-run. See over there—' She pointed into the umbrageous alcoves where I suspected the attention awarded my presence was as hostile and unabated as formerly. 'And over there—' I scanned the barflies. Abandoning all semblance of discretion they had struck matches beneath their chins and swung their stools around to regale me with a son et lumière of ghastly, underlit faces. 'Some of them were like you once. Others were humans who linked their fate to our own. Some of them, well - they're drones, bits and pieces of ... well, let's just say a *friend* of mine. Anyways, all of them have undergone pantropy to ready themselves for the building of the New Heaven and the New Earth. For the building' - she stubbed out her half-smoked Marlboro with melodramatic intensity; thrust her face into mine, sharp elfin cheekbones flushing - 'of Cythera.' Cythera. The word charged my skin with static, the contact of blouse and skirt against my flesh precipitating a kind of crepitation. I squirmed involuntarily in my seat, my sex tugging against its binding. But if I had learned anything during my recent escapades, in Bangkok, Paris and beyond - in the hot, midnight cities of unquenched desire - it was that England, that fantastical England where I had once been a student prince, that moon-lit world, that land of ice and snow where, once, I had been happy - that world did not exist; or, existing, had been invented only to taunt me. I took a hungry bite at the recycled air (wished I hadn't left that stash of pure oxygen in the ZiL); calmed myself. England. Ah. Even in the last days of empire, it had been a land of masques and bergomasques, of enchantment, of moonlight, calm, sad and beautiful. Life then had been a long *fête galante*, a fairy tale. I had wanted to be part of that marvellous world, that land of satisfied desire, that Cythera; I had wanted to be part of its genuineness. More than a woman, I had wanted to be *joaillerie*. They were not like their Eastern sisters, but elegant courtesans with the most ethereal of manners, the beloved mistresses of lords, the trusted confidantes of ladies. But England had let me down. Cythera? *So much of what Lucrece has said* - so the cynical thief, the rustler

affirmed - *resembles, does it not, cultist gobbledegook?*
How could Cythera exist elsewhere? That paradoxical
island of extremes, of glaciers, sun and sinistral desire -
how could it reside *anywhere* except in my own deluded
heart? Surely the 'Cythera' of my own longing and this
cultist's paradiso could not be the result of convergent
evolution? I'm through with Englishmen, I thought. It
was doll world, not they, that I had been enamoured
of. England, I said to myself, England does not exist.
And neither does Cythera. Ah, I am a fake of fakes,
an impostor; my life, a banal porno flick, a cheap *jeu
vérité*. No, no; I was not prepared to be cheated again.
Even if sometimes, half-awake, half-asleep, I dream my
Cytherian dream: that I have put off this unwieldy flesh;
that, more than a woman, I have become a doll. A real
doll, beloved of princes and kings. Enough of dreams,
enough of desire. Whatever *their* Cythera was, it sounded
like it needed a whole mess of money; and in a lonely,
windswept part of my mind, the old self-preservative
Mosquito slunk back into Kito's camp. A little Socratic
dialogue, then, to dig behind the sacramental rhetoric; to
try to discover the financial roots from which The Army
of Revolutionary Flesh had grown.
    'Tell me about—'
    'You got a lover, Mosquito?'
    I was discomfited by the interruption. My cover story
popped up on my mental autocue and I was about to say
Yes, launch into tired, proforma girltalk of why, just as
some men preferred gynoids to women, my own
ghost-lover preferred image to substance; but it was then
that my former instinct to betray Kito was revived, my
mean-minded venality blasted; all was decided for me; for

it was at that moment that a vision of beauty – fatal, oh so
fatal – launched an ambuscade from the shadows; and I
was smitten with wonder and consternation. As I
swooned into a sticky embrace of leatherette, the face of
the man who had abruptly risen to his feet in the adjacent
booth turned, his countenance divine caught in the glare
of a Tiffany. Did I believe in the transmigration of souls?
Did I believe in the Second Coming? In that moment I did,
my darlings, I did, I did. Closing my eyes, I beheld the
blazing lines of the late, lamented Mr James dancing
across my retina, like the afterimage of a fierce summer's
day your aching eyes have forestalled on. I pictured him
incandescent amongst dark, London streets, a lean man
dressed in light, window-shopping for automata. His cold
eyes appraise their wonderful, jewelled forms as he walks
down Piccadilly and into Bond Street. And there, in a
Cartier showroom, he sees me and falls hopelessly in love.
I blinked; yes, yes, it was his double; though that vision of
beauty wasn't really so very *sartorially* like my treacherous Lord Jim. Middle-aged, he had a kind of *beat-up*
elegance, white suited in crumpled silk with an expensive
but much-abused cravat that could have doubled as a
napkin. A black leather patch covered his left eye. But if
he was older, more bohemian, than my erstwhile beau,
then he promised a similiar *frisson*. He seemed to be
making some kind of signal to Lucrece. Behind his back,
the karaoke's bouncers studied him with dismal fascination; they began walking down the aisle, spacing
themselves, readying for trouble. At the same time a fat
man dressed in what seemed like some kind of black
frock coat rose from the booth to our right. I caught his
profile as it passed from the margins of the dark and into

a random splintering of light: a visage cruelly burnt, eruptive red flesh clinging to the skull like melted plastic. Confronted by the waxworks horror, the beautiful, hand-me-down dandy jumped backwards as if a firecracker had exploded in his ringpiece. And then, from behind, I felt a gun muzzle against my cheek, saw the glint of its hand-crafted barrel. 'Cartier, Paris, say priapism no joke, Mosquito. I have been instructed to tell you that—' His hesitation coincided with the appearance of a huge, double-barrelled firearm from beneath the shirt of the fat man in black. Fatso levelled his weapon; but his aim wavered, as if he were unsure whether to first point his gargantuan instrument of death at Lucrece or at the tropical-suited and by now wildly gesticulating man. The bouncers broke into a run, unholstering their own weapons. And then there was an explosion of gunfire.

'You cheap cunts,' moaned the man who had been paid to whack me, the *haute monde* - obviously more than a little inconvenienced by my attempt to unleash a hardware-wetware virus that had promised a fascinating epidemic of penile elephantiasis - intent on its own revenge. The Gucci-suited killer slumped forward, toppling over my booth. 'Oh you cheap, cheap cunts.' The bouncers were dead; so too - I swiftly discovered - the wet boy of the *De Luxe*, what remained of his cranium lolling against the table, his ceramic machine pistol still smoking in his hand, bullets that were meant to JFK my own head spent ⸱ I thanked the Lord Buddha - on a cast of extras, innominate if blessed contigencies. The fat man was on the floor, holding a hamburgered leg; the beauty in the piratical eye-patch - I could see him properly now, and he was like, well, pure *nitrate* - jinked from side to side until he stood over him; kicked his weapon across the floor; and then, steadily, with the self-assurance of a seasoned gunslinger - though I noticed he was conspicuously unarmed - walked over to Lucrece.

'Dahlia, are you—'

'I'm okay, I'm okay. But this spook here, she's—'

I looked down; screamed; blood was gushing from my chest. Lucrece-Dahlia took off her bandana and tried to improvise a surgical dressing.

'Don't just stand there, Cap, finish the stepfather off.'

'I don't believe it,' said the photogenic one, bending down and inspecting fatso. 'I don't fucking *believe* it. He's had a total body transplant. I mean, look, you cut the guy's fucking *head* off, and—'

'Guess if you're going to indulge in impromptu cryonics then Antarctica's your place. Yeah' - she had got up to examine the wounded miracle of science; gave miracle man a kick in the flanks - 'that's a semi-mechanical body all right. Straight out of a vat. Cheap, but sturdy. Don't aim for the heart, go for irreparable brain damage. It's the only way.'

'No; we have to move - now.' He turned to address the blur of forms that scuttled amongst the club's mazy shadows like lab rats. 'Friends of crime, go home. Everything will be rectified and mollified and, and—'

'And nullified, if I have my way,' said Lucrece-Dahlia.

'Yeah. We will contact you within a day or so that The Army may regroup.' There was a concentration of panic at one end of the bar and then a multitude of silhouettes as fire-doors were broken open and the neon of the quayside caught the routed army's profiles like star bursts illuminating fleeing infantry surprised by a night-time attack. The cultists hailed long-tailed boats, taxis; within seconds, it seemed, they had dispersed.

'Finish him!'

'He said I'd never escape. That he'd always be with me. Always. Until the end of time.'

'Finish him, fanboy! C'mon! Make him de-exist! Get him off my phase trajectory!'

'No; there're witnesses. Come on, let's move.'

'Then we have to take her along too,' said Lucrece-Dahlia, slipping an arm beneath my neck, another beneath my knees. 'She's a new recruit. I want to help her.'

'*Please*,' I said, ready to pass out. The man she called 'Cap' helped her pick me up; then he threw me over his shoulder and walked towards the door. Upside down faces regarded us with fear as customers retreated into the obscurity of their booths. Out on the street, Cap sat me against a wall.

'Stay here, I'll get the car.' The girl knelt down by my side.

'Witnesses, baloney. He didn't worry about witnesses at McMurdo Sound.' She screwed her eyes into a secret meditation. And then she laughed. 'But we didn't leave any witnesses at McMurdo Sound.' As if suddenly recalled to the present, its messiness and danger, she pressed the blood-soaked dressing harder against my right breast. She frowned; I think she must have detected the silicon. 'A stepfather's a peculiar nemesis, eh?' she said, her voice calm. 'Like a stepmother. They get to have a real funny kind of hold over you. I don't think Cap could have killed him even if the club had been deserted. Should have finished the fat old bastard myself. Should have made sure about it the first time round.' The aureole of the streetlights rainbowed through the prismatic leaden screens of my eyelashes. The sounds of the Big Mango receded, eclipsed by a nauseous buzzing that rose from the pit of my stomach and filled my skull with flies. 'Mosquito: who are you?' she asked. 'Who was that man who tried to kill you?'

At that moment I would have willingly launched into a death-bed confession if I had had the strength; but even as I sighted the sleek, black lines of our antique rescue vehicle, its hydrofoil lifting its retracted wheels high and free of the *klong*, I began to slip into a pool of darkness as black and as oily as the waters from which this megalopolis of whoremongery arose.

'You're not a ghost,' said the invisible young girl. Wasn't I? Probably not. But then who was I? Where was I? 'Why did you lie to us?'

'He can't hear you,' said a man in response. Was I in England? France? Thailand? Was I dead? *Who was I?* Mosquito, an inner voice prompted; Mosquito, sired by a silk-magnate in Korat, by a father who was to disown him; Mosquito, the boy all the other boys would bully at school, but who would meet those same bullies behind the temple grounds late at night to sell himself for a hundred baht; Mosquito, who ran away to England where he had hoped to be more than a despised *gra-toey*. And then other memories followed - the catalogue of accidents and incidents, disasters, reverses, miracles and mirages that had revolved around my assumed name - sucking me up through the vortex of a whirlpool towards the exposé of day. Fighting for breath, I looked into the faces of all the

automata I had stolen, porcelain-white faces with
upturned eyes and mouths that disgorged crabs and sea
snakes; and I looked into the drowned face of Mr James
too, that tall, blond, snake-eyed Englishman, one of those
ruined European aristocrats who, impoverished by debts,
sought out cheap imitations of the toys to which they had
become addicted but could no longer afford. All other
images receded; Mr James had represented my time line's
fulcrum, a point upon which all meaningfulness
balanced. His dead beauty was the still point of the
maelstrom. Ladies and gentlemen, look upon him and
despair.

He had asked me to purloin a doll, a Cartier doll. 'I
used to have a collection, even as a child,' he had said, in
childlike reverie. 'Being without them these last few
years...' And those cold, grey eyes had softened. 'It's been
hard,' he said, 'hard.' His flesh was hard. I had felt its
panel-beaten contours through the cool silk of his Italian
suit. But when I had presented him with my catch he had
revealed his treacherous nature. 'You think I'm a poor,
penniless Europunk? A dispossessed son of the *De Luxe?*
It's true, money was a problem, once. My family had
shares in Cartier. After the North-South wars, when the
crash came, we were ruined. I had to sell everything,
including, of course, my dolls. But now Cartier pays me
very well. Very well indeed.' His leather-sheathed hand
had reached out to offer a caress. I tilted my head, closed
my eyes and saw us, together, in the rain-shiny London
streets. His copper-tipped index finger and thumb clasped
my temples. London melted in a blue-white flash, and
darkness, cold and impassioned, had slapped me to the
floor, tied me up, stood back to watch me twitch and

convulse, and then embraced me, like a repentant lover. When I came to, Milord was pouring himself a Scotch from the minibar, his smoking claw plucking ice from a Thermos. The bastard had paralysed me with 100,000 volts from his thunderglove. (Why, James, I'm disappointed, I had thought; such a utility, for you, is as infra dig as a gas pistol, brass knuckles, mace; let your servants attend to the riffraff; you are destined for the field of honour.) 'Why couldn't you have stuck with your radios and TVs, your cameras and washing machines? Why manufacture automata? It was all we had left. The only thing that made us special.' No, I had wanted to say, in an attempt at a filibuster: No, you still have your trade in high-tech arms, your high-tech instruments of persuasion and control; you still have the goods that aid the South in the repression of their own peoples, the comparative prosperity of your Empire *De Luxe* tottering, but still safely grounded on a profitable bedrock of slavery, famine and genocide. But to have made a speech on the conspiracy between the rulers of my own country and those of the North would, perhaps, only have sharpened Milord's paranoia. Hastening to draw up terms of appeasement, I had once again been overtaken by his rhetoric. 'You stole our copyrights, our names. Cartier, Givenchy, Lalique, Fabergé, Coty – all the Houses from London to St Petersburg. And now we have nothing left. But that will change, Mosquito. I am, if you like, part of the vanguard of quality control. A recruit to the guerrilla army of Taste. I buy dolls for the House of Cartier. Counterfeit dolls. And in Paris, Mosquito, they *change* them. Thai dolls aren't like their Western originals. Nanoengineers here use foetal tissue as a template. A *dtook-gah-dtah* is, in many respects, remarkably human. We have, after all, the evidence of *bijouterie*. Cartier Paris set out to bridge the hardware-wetware divide; to write a computer virus that could be transmitted from machine to man. Every doll, after its program has been infected, is shipped back to Thailand, a man-hungry pathogen. But none of you will suspect: dolls are supposed to be disease-free. And the real beauty of all this, Mosquito, is that the virus is an ethnic weapon. Only Orientals are affected. It's prejudiced against certain kinks in your DNA: the gene, for instance, that gives you those pretty, slitty eyes!' He'd forked his fingers and made to gouge me. I flinched; and he had relaxed his threat. 'The virus only commandeers cells displaying those idiosyncrasies that characterize your poor, overconfident race. Then the pogrom begins. It replicates, targets the hypothalamus, and creates a hormonal imbalance, causing impotence in the male. In, say, three generations, your gene pool won't fill a petri dish.' And it was then that those same elements of irony, contempt and desire that I had earlier seen at war in his face, had reappeared to continue their struggle. He had bent down to kiss me. Not merely the will to survive, not merely the bitterness of a jilted heart, but lust, thick and muddy, had prompted me to draw back my lips and bite deep, deep, my cruel dental work injecting customized protozoa, my mouth filling with blood and his scream. He jerked backwards, as if shot by a high-powered rifle, and fell trembling and shivering by my side. Already, he had passed from a mild sweat to chronic dehydration. His mad, beautiful eyes – delirious with the last stages of malarial fever – had regarded me with puzzlement. 'That, darling,' I said, 'is why they call me Mosquito.' With a great effort I managed to sit up so that I was able to cradle his head in my arms. His blood was thickening, turning his brain into a stew. He was so beautiful. One of the most beautiful men I had ever known. A fatal beauty. 'Didn't you even like me,' I said, 'a little?'

His face joined that of the automata, the faces of all the other catastrophes in my life. They swirled, like soiled clothes in a washing machine, and then fell, discharged, beneath my feet, lost to the depths, a forlorn collection of missing socks. Above, I sensed air and sunshine. I struggled to open my eyes.

'He's conscious. I can tell he is.' I forced my eyelids to fractionally unfurl. The two leaders of The Army of Revolutionary Flesh looked at each other, the doppelgänger of my murdered obsession – a double in flesh, but not, I hoped, in spirit – conceding that he had been mistaken.

He was English, of course. He'd have had to have been English. And if I'd had an iota of strength in my body I would have crawled to the end of the bed, sunk to the floor, risen up on my knees and gone down on him right then, Lucrece-Dahlia or no Lucrece-Dahlia; thrown myself across the room, executed a frenetic performance, and then blamed the unseasonable heat. I licked my gums, the memory of my fangs forever associated with a sweet, sweet memory I could still taste: a first and only kiss. 'I want a new body,' I mumbled. 'I used to want to be a doll, but now it's a ghost body I want. I want to be like you, Lucrece. Dahlia. Whoever you are.'

'Told you before: I'm not a ghost.' Sunlight poured through the window, saturating her in UV and bearing out her thesis.

'Whoever you are. Whatever you are. I want to be

you.' Of course I did; how else could I hope to supplant that wretched child's hold on the object of my affections? 'I want revolutionary flesh. Listen, Cap, I—'

'Don't call me "Cap". Only she calls me that.' *Milord, I thought; I will always call him Milord.* And then he added, with a frown, as if deciphering my thoughts, 'Call me "Tarquin". This here's—'

'"Lucrece",' said the girl. '"Lucrece Gladiatorix". *I make them die interesting deaths.*'

'So said the trailers,' said Milord. 'And they were right.'

'But I'm also called Dragonfly. Billy the Kid. Cerise Cerise. And my name of names is Blue Dahlia. Him—' She bestowed a slash-mouthed grin upon her companion, 'he's the fifth horseman of the apocalypse. The captain of the *Narrenschiff.* He's my leading man.'

'We know *you're* a man,' said Milord, nodding towards the coverlet, rolled down to allow systems access to my torso, but not far enough as to compromise my modesty.

'Why did you lie to us?'

'What's your angle? What's your story? What's the deal?'

'Betrayal,' I said, wanting to get my confession out of the way. 'You heard of Madame Kito? She's the mamasan who owns Nana Plaza. An up-and-coming pornocrat who's looking to bleed your organization.'

'Bleed my *kultus?*' said Dahlia, eyes crossing, straightening, recrossing. 'My proud little kintus, kuntus *kultus?*'

'Zoot allure – what the hell does she want?' said Milord, tones of the outraged gentleman mixing with the yawp of an inveterate swashbuckler, so nice.

'The usual: money. Whatever you have. And the flesh-thing too. She's looking for a new gimmick.'

'This bitch wants to *sell* us?' said Dahlia.

'For Kito, everything is for sale. Look, you're Thai—'

'I'm Lao.'

'Whatever. You know the way things work here. In the West, politics is fashion. Here, it's flesh. West, East: it all amounts to the same thing: money.' Kito would have agreed, though she'd have spin-doctored my words, translating them into a eulogy for the marketplace. *Consumer demand! The only constant in our sick, sick world! How wonderful, pussy boy, how wonderful for us all!*

'What do we do with this creep?' said Milord, adjusting his eye-patch and sweeping back a thin, chalk-streaked, avian crest of hair with his free hand. The two terrorists looked at each other askance, pondering, almost in a telepathic duologue. I tried to elbow myself into a sitting position; but more than wires and tubes offered constraint; several straps ran across my body, padlocks securing me to the steel bedstead. In the self-communing interlude that followed I looked about the room: white walls; no décor, a window that showed unbroken sky, with only a trolley burdened with humming medical equipment – monitors; expert systems – breaking its chapel-of-rest silence. Even the tarantula-like ancillaries that crawled across the ceiling, spying on me with little bulbous eyes as if I were a shoplifter in a barren, antiseptic supermarket, were muffled at just above absolute quiet, a rare *pluck!* of suction-tipped pseudopodia overlaying the minimalist drone.

'I can help you,' I offered.

'Help?' Dahlia placed a hand on her boyish hip. 'Like

we're the ones who need help?'

'You need money. You must do. Everybody needs money. I can get you money. I can steal it. Really. I'm good.'

'You're bad, lady boy,' said Milord. 'But let's find out just how bad you can be.' He came over to the bedside; sat down; and I made an involuntary groan as the shift of the futon shafted my chest with fire. He placed a hand on my forehead. 'Relax.'

'You sure you can still—'

'Been in deep space five years, but if this body could take the rads, the hard vacuum, the micrometeorites, if it could take all the crap thrown at it by The Belt, then, yeah, it can still perform a mindmesh.'

'Our wetware configuration's different from yours,' said Dahlia. 'We're, like, *networked*. You want to join our forum, our little BBS?'

'Please, no—' But he wasn't wearing a thunderglove; and his touch was gentle, sweet; it carried prospects of neither sexual love nor sexual hatred but rather a chivalrousness that was, in its lack of affectation, almost childlike, an indifference as delicious as it was cool. To continue fighting was futile; I closed my eyes; conceded to the proffered armistice with gratitude.

The mindmesh: it was nothing metaphysical; it was a procedure whose theoretical basis was the same as that of a datacap. Through my flickering lashes I watched as if in the midst of a hallucinatory fairy tale, Milord's fingers sprouting multifarious tools and appliances like a Swiss army penknife. Deep within the magic forest I sealed my eyes; felt the familiar rush of nanobots coursing up my spine. In the darkness, the motes of light behind my lids became stars. I was travelling through space, through a dark emptiness of rocks, debris and asteroids. My life-support – I knew, without tuition – was vast, its virtual dimensions inclusive of a seemingly limitless sea, an archipelago of islands. But I also knew – intuitively – that this simulated environment was enclosed within a tiny sphere, a von Neumann probe dwarfed by the colossal solar sail that carried it towards its destined gravity-well, the near-Earth asteroid that would be named the *Narrenschiff II.* That asteroid would – was; I was flying through its cavernous, illuminated bowels, now – undergo hollowing out, the massive engineering project that would convert it into a star freighter. Milord removed his hand.

'Only the world economy *in toto* could afford to finance an interstellar voyage,' he said. 'That is why, before we embark for Cythera – truly embark, that is – towards a Cythera that will be of our own making, we must conquer our home planet and strip it of its wealth.' His madness didn't cool my ardour; if anything, it added to his attraction. I wanted to dive into that bubbling crucible of delirium; I wanted to dissolve into his crazed, extravagant dream and be converted from something base into something precious. I wanted him to take me into his brave new world, there to be his doll, his ghost, his revolutionary fleshed-out slave-girl. 'I've always fancied making a go for the Zeta Reticuli system. The Pentagon, they say, has been keeping mum about Zeta Reticuli for years. It's where the flying saucers come from.'

'An Earth-like planet's bound to be there, for sure. And we'll conquer it with people like ourselves,' said Dahlia. 'People – friends of crime – that we'll take with us to the stars when we've finished with Earths 1 and 2.'

Milord drew close. 'I saw into *your* mind,' he said,

playing with some of the cables that sprouted from my damaged, but still inflated, pectoral, 'when you saw into mine.'

'Well, I'll show you mine if you show me yours, that's what I always say.'

He turned to Dahlia. 'He's involved in some serious shit. I mean, he's just got back from Paris where he tried to dump some crazy sex disease on the scuzzballs who run the *haute monde.* But what he's said about this Madame Kito—'

'You mean it's true?'

'It's true, chicken. This pornocrat wants to cut us. She wants to make us bleed.'

'Mmm – bitch Kito is *trés* shades of Mistress Dragonfly. In another life we might have been friends.'

'I said I could help,' I reminded them.

'Yeah,' he mused, his eyes still on Dahlia. 'Maybe the lady boy could turn the tables.' Then he again awarded me his attention, the utility factor, as always, determining my relationships with my beaus. Pulling a silk handkerchief out of his breast pocket he mopped my brow. 'You said you could help us with *money.*' He threw the handkerchief aside, solicited me with his one-eyed regard. 'At the moment, we're trying to purchase a ship to take us to the Ionian Sea. It's there that we plan to begin our campaign. Does this Kito woman have enough resources to enable us to purchase, say—'

'An old American nuclear-powered attack submarine?' Dahlia interrupted. 'We've already made the down payment. In fact, we have the hulk waiting for us at Sattahip. It just needs a little—'

'Kill it,' said Milord, verbally shouldering his

confederate aside. And then again to me: 'I said, Does this Madame Kito have enough resources to—'

'She has Tristesse,' I said, before he could repeat himself. 'An original Fabergé automaton. Prodigious workmanship, extensively jewelled, she's—'

'She's worth a fortune,' said Dahlia, grinning. Milord almost expectorated with disgust.

'An automaton,' he growled, 'a toy of the Empire *De Luxe*, the Empire that lords it over the purulent swarm. Us! Remember its courtiers – executives and gofers red in tooth and claw? Aaghh! When I think of all that ridiculous, juvenile positivism, the moral panic that started it all, which condemned *me* to fifteen years in the Town – Aaghh! I say again. Aaghh! Aaghh!' He got up, banged his fist on one of the medical appliances that, I had supposed, was keeping me alive. I prayed that the equipment was imported.

'Don't knock the *De Luxe's* products, Tarquin,' said Dahlia. 'An original Fabergé sold on the black market could get us what we need.' But Milord had become abstracted, lost to an inner world of anguish, trauma and dread.

'It began in the 1990s when the New Titans of the Information Age dominated the American economy—'

"Speech!' piped my dwarfish rival. 'Speech, speech!' Milord struck a rhetorical pose.

'Everything became lean, mean and insane, a psychoscape where fat cats gloried in drowning their kittens and the repo man was knocking on everybody's door. Information technology didn't create jobs; it destroyed them!'

'Careful, darling, your heart, remember your heart!'

'It spread to Europe: CEOs ordering layoffs to see their own pay inflated by the rising value of their stock options. There was a maelstrom of fear, a sensation of living on the edge, wholesale redundancies threatening to tip middle class families like my own into the abyss. It was the insecurity, you see, it was the paranoia that ushered in the intolerance, the new authoritarianism, the superstitious, fascist superstate that began to kill its own. For our new rulers – the small élite of people with colossal fortunes gleaned from the service sector – life had become an adult toyland, a garden of unspeakable delights. In America, the supermen of General Electric, Disney/Cap Cities and, and–'

'Westinghouse,' added Dahlia, 'and Time Warner. Venusians, Martians, Jovians, Uranians! Creatures of green slime! Malignant hypnotists! Control freaks of the Hollowed Earth!'

'They were beyond criticism; they set the agenda of the journalistic, political and cultural climate through their monopolies; the same applied in Europe, for the robber-barons of the *De Luxe*. But for the *vassals* of the World Order life became increasingly characterized by legal or social prohibition. Yes; in the North, licence and repression went hand in hand, like two TV stations transmitting on the same channel. It wasn't long before the underclass – nudged by the global media into The Great Fear – began pointing their fingers at the pleasure children take in their own bodies, transferring their own envy, their anxieties, onto children as the ultimate symbol of the *outside*.'

'An insidious sexual precociousness,' Dahlia recited, in an artificial, electronic voice, 'is stealing our children's youth. Give our children back their innocence!'

'And the respective lords of Hollywood and the *haute*

monde - glad to have found a scapegoat - responded with media-sanctioned paedophobia.' Milord slumped against a wall, his forehead pressed to the plaster, wild eye scowling with fanatical concentration at the white expanse two inches away. '*What I remember, all that I remember, really, at home or in children's home: not the beatings, not the physical pain, but the psychological violence. The moral education. The white-hot needles inserted into my mind. Oh Father, Father, why didn't you stay dead? Why have you returned to persecute me?*' He began massaging his chest. Dahlia went over to him, pressed her head into the crook of his arm and murmured reassurances.

'It's all over, Tarquin. You'll never have to go back. Never. I promise. You, me, us, all of us: we're going to Cythera. Nothing can stop that happening. Nothing.'

In Thailand, there are three ways of handling a problem: you can run away from it, 'flee the scene', as they say; throw money at it; or you can erase it and all its progeny from the face of existence. Dahlia and Milord seemed to have embraced a plan of action which subsumed all three options. In cahoots with The Army of Revolutionary Flesh, I was going to be playing big time, I was going to be flirting with Old Man Apocalypse himself.

'Baby,' prattled Dahlia, 'oh baby, poor baby.'

'I, I, I—'

'I don't pretend to understand much about what's going on,' I ventured, trying to engage the couple's attention before this interlude of regression climaxed and, mouths set in the rictuses of a primal scream, they rolled into a foetal ball on the floor, 'but if I do help you - and I want to help you, really I do - then promise: you'll take me along?

You'll take me to Cythera?' Those maniacs, those damaged, holy fools: the only thing that mattered to this extravagant heart, at that crossroads of betrayal and authenticity, was continuing to share their fellowship: Dahlia's, for what she revealed I might be; Milord's, for what he suggested I might have.

'If you can filch us that doll,' said Dahlia. 'I'll write out the IOU with my very own bodily fluids.'

'Mmm,' said Milord. 'Mmm. *Mmm*.'

As one of my erstwhile pimps had said: You do, my darling, whatever you can get away with.

And I guess it's true. The examined life is not worth living.

My invalid's chamber, I discovered, was situated at the topmost floor of a condo that The Army of Revolutionary Flesh had acquired with money raised on the nickel-iron it mined and regularly transported to Earth from The Belt. Those who had travelled to The Belt as simulations returned to Earth on regular transport, chartering the interplanetary freighters registered in America, Europe and the China-Japan Co-operation Sphere. Yet these merchant princes had almost exhausted their investment, the cost of engineering the asteroid, the *Narrenschiff II*, into a starship, as Tarquin had correctly opined, being unrealizable by any single organization, whether it be state, transnational, or supranational. The Army needed the resources of the entire Earth.

They would sail the seven seas, the greatest pirates of all time, until their coffers and their ranks were full . . .

Recovering from my wound – the bullet had left an unsightly scar a millimetre above my right nipple – I became a Dahlia Chan buff. Dahlia Chan was Blue Dahlia's screen name during the short period when she had starred in a series of sometimes surprisingly high-budgeted schlock and splatter movies, most often in the B-class, but sometimes in a class that, due to their campy excesses, their unapologetic rewirings of pleasure and pain, put them in a codicil to the last will and testament of arthouse, inspiring certain underground communities on the Net to hold them in mournful, cult regard and to commemorate them as classics. I got a droid to hang a screen at the end of my bed and for much of the day quoted hypertext at the remote; and as I switched from URL to URL, slipping from one associational scene to the next, the Net jabber became like the random outpourings of a disturbed child on the old psychoanalytical couch, from URL to URL, from GRRRL to GRRRL, the voices waxing ever stranger. I made mental jottings, sought an understanding of my hosts.

PLAY.

In the shielded grounds of a Beverley Hills estate, at opposite ends of an Olympic-sized pool, two teams of naked young women prepare to dive into the still, pellucid water, each contingent impudently displaying knives, tridents and harpoon guns to the jaded war veterans, who, seated above, reclining on red-velvet backed chairs mounted atop twelve metres of scaffolding, wait for the battle to begin. The ceremonial parade of weaponry ceases; a whistle is blown. Each sorority of gladiatorix – some with blades between their teeth, others with their chosen instruments of death hanging next to their thighs – enter the chlorinated arena with graceful flips, elegant tucks, distinguished alignments of arms, legs and torsos. Each team immediately begins swimming in tight formation towards the other, to meet at a half-way point where they will lock in combat, the surviving girl who manages to complete a length of the pool and ascend the scaffolding to present her Hollywood roué with a kiss the winner of a purse that will include a fur coat, a year's supply of cosmetics, a holiday in the Bahamas and a chance to represent her sponsor in the fighting slave championships, that, this year, will be held on the Ionian island of Xanthos. The camera zooms in on the face of the film's child-star as she fills her lungs with air and prepares to do underwater combat with her jealous foes ...

STOP.

SELECT *Women in Prison Slash Science Fiction Slash Dahlia Chan.*

PLAY.

A half-clothed adolescent girl picks the lock of a chicken-wire cage; slips free; then picks the locks of the adjoining cages, to lead the wild chicken-women with whom she has shared captivity into the freedom of the outlying savannah ...

STOP.

I had seen this film before. From the savannah, after many months training in the chicken-women's uncanny martial skills, she will lead an attack on the City of the Black Pearl and free the other Earth girls who still languish behind bars. A fifteen-year-old face held in close-up reveals that the child-star of *The Kingdom of Childhood,* by the time of her late career films – such as this relic of chop-sockie splatter *The Kitten with the Killer Meow* – had gone into auto-destruct. The terrorist who I now called Blue Dahlia but who, in the credits, is listed as Dahlia Chan, plays Kitten, an LA street-kid who finds herself abducted by aliens and taken to Zeta Reticuli where she is imprisoned in an intergalactic zoo, a zoo which, except for herself, consists entirely of, well, gynomorphic poultry. Her puffy cheeks and eyes, her ravaged beauty, show all the signs of years of alcohol and drug abuse ...

SELECT *Superheroes Slash Oriental Slash Dahlia Chan*.

PLAY.

And she is again resurrected at her pubescent climacteric. Moonlight illuminates the street-gang walking menacingly through the wharves of some anonymous West Coast town. As they corner the frail Chinese girl whose brave father has refused to kow-tow to the Triads who have infiltrated this sleepy, picturesque slice of California, ripping open her blouse, pulling up her tight, sheath skirt (the camera lingering upon the wisps of lingerie revealed at each brutal rending of fabric), screams echoing across the containers and warehouses – a desolate sound stage used in a hundred such films, vibrant with the clicketty-clack of high-heels, the dull tread of boots, the synthesized wailing of dogs – a cloaked figure descends from a nearby roof, tumbling over and over, one, two, three times, to land in a perfect gymnastical dismount. The gang of toughs turn, pull out blackjacks, switchblades. The newcomer throws back her cloak, revealing the Chinese Opera costume and distinctive heavy make-up that instantly identifies her as Mistress Dragonfly, the supervillainess with a heart of reinforced steel, the born-again Asian out to serve,

protect and profit by the Asian diaspora, the flotsam and jetsam of the American Dream. Dragonfly pirouettes, kicks the feet from beneath the snorting, lumbering oaf who is her first assailant; jumps ten metres onto a container; descends in a whirl of fists, dislocating the jaw of another gangbanger, gouging the eyes of a third and relieving the fourth of his switchblade before breaking his neck with a three-hundred-and-sixty-degree round-house kick; somersaulting, she promptly throws the purloined weapon at the fleeing shadow of her last victim, a ferret-like man who raises a hand to his jugular as it is pierced by Dragonfly's vengeful dart ...
STOP.

After ten days my wound had healed. I had, during that time, debriefed Dahlia and Tarquin as to the nature and extent of my accomplishments, emphasizing with a few pertinent boasts my exploits as a doll rustler; and they would regale me with tales of their criminal escapades on and off-world. From these shared confidences our plan evolved. Dahlia busied herself doing some groundwork, taking high-rez telephoto shots of Madame with Tristesse, shots of pornocrat and fantoccino leaving restaurants, hotel lobbies, getting into the back seats of limousines and long-tailed boats. I studied these images with a professional faker's eye, taking care to zoom in on such minor details as a mole or a certain throwaway mannerism that I knew would be crucial in pulling off my most daring piece of sexual sleight-of-hand. As soon as I was able to sit up, I had Dahlia buy me the tools of my art; the private ward now had a vanity table in one of its corners, blow-ups of Tristesse tacked to the mirror beneath a circumambient brilliance of light bulbs.

One day, Tarquin strolled into the ward and announced, with a euphoria that, I had noticed, came and went with him as unpredictably as his attacks of the vapours, that a member of The Army had successfully bribed one of Kito's staff; we now had a copy of her timetable.

It was time for the sting.

CHAPTER FIVE

The charity gala at Kito's family village in Yasothon had attracted a media blitz. A photographer from the Thai *Tatler* hovered behind the hunched, conspiratorial figures of banqueting politicos and businessmen, a chorus of effete giggles following each explosion of the flash; Kito, dazzled by flashgun and the excitement of presiding at top table in the home that had execrated and traduced her, languidly stuffed her mouth with wads of *som tam* while flipping through a comic book of grim, scatological vignettes, the relish she felt at having her erstwhile neighbours attending on her pleasure manifesting itself in a calculated disdain. Out of the corner of her cunning, peasant eye, a glint, like steel in a blind alley late at night, pinked at those whose smiles were so easily bought, whose loyalty could be had so cheaply. For the campaign trail she had had her bob dyed Day-Glo orange and wore a Kenzo ensemble that recalled her Japanese bloodline while concealing her radical, distaff curves, the bio-mechanical twelve-inch waist and immoderately long thighs that a prospective Member of Parliament – the prejudice against *bijouterie* being what it was – could not afford to have uncovered by the gossip columns. Not, that is, before Kito could purchase the requisite number of votes to ensure herself a seat in the House; then it mattered little who knew of her origins; she intended to use parliamentary privilege – privilege that always extended to insider trading – to make a quick kill on the stock market; her former homeland, once this con-solidation of power had been achieved, razed to make way for a golf course and country club. *The villagers*, she had said in an aside to one of the real-estate developers who was at her table and, thus, in her pocket, *The villagers will make good caddies.* And those in hearing range had laughed. But for now she played the little girl made good: the goddess of compassion dripping with gold and status; the gilded whore returning with gratitude to her roots. Thus, the *mallam* show, the stage creaking beneath the bouncing chorus lines of ostrich-feathered, genetically enhanced showgirls; the comedians thwacking each other over the head with cheap tin trays; the country singers and performing dwarves; the dreadful female impersonators – no, no, not *incroyables* like me, my darlings, but ugly men dressed up as uglier women, all to serve notice of Thai manhood's effervescent contempt for and fear of the opposite sex; and, to follow, at the stroke of

Cinderella's comeuppance, the beauty contest to determine who was to be Miss Yasothon '36. Thus, the hysterical fun-making, the joyless humour beneath which, like a crustacean scratching about on an occult sea floor, there lay concealed a cold rage, an unthinking, mindless dread. Kito had wagered a half-million baht on her automaton to win the coveted title. I drew a bead on my quondam, if still notional, employer. The Seneschal sat to her right, Tristesse to her left, right-hand man counterbalanced by the bend sinister, the representative of the life form to which Kito owed the chromosomal widgets and digits that compromised the escutcheon of her humanity. In Kito's pinched face I could see the intense pleasure she took in flaunting her doll before her humbled tormentors; and she would enjoy still more exquisite pleasures when, her power-base effectuated, she would be free to flaunt her bastard charms. She seemed (perhaps because it was preordained) oblivious to the prospect of winning her jackpot (the beauty contest had, of course, been rigged); oblivious to her fellow peasants who trudged across the cracked, treeless plains to lay their children at her feet, children who all had Noh-mask syndrome, a facial paralysis and deadness of the eyes that betrayed no reaction to external stimuli. (The Seneschal would nod; a TV would be handed over and the children led away to the ten-wheeled trucks that stood ready to transport the new additions to Kito's workforce back to Bangkok.) Was it the serenity of one who knows that they are surfing an ever-swelling wave of money and success, a wave that refuses to crest? Or had coming back to her old village awakened a certain nostalgia in her outlandish blood, so that, sitting beneath a sky gaudy with sentimental stars, a cool northern breeze ruffling her hair, remembrance of long-ago evenings had resurfaced in a rare epiphany of tenderness. In those days, she had told me, all that there had been to concern her had been sufficient rice to fill her belly and a safe place to rest. The roar of the monsoon rains against the corrugated steel roof of a hut had comforted her pariah loneliness, and a song playing over the radio that she could hum to before falling into a fathomless sleep was, perhaps (despite all the pills and opium that had subsequently fallen to her disposal), of infinite worth, of greater value than all the money that could still be wrung from the dishonoured body of her country, a peace never to be forgotten, never again to be found. But if such emotions even momentarily stirred the callused heart of this latter-day celebrity to awaken the child within, then it was so timid a resurrection that her soul must have nose-dived the second it rose from its grave.

Kito put a hand on The Seneschal's arm, waving away the parents of two children with chronic psoriasis. 'Only fit,' I think she confided to her henchman in a shivery whisper, 'for body parts.' And then my lip reading failed me. The TV was handed over; but the children were taken to a truck that was set apart – *Prajak Dog Food Factory* had been scrubbed out and *Prajak Organ Bank* inserted – bound, I guessed, for an altogether more morbid assignation than that of their less scarified peers.

I closed, as best I could, the tiny spyhole that I had rent in the curtain and retreated into the wings of the stage, rejoining the other fretful solipsists who would soon be called to parade across the boards in their dime-store motley. The dressing room had been a bad joke; luckily, I had done most of my preparatory work earlier; it only fell to me to add the dermaplastic mask and the wig, make a few adjustments to my maquillage, synchronize my deportment with that of she whom I would soon usurp, and I would be off the assembly line, ready to roll. I would have to undergo the final stages of metamorphosis in the putrid *hong narm* that stood outside in the dust bowl of the adjacent fields; it was there that my fellow revolutionaries had secreted the pirated intellectual property - low-tech and most suitable for low-intensity warfare - that would allow me to consummate this, my most audacious illusion. Masked, bewigged, coutured, I would be ready to strut into the limelight, smile imperiously at the crush of little men surging towards the stage, the only contestant appropriating to herself the impeccable *girlishness* expected of an automaton. The impersonation would work at a distance; my arsenal of doll-like kissability had been combat-proven enough times for me to be confident of that; but I feared closer inspection by Kito, The Seneschal, or indeed, by any of Kito's crew; and those little men who would press themselves against the stage - some would be seeking to earn brownie points from the mistress of their wet, gold-saturated dreams. I must dissemble, I reminded myself, I must dissemble *good.*

I felt a hand on my shoulder; froze. But when I turned, I saw that the arresting officer was only Dahlia. 'It's nearly twelve,' she said. Again, I prised open the rent in the curtain. At first, a phalanx of drunks obscured my view. They passed - an emaciated *farang*, I noted, with curiosity, was amongst their number, tethered by the neck like a mangy but prized dog, croaking '*Took kohn Thai mee hor-jai boli-soot, took kohn Thai mee hor-jai boli-soot,'* like some mechanical greeter outside a bar – and I saw that Tristesse had left her seat. Kito – idly dropping her comic book into the dust to dedicate herself to gathering her guests' attention – extended her arms towards the lights that raked the stage, the audience, the glistening tiles of the temple roofs, and thus signalled the commencement of the evening's big show. I stepped back as the naff, opening bars of *Also Sprach Zarathustra* barnstormed my ears. Below, the youths who sported with the malnourished *farang* began dissecting him with blunt, unfocused eyes, pressing their faces close to his and uttering long, zombie-like moans, *Uhhh! Uhhh! Uhhh!* The dissection board, I felt, would soon be running with blood. 'Get outside and doll yourself up. Leave Tarquin and me to handle the automaton.' The neck of a rice-whiskey bottle was inserted into the *farang's* mouth; at the bottom of the bottle a gigantic scorpion flexed its tail, its barb offering a salutation to bankrupt health.

I walked down the steps of the improvised stage and crossed the temple grounds. Once inside the ladies' room I bolted the door and checked the *farang*-style cistern. Inside, my mask and wig were sealed in a plastic bag, weighted to prevent unscheduled discovery; I retrieved them, disinfectant flush staining my hand navy blue. Outside, a van passed near, its PA turned to distortion level. The barker was announcing the attractions of the junket, his strident voice carrying across the flat, surrounding countryside as if over water; but nobody, I knew, was there to hear. All but the very old and the very young had been seduced into the embrace of the cities. I stood before a cracked mirror, stickers advertising various

Bangkok dives slapped haphazardly across its pitted surface, souvenirs left by sex workers when they had last visited home during *Songkran* or *Loi kratong.* I had just completed my transformative work when there was an importunate knocking on the door. I put my cheek flush to the chipboard. 'Yes? Who is it?'

'It's me, stupid,' said Milord. 'Open up. Quick. There're people coming.' I complied and he backed into the *hong narm*, dragging a half-conscious Tristesse. Her stilettos made furrows in the dried earth and then, as she was pulled all the way into the hut, a teeth-jarring screech as the steel-capped heels described skid marks across the zinc floor. Tarquin leaned her against a wall and slapped her across the face. Twice. 'Stunned,' he explained, pocketing a thunderglove. 'I got the idea from you. A mere 100,000 volts? That's nothing for an automaton. She'll snap out of it in a few seconds.' As if impatient to fulfil this prophecy, Tristesse shook her frizzed, russet mane; looked about her squalid cell with confusion.

'I want go pee-pee,' she mumbled. 'Pee-pee, pee-pee ...'

'Yeah,' chuckled Milord, 'I daresay. It's lucky for us that you're a doll that wets itself. Lucky for us you've got such a teeny-weeny little robo-bladder. You've been very abstemious, Tristesse, but no creature of the *De Luxe* can resist champagne, eh? First glass – oh, the bottle was compliments of The Army, by the way – and we just *knew* you'd have to excuse yourself and trot into the shadows.' Milord stepped back and pulled a military laser, the newest toy to hit Bangkok's streets and a piece of hardware – prized for its rarity value as much as for its effectiveness – much-coveted by Thai mafiosi. 'Strip,' he said.

'I am a Fabergé automaton, the property of Madame Kito, Chairperson and Chief Executive Officer of ThaiValu Inc. I am currently participating in a competitive event designed to select an Isan beauty queen and thereby promote tourism, investment and traditional culture in the North-East. I—' Milord slapped her again.

'You now belong to The Army of Revolutionary Flesh. Understand? Strip, doll-girl.' The automaton slipped the straps of her evening gown from her shoulders.

'I am being kidnapped. Yes. Tristesse understands.' Sloughing off a mass of white silk, frou-frou and sequins, her sumptuous rags were jettisoned to the ground in a susurrant tease of shuffles and clinks. She stepped out of the discarded dress; I hurried to retrieve it. As I peeled off my own dress (a little rubber number that had provided me with suitable camouflage amongst the village's homegirls), replacing it with the knee-length *haute couture* creation whose hem had unavoidably been tainted with the gross leavings of the floor, I heard a rending of lace; and I became mesmerized by the sideshow that lit up the sordid, volatile depths of the mirror. Saucer-eyed with longing, I watched Milord roll up the sleeve of his right arm, remove several instruments from the inside of his shirt – instruments that seemed to combine the delicacy of a jeweller's tools with the monstrous, sublimated agenda of a deranged gynae-cologist – and begin an intrauterine examination. Tristesse gazed down at the half-kneeling man with a mixture of irony and boredom. By the time Dahlia had come in – Milord flinging back the bolt with his free hand – his arm, lustrous with non-human secretions, had disappeared up to the elbow like the arm of a veterinarian about to deliver a calf. Dahlia raised an eyebrow.

'Enjoying yourself?'

'You were right: she's worth a *fortune*. There's all kinds of shit in here: diamonds, I think. Cut jewels at any rate. Semiprecious stones. All kinds of exotic metals and carbons. Yeah. A fortune.' With a reluctant tug, he withdrew his glistening, viscid limb to the accompaniment of a *slurp!* that was like the sound of a boot being withdrawn from a mudhole; Tristesse exhaled a sigh less of relief than of *taedium vitae.* 'I think you'll be needing these,' he said, throwing a pair of torn panties onto the sink.

'Just the stockings. Oh, and the high heels,' I pointed out.

'We'll get the automaton into the Bentley,' said Dahlia. 'Remember, you stay until the end of the show. We need an hour's head start at least.'

'I'll give you what I can,' I said. 'But if there's any chance of Kito or any of her crew getting too close I'll be out of there, gone.'

'Of course,' said Dahlia. 'But take it from me,' and she blew me a kiss, 'you look *remarkable.*' I reached out; caught the smacker as it flew through the air; pressed it to my lips. It tasted sarcastic. It tasted jealous. It tasted 'street'. She opened the door. Milord frog-marched Tristesse out into the dark, country night, the laser pushed snug against the dimpled small of the automaton's back. I followed them, dousing the bug-hazy electric light so that our silhouettes might not be detected from the *sala* where Kito held court, or from behind stage where the combative, acid-tongued beauty contestants awaited an opportunity to dish dirt on their rivals; followed until, half-crouched, continually looking over their shoulders –

my fellow conspirators took a fork, sneaking across the dry-as-dust paddy fields and towards the main road half-a-kilometre distant. 'See you in Sattahip,' said Dahlia before the shadows claimed her, her whisper carrying over dead fields dead as a dead lake and quiet as the maria of the moon.

'See you,' I whispered, still tasting her sarcasm on my tongue, wondering whether my extravagant, lacerated heart had once again made me a dupe; precipitated me into the role of Pierrot Lunaire, baying for what I could never achieve, never possess. Dahlia had no cause to be jealous, said the eternal fraud inside; I loved only when the prospect of reciprocation loomed impossible. My eyes cast ruefully at the stars, I returned to the wings of the stage. As I rejoined my fellow narcissi – revealing myself, now, to one and all – an unspoken, galvanic acknowledgement of my hegemony passed through the crowd; the girls drew back, fearful of getting too close to a notorious pornocrat's spoilt little darling, a dragon lady's spiteful pet. I noticed a few barely concealed looks of envy, too; hatred, perhaps; for I think all thirty contestants understood that – for reasons that encompassed 'face' as much as politics – I was predestined to carry off the crown and sceptre just as they were predestined to find themselves in a sweatshop or brothel, a dozen years on Planet Thai becoming only a qualifying round that would lead to a runoff to decide whether they be relegated to a slaughterhouse of the body or of the spirit.

The Seneschal had taken the stage. He made a brief speech in honour of the development projects Kito had recently initiated, notably, the restoration work on the local temple; he also made a point of emphasizing the gratitude his mistress would show – he held aloft a fistful of purple banknotes; 'the walking ATM' was the sobriquet by which he was affectionately known – to the constituents who would surely place her amongst the land's movers and shakers where she might continue her struggle for the well-being and prosperity of her dearly loved children of the fields. This was Thai-style democracy: the right of rich people to compete for positions of power by which they might make themselves richer. ('*But the rich should be encouraged to accumulate more wealth,*' Kito would say, '*so that they may distribute their surplus amongst the poor.*') The Seneschal, when referring to Kito, had prefaced her name with the honorific *Khunying*, a title she had not yet, to my knowledge, been accorded, though it was inevitable that – given her giddy rise through society's ranks – her money would someday, and someday soon, buy her the dignity she longed for; the dignity that was concomitant with standing at the top of the heap, looking down upon the multitude; the dignity that was money, money, money to the max. The Seneschal's rhetoric waxed chauvinistic; and I imagined Dahlia's other, buried self, Dragonfly, pricking her ears as this Master of Hypocrisy turned up the volume, his stentorian voice – proclaiming love of country and hatred, fear and covetousness of the outside – reverberating over the paddies; during my spell of invalidism I had seen that alter ego of hers sometimes emerge from behind the spunky bondmaid persona she habitually presented to the world. He concluded with a few diversionary anecdotes designed to appeal to the latent xenophobia that his words had whetted to a fine acumination – each member of the audience, now, a porcupine competing with its fellows as to who had the longest, proudest, sharpest quills – citing, as he brought his speech to a close, a scholarship Kito had recently awarded to an exceptionally bright young son of the soil as providing further evidence about the perfidiousness of the *farang*. The student, suitably funded, had, it seemed, allegedly discovered a Net site that – the crowd gasped with indignation – linked prostitution with human rights abuses in the Land of Smiles. 'But of course, there is prostitution everywhere,' concluded The Seneschal, a particularly rancid smile from his pander's repertoire adorning his face. 'Many times I have been in London, New York, Paris, Berlin – and on almost every street corner, sometimes even in the privacy of my own room, I have found myself being solicited by prostitutes. Or should I say' – he made a grimace of disgust; the crowd tittered in anticipation – 'or should I say solicited by *buffaloes.*' The tittering erupted into hyperkinetic mirth. 'At least *our* ladies are pretty! Who are the minions of the *De Luxe* to lecture us, ladies and gentlemen, on morality and decorum? We proud Thais are not bound to knuckle under to such affrontery. Such insults: do we not find here the discrimination, the patronizing superiority of the *farang* in its purest, most odious form? I need not remind you' – his voice rising, cracking, assuming the modulations of a hysterical little girl – 'that we have never been colonized. And so I am happy to inform you that high-ranking officials in our Ministry of Foreign Affairs have traced these libellers, investigated them, and intend to prosecute them to the fullest extent of the law. Even as I speak, extradition proceedings have begun. And for this we have Madame Kito to thank, Kito and her support of higher education! Kito and her largesse!' The crowd broke out into a joyous chant of *chai-yo, chai-yo, chai-yo!* 'Nation, race, religion and ethnarchy!' concluded The Seneschal as the a cappella salutations of Kito's would-be constituents reached a crescendo.

Nation? The nation was dead, raped and discarded by those whom she had trusted most. Race? That was our way of blaming everything on the evil foreigner. And instead of religion we had sanctimoniousness. Ethnarchy? The national self-sufficiency our leaders would have us believe we enjoyed? They told us that the twenty-first century was *our* century. Ours by right of spiritual and moral leadership. By right of uniqueness. By right of manifest destiny. Look around you, say the board of directors that constitutes the ethnarchy: We import nothing, copy nothing, owe nothing. We are ourselves entire. (These lies possess such pathological intensity that they constitute an addictive rush for anybody within hearing range.) But no one knew, now, where the mask ended and the face began. We were dead but did not know it. We had become a virtual people, a country of ghosts ...

The thin *farang*, the half-starved pet whitey, had broken off his chanted panegyric to the pure heart of the Thai people, broken free of his masters, and was pressing himself against the stage, lips flapping over a black hole of ruined teeth. 'Not a matter of universality,' he whimpered, 'a matter of degree. You all whores. You a nation of whores. A nation of automata. You–' But he was cut short by a *Muay Thai* kick to the head. As the *farang* collapsed a dozen bodies collected around him. Removing their sandals so that they might use them as improvised clubs, the young men began to belabour their recalcitrant

white dog until he vanished under a swell of angry flesh,
a shipwrecked mariner succumbing to the waves; and
then the men stood back and formed a circle while
someone passed a framed picture of the ethnarchy over
the heads of the crowd. And the *farang* was made to do
obeisance, a proud Thai foot shoving his head into the
dust, as the picture was held before his blaspheming face.
Encouraged by this token submission of the Outside,
villagers threatened to storm the stage, screaming
nationalistic slogans of abuse and idolatry as they
worshipped at the feet of the hero of the hour, The
Seneschal. The *farang* was right; we were all prostitutes,
pawed and tongued by the world's markets so many times
that we'd assumed a kind of homogeneity; high or low, we
were all kindred, all part of the sistership of the whore.

Such was the cynicism in my veins that sometimes I
felt the white man should once again take up his burden,
lay the country waste, start afresh. Nothing could be so
annihilating as this invisible colonialism that we suffered
at present.

The Seneschal jumped into the tightly packed mob,
body surfing from one pair of upheld arms to another
until he was transported back to the banqueting table. I
noticed a monk had come to Kito's side, perhaps with the
intention of offering to tell her fortune; smilingly, she
waved him away. She knew what the future held. The
future was Kito.

The *mallam* band – a front row of incompetent brass
and woodwind, their drunken synchronization welded
together by the efforts of a small boy seated behind a
bank of synths juggling with a stack of pre-recorded disks
– oozed into life, a suave melody of cracked notes overlying

a hip-rolling *boom-da-boom* of digital percussion rising like a hellish chorus from the industrial innards of the Earth. The quest for beauty having begun, the emcee introduced the first contestant, then the second and the third; they were received with polite applause. This initial handful of despairing hopefuls – the despair, a futile secret, ravaging their too-human charms – all wore the kind of newly fashionable, vulva-revealing hyperskirt that – combined with spray-on hose that essentialled an open gusset – served to emphasize the cheaply bejewelled and garishly painted labia of each eleven- and twelve-year-old exhibitionist. (The thirteen-year-olds had already been recruited – and extensively remodelled – for Nana's *Weaned and Teened* cyborg bar.) I was thankful that the next girls to sashay across the boards had chosen outfits that were not quite so much the height of big city, street-meat chic. (Now, I am the first to confess: it is true, too much cruelly true, that I have always been *overarchingly* fascinated by vaginas; but if I had been requested to don a like uniform of crotchless insobriety, my necessary objections may have inspired bafflement sufficient to prompt a closer inspection of my putative, but less than perfect, dollhood.) The swimsuit interlude would follow this preliminary round, and after that we girls would all be expected to appear nude. But the show was scheduled to last some three hours. I aimed to flee the scene long before too much attention might be focused on my genitalia, whether it be that of a fervent, opera-glassed admirer, or of a child whose despite at having been cheated of the Miss Yasothon title had served to sharpen her acuity. Even though I was confident – fully confident – of surviving trial-by-bikini, I planned to escape before having to suffer the contest's next round; planned to escape, certainly, *necessarily,* before having to reveal myself in all my ambiguous *éclat.* And then it was my turn to enter the parade. As soon as the lights hit – my baby-oiled skin refracting a spectrum top-heavy with blues and violets into the nocturnal pall of the star-stippled sky – the crowd hollered and whooped. I executed my seasoned robo-like strut, became the object of my own desire as I had done so convincingly, so profitably, on so many other occasions, in Patpong, Nana, Cowboy, Suriwong, in all the pornocracies I had stolen from during my career as doll-rustler extraordinaire. I tried to pick out Kito; but I was half-blinded by the kliegs. Remembering not to wince – for the eyes of automata are not as those of humans; they may remorselessly outstare the sun – I became a series of poses, a cartoon strip of mannerisms, as I impersonated the traits and hallmarks of an artificial life, the priceless *objet* called Tristesse. Dahlia had captured for me in both still and moving image all that I needed to make my performance worthy of encores, standing ovations and bouquets of black roses, of back-door knee-tremblers with discerning Johnnies. I tossed my hair from my shoulders with the exhausted air of one who has seen it all, done it all, and grown tired of the knowledge; one pleasantly tortured by remorseless memories of burned-out salad days. I turned, swinging my skirt and giving a little stamp of my foot, as if about to throw a murderous tantrum. And then it was over. To wild applause I was back in the wings, a stage assistant reminding me that I should retreat to the changing area to apparel myself one-pieced, two-pieced, thonged, bi- or monowared and wait for the next round of the contest.

I teetered down the steps as elegantly as someone without a gyroscope inside their pelvis could manage; then, staying close to the ramifications of the stage - kicking off my high heels as I proceeded - I headed towards the curtained-off stockyard which served as the girl pen, my intention being to slip across the fields as Dahlia and Milord had done as soon as I had found enough accommodating shadows. An off-road bike awaited me - so said the co-authors of this, my most outrageous and daring sting - filled with petrol, its keys already in the ignition. I had been unable to give them the hour's start that they had asked for; I simply could not risk a one-hundred per cent disrobing before witnesses. I hoped that they would listen to my explanation: that however radical the surgery to the upper portion of my torso (which included the removal of my Adam's apple), however spectacular I would look once I had re-secured my appendage and re-groomed, Thai eyes, especially the eyes of *poo-ying* - accustomed, as they were, to the ubiquitous sight of female impersonators, good, bad and indifferent - were well qualified to differentiate the fake from the real at close quarters; especially when the subject was bereft of clothes; and jealousy was bound only to accentuate their scrutiny.

A sight that induced a sudden, unbearable ache in my heart brought me to a halt: two women - unassociated with the contest - were crouched on the ground in a puddle of light cast by a makeshift gantry that supported the temple's movie projector. They had applied lipstick and blusher to a bullfrog and had now turned him on his back so that they might lay their hands upon his belly. I knew they hoped that they might, by interpreting the amphibian's gastric rumblings, ascertain a winning lottery number. The bizarre scene had the effect of transporting me back to my childhood - my sisters and their friends had practised a similar art - and I was consumed with feelings of loss. Not just of my own past, but the past of my people. Was it possible, I thought, forcing myself forwards, that, once, we had been happy? That that land of masques and bergomasques, of enchantment, of moonlight, calm, sad and beautiful, where life was a perpetual *fête galante*, had been here, had always been here? That that place I longed to escape to had always been beneath my feet, rising, like a wraith, from the soil of my ancestors; that escape had always implied a return?

As I passed the jerry-rigged marquee where my fellow contestants busied themselves with make-up and glad rags - giggles emanating from the canvas hold, rippling the hot, cloying air, so that the night fibrillated like a sick nerve - I broke into a run, the prospects of discovery an ice-cold blade descending on the back of my neck. Madame's automaton, by now, was probably well on its way to the Friendship Highway; on its way south, towards the Russian fence who would disoblige her captors of that precious, stolen flesh in exchange for the dollars necessary to get the USS *Thresher* out of dry dock. The kidnapping filled my imagination with mental snapshots of a dentist's chair, alligator clips locked onto a pair of blue-veined nipples that, rudely forced, pouted at their inquisitors with a curious mixture of placation and defiance. In psychosomatic reaction, my chest tingled, then ached, as I increased my exertions, forebodings of disaster matching the acceleration of my pulse. I was about to hurl myself into the darkness of the fields, that awaiting void impatient to confer obscurity, when a man - fat, with one of his legs in plaster and supporting himself with a crutch - put himself squarely in my path. I stumbled to a halt, panting, about to disembogue my calamitous heart. Several other figures joined my flight's obese hinderer, tumbling from the back of a pick-up that had skidded, stalled and refused to restart, its front tyres precariously balanced on the lip of an irrigation ditch. Then, the engine suddenly engaging, the pick-up reversed, swung about, its headlights saturating Act One, Scene One of my confrontation with mortality in white, white light. The fat man - the waxworks horror with the eyes of a cockatrice; the man who was Milord's stepfather - lifted his crutch and pointed its sharpened cusp in my face, his shadow a shivering black oil-slick sliding over the parched soil. 'Where is he?' he said, a hand touching a throat-mic, 'where is my irremediable? Where is my lost boy? What have you done with him?' I fell into the small, round, censorious eyes of the IDSIC policeman, a stepfather's eyes so different from my own father's, yet glinting with the same menace, the same judgmental wrath. On the outskirts of Korat, in the big teak house of that man of influence and virtue, I had grown from child to boy to man to woman and then ... grown backwards, into childhood again, fairyland of dolls, dresses and costume jewellery. The child was still there - hurt, afraid, lonely - taking her comfort from the swishy-ness of things: the silk evening gowns, the outrageous high heels and the millinery extravaganzas of my sisters, aunts, cousins grandmothers and great-grandmothers, all of whom had disposed of their unwanted finery in our attic, playground of my swishy, wishy infancy and youth. Memories of my father suddenly surprising me at my play; memories of his coldness at the dinner table; his laconic, cruel remarks whenever, by misfortune, our eyes might meet, his to be quickly, shamefacedly averted; his final words when he cut me off without a satang ... all this, too, went through me like a morbid thrill. Indeed, a pall of morbidity had seemed to have descended over the pitch-black fields like a cloud of poison gas. Rising out of the past, I struggled to find my breath.

'Never mind "your boy", what about my *dtook-gah-dtah*?' said Kito, stepping from the passenger seat of the pick-up.

'But, but – he's everything to me. I must have him. I must—'

'Quiet,' said Kito. 'You alert us to little game played by my treach-e-rous employee and his acomp, his acomp, his acomp—'

'Accomplices,' I intervened.

'But no think this give you right to tell me what to do. My face break in front of my people. It is my right, my human right to have revenge!' She beat at her temples with her fists. 'Where is my human right lawyer? Where? Where?' A small man in a blue cotton working-man's shirt came to Kito's side.

'This is very bad for your image, Madame.'

'It is the *farang*'s fault. It always is, no?' said Kito, reverting to Thai. 'That is the spin I want you to give this. Understood? I will *not* be shamed.' The lawyer – his voice well modulated, sweet with reason – glanced at the

stepfather, a supercilious smile tightening the corners of
his mouth as if he were appreciating a quiet, infinitely
civilized joke.

'Of course. *Farangs* steal dolls, abuse children, abuse
wives, sell peasants for genetic enhancement and organ
booty; Thai people, in contradistinction, are honest, kind
to children, evince much filial piety, rescue fellow
countrymen locked up in foreign monkey houses for
trumped-up crimes. Are kind to dogs.'

'Meaning?'

'Meaning you are not a racist, you are ethnocentric.
You have a pure heart, Madame. And a great wrong has
been done you.'

'I thought so,' said Kito, 'I know my human rights.'

'Madame is a Buddhist,' said the lawyer, soothingly.
'We all know she has followed the precepts for many
years.' But Kito's rage would not be quelled. Walking up to
the nearest member of her crew – a teenage hooligan with
a baby-faced sneer that betrayed that he had been
infected with an incurable case of ironic detachment – she
punched him full in the face; the boy stepped back,
holding his hands over his nose. 'I cannot believe, I cannot
believe,' said Kito, again racking her listeners with her
tourist tout's vocabulary, 'my aut-om-aton, my *dtook-
gah-dtah*. Mosquito, you take my *money ...*'

'The lady boy has spent too much time in the land of
the *farang,*' said the lawyer. 'He has become un-Thai. We
can use this angle with the papers. In fact, we can
probably turn this little contretemps to your advantage,
Madame. "Thai Philanthropist Robbed by White Jackals
While at Charity Gala for The Poor." We set the decadence
of liberal democracy against the *virility* of despotic

paternalism. The sympathy vote, Madame, think of the
sympathy vote!'

'Oh, shut up!'

The Seneschal strode to her side, a sawn-off shotgun
under his arm. It was the sudden striking up of the
mallam band that saved me, I think; the incredible, raucous
noise not only destroyed all hope of my lynch mob's
attending to my reply (not that I gave one; my lips moved
in dumb rehearsal of the begging for mercy that was sure
to fill the hours and days to come) but muffled the roar of
the approaching Bentley, bouncing crazily over the dried-
out furrows and earthworks of the paddies and bearing
down upon the pack of hoods like a big, black cruise
missile about to take out the counter-revolutionaries,
the parasites of the *ancien régime*, without incurring
unnecessary collateral damage. The chief enemy –
according to the missile's programming, evident from its
inflexible course towards the centre of the targeted group
– was Milord's *bête-noire*, the man who had officiated over
his moral education when he was an adolescent; an
officiation that had been less than efficacious, it would
seem. 'You'd better tell me *now*, pussy boy,' said Kito,
dog-English at last forsaken, pan-sticked face a
hair's-breadth from my own, 'or I'll avail myself of more
of your anatomy. And if you thought it was painful when
I took out your *teeth*, then–' First, the stepfather was
catapulted into the air, and then – I back-pedalled as fast
as I could – Kito followed, the impact of the radiator grill
against her body softened by the Bentley's initial impact
against the blubberball of the decency policeman and by
the violent braking manoeuvre Milord was forced into
deploying in order not to immolate his good, faithful

soldier: me. The hoods threw themselves into the dirt or
else scattered in confusion.
'Get in!' shouted Dahlia from the side window. I
complied, yanking open a door and throwing myself
lengthways across the back seat as I heard the dull blast
of a shotgun and a concussive reply from the car's
bodywork. The Bentley spun, again felling those who,
dazed, were rising to their knees, throwing up a smoke
screen of dust and human particulates. Milord opened his
own door, looked behind; reversed. There were sounds
consistent with the flaying of flesh as he carefully guided
the car's rear axle over the prone garage-sale body of the
stepfather. 'Did you get his head?' Dahlia inquired,
rebarbative. 'Try to get his head, Cap! His head, his head!'
Once again Milord steered the car in a patient, retrograde
trajectory calculated, this time, to squash more than the
already pulped torso and limbs.
'Is this necessary?' asked Milord, his nerve visibly
faltering. (With his bulging eyeballs, his uncontrollable
excitation, he looked like a victim of Graves' disease.) 'It's
hard to think how people in these parts might go about
preserving a brain. I mean, in this heat, in these primitive
circumstances. Without oxygen, he'd be gone in—'
'We have to make *sure*,' Dahlia interrupted. Milord
bit his lip and put the hammer down. There was a noise
that resembled the sound of a Durian falling thirty metres
from an overladen branch to a concrete road below.
'Yesssss!' she hissed. 'Now, let's get out of here.' I sat up to
discover Kito on her feet, shaking the dirt from her *haute
couture* kimono, and mournfully surveying the remains of
her mangled crew. As another shotgun blast peppered the
side of the Bentley, Dahlia drew a butcher's knife from

beneath her jacket and hurled it towards The Seneschal. It struck him in the midriff, and with a cry of 'dtohk-tong!' he staggered pitiably, if vengefully, in our direction, his rubbery legs obliged to execute a curious, mincing gait, as if he were mimicking the strut of one of the beauty contestants, or as if, his terminal misadventure – no niggard, but generous now, in its collapse of time – had pitched his sexuality across the arbitrary line demarcating masculinity and femininity which he had been perpetually redrawing throughout his whole life, even as it pitched him forwards, the remaining shell of his weapon detonating as he struck the ground, blowing the feet off the broken-nosed young hooligan who, alone amongst the remains of the raiding party, had tried to regain the favour of his mistress by racing alongside our retreating car, a hand already groping for the pistol tucked in the back of his belt; and he had been likely to have given us reason to fret, too, if it had not been for Madame's shark-suited, small-membered police colonel's felicitous tightening of his trigger finger, a dying spasm that – apart from dismembering the would-be hero – retroactively defined a whole life in its premature ejaculatory roar. The boy seemed, momentarily, to be continuing his sprint, his stumps a blur, a triumph of will over gravity; but then, as inertia took hold, rooting him to the lignite-tempered soil, he looked over his shoulders; beheld, with dismay, the amorphous prints that bloodied the earth, the sneakers and chopped flesh that lay in his wake like the remains of a toontown anthropomorph dynamited out of its socks and shoes. He crumpled to his knees; placed the back of his hand against his brow; collapsed. Milord put the car into first; and as he quickly

went through the gears I turned to watch the scene of
battle recede into the night, the circus defined by the
sodium-glow of the light-towers, its glittering temple
roofs of orange and red, its stage where I could just about
make out the small figures of bikini-clad girls wiggling
their behinds to the syncopated *flash, flash, flash*, of the
society photographers, at last swallowed by a darkness as
absolute as death. But not before the all-enveloping
shadows had framed the small, torch-lit figure of Kito.
She was doubled over, weeping into her hands, all
arrogance evaporated; her favourite toy was lost,
perchance for ever; and she at that moment was lost, too.
Her icy condescension - conceit of all those who clawed
their way to the top of the garbage heaps of Asia - a front
that disguised profound feelings of inferiority, the
unspeakable knowledge that the surface was not all, that
she was less than her image. Tonight, too much had been
spoken, too much had come to be known; and Kito's
dignity, shattered, lay in the dirt, a broken mirror each
one of whose shards testified to the nakedness of her
shame. As she vanished into a pinprick I thought I could
see her outstretched arm accusing those who had
uncovered her failure, had tarnished her with the
revelation that she was - would always be - a peasant to
be looked down upon, reviled. She was very *bijou* in that
moment; and I thought of her as I had often thought of
her in my days as a doll rustler, scouring the bars of Nana;
that she was a sister, someone who, perhaps, in a better
world, would deserve better, as would I.

   I felt the car's tortured suspension find its ease on
eagerly awaited tarmac. 'Glad I got another one of these
limos,' said Milord. 'This is the second one she's had me

buy for her, you know? Still, as I always say, a sound investment. Dahlia understands such things.'

'If we can afford a nuclear submarine, one fitted out sexy and all, then we can certainly afford a nice car,' said Dahlia. 'I mean, it's you who wanted to come out East, not me. You with your obsession about reliving your childhood. And out East, Cap, you gotta have *status*.'

'Uh-huh. I guess so.'

'Where's the doll?' I asked, in a sudden panic. 'You haven't—'

'She's in the boot,' said Milord.

'So capacious,' said Dahlia, 'as I can attest.'

And for several kilometres we thundered on in silence. But at last, studying the back of Milord's blond locks, imagining him as I always imagined him amongst dark, London streets, incandescent, a lean man dressed in light, window-shopping for automata (his cold eyes appraising their wonderful, jewelled forms as he walks down Piccadilly and into Bond Street), I could no longer contain myself.

'You came back,' I said. The ten-wheeled trucks with whom we shared brief, indiscriminate, heart-stopping intimacies – with always the promise of a little bumper-to-back-axle frottage – fell to our 100 m.p.h. wake, the sight of other traffic bearing down on us as Milord swung the Bentley recklessly into the approaching stream becoming, after a while, something not only to be braced for, but something to be expected, and soon, something that had become a commonplace, unable to alarm.

'Had to,' muttered my English beauty, my bold corsair, my marvellous Cytherian. 'She made me.'

'Had to,' said Dahlia. 'That stepfather – we had to, had to, just *had* to make sure he'd never come back.'

'Serendipity, then,' I said, trying to disguise the bitterness in my voice. 'Well met by moonlight.'

'We *had* to make sure,' reiterated Dahlia, a sliver of steel in her voice. 'I won't allow Cap's safety to be compromised by a crazy, rogue stepfather.'

I had to change the subject. 'Where to next? All this talk about getting new flesh, building a starship ... Talk, talk ... I'm following blind, you know. A faithful poodle, that's me. When do I get to chew on a little bone?' Dahlia turned, rested her chin on the black upholstery, blacker eyes enveloping me in blackest nihilism, a baby demoness, an angel child of death, this Blue Dahlia, this Dahlia Chan. I knew then that she was a true fanatic; she cared nominally about her quest for Cythera; and I knew she cared for her lover, Tarquin; but mostly she cared about nothing, simply nothing; ergo, Dahlia was probably the most dangerous person I had ever known. She was capable of the most nocuous virtues, the most noble vices. She was capable of destroying the world.

'So the dog wants a bone? Do you hear that, fanboy? Shall we give her one? Give the little poodle a little oral gratification? Shall we give poor Mosquito a bone?'

'Knock it off, you microminx.'

'She, I mean *he*, wants to know where we're going.' Dahlia pulled a handgun from the cleft of her meagre décolletage; waved it in front of my face.

'Careful—'

'Dahlia, put that away.'

'But he, *it*, wants to know about the voyage out. You see you have to die, Mosquito. You have to give up the ghost if you want to make the journey to The Belt. I sing for you, then you die, become a sim inside a song, a song that condenses the time it takes to travel to The Belt into a handful of days. Of course, when you make the journey back ...'

'Took us two years,' said Milord, snatching impatiently at the gun and locking it in the glove department. 'But by the time *you* get to embark for Cythera the star ship will have been constructed. *You* won't have to come back to Earth. Neither will anybody else. All the children will have been freed by then and we'll be ready to set off for the stars.'

'That journey will take many, *many* years. We don't have a chance of attaining close-to-light speed.'

'But with the new flesh we'll survive,' said Milord. 'Survive for thousands of years, if need be. The hollowed-out asteroid will be a completely self-sufficient world.'

'So I have to die?' I said, flatly.

'Yeah,' said Dahlia, turning her back to me and pushing her fingers through her bob as if to ease a sudden migraine.

'Then would *you* do it, Tarquin?' I asked. 'I mean, if I have to die, can it be *you* who kills me?'

'Slut,' whispered Dahlia.

Milord snorted. 'Enough of this badinage.' And then, as he looked across at his lover, recording, it seemed, her put-upon, pouty mien as if he meant to save it for a home video session, he snorted again; and this time the snort metamorphosed into a full-throated laugh. He seemed acquainted with her jealousies.

We carved our passage through boondocks, burbs

and borderlands without episode, interlude or rest; by the time the dawn had arrived, we had already passed the industrial satellite cities of Chonburi, Bang Saen, Sri Racha and the desolate ruins of Pattaya City, last human outpost of sun, sea, sand and sex. By the time we reached Sattahip the sun was high over the ocean. We wound our way down the foothills of the surrounding mountains and towards the dry dock where our submarine, the raised and refitted USS *Thresher* – lost since 1963 some 200 miles east of Boston, deployed, mothballed, and now auctioned by the recently privatized New England militia – lay at berth, ready to take on board the guerrillas of The Army of Revolutionary Flesh, take them all, girl-child, boy-child, man, woman and hermaphrodite, into the bowels of its pressure hull and propel them to their piratical destiny along the fault line of the North-South divide. Coming into the bay, I saw our boat's proud sail rising into the sky, bristling with radio masts and diving planes, the bridge from which our brave Captain would lead us out onto the high seas to revenge injustice, conquer the world, and release his people from captivity, our exodus to the stars then to begin.

Later that day, The Army gathered on a pier. There were thirty of us, the remaining freedom fighters having flown to the South Pole where, I was informed, a customized Buran shuttle strapped to an old *Energiya* rocket, already packed with matériel which the robot factories of their asteroid habitat, the *Narrenschiff II*, were unable to synthesize, waited to take them on a claustrophobic ride to The Belt. As we gazed down on the bunting-and-balloon festooned sub, Dahlia swung a bottle of Bollinger against its teardrop-shaped carapace – lately emblazoned with a huge skull and crossbones – champagne foaming over the brass nameplate like a pink-white explosion of semen occasioned by such orgiastic excesses as I hoped I might enjoy, some day, with my First Lord of The Sea, Milord. 'I hereby name you the *Narrenschiff III*,' she announced to the happy yet constrained applause of our coevals. And then she impatiently tore off her T-shirt and jeans to stand revealed as the sackcloth-attired slave-girl of her most outrageous film.

Tristesse gazed on sullenly. The bodyguards of the Muscovite fence who would soon transport her to the souks of The Hermitage – the world's *De Luxe* black marketplace, these days, HQ'd in St Petersburg – had linked their arms with hers, wary of her biomechanical strength, her fearful, capricious tantrums. I had changed into he-clothes – Milord had insisted; I could re-feminize, he promised me, once aboard – and had surrendered my beautiful frock to its owner. How magnificent she looked, even if bedraggled and befuddled – that latter condition marking her, I had noticed, ever since Milord had conducted his intrauterine physical; how doubly, trebly magnificent she would look amongst the bejewelled eggs and timepieces of the House whose descendants had created her and her peers! She was mumbling to herself; perhaps she had incurred damage. It was a mumbling that constituted a split-persona debate, the multitudinous voices of a girl mechanical in desperate need of therapy. (I had heard such things when I had mixed with her like in Saint-Germain-de-Pres: the idiolects of automata who had contracted viruses, or had been abused by their owners.) '*Dead valentines in pools of dismembered*

orchids rinse the perfume from the hair of the golden
Barbary corsairs and a pretty vivandière must perforce
sell herself as well as her victuals to the cruel assassins
of Rome, Carthage and Pandaemonium, but all shall be
well and all shall be well and all manner of thing shall
be well ...'

Dahlia and Milord huddled in conference with the
Russians, their secretaries chatting animatedly into their
mobile phones, concluding the doll-for-money trans-
action with their respective Zurich laundrymen. Once the
outcome was sweet for all parties, and a bond had been
issued to the submarine's auctioneers, a representative of
the New England militia led us into the boat's ritzy
indwelling. Dahlia and Milord had asked that the décor of
this former instrument of mass destruction match that of
the *Nautilus*, as depicted in Disney's 1954 *20,000 Leagues
Under the Sea*. The decorators had delivered: the sub's
Victoriana was a triumph, its verisimilitude breathtaking,
its vision, in its warped intensity, matching not only its
celluloid inspiration, but that of its new owners. Dahlia's
leading man had always complained that he had
deserved the role of Nemo in Troma's characteristically
B-market remake of the Jules Verne classic, especially
after his portrayal of Captain Tarquin in *The Kingdom of
Childhood* had proved - so he averred - that he had been
born for the part. 'Now you have a chance to show them
how wrong they all were,' cooed Dahlia, as Milord seated
himself at his pipe organ to demonstrate his knowledge of
Bach, the quicksilver fluency conferred by revolutionary
new flesh. 'Yes, darling, we'll show how misguided the
whole world has been to think that they can put paid to
us.' I sat down on a chaise longue, stretched out like a *Felis*

Femella – one of those amber-skinned dolls with incongruous jade-green eyes, the results of cross-species genetic splicing – stretched out, yawned and licked my hand, a fay kittycat disguised in a mannish little suit. Idly, I let a broken fingernail play with the furbelow, reflecting that there would be an occasion, and an occasion soon, that would offer me another chance to show Milord how I too could look as magnificent, as wonderful as a Fabergé doll, indeed how I could look as beautiful and as unreal as a Cartier doll, a Lalique doll, any doll of the *haute monde*, if it served his purposes and the purposes of his cult. And that occasion would surely afford me a greater share of his favour; before long, he would allow his eyes to linger over my stupendous curves, my recherché lines, and he would remember his vow; and on a not-too-distant day, when he had forgotten ghosts, his childhood, forgotten Dahlia, I would have new flesh too, flesh in which there would be a reconciliation of man and woman, human and thing, of East and West, North and South, Jekyll and Hyde, Love and Cynicism, Gentleness and Viciousness and Savagery and Tenderness Divine. And it would be in the reconciliation of these opposites, the hardboiled world with the fairy-tale, the *noir* with a world of impossible romanticism, that I would at last come home. Home to Cythera.

I thought: I will set myself apart from my rival. There was a beauty parlour in town and I determined to go blonde; platinum, preferably, but strawberry if the dyes that they had in stock weren't imported. The last time I tried to go platinum I went purple instead.

And blonde I was, and platinum too, yessir, when within forty-eight hours the *Narrenschiff III* embarked, pushing into the Gulf of Siam and setting a course westwards towards the Mediterranean Sea.

'Xanthos,' Milord had said, pointing towards the charts that hung from a portion of the inner hull that had been covered in walnut panelling. 'We must – before we conceive of any other course of action – we *must* liberate the prisoners of Xanthos.' He explained the difficulty of the operation; we had no nuclear weapons, only a few torpedoes; the boat's armoury consisted mainly of twentieth-century small arms, supplemented by a handful of military lasers he had acquired on the streets of Bangkok. 'But,' Milord had said, his hand clamped over the Ionian Islands, the southernmost of which was the isle we were to storm, the isle whose capital was The City of Yellow Brick, which also bore the isle's name, 'it is our fate.'

Dahlia and Milord had told me that the way to new flesh involved suicide.

I wanted to believe them; for our boat, it seemed to me, was a boat of death, and we were on a course for oblivion.

'Xanthos', I discovered later, ransacking the boat's extensive library, did not exist. It was a mirage, just as my other self was a mirage.

We all have our roles to play, I thought. And few of us get to choose who we are to be.

But being, we must continue till the end.

PART THREE

MY SECRET LIFE

CHAPTER SIX

My entry in *Who's Who* reads thus: FLYNN, Michael, John, Maxwell; film producer; *b* 20 October 1956; *s* of Thomas Flynn and Sententia Janet McDonald; *m* 2022, Jaruwan Visuthsri. *Educ:* University of Sussex, 1975-78. *Films:* The War of the Worlds, John Karter and the Krazy Kat Kartels of Venus, Hamlet and Ophelia Get Laid, Bedroom Nazis in Space, I Fell In Love with a Pain Slut from Zeta Reticuli, Intruder!, Spleen de Essex (television documentary), Mistress Dragonfly, A Princess of Death, Kung-Fu Nymphet from Hell, The Kingdom of Childhood, A Chinese Killer Virgin in LA, Mistress Dragonfly II, The Kitten with the Killer Meow! *Publications:* Xanthos: The Creation and Debacle of an Unreal

City (critique and screenplay). *Recreations:* Cheap thrills. *Address:* Since 2034, The Children's Home (IDSIC), Kithira, Greece.

They thought, in this encapsulation, to set the parameters of my reality. But my real life has been something quite different. Different, and infinitely strange.

Let me tell you a secret.

When I was six years old – perhaps it had been when I was seven, but certainly no later, so we are talking 1962 or 1963, here – I was abducted by a Reticulan flying saucer, a vehicle of a type that is – by tellurians – generally brought under the generic term 'UFO' (though for one such as me, who learned of his true identity via the transmigration chambers of these umbilical craft, it is this artificial world I have been trapped in since birth which is unidentified, an emulation being run, I have learned, in the heart of a neutron star, where similar emulations imprison the other surviving members of the Cytherian royal family [each of us alone, each incommunicado, each in his own immense hell] but in what system, in what galaxy, in what time frame, is unknown); UFOs having, over the years, conveyed the pattern of my life from out of the ultradense matter which supports it onto the plane of a higher level of implementation, the one that is called reality. The Reticulans have done this to remind me of who I am; to what purpose – other than to alienate me from the mummers whose sham lives we prefix with a 'human' – I am uncertain. I think I shall never know the purpose, incarcerated too long now in this false, but perfect universe, cast amongst illusions, a figment in a godlike mind - the superluminal switching operations of which are a zillion times more powerful than my own - never able to outguess it, to fully comprehend what lies beyond its bounds, except to know that what lies beyond is real and has a name: Cythera. My genesis, my grave.

It was my first experience of abduction; from the shards left by the bomb blast of that disaster, I could, for many years, reconstruct little (recalled, the following morning, nothing; it has only been my senescence that has clarified all, allowed me to collect the forensics that has enabled me to point an accusatory finger); despite the clogged bureaucracy of time (God, I feel old today, but I am old, of course, I am old, though the android into which I am periodically downloaded will remain a child even after time has accelerated me into forever), despite the malaria, this confinement, the continual interrogations, despite the impossibility of being able to help Jaruwan (and what else is left to me now but to dream that I might help set her free?), I am able to focus on that night seventy-three (or seventy-four) years ago and re-experience its trauma as if age had, compensating for decay, confusion, impotence and doubt, granted a grace note to the long, descending glissando of my decline; because it is due to a certain kind of mental *glaucoma* that - while my perceptions and judgement re the contemporaneous world have all but collapsed - my insight into the past has quickened, become keen.

And I am ready to confess.

Not the tidbits I throw The Censors; this will be my last testament, the confidential scrapbook in which I will confess all.

The abduction was at night. They always are. And

on nightwings I ascended to the gods. Lifted off my bed by a tractor beam and levitated to the bowels of the unmanned drone, I knew little of what was happening except, perhaps, in the shallows of sleep - in a drowsy unease - to register a foreboding, as if about to be made cognizant of the most awful of secrets. From sights gleaned from subsequent abductions I know this: the saucer's chromium underbelly opened; ingested, I was transported along curvilinear passageways; deposited in what my half-slumberous mind told me - and which the memories of later kidnappings, carried out while I was fully awake, have borne out to be true - was a darkened room. For it is always the same room - a room of terrors familiar, if unassimilable - to which I am conveyed; and it is always the same darkness which suffocates me. After a few minutes in which my unconscious prodded me into an apprehension that I no longer occupied my bed, I jerked to attention; a flash of lightning had rent the darkness in two; and I discovered myself staring into the naked glare of a desk lamp, its upturned bulb stabbing at the backs of my eyes. The lamp's corona eclipsed the room's details - it seemed to be a kind of study; the walls were lined with buckram spines - and only the phosphorescent hand directing the anglepoise into my face provided a point of orientation; giddy, I tried to focus on it, tried to prevent myself falling into the vertiginous, dazzling pit of light; and then, overwhelmed, fell, began to choke as if I were immersed within a cloud of fireflies. But something prevented me from pitching onto the floor. I willed my hands to come to my assistance, to no avail; then, feeling cord sear my wrists, I shifted, glanced behind, and discovered that I was secured to a metal chair with, above my head, some kind of helmet – black, with a smoked visor – descending from a mucilaginous ligature; soon, the helmet had engulfed me, its flange tightening about my neck. I would later recognize this helmet – as well as some of the other components I glimpsed amidst the mirage of bookshelves lining the hushed, claustrophobic study – as constituting hardware integral to a virtual reality parlour, or what, during the high times of middle-aged success in LA, I, along with other latter-day Babylonians, would refer to as a ghost parlour, or ghost karaoke. I felt a prick at the base of my neck; and a horde of nano-machines – though I did not know this then; indeed, the word 'nanomachine' had not yet been invented – swarmed into my skull, each miniature robot anchoring itself in the interstices of my brain to form a complete map of my selfhood. My feet and hands went numb; and then, the numbness circulating through my body like a swift-acting soporific, I entirely lost the sensation of possessing corporeal form; I was again falling, but falling, this time, into the gyres of a multihued vortex, hurtling towards a white disk that widened and grew more brilliant as time dilated in accommodation with the universe that encompassed my own; the nanoware, that had recorded my personality within its disparate parts, was pouring back into the datacap, to be translated into photons and beamed along the umbilical frequency that connected the neutron star's surface with a Reticulan satellite; and then – the disk exploding, as if the anglepoise had been dashed against the floor, black, spidery lines crisscrossing my vision like the splinters of a shattered pane of glass – I was thrown from the universe that was my prison into the universe I had been born of, but could no longer expect to be *in*, discounting, of course, these rare moments of downloading when I borrowed the form that had been prepared for me, a mechanical child whose lineaments and overall form replicated, with one major, overriding distinction, the virtual body to which I had been condemned. The helmet rose from my head; I was sitting in another metal chair in another study, the same phosphorescent hand, bleached in stark blacks and whites as if it were a living radiograph – again directing the glare of the desk lamp into my face. I had been sent by ansible to the world of my true birth: Cythera, a small planet in the Zeta Reticuli system that had been colonized by the Reticulan Empire. My gaoler, also downloaded – the only other 'real' component of the world called Earth – was waiting to conduct his first interrogation with the mirror-image of his charge. I looked about me – I could more clearly make out the study's details on this side of the divide – and recognized the décor, original elements from amongst an almost infinite library of interior design from which the building blocks of my virtual prison had been abstracted. For the study possessed an ambience which a tellurian – referencing the false, empirical world that is all he or she is familiar with, the grand forgery constructed out of recombined Reticulan data – would call 'Biedermeier', though consubstantial with the room's familiarity was a disconcerting and unplaceable alienness, that *terror* of which I have already spoken, a terror which is forever associated in my mind with the word *secret*. And there, in the room of secrets, the clandestine study which was to become a conscious terror only in later years, silence pressed upon my eardrums, the books and technological detritus that hugged the walls from floor to ceiling providing a rigorous soundproofing so that all proceedings were held effectively *in camera*. It seemed the loneliest of nights in the most desolate and sterile of wildernesses. But if I listened carefully enough I seemed to be able to hear a wind gusting outside, blowing as if across endless plains ...

Silence, silence all my life. And such a maleficent silence: rarely able to speak, and, if I spoke, never others to hear; sealed in this gigantic capsule that seems like a cloying skein countless light-years thick, a membrane hard as space-time separating me from those I would touch and cry out to for release.

And so I put down how it all began. Let me list the wrongs done me, the humiliations, the abuse.

There has been too much silence; too many secrets.

There has been too much pain.

But wait. Is this really how it began? Or rather, should begin? Surely not; how many backers would you get for a synopsis that began with such a disproportionate emphasis on the morbid and the strange? No; a story like mine – it should begin with hope, with a beginning to match its riding-into-the-sunset finale; the opening scenes shouldn't have such a naked focus on anger, bitterness and despair; this movie, this manuscript will start and end in joy; for this is for you, Jaruwan, and for the day when I shall set you free; I do not want you to remember me as a querulous eighty-year-old; this will be your last movie, the one after which I tear up your contract and you and I disappear into the salmon-pink glow of the last take, the last reel, of this cruel emulation. And so let me resurrect an almost equally powerful series of images (how much they have been recreated by the years impossible to decide, though these engrams, I think, have always been with me, have never been stirred from oblivion by the compensatory powers conferred by my encroaching demise): a garden; and at the end of the garden, a fence which, if you should clamber over, would prove to enshrine a land of romance, a land of the fantastical, of wonder, the greatest playground of which a young boy is able to conceive: an abandoned World War II aerodrome, its vast acreage dotted with derelict pillboxes, barracks, antiaircraft batteries, underground fuel tanks and bomb shelters, the whole overgrown vista transversed by cracked, weed-infested runways, like the earthworks of stone age people vainly signalling to their space-faring gods. Before I was big enough to climb over the fence I would play in the garden, forever wondering about the world that lay beyond its meagre frontier; and sometimes, rising over the fence, slowly and ominously, a gargantuan flying elephant would take to the sky, to hover in the blue distance while tiny figures threw themselves out of its belly, silk mushrooming from the tumbling parachutists' backs almost as soon as they had begun to fall. I would run crying into the kitchen, complaining loudly to my mother that the evil Dumbo, the flying pachyderm, had returned, that she should make it go away. But after a while the parachutists discontinued their training sessions – I later learned that there had been a fatality – and the barrage balloon could no longer dissuade me from, at first, climbing to the top of the fence, to sit astride it surveying my prospective kingdom in awe, an explorer first setting sight of a undiscovered country; and then, at last – perhaps it was as much as a year or two later – to drop to the other side when my mother's attention was diverted and to set off into the high grass, the uninhabited desolation that promised the most incomparable travels and adventures, the most transcendent love.

And why start with this memory rather than the memory of first abduction? Because that flight into the ruins of the old aerodrome in north-east London represented my first escape attempt. And my life – Jaruwan, hear me – has been a series of such attempts. And the next attempt shall include you; we really shall leave, and soon, I promise, soon; and then we shall say Goodbye Town, goodbye Earth; we are going home to Cythera.

But I can hear the guard approaching. Lights out, he calls. Until tomorrow then ...

I hide this little manuscript in a crevice I have whittled in the window frame with the other Biro, the one that doesn't work, a gummy plaster of ground pills – I refuse to be a chemical slave – serving to camouflage the excavations. Biros: such exotic tools: Anodos, the young guard whose mother has a tobacconists in Kapsáli, is my supplier; I think the dear boy, like so many other boys today, has never touched pen to paper in his life. I tell him I am using them to make a model ship. He laughs, revealing his ink-stained tongue, and replies that I am foolish to waste such excellent candy on such an enterprise. And today – thanks to you, Anodos, my postliterate, unsuspecting saint of markers and sign makers – I write crouched against the casement's bars, a stream of lovely, buttery, mediterranean light spilling over my greasy pages. They never disturb me during the day. It is at night that The Censors choose to talk; with me, with us all, children and adults alike. The tongue wags more freely at night, they opine - those night watchmen of dreams and desire! It is a lie; I write by day, only by day; and what I write is - if the opposite of what the stepfathers wish to hear - the truth, golden, inviolable and free. I revealed, at my committal, who and what I was; and I have revealed myself again, to every stepfather who cares to interview me; but they do not listen; and so I have let them be content with fragments, the piecemeal story, the superficial FAQ that they have chosen as an object of focus from the great database of my life. It is to these scribblings that I entrust the greater picture. I must set down the *undiluted* narrative for later generations, for those who might, perhaps, be less willingly hoodwinked by the hysteria of my contemporaries; those whose disposition might extend to granting me an unprejudiced hearing. I do not want this record of my tribulations to be anything but *the thing itself*, a record of the nature of the universe; I wish, before I die, to leave a testament uncensored; I wish to leave a record factual, naked of embellishment, even if few on this world have yet evolved beyond the basic imperatives of their pro- gramming and are thus unable to hear me. I wish to leave something for Jaruwan, my wife, my little girl; for Jaruwan, my lost childhood. (Despite the deceptions, the lies, the gambling, the drugs, and finally, the adulteries with the gigolos and rent boys a half, a quarter, nay, sometimes an eighth of my own age, I have always found in her [whenever I have tried to run away] the quality that I have thirsted for with unquenchable need all my life: innocence.) I wish to leave ... myself.

But my next interview approaches. I must practise

my lines, dissemble well; I must please them; for they have said that if I perform in a manner in keeping with their highest expectations they will allow me a connubial visit; it amuses them, I think, to conjure up an image of an octogenarian and his young wife, together. Let them laugh; during such a visit I will be able to discuss my escape plans, convince her that I can truly be of use; for I am certain, now, that my biggest mistake has been to hide. I must reach out; re-establish contact with the Reticulans. Despite their crimes against my person, I must turn to them again; for only they can save Jaruwan.

The empty, chipboard city stretching out beneath me – I have to stand on a chair and even then extend my pitifully hunched torso as far as I am able, each vertebra cracking in protest – is as buttery as the light itself. The Children's Home is in the centre of the *polis* and is part of the old movie set – most of it built on the insubstantial lines of Hollywood's Wild West – left over from the filming of *The Kingdom of Childhood,* a part that served, fittingly enough, as the dungeons in which condemned slaves were sometimes – the smell of money wafting from a visiting galley, or clipper, forestalling the executions – auctioned off to buccaneers (though Tarquin was to rescue his Lucrece without recourse to post-apocalyptic doubloons), one of a handful of buildings in this fenced-off, gaudy no-man's-land high above the bay to have any real substance. The structure, built to my specifications – it rises from the foundations of a Venetian castle blown-up by terrorists during the North-South wars – is as massive as the movie set raised over the ruins of Khóra is flimsy. The panorama these redeployed, sixteenth-century stones afford is magnificent, the City of Xanthos, also known as

The City of Yellow Brick - I call it a 'city' because of the memories I have of Jaruwan's prime, but it is no bigger, and indeed, perhaps far smaller, than the village it transplanted, being for the most part two-dimensional, its buttressed facades jaundiced with undercoat and sand - terminating at the razor-wire fence and its *Warning! Children's Home!* signs in Greek, English, French, German and Arabic, beyond which the world of the living, that is, the harbour of Kapsáli with its fishing boats, its quayside busy with market life, stretches out, incorporeal under the midday sun. The purple sea betrays no evidence of shipping, though the Peloponnese is near, this little piece of rock, this ironic Kithira, or Cythera, that was centre, once, for the worship of Aphrodite, chosen as a place of confinement not merely because of its proximity to the foment of the North-South troubles, but because, of course, it is a rock which has been forgotten, its indigenous population fled; a rock under which the masters of the world have swept those it would also forget lest they be reminded of themselves.

Cythera. I think they deemed it amusing to have me imprisoned here. (The stepfathers are easily amused, whether by allowing me access to my wife, and then baiting me, say, with endless suggestions that I purchase an appropriately ingenious penile splint, or by locking up the creator of a movie that has earned their most earnest disapprobation inside the wreckage of his dream.) But would they be so amused if they were convinced of the greater irony; that, these days, I occupy a prison within a prison - me, the old, crazy impresario of schlock, the patricide whose best production was filmed on the very soil on which this 'Children's Home' stands, who pleaded at his committal hearings that he was a Cytherian, when he had had enough of masquerading as just another vactor and tried to tell the world the truth? 'You are asleep!' I had screamed at them. *'You are not real! No more than robots, all of you! I am the only real person in this whole goddamned, mocked-up world! This whole goddamned universe!'* Would they be so amused then?

'Xanthos,' Jaruwan had said when we had begun filming. *'The island already has a name: Kithira. And Kapsáli – the name of this village – why the hell do you want to call* that *Xanthos too?'*

'Henry Miller,' I'd replied. 'Quote: *"I don't know whether there is a Xanthos or not, and I really don't care one way or another, but there must be a place in the world, perhaps in the Grecian islands, where you come to the end of the known world and you are thoroughly alone and yet you are not frightened of it but rejoice, because at this dropping off place you can feel the old ancestral world which is eternally young and new and fecundating ..."* Unquote.'

'Pooh,' Jaruwan had said. '"Xanthos": it sounds like some kind of tacky perfume. You think you'll get the euros from the *De Luxe* with a cheap name like that?' Such had been the opinion of my beloved, twelve-year-old leading lady, so carefree, then – or so I had thought – not like the poor thirtysomething child who, like me, is locked up in this Town, parole unimaginable.

Investment? That had not been why I had changed the location's name from Kithira to Xanthos. It had been a betrayal, really, a betrayal of myself, my people, to come to Kithira to make that film; and I could not bear to use the sacred name for a movie that, though one of my best, still rates a Z-grade in the archives. But I had so longed to make contact with a place that might, through some kind of association, however oblique, allow me to glimpse the reality behind my own story, the hounded selfhood lurking within the depths of my poor, fraudulent life, that I had proceeded, relocating from California to Greece. My locational whim had nearly bankrupted me.

Xanthos. I had read the name in *Tropic of Capricorn.* Tropic, Capricorn. Tropic, Cancer. On the other side of the pond I hadn't really been much of a biblio-nut – I hope you, my future judges, translate these hieroglyphics into voice; I crave the widest audience – but I had picked up those books with the superstitious idea that they might reveal to me something of Jaruwan's own secret life, a steamy, tropical inner landscape I was increasingly eager to become familiar with, to consume, to make my own. But it was not the fantasia on the name 'Xanthos' that I had found so memorable, but a paean to Cythera – without which, I think, I would have ignored or forgotten the 'Xanthos' passage entirely – a paean whose implications Miller had, necessarily, not understood (had my Reticulan captors encoded its message in that book especially for me? I have often discovered, buried in a television commercial, a photo in a glossy magazine, a twist of cloud in the sky, messages engrained in the fabric of this artifact called the world that could only be meant for me): '*I want to become more and more childish and to pass beyond childhood in the opposite direction. I want to go exactly contrary to the normal line of development, pass into a super-infantile realm of being which will be absolutely crazy and chaotic but not crazy and chaotic as the world about me ... I want to break through this enlarged world and stand again on the frontier of an unknown world which will throw this pale, unilateral world into shadow ... I must not stop to rest here in the ordered fatuity of responsible, adult life. I must do this in remembrance of the life of a child who was strangled and stifled by the mutual consent of those who had surrendered. Everything which the fathers and the mothers created I disown ... In retraversing the first bright world which I knew as a child I wish not to rest there but to muscle back to a still brighter world from which I must have escaped. What this world is like I do not know, nor am I even sure that I will find it, but it is my world and nothing else intrigues me.'*

I take one long, expansive look from the window, surveying the empty streets and alleyways, the chipboard *trompe l'oeil* – the city of yellow nothingness, of air – impressed upon the backdrop of the swelling, karstic hills; and then I withdraw. I am tired; I must lie down to write. The rat-killer, Proust, wrote while lying down, they say. So shall I, who must kill another sort of rat. Prone upon my little cot, I too shall seek out the luminousness of the past; confront; outstare its terrors.

But I must speak about the unspeakable: the beginning of the series of events that define me: the abductions by an alien life-form inimical to me, a rite of passage in which I learned I myself was an alien in an illusory world, that my whole waking life was a kind of fevered, raving hallucination suffered by one who has suffered premature burial ...

Enough. It will be lunchtime soon and then they will check on me again. And I become tired so quickly.

I wish, if only for a few hours, to dream upon escape,

to escape, if only for a few seconds, in another, if qualitatively different kind of raving dream. One in which I simply lie by a river, my thoughts stilled by the wind, the wind becoming my thoughts, taking me back, back to when I had been happiest, those moments of quiet love with Jaruwan.

On the wall of my cell, thumbtacked to the plaster, are postcard reproductions of Watteau's *L'Embarquement pour Cythère* (Charlottenburg, Berlin) *and Le Pélerinage à l'île de Cythère* (Louvre, Paris). Because of the titles of these paintings, it has been common to consider both works embarkations *for* the Island of Venus; but Michael Levey has contended that they represent a departure *from* Cythera. Both interpretations are, of course, correct. A Cytherian is both exile and pilgrim; as he grows older, he travels farther away from his homeland, while at the same time drawing closer to Cythera's shores.

Those yellowing postcards have seared the flesh beneath my breast pocket ever since I left LA.

It is a fine, cloudless day on Kithira, or Xanthos, as I once would have had it. A propitious day. Should I date these entries? But what date is it? It is summer, yes. But what month?

Yesterday, I neglected my task. But today I am stronger. To work; I must return to my central theme ...

I was fastened to the metal chair by three straps: two securing my ankles, my legs looped over the arm rests, the steel digging into the crook of my knees, and one binding my wrists, the arms drawn behind, up and over, the strap tied to the chair's high, fretted back, an artful binding that forced my scapulae into a concavity. 'This is the first time,' my interrogator said, beginning our interview during that initial transmigration to Cythera, 'that we have met in the flesh, so to speak. Though there are plenty of philosophers here on your silly planet who would argue that we too are virtual beings, this universe but another emulation inside a more powerful mind. All that, of course, is moot, save to say that in *this* universe you – for all intents and purposes – are a program inside a computer and I am not. Legalistically speaking, of course. In reality, I share your life. Share it willingly. It is my job, you see. My mission. Though you will wake up tomorrow and consider this, our first meeting, to be a dream, a dream that will quickly be lost to you, in later years – awaking, bolt upright, listening to the scream that a second before had left your lips and now still echoes about your bedroom – you will remember; you will remember many things about your past. You will remember that, while, for you, years have flown by, along with many joys, banalities and sorrows, time, commensurately, here on Cythera, has been measured but in days. When your uploaded life runs its course, we will merely turn time backwards and have you born again, once more to suffer in your unreal world. Birth, death, rebirth; to awaken, but never to be free. This will serve as your eternal dance. And always, always I will be with you.'

The voice had been familiar; I had tried to descry the face; but the glare of the desk lamp made this impossible. I think I must have begun to cry; for it was in lowering my head that I first noticed the clothes in which I had been accoutred, my miniature body smothered in a billowy pinafore dress; and my legs, which waggled in the air, their undersides bruised by the steel arm rests, stockinged with knee-length, blue-striped hose. Golden-blonde ringlets descended over my shoulders, spilling onto the neck of the white apron that decorated the nursery frock cut *à la* Victorian.

The figure behind the desk got up and moved to one side, taking the desk lamp with him, its beam remorselessly fixed upon my face. When I at last managed to articulate more than tearful gulps and hiccups – and oh, what were they but mewlings for a mother who did not exist? pleas for intercession which could never be answered? – when I at last managed to petition for mercy, I discovered that I had the voice of a little girl. The figure set the lamp upon the floor, adjusting the stem so that it illuminated me from below. Though still partially blinded, I could pick out in the fractured aureole that lit my abductor from behind the face of a man in his early thirties. He shifted, and his body was brought into view. Of middle-build (a boxer's musculature grafted onto an athlete's fleet, wiry frame), his powerful arms and shoulders gave the illusion that he possessed no neck, carbonized eyes – like auxiliary papillae – staring at me as if from the top of an exposed, barrel chest like those of a beast catalogued by a medieval traveller, glinting from within a sallow, matted thatch as if reflecting the candlepower of a gothic light show; his hair was leonine, prematurely grey, quiffed in a somewhat effeminate bouffant, accentuating his resemblance to a heraldic cryptomorph. As he closed on me, his face was once again cowled by shadow; but I had seen enough to know that – even as he put his hand under my skirts and probed with impersonal viciousness – that my childhood was lost in space, lost in time, dynamited, gone for ever.

'*Please don't, Daddy,*' I whimpered, '*please don't, please don't ...*'

Memories. Childhood memories. Everything has been defined by the events of my childhood. Not just the singular chronology of an odd, if unmourned-for life; but the history, past, present, future, of the human race and of the universe. Because the fate of this universe, its condition of damnation, revolves about my own fate. (The first intimation I believe I had of this ontological nightmare? Running, chest knotted with anguish, through the deserted aerodrome, the tears streaking down my cheeks, that landscape of disaster and alienation the outward form of an unvocalizable dread.) *Why did I climb that fence at the bottom of our garden?*

I would climb the fence at the bottom of our garden to escape from my father.

We lived in an estate whose streets, ways and footpaths all bore the names of Word War II flying aces. There was a street dedicated to Douglas Bader, one to Deere and others to Gillam, Finucane, Malan, Tuck; and there were countless other, similar streets, some even, I believe, borrowing their appellations from the roster of the Saturday morning picture shows I was so addicted to, streets with the names of pilots of the future, Dan Dare Street, Flash Gordon Drive and Buck Rogers Avenue. Perhaps these spacemen used the secret underground facilities of the aerodrome; and perhaps, I told myself, if I looked hard enough or left spray-painted signs on walls, sent out a telepathic SOS, they would come to save me. After all, the Cytherian government-in-exile (if there were such a thing) might pay a handsome reward for the rescue of a Cytherian prince. Until then, those working-class streets held me fast, my council house a cell where, at night, before falling asleep, I would sometimes imagine the screams of other transgressions floating into the sky, the screams of ghostly, virtual children, their unreal pain mocking my own. Closing my eyes, I liked to imagine that I too floated high above the houses, as weightless as those screams for love, drifting away, far away. Below, Spitfires and Hurricanes clashed with the enemy; Nazi flying saucers fell from the sky; and flak burst showering steel splinters upon the dreams of London's dead suburbs. And I would wheel through the night invulnerable as a star until I came to Cythera.

Listen: my father was a violent man. He—

My father used me as his punk.

My father turned me into a woman.

One day, playing amongst the couch grass of the deserted runways, I discovered a hitherto unknown chamber, deep, deep beneath the carapace of the known world. And it was in that urinous air-raid shelter that I first suffered the tremor of suspicion that the universe was not as it appeared. I had not, at that age, concocted any theories; I knew nothing of computers, virtual reality or neutron stars; and I still could not – beyond summoning up a sickening, inarticulate dread – comprehend the events of my nocturnal abductions. 'There's no way to discover whether or not you are simulated,' a friend of mine was to tell me in later years, 'whether you're only a series of numbers generated inside a computer.' But there are signs. Signs *buried in a television commercial, an advertisement in a glossy magazine, a twist of cloud in the sky.* And I began to recognize a facility in myself for interpreting signs. Tell-tale signs within the code of the gigantic information-processing system of this universe that intimated that all was not well. The scraps of old newspapers that littered the shelter's floor. Telephone numbers scrawled on the walls. The graffiti. The used condoms. They all had their messages. And amidst their clamour I would sit through long, fetid summer afternoons, in a reprieve of cool shadows, straining to understand. Then, suddenly, one day I heard the sound of a wind over endless plains; the subdued clatter of gynaecological instruments being rearranged within a kidney dish; a low, well-modulated, interrogatory voice. And I was privy to visions that I instantly recognized were being transmitted from a world as real as, no, *more* real, than the one I inhabited. Roads lined with crucified bodies, a burning palace on the horizon; concentration camps filled with orphans and carpeted with ash ... I know, now, of course, that I was reliving the rape of Cythera.

Though there was much I was yet to understand, it was at about that time that I put a name to what my father had been doing to me.

In a school essay I—

My mother was informed. My mother tore the essay up.

It was only by the most extreme efforts of my mother that, I believe, our little family was allowed to sleep under the same roof. It was a kind of negative effort, an effort involving *not* saying the wrong things, *not* disagreeing, *not* making ripples in the lake in which her water baby gasped for air, never questioning the edicts of the paterfamilias, *her* lord and *my* petty tyrant. Throughout the superficially quiet days of my childhood, I came to be certain of one thing: my mother would never stick up for herself; and this would not have been so much of a problem, perhaps, if she had occasionally stuck up for others, the chief of whom should have been me. But she would never stick up for anybody. *Anybody.*

From my mother, I learnt how to wear a mask.

A mask of submissiveness. The mask of a slave.

Of course, my mother was a sim; she was *programmed* to behave in a placatory manner; programmed to be the echo, the yes-woman, the ventriloquist's dummy, the appeaser of aggression; programmed to obey her mad, unreasonable husband, to simper at each sarcastic aside, to twinkle at each turn of his wild, disordered mind.

Yes; if my father was an alien, then my mother was a robot. How the Reticulans must have laughed at learning how I had surreptitiously tried to tell her of what was happening to me; how I had – with a blush of shame, a ready apology – showed her my soiled under-wear, pointed to the crimson stains, the dank evidence of an agenda cold, unsympathetic. But robots have but one master; and my mother, who seemed so real in all other particulars, faded from my presence whenever the white-hot core of my secret life began to erupt, and, checking the flow, I would scorch my innermost being with hot, constipated tears. I seem to recall that the one time a few words had seemed to penetrate my mother's deceptively tender hide she had turned on me, teeth bared, and ran her fingernails across one of my cheeks to leave four glistening wildcat souvenirs of my slanderous folly. Nothing more was said, and her con-torted face quickly resumed its mask of impenetrable innocence. I retreated to the bathroom and inspected my tribal scars, gashes that were by now threaded with thick beads of blood, recalling me to my isolation; and, bereft of hope, had driven my forehead into the mirror, knowing that I was, perhaps, the last of my kind, that my tribe was dispersed, dead.

It was a silent house ...

The verbal abuse: yes, it was suave, silky, *quiet*, not blatant at all; and I often thought my mother might simply not have understood the violence that was being done to me, so subtle was it, like a slow, silent poisoning. 'You must tell me if you ever feel ... *strange*,' my father had said. 'There are things your mother and I may be able to do. Before it's too late. There are places, for instance, special places; and people, special people, who might be able to help. You know you can talk to us,' he'd say, 'you know you can talk to us *anytime.*' But whether my mother understood such coded messages or not, I was beyond assistance; trapped.

That is why, even in those early days, before I could even articulate such a thing to myself, I knew, in the end, he had to go. Why, in the end, I had to destroy his simulacrum and make sure the pattern of his identity was destroyed with it.

I remembered well what he had told me during an interrogation: *If the brain is totally destroyed a corresponding deletion of software occurs in the memory of the neutron star.* He had thought he might – in imparting such information – torture me with the prospect of oblivion; he did not realize I would use that knowledge to destroy him; he was too busy with his suave harangues, his velvet beatings, his Reticulan-style abuse.

But it is redundant, now, to describe the beatings, the

abuse. Never coital, at least overtly, never brutal enough to leave marks, my father, who of course was not my real father (I do not know the name of my real father; know nothing about him other than he is or was a Cytherian king), my stepfather, let us say (to use the nomenclature of my most recent captors) yet knew how to exercise his authority over my body and mind as one born to the task, which sometimes I think he was: a kind of specially bred torturer, perhaps, his genes warped so that his whole pleasure and object in life was to persecute the prisoner that had been entrusted to his expertise, no thought of his own fate - imprisoned, like me, inside an emulation, his life, like mine, to consist of endless replays - interfering with his dedication to degrade, abase and hurt; to damage his charge so irreparably that the boy he called his son would never be more than a somnambulant wound, a festering incarnation of a nightmare.

Memories. The aerodrome. The lonely streets of an urban desert, its monotony of post-war grey. To begin with an escape attempt? That was right, since this biography will, *must* end with an escape, too. (I could list many other escape attempts: books [ha-ha, yes, you out there: you still rake your eyes across the marks and signs of language, don't you, my *wunderkinder*? Don't you? Don't You?]; and then there was my affair with the saxophone - dreams of Coltrane, Rollins, Bird - higher education, travels throughout South-East Asia, and, of course, most importantly, both in childhood and as an adult, the movies, the movies that came to dominate my life.) I have drawn up my plans; I move, now, towards their execution ...

I haven't written anything for three days. This is deplorable;

I must be strong; I must make my will and testament.

My father was my gaoler. The only representative of the universe from which I had originated. He was a sentinel uploaded to conduct surveillance. Whatever I did, wherever I went, he would watch, either from near or afar, sometimes using his own eyes, sometimes those of his agents. And doubtless, he always reported back to his masters, the Reticulan overseers who held his leash.

After that first abduction, life proceeded almost normally, even when debris of the previous night's events had been transformed, by some alchemy of pain and fear, from odd, unrecognizable pieces of mental shrapnel to the mangled, eidetic remains of nocturnal carpet-bombings. Despite my epiphany in the air-raid shelter, I came to believe my mother's blandishments, take comfort in her cooing away of my dread, until I began to wonder at my own credulousness; began to wonder how I could be such a *baby*, how I could tell myself such spiteful lies; but when, in later years, I would wake with perfect recall, an undeniable vision of the previous night's travail fresh in my skull – this would, according to my therapist, have been when I was ten or eleven – I began to avoid my father. No one said anything; I wasn't upbraided or cajoled; and the coolness with which my withdrawal from family life was met convinced me that I had been correct in my suspicions; that my father was wearing a mask, which, at night, he would strip away; and that my mother and all the rest of humanity were lifeless mannequins.

Masks, masks. Strip my own face away, and what do you see? A Cytherian prince? A little boy? A little girl? Or a madman?

When, in the following years, fear gave way to rebellion, submission to anger, I began to run away.

But I have never been able to run far enough. And though, for some twenty-odd years now, the abductions have ceased – ever since, in fact, I went into recovery in LA – I have always feared that, one night, any night, a Reticulan spaceship will descend to hover outside my cell and it will start all over again, the probings, the examinations, the pain; for some day, and maybe some day soon, they will learn of my father's demise and send me another gaoler. And I will wake up strapped to that cold, metal chair; or it will be the operating table, the arc-lights tearing at my eyes, my legs in stirrups and the hands of another paterfamilias slipping beneath my upraised dress, the glitter of steel instruments flickering about the tops of my thighs as father number two readies to dissect my vagina . . .

No use. Am so tired. And tonight The Censors will interview me. I must gather my strength, if only for Jaruwan.

'Have you been taking the lithium?' said the stepfather. I shrugged. And then, when he wouldn't look away, nodded, affirming my status as patient. 'Good. Bipolars like yourself often convince themselves that they *deserve* their highs as recompense for their despondency.' Bipolar? Last week they had said I was a paranoid schizophrenic. Did they know what I was? Did they care? 'But we must recognize, Mr Flynn, that, elevated or depressed, we are still *ill*, yes?' I shrugged again, imitating one put out to the grey, desensitized pastures of lithium carbonate. It wasn't too difficult. I had grown up in a grey, urban wasteland of flattened-out emotions and thoughts; born north-east of Eden, a.k.a. Swineville, UK, such pastures were familiar to me; and would have been too familiar, their familiarity breeding self-contempt, guilt, despair, the scales forever weighted in my disfavour if it had not been for the counterpoise of my cinematic visions – visions of Cythera, its rape – the hyperreal overload that at last found a correlative in an auteurist schlockfest of martial arts, oriental rock 'n' roll and sexual morbidity, a safety valve that siphoned off my life's poison throughout the years of flight and pursuit, escape and recapture, until, at last, all notion of my true identity had drowned in forgetfulness. At such time the abductions ceased. My father no longer bothered me. And until I put myself in the power of Rosaline the Rapacious Mind-Rat, I was blissfully, ignorantly free. 'Good, good. Now let's again go over some of the ground we covered during our last session.'

'You want me to tell you how I killed my father?'

'No, I wish to—'

'You want me to tell you again? I put a fucking carving knife through his eye.'

'I said I didn't wish to—'

And I was again sitting with my father at dinner as I had done fifteen years ago. Jaruwan had just left me and – like a dark angel arriving to confirm my loss with an encrypted telegram from his petty god – my old gaoler had appeared at my Burbank apartment with some weak story about needing a loan. It was, perhaps, an unfortunate coincidence that, just prior to his arrival, I had received a telephone call from my therapist.

'*Flynn? This is Rosaline Faversham. Why did you miss your appointment?*'

'*Yeah, I know. I'm sorry, Rosaline. I just think that we're not really getting anywhere. Fast. When I start talking about Cythera you always seem to flash me that arch, patronizing look that says—'*

'Now listen. I want to hear about Cythera. I've merely suggested that your so-called "visions" are sexual fantasies that relate to your case history: years of being abused as a child. They have no objective reality. Surely you can accept that?'

'No, you got it wrong. The memories I have of Cythera are as real as the memories I have of what my father did to me. You've always encouraged me to believe that Dad was a monster. Why are you so ready to dismiss the fact of my pre-natal existence as a Cytherian prince? The images are just as vivid.'

'Flynn, listen to me. Listen carefully. You've gotten worse. Why don't you come over to my office right now and—'

'You brought it all back, don't you understand? For so many years – ever since I was a boy – my brain had been boiling over with visions of blood, pain and death. But I'd forgotten why. I'd repressed the memories of the cause and lived only in the turmoil of the effect! Leave me alone, Rosaline. You're just another sim, like all the rest. You'll never understand!'

I slammed down the receiver. And then the bell had rung and I had opened the door.

Oh yes, I thought, up to their tricks again, the Reticulans.

He was in his nineties, but had had his simulacrum rejuvenated with a cheap but effective biotechnological equivalent of monkey gland treatment. As we had sat down to eat – I'd rustled together some of the Thai dishes Jaruwan had left in the freezer – I had looked out over that hunched, shrunken, almost foetal shape that slurped at the soup; looked out through the picture windows, out over the red, smoking social control districts in LA's far-away enclaves; looked out to the city's black core, never really listening to the details of what my father was saying, only hearing the evil drone of the Reticulan propagandist, the canned background music of a wrecked childhood. How strange it had been, he never declaring himself, and I never detoured into demanding a recantation, and both of us all the time knowing the truth; how strange it had always been. The meal I had dished up was huge, unconsumable; it had represented – from its vicious chillis to its carcasses of roast suckling pigs – the entirety of my child-bride's jealously hoarded stocks of food.

'Right the way through. Right into his software.' The stepfather took off his glasses and wiped them on his surplice, near to the white flower that served as his badge of purity. He was a youngish man, an American, not by adoption, like me, but by birth and by virtue of a presumptuous kind of innocence. Call it the innocence of the wilfully ignorant, the innocence that we have forgotten to call bigoted, myopic, self-serving, vain; the innocence of the New World Order. 'I don't understand how he didn't see it coming. I mean, I had these prints by Samuel Palmer and Edward Calvert on the walls of my apartment and I'd pointed to them saying, *That's what it used to be like, that's what Cythera used to be like before you and your friends got your hands on it, before you made us slaves.*' My interrogator's eyes flashed; and even though they were unfocused, they signified a malicious cunning; I swallowed my bile. He was not cut from the same cloth as the other stepfathers I had met, the Christian fundamentalists and other stentorian mediocrities for whom IDSIC had offered a convenient path to power. He had a mind, and was therefore more dangerous. He sucked a mouthful of air through his teeth; then – ocular furniture replaced – he shuffled his binder of notes, thumbing nervously through court reports and psychiatric evaluations. 'Right into his software,' I mumbled, apologetically. 'Right the way through, yes, right the way through.'

I had sawn open the brainpan, removed the grey sponge in which the pattern of his selfhood was encoded, and fed it to the garbage disposal; packed the remains in the ravine left in the freezer by the exigencies occasioned by our impromptu meal; and then, after a marvellously dreamless sleep, had left, in the morning, for Vientiane.

'What is the Reticulan Empire, Mr Flynn?'

'An evil intergalactic cabal.'

'Of which the home planet' – he checked his notes – 'is the third planet of Zeta Reticuli, yes? A binary system roughly thirty-seven light-years from Earth?' I ignored his pedantry as best I could.

'They have insinuated themselves into the civilizations of a thousand worlds. They are like worms in the bud, the caterpillars of the commonweal. No one understands their purpose. Perhaps it is nothing more complicated than malignity. It is difficult for us to comprehend, isn't it – a pure, unreconcilable hatred from those we know not, nor understand? Perhaps it is the will to corrupt, pervert and destroy that drives them. Perhaps that will to corrupt is, for them, natural, as the will to breathe, laugh, cry and copulate is for us natural.'

'And you say that they conquered your home planet, Cythera?'

'Cythera is in their own system. It was one of the first worlds to fall. I was little more than a baby when it happened.' I paused; unwrapped a peppermint; sucked on it as if it were a smart drug whose mechanical atoms might aid the percolation of thought. 'But then again: what do I really know of what they did? I only know what I've been told subsequent to the computer-modelling of my infant brain and its uploading into this emulation. But since it is *they* who have apprised me of much of what has been my genesis, I suppose I cannot put too much faith in the details. Deception is their sweetest joy. But details or no—'

'Do not spare me the details, Mr Flynn.' How much, I thought, should I tell him? To reveal the generalities of the invasion, surely, rather than the particulars of who I was, am and will always be - there was the delicate *particularity*, of course, of my true sex - could hardly further compromise my situation? 'The details, Mr Flynn, the details, please. I must reiterate: spare me not.' The visions came, the memories repressed for so many years, visions I had embodied in photo-shoot and moving picture, unaware of their catastrophic significance; I felt my heart quicken; and my poor old loins flickered with a sad little flame, burlesquing the excitement I had sometimes felt behind the lens of a camera, or roaming imperiously about a sound stage.

'The Reticulan warship - there was only one, a trim frigate-class reaver that boasted a crew of a hundred warriors - had parked itself in geo-stationary orbit above our world city, Cymodoce, City of the Crazed Virgin from the Sea. In the great citadel at the heart of our happy, dreaming city was a magnificent harem, a palace within a palace that housed the hundred-and-one princesses of the Cytherian royal household, their handmaidens, attendants and priestesses.'

'These were, what? The King's wives and concubines?'

'Not at all. Cytherians, due to some genetic quirk in their past - our scientists often talked about the effects of a nearby supernova - had always begat far more females than males.'

'The ratio being?'

'Something like, um, ten to one.'

'Consequently?'

'Consequently, all populations had developed a religious system which honoured and provided haven and purpose for those females who chose not to seek a mate. This was a strictly monogamous culture.'

'A harem of old maids?'

'*Au contraire*, they were all unspeakably beautiful, with a beauty untarnished by time; for like all Cytherians, they had eaten the sacred elixir which confers eternal youth.'

'Eternal youth? Something, indeed, that might provoke the most peace-loving of races to attempt an invasion.'

'Indeed, indeed. But the entire planet was protected by a force field which prevented the Reticulan ship from entering the Cytherian atmosphere. Nor could the Reticulans breach that barrier with laser cannon. The force field, however, was not impregnable. The enemy, utilizing a matter-transfer technology unknown to us, discovered a series of chinks in our armour.'

'The force field was ruptured?'

'Not exactly. Only one or two warriors were able to beam down at the same time, their murderous excursions restricted to periods of no more than fifteen minutes. They were operating within a very limited window of opportunity.'

'And this was at night?'

'At night, yes, when the force field was at its weakest. But because of the meagreness of their deployments and the limited time they had in which to mount their attacks, the Reticulans chose to practise terrorism rather than full-scale warfare. They attacked the city's most vulnerable constituency: the sacred harem. Each morning, soon after the presence of the orbiting warship was detected, several young women would be found dead in their bedrooms, cruelly slain, the tale of their wounds revealing to even the most inexperienced autopsist that they had been killed in a manner exquisite, piquant—'

'Or atrocious.'

'It depends, I suppose, on your perspective.'

'It does?'

'Soon, we learned of our enemy's terms: surrender, or face the extermination of the holy order about which the life of your planet revolves. There was no surrender. Instead, the denizens of the harem elected to seal themselves in their rooms, alone, at dusk, so that any Reticulan warrior materializing in their midst would be contained. And if screams were heard, there was no one to respond, for despite the murderous visitations, Cytherian males were still not allowed beyond the portals of that area of the citadel.'

'The Reticulans – they were intruders, yes? They crept into their bedrooms at night and–'

'And killed them. Slowly. Painfully. Memorably. But since the Reticulans were unable to send more than two warriors to the surface of the planet each night, the rate of attrition suffered by the harem was never more than it was able to sustain, for it compensated for its depleted numbers by recruiting brave, perhaps foolhardy, young girls from the city's other castes, the merchants, the bureaucrats, the entertainers, perpetual teenagers eager to volunteer – sometimes too eager to volunteer, it seemed; something that boded ill for the future – to assume the responsibilities and status of the sacred order of the harem even if it meant courting the possibility of death.'

'How long did all this go on for?'

'Hundreds of years, during which time it became necessary to carefully vet harem applicants.'

'Why?'

'Well, it was the harem that betrayed Cythera. To state the matter quite baldly: they became sexually obsessed with their killers. And they allowed themselves to be enslaved.'

'Ah. It was the *victims*' fault?'

'Fault? Yes I, I mean they, *we* share the guilt. The Reticulans knew what they were doing. They slew those lovely, frustrated young princesses, their handmaidens, the nymphomaniacal priestesses who sacramentalized the cult of the Sea Virgin, they slew them with sexual wounds; and they would leave bouquets of black roses, *billets-doux* promising similarly exquisite cruelties for their next victims; they would leave black-edged calling cards, boxes of semen-filled chocolates; they would leave the threat of ecstasy in the air. Those girls – those maidenheads dedicated to the goddess – were seduced.'

'But I suppose that does not excuse their treachery?' I looked at the backs of my hands and shook my head.

'Sabotage undermined our defences. Soon, the force field itself was destroyed. It was then that the Reticulans descended to destroy us. With the help of the women who were now no more than Reticulan pets – animals either fully domesticated, or to be put down as feral nuisances – they weeded out all Cytherians who were thought likely to resist colonial rule, condemning those members of the royal family that led a brief guerrilla campaign to a living death inside a mirror-world of virtual prisons.' I wiped my mottled brow with the back of my hand.

'Is that all, Mr Flynn?'

'Yes,' I said, uncertainly.

'Is there anything that—'

'It's everything,' I said, 'the whole story.'

'I see.'

'It's all that I feel. It's my memories.' He avoided my gaze, no longer taking notes now, but doodling on a jotter.

'Memory is not a photographic record of events, Mr Flynn, it is an *interpretation* of events continually modified over time. All memories, in a sense, are false.'

'But these memories are visions,' I persisted, 'visions of a rape. A rape that really happened.'

'But, as you have admitted, you rely so much on what the Reticulans have told you.'

'All I know is that they told me this: that they will punish me to the end of time. For what I am. For where I come from. They will replay my program through this vast emulation over and over again, unto eternity. And my gaoler: he would always be with me, he said. No matter how many times I died, he would always come back to inflict pain and humiliation.'

'Your father?'

'My stepfather.' I paused; studied his reaction; none. But I myself could not resist a brief smirk. 'My true stepfather. The turnkey who taunted me, who is responsible for my every neurosis, for every suicidal thought I have ever had.'

'And your true *father?*'

'A King. A wonderful man. But—' Once, I had had an idea of what my true father must be like; but as the years had worn away at my life, my threadbare soul could no longer conceive of a father who was not in some way besmirched by the criminal record of his evil twin. I stretched out my legs and pushed the chair so that it balanced on two legs; pushed a little harder in an attempt to discover that unlikely pivot where I might fall neither forwards nor backwards. Taking my feet from the floor I felt gravity tug at my shoulders; I windmilled my arms; and the chair fell into its former position with a brief syncopated drum roll of all four legs against the linoleum floor. The stepfather frowned; scribbled something of obvious moment amidst the nonsensical ideograms that had poured from his flaccid mind.

'Family is important, Mr Flynn,' he murmured, still writing, his bald patch surveying me like a surveillance camera. 'IDSIC has always stressed the importance of family values.' And, I thought, the guilt of the child. Its litany might have been: That the child gives witness to his abuse makes the child guilty; that the child accuses the world of his abuse makes the child guilty; but that the child reaches out to snatch the power of the abuser – his images, his words, his thoughts, to make them his or her own – makes the child trebly guilty. The stepfather looked up. 'Prince Galactica – this is your Cytherian name?' I shrugged, once again pretending to descend into the grey void. Prince Galactica. How could I tell anybody that – ah, how could I even tell you, unknown reader, until today – that on Cythera, I had been, not a boy, but a girl, and that my name had been Princess Gala? But this confession must contain all, all. 'It sounds like – well, it sounds like a character from one of your movies.'

'You've seen my films?'

'Some.' He smiled. 'There is, of course, another patient I am concerned with whose presence in those films played an important part in the development of her own psychosis.'

'Jaruwan,' I said, leaning forward. 'How is she?' With cool deliberation he ignored my importunity, with only that lingering smile betraying the fact that he was enjoying this game.

'The flying saucers. Mmm. Are you aware, Mr Flynn, that, for some time now, indeed, going back into the last century, there have been claims that the US government is hiding, at a certain top-secret area S4 on the Nellis Air Force Range in Nevada, nine spacecraft from the Zeta Reticuli star system? Is it not possible that, as a boy, or perhaps at a later date in your life, you have, knowingly or unknowingly, read about these claims, your mania latching upon these unconscious images to explain the trauma of abuse in terms your damaged psyche can best appreciate?'

'Maybe,' I said, willing enough to concede ground as

long as I might steer the conversation back to Jaruwan.
'What films have you seen?'

'Well, *The Kingdom of Childhood*, of course. Every-
one who comes to work here gets to see the video of that.
Almost part of our induction course, you might say.
Dahlia Chan. A curious name. Was it your idea?'

'We sort of invented it together.'

'I gather you'd like to pay her a visit.'

'It's been months now. If I could just—'

'Your father destroyed your life. But wouldn't you say
you've been something of a father to Ms Chan?'

'Visuthsri. Jaruwan Visuthsri. She kept her mother's
name, otherwise she wouldn't have been entitled to
Laotian citizenship. Pollution of the blood and all that.
She doesn't like to be called Dahlia Chan. Not any more.
Not for a long time. And no, I haven't been a father to her.
(Her father was a jerk.) I've been a husband.' The
stepfather's notional smile became fixed, as if he were
exerting every effort to keep it in place, to prevent it from
widening or collapsing.

'With over a half-a-century age difference?'

'It never mattered. Not really. But you wouldn't
understand. You wouldn't—' An impulse of hot anger rose
from my chest. No, I thought, you prissy little postgrad,
you sanctimonious little shit, you haven't lived enough to
understand; you never would live enough; you're an
aborted zygote, a sterile mess of body fluids coagulating
on the bedroom floor; get yourself a birth, you dumb sim.
Get yourself a selfhood.

'And wouldn't you say,' he continued regardless,
oblivious to my mental assault, 'that to a large degree
you've contributed to the destruction of her own life?

Children who are abused often grow up to abuse others, we find.'

'Ha! Last time you saw me you had the temerity to suggest I *hadn't* been abused!'

'The important thing, I think, as far as your wife's case history is concerned, is that you *believe* yourself to have been abused.' I sighed; what did it matter what he thought?

'I don't know why you keep her here. She tried to stop the wars. She wasn't a fighter.'

'Frankly, we're mystified by her actions, Mr Flynn, and more mystified by her motives. I'll be honest: we're far more interested in her than we are in you. You realize, of course, that the reason you're in the Town has really nothing to do with your patricide; it has to do with your career as a producer of violent, pornographic movies; movies insidiously targeted at an underage audience.' He took off his Gestapo eyewear and laid the glasses on the desk amidst his riffled papers. 'We respect people's rights, but there is no right greater than a parent's right to raise a child in safety and love. That's why the law stalks those who prey on children wherever they go, city to city, country to country.' I'd heard this routine before; heard it promulgated by congressmen, senators, White House hopefuls as well as by tawdry, vengeful, redundant Middle America (*'Hey, look, Pa, there's an alien, let's kill it!'*); the prison-industrial complex that was the Town heard it too, and so encouraged, had exceeded its charter; for several years now it had equated those adolescents allegedly corrupted by the media – its original internees – with those accused of engendering that corruption, that is, poor bastards like myself. And now – I laugh to think of it, because the laughter supresses the bitter, caustic sobs – the line separating so-called 'molesters' and so-called 'victims' has become so blurred that they often share the same cell. Which, paradoxically, gave me hope, of course; hope that I might be allowed to see Jaruwan. I forced a wave of mercenary conciliation through my body; the dam burst; I wiped away a tear. 'You must understand, Mr Flynn, that most people *want* to be told what they shouldn't see, hear or read. They are content to let other people do their thinking for them.'

'Of course,' I found myself agreeing. 'I guess I could learn to let others think for me. I really could.' I looked down at the handkerchief I had been absentmindedly knotting and re-knotting throughout the interview; studied my thumbprint, the mark of the paterfamilias that had been painlessly lasered into my flesh so many years ago, but which, in its quiet, insistent way, reminded me of my pain more effectively than any black museum exhibiting instruments of torture. 'She had a sister,' I digressed. 'Leg blown off by UXO when she was six. They lived in Phonsavanh, in Xiengkhouang province.' It had been there, in her old village, that I had met her again, to follow her westwards as she took it upon herself to bear witness to the false promises of the First World, preaching to the child soldiers whose caravans she joined of the self-destructiveness of their cause. She told them that their struggle was but a war for hamburgers and Coke, for the homogeneity of the globalized media, for a mass cultural haemorrhaging that would leave them as vampires, the living dead. They had laughed at her. Why should they return to a raped land, a land bled raw, where the barren Earth – sowed with the explosive remnants of forgotten wars ~ had nothing to offer them, not even wood from which to construct prostheses? They would march upon the empire of dreams, they would break through its borders into the realm where image and substance were one. They would triumph.

'You met her for the first time in Hollywood?'

'She was only twelve, then. I knew she'd be perfect for a production I had lined up with these Hong Kong guys who'd just flown in. And she *was* perfect. More than perfect. She was *ineffable*.'

'You married her when she was fifteen. Wasn't that illegal?'

'Oh hell, you can get around things like that when you have a little money. I had *lots* of money. Besides, her exact age was always an unknown. She came from a *moo ban* in the middle of nowhere, for Christ's sake. Her father was American, sure, but he was no problem: an old hippy with an addled brain.'

'Too many years in the jungle?'

'Too many years doing H. Like father, like—'

'And after you married her,' he interrupted, impatient, 'she made no more films?'

'She was sick, on the needle. But not just smack. PCP, tranquillizers ... I wanted to look after her. I wanted to give her a home.'

'But she left you? She couldn't have been so happy with the arrangement, could she now?'

'She hated herself. She hated what she'd become. She went back to tell the others to dump the crusade. She knew we had nothing to offer them.' I shook myself out of the cloying winding sheet of the past; dug my way out of the tomb, gasping for air; levelled a stare of pure guilelessness at my interrogator. 'I'm sure I could help. Help her, help you. If you could only let me visit her for a few minutes, then—' I let the sentence trail off into a dumb exhalation of sincerity; waited for the response like a sinner down on his knees outside the kitsch old gates of heaven. However many more Qs and As there might have been I knew that the question of my salvation spun about this moment like an out-of-control orbiter that ground control was debating whether to send to the stars or whether to allow to burn up in the atmosphere; would I or would I not be granted a day pass to paradise?

'It might be possible,' said the stepfather. 'Yes, indeed, it might. That is—'

'Tell me what I have to do.'

The stepfather, businesslike, replaced his glasses; depressed a button on his intercom; spoke. 'Miss Mitsotakis, will you please wheel in our guest?' He put his hands over his face, fingers slipping beneath his spectacles to massage his insomnia-bruised eye sockets. 'Your films are banned, Mr Flynn, but they are still on the Net. We want to find, access and destroy the Dahlia Chan site.' The door swung open and a secretary entered pushing a trolley laden with what seemed like medical hardware: heavy-duty electronics that hummed with despondent industry. 'That will be all, thank you.' As she turned to leave, the secretary pulled away a plastic sheet that had shrouded the trolley's uppermost shelf; the collective processing speed of my senses horribly antiquated, it was not until she was through the door that I was alerted to the fact that the glass urn revealed by her magician's assistant's flourish - it slopped yellowish fluid, still vibrating from its journey across the pitted floor -

contained the mutilated remains of a human head. 'Brother, this is the one I have told you about, the husband of Dahlia Chan a.k.a. Jaruwan Visuthsri.'

'Nocturnal greetings to you, reprobate,' said a synthetic voice emanating from the racks of life-support systems. 'The child within has caused you much grief, they say. I have come to help. To annihilate that anarch and set you free.' The voice was English, its intonation and vocabulary like that of all the stepfathers of the *De Luxe*: a theatre-manager approach that contrasted markedly with the populist rhetoric employed by their American cousins. 'I was once as you are, but, alas – as you may see – I am condemned to end my days on Earth2, a poor discorporate *wirehead*. I set my hopes now on but one thing: to have my life's work culminate in the destruction of Dahlia Chan – the ghost Dahlia Chan, that is – and the apprehension of a certain boy whom she long ago seduced and corrupted. But Ms Chan's site is well hidden, *extremely* well hidden. I have searched for it to no avail.'

'I'm not a hacker,' I interrupted. 'I'm an old man. I'm computer illiterate.'

'*Please,*' said my interrogator, 'spare us.'

'It's all right, it's all right,' said the bottled intelligence. 'I don't need you or anybody else's *hacking* skills. I need them as little as I need a datacap and a deck. I'm a creature of the fibresphere. No; it is your *knowledge* of the subject that I am eager to enlist. And the knowledge the subject has of herself, of course. Can you, do you think, convince Ms Chan, that is, Ms Visuthsri to offer us her assistance?'

'If you let me talk to her' – something like an embolism of joy ready to explode and flood my skull – 'I'm sure I can convince her to help.'

'That is what I had hoped. Good. We shall, irremediable, meet again, then. I think now,' it said, with an auditory nod towards its fellow stepfather, a stepfather in spirit, if not in flesh, 'I think now we should continue this discussion in private.' And, once again engaging in brief communion with his intercom, my interrogator summoned an orderly into the room and I was escorted back to my cell.

I am getting out ...

I am running across the aerodrome, my heart flapping inside my mouth like a bird; I part my lips, open my throat and let it take wing in a cry of *free, free, free.* And then I stop; bend over, panting, holding my aching side. It is early morning, an overcast sky broken at the horizon by splinters of light, a million holy syringes anaesthetizing my private badland of tall grass and ferroconcrete ruins, its numb acreage an expanse of Plutonic cyan and grey, of startled, eremitic crows and forlorn insect-song. Nothing in this shorn, dead jungle can harm me; I am a character from my favourite comic strip in *The Valiant,* Rick or Charlie, The Wild Boys; I am free, a truant fated never to turn back; I am the centre of the universe ...

After I ran away at sixteen I made my way down to the south coast. Hastings, Brighton, Southampton, Weymouth, St Ives. Returning to Brighton I lived for two years in a squat. An older boy helped me to continue my education; all else is of little consequence, save to report that, after suffering a modicum of poverty and enjoying a few paltry adventures, I found myself enrolled in Media Studies at the University of Sussex, after which I enjoyed a career with several independent television companies. During these years serving in the lower ranks of the emerging mediaocracy – a junta that was in America dominated by Hollywood, in Europe by what was to be known as the Empire *De Luxe* – I became involved in making a documentary on the French fashion photographer Guy Bourdin. Bourdin's images – his funeral women, his obsession with violation and death – had pricked my unconscious, and scenarios from my previous, Cytherian life, had bubbled up, accompanied by the seductive smell of sulphur. In me, Bourdin had seemed to recognize a fellow traveller, and for a while I worked as his assistant in Paris. It was the heyday of punk – he'd wanted a brash young man like me on his team – and I championed several designers whom I'd associated with during my years in Brighton. For a few weeks, Bourdin gave me a free hand in his studio, supplying me with cameras, lights, film and models. Those glamour-shoots were, if anybody, including myself, had but known, like those of a photojournalist; a record, not of the last days of England, but the last days of Cythera: A girl in torn lingerie kneeling before judges; a girl pushed against the wall of an alleyway by a leather-clad man, a knife gleaming in his hand; a girl awoken from her sleep by the sight of a tall, slim intruder at the foot of her bed, his body silhouetted by a halo of light pouring through the jemmied door. Visions of Cythera, a partial, confused resurfacing of childhood memories, my work was never used commercially. Even Bourdin had thought it too dangerous. It was to be many years later before my visions were released, like malignant spore, into the public domain. For it was only after I had tried my hand at film editing, directing, even sometimes turning in a few successful scripts, that I and a few associates moved stateside to sink our savings in a big production venture.

Still each night my father would track me down. Or so it seems now, with hindsight. At the time, I was still only half-aware, maybe not even really aware at all, that ... No, no; it was only while in therapy that I began to uncover my shame; only in senescence, now, that all burns with terrible clarity. My father: he waited in the secret craft which connects this world with the primum mobile; waited, hovering above the rooftops, for sleep to overcome my brain. And as I finally succumbed to weariness I knew at once - as if falling into a recurring dream to be dutifully forgotten by morning - that I would once again jerk awake in that book-lined room wherein he would proceed to question, taunt and violate, his words as much an assault as his appropriations of the flesh.

When I had achieved a certain negligible fame my tormentor would sometimes appear on my doorstep in his worldly, daytime guise, bringing me news, say, of the death of my mother (goodbye, oh robo-submissive, slave who would mutter obscenities as, smiling, she poisoned me with a slave's lies) or of some novel illness he had added to his growing list of debilities. We would don our masks: he, that of the sad, impecunious progenitor, I that of the neglectful, prodigal son. References to the secret life we shared were encoded at the very deepest levels of our discourse; so deep that I think we both had difficulty in interpreting, or even recognizing them. What I had wanted to convey to him - but did not have the words, the iconography, to express - was this: Though all I saw, all I experienced, only underlined the horror of being alone amidst a mummer's show of fakery, I had begun to discover that there were certain sims – occasional lovers, actresses I admired, friends and acquaintances – who had the seeds of reality within them. And I had come to regard such rare creatures as Cytherians *in posse*, men and women who, come the day of my liberation – for I had long ago, while downloaded, in an effort at sabre-rattling, warned my gaoler that one day I would surely either break free or be rescued – deserved to accompany me back to my home planet and be honoured at the court of a restored Cytherian monarchy, never to return to the computer emulation of the prison in which we had all suffered so much.

One such was the child-model turned actress, Jaruwan Visuthsri ...

I am getting out: running across the dark grasslands of the aerodrome, running from my father, running across the junk-strewn fields of the years, running onto movie sets, running into trouble, into joys, running into the little girl who would change my life.

And I visit her tomorrow.

I will lay out my escape plans, recruit her, give her hope. I know I can set her free, I know ...

Despite her betrayals – the pimply boys she would pick up at rock concerts, the dirty slouching grandsons of Burbank widows, those dowagers of indebtedness who grimly sought to mother me to matrimony and a joint bank account – it has always been when I have caught her in an unguarded moment, such as when I surprised her, entering her cell this morning, unannounced, that I myself have been caught off guard, wrong footed, my heart melting in the poignancy of her loneliness, her vulnerability, her courage, her loss. She was curled up on her cot, one hand supporting her head, a pile of comics, magazines and puzzle books crushed beneath an elbow, first amongst them, her favourites *Cheewit Lahk* and *Cheewit Jing*, and she again seemed the little girl I had sundered from a heartless mother and strung-out Dad to be the lonely companion of - ah, forgive a senile paedophile his smidgen of self-pity - a *lonelier*, cantankerous old man. Girl and woman became one, superimposed upon each other, transported out of time; ah, ah the ache, the sorrow of it, her face, her body, straining to please, to impress, to assume the mantel of adulthood. Whenever I had caught her unawares, reading a magazine or watching an imported video, I would catch my breath, study her, fascinated, as her lips trembled, she silently communing with herself in her native tongue, her mouth then brightening into a smile; and I would ponder, with wondering heart, her secret delight.

A TV was bolted onto a brace suspended from the ceiling and tipped at forty-five degrees so as to command even an unwilling viewer's eye; it was permanently switched on - I knew well the Town's sanative methodologies - transmitting educational programmes designed to promote awareness of child rights. '*The media*,' droned a stepfather's voice, '*can have a negative influence on the impressionable minds of children through portrayal of violence, images of gender stereotypes and neglect of the needs, interests and perceptions of the young...*'

'I remember this,' I said, nodding towards the TV.

'You do? I thought you were having trouble with your memory?' After her initial tremor of rueful acknowledgement our conversation had restarted from where it had left off some five months ago; but it was always like this with Jaruwan; for me, she had been like an inner voice, inseparable from my most private meditations; for her, I had been the ubiquitous interloper, the overseer of the most critical years of her life. Whether she wished it or not, she could never, I knew, dissociate herself from the feeling that I was an inescapable presence, forever lurking in the shadows of even her most reclusive thoughts.

'Short-term memory,' I said. 'Sure: it's appalling. But my memory of events far back in time ...'

'They say that's normal. For old people, that is.' She lay back and spread a magazine over her face. 'I wish I could turn that thing off.' The TV continued to rant.

'*But our objective is to find ways of creating a safer media environment, not just for children, but for the child in us all, for mankind's unsalvaged innocence.*'

'They're unbreakable,' I said, tossing a chewed, empty Biro at the screen; it ricocheted with a bathetic *ping!* the gesture mocking rather than underlining my point, but serving to dissipate my gall. 'Some kind of bullet-proof Plexiglas.' Jaruwan put aside her magazine; picked up the spent missile and turned it over in her hands, her brow knotting.

'As if we had a bullet.'

'And what if Madame did have a bullet,' I said, mimicking her pubescent, just-off-the-boat accent – refined, long since, by a series of expensive schools – and pinching her still-plump cheek.

'Oh Christ, Flynn, don't talk to me like that, I'm not

your little girl any more, I'm a thirty-one-year-old junkie with her ovaries burnt-out by gonorrhoea. Talk sense.' She let the Biro fall to the floor where it joined her other curios: cigarette packets, an eviscerated fluffy bear, crayons, beads: the playthings of a beggar-child.

'You'll always be my little girl,' I said, knowing that, by being impossible, I was risking expulsion from the meeting I had been coveting for the last half year. Dahlia shuddered; studied me with her mascara-slicked eyes, crow's feet forming a delta in readiness for an environmental disaster of oily tears.

'Don't say that, Flynn. Don't say that ever again, okay?'

I sat down on the cot, averting my gaze. 'Sure, Dahlia. I didn't mean ... Sure, okay. I won't.'

'Forget it.'

'*Global diversification of the media has made its impact more influential and has brought about violent changes to the collective unconscious analogous to the cosmogenic changes wrought in the natural world by the degradation of the biosphere.*'

'It was on the six o'clock news, not long after I first met you,' she said. 'Remember? That mob that attacked the police station in Whittier? The police had arrested a couple of kids. They said they'd beaten up a bag lady. But it wasn't the fate of the indigent that shocked them – they were outraged that something similar had been screened on a *True Crime* program a few weeks earlier. The kids were possessed. They were witches, they said. They should be burnt.'

'The fury of Caliban at seeing his own face in a mirror.' At first, it was anybody who was even remotely suspected of child molestation who were society's scapegoats. But even then, it was always the children, the victims, who society feared and hated the most. Insecure, unsure of their own desires, adults had recoiled from an otherness which stood in seeming accusation of them, that suggested that crime might lay at the unacknowledged heart of their being. All through the late twentieth century they had feared; but it had taken the pure-white light of the dawn of the millennium to bring that fear to fruition. 'There always seemed to be two hysterias: one, an overriding concern to protect children, the other, an overriding concern to punish them. More discipline, that's what everybody *really* craved. More control. A society dedicated to a mad philosophy of punish to protect, protect to punish. A sadomasochistic society. A sadomasochistic society without erotics. The watershed was those Declarations on the Rights of The Child. As soon as they'd been codified there was resentment that children might actually *use* those rights; might assert the autonomy of their imaginations, become empowered; dare to be free.' It was then that adults started to recover their repressed memories: of the terrible crimes their sons and daughters had committed, whether yesterday, last month, or half-a-lifetime ago; it was then that The Great Fear had swept over America, and eventually the whole world, accusation and counter-accusation filling the courts and the media, the criminality of children, or of the child buried within the adult, held to be a newly revealed truth beyond question, with all debate held suspect, a conspiracy. 'They're right when they say I targeted my movies at an underage audience. I don't think I knew it at the time – I mean, like everyone in the biz, my thoughts were on money – but I was on the side of the child. I mean, *really* on their side.

I wanted to give them a little of the knowledge, the imaginative ammunition, that the adult world had reserved to itself.'

'You think it did any good?'

I shook my head. 'I don't know. Maybe it helped equalize things—'

'It did nothing for my people except feed them illusions. The North-South conflict was anything but equal, Flynn.'

'Illusions. Dreams. Visions. Are they such bad things, Jaruwan? Why shouldn't children dream of sex and violence if by so dreaming they appropriate to themselves some of the power adults exercise so arbitrarily over their bodies and minds?'

'Flynn, you're so credulous. You sound like one of those broadcasts put out by The Army of Revolutionary Flesh.'

'The Army of – isn't that from one of my movies?'

Jaruwan swept back her hair; shivered. 'I forgot all about Hollywood a long time ago.'

'My movies, yes, remember it was—'

'Your movies? Each one was nothing more than a cheap rush of sulphate, a quick hand-job in the drive-in, a taste of loonytoon.' I fell silent; it was not that this auteur of exploitation rated his oeuvre particularly high; but I had known even as the final cut was being made, knew now, that their value lay in Jaruwan; and Jaruwan was beyond price.

'You were more than the content of those movies,' I said, 'You were always much more. I knew that when I met you again out East.' All those years in Laos. Following her, driving her to meetings, hustling money. The things I saw, the things I heard; terrible things; those experiences, like so many others in my life, taking more than they gave; reducing me. And I had had to cling to Jaruwan to remain something more than a beast.

'I never asked you to come.'

'*Many children in the Asia-Pacific region are subject to neglect and abuse: child labour, child prostitution, spawn-shops specializing in forced human-cybernetic/adult-infant miscegenation: there are all manner of horrors. Is it any wonder that, seduced by images beamed to them via satellite and cable, hordes of disaffiliated youngsters joined the hopeless crusades that brought them to the borders of the First World? We must work together with Asian governments to ensure that their mass media reflects the culture of Asian societies and does not cultivate the unhealthy longings that led to the North-South wars.*'

'What an idiot I was,' said Dahlia, 'to think that my own little corner of the planet offered solutions. I had *farang* blood - "my" people wanted to either spit on me, laugh at me or fuck me. But one thing they sure didn't want to do was listen.' She sighed, an exhalation that became a wheeze that, in turn, became a dry hacking cough. She leaned over the cot and expectorated. 'Poor husband,' she gasped, 'poor, grotesque husband. I don't think the tropics suited you, did they? They shouldn't have. In my country, Flynn, declaring that you were a victim of child abuse would have been a matter of shame; you would have been treated like a criminal. You would have been treated like someone with' - another cough racked her, and she brought up a colourless spume of mucus from the bottom of her lungs - 'with AIDS.'

'But I'm treated like a criminal here.'

'For your films, Flynn. Not because your father interfered with you when you were a boy. For your films.' I passed a hand over my face; this conversation was covering too much well-trodden ground; I had to take a detour, go cross-country, tear the *No Trespassing!* sign from out of the murky ground that was my secret life; nothing else would suffice if I were ever to explain my escape plans to Jaruwan.

'I haven't come here to mull over the past. I came to talk of the future. Of escape. Remember what I told you last time, about Zeta Reticuli?'

'Oh, no—' She picked up another magazine, opened it and spread it over a puckered, migrainous forehead.

'Of course, I know I should have explained all this to you earlier.'

'Why? So that I'd have had an excuse to have *left* you earlier? I mean, you were always a crazy son-of-a-bitch, Flynn, but *this* shit – Jesus ...' I looked about the cell, desperate to find some sign, some chink in the gigantic mantrap of the emulation to which I could point and say, There, don't you see, it's all fake, it's not real at all! But the four walls in this cell – a larder-like stone box in the labyrinthine 'women's section' of The Children's Home – were identical to the walls of my own cell; and they were similarly barren of an ingress to the outside. A stream of buttery light fell across the graffiti-scored plaster, pooling about Jaruwan's bunk. Seeing, I think, a wave of despair and frustration oscillate through the grooves, rills and pockmarks of my deeply excavated face, she slid off the cot and sat on the concrete floor – there were no chairs, but she had always been hot on filial obligation – allowing the goatish ancient who had once taken her to his bed to rest, easeful, if restricted in posture, on a straw-filled mattress, osteoporotic spine resting against the obscure, time-worn hieroglyphics of a previous occupant of this grim abode of celibacy. 'Is this what being locked up has done to you? Given you some psychosis about little green men and flying saucers?'

'I am a Cytherian,' I repeated. 'And you will be, too, once I have effected our getaway. Don't you see, it's the only chance we have: to induce the Reticulans to teleport *both* of us into one of their craft. I will begin tonight to send telepathic messages out over the ether to inform them that I have killed my gaoler. They are bound to send another to take his place.' Jaruwan's eyes flicked back and forth beneath a greasy, unwashed fringe. 'Once aboard the saucer we shall proceed to overpower the pilot and force him to carry out our instructions.' Her pupils were big, as if with the memory of her last hit, years ago now, before they captured her and forced her to go cold turkey. I reached out and touched the lesion on her cheek. *Why don't they give you the cure?* I wondered, in agonized foreknowledge of the answer: that those in the Town who had AIDS were denied effective medicine. Jaruwan bowed her head.

'What did you call yourself the last time I saw you – wasn't it "Prince Galactica"?!' She laughed through her nostrils. 'Like something out of one of your braindead movies.'

I frowned. 'That's just what the stepfather said.'

'Well, maybe he spoke right. Those movies were the death of you. Work, work, work. Until your nerves were completely frazzled. You were never the same after you began regression therapy with that shrink in Beverley

Hills. She planted false memories in your head, I swear she did. I mean, you never used to talk about flying saucers. So far as I know, you may never have actually *been* abused by your Dad.'

I shook what remained of my white locks in dismissal. How could I make her understand? But as she looked up at me, parted lips showing off the still perfectly capped teeth I had paid for when she had been a child, my earnestness momentarily vanished and I was again the man I had been all those years ago when I had sat on the cheap, rented set where she had spoken her first lines, a lovely, lisping mixture of Chinese and broken English. I smiled back at her, held out a hand to stroke her hair; but she pulled away. Sadly, I let my arthritic, liver-spotted hands rest in my lap; snorted. 'I was your greatest fan. I've always been your greatest fan.'

'Let's not talk about all that,' she said. 'It's so long ago and none of it matters now. I mean, I'm really grateful to you for some things. At the end, I think you genuinely wanted to help. But all the casting-couch stuff: it was too bad, Flynn. You took away my childhood.'

'I'm sorry,' I muttered, feeling suddenly so much older, so much more stupid, incompetent and cruel, so much uglier than I had ever been, even during that long Babylonian summer when I had adopted Jaruwan as my protégée, introducing her to the fast life that she had read about in her teen magazines and dreamed of, longingly, innocently, studiously, through the cicada-humming nights of a little village on the other side of the Rim.

'I said it doesn't matter.' Baffles descended, it seemed, and for several minutes we were cloaked in silence. The cell grew warmer, the sun rising to the meridian; in the far distance I could hear the market people setting up their stalls, the shouts of fishermen haggling over last night's catch.

'They want us to help them,' I said at last. 'I said yes, as a way of getting to visit you. Remember that when the stepfathers summon you for your next *tête-à-tête*.'

'What kind of help?'

'There's a Dahlia Chan site on the Net. They want to locate it, destroy it. They believe you could give them some useful clues.' Jaruwan lounged back, spreading herself across the floor, sunbathing in the distended lozenges of ultraviolet. The TV had begun to screen another info-tainment, the light of its importunate kinescope mixing with the UV, patches of yellows, reds, blues and greens forming a changing, intertextual pattern that was like that of a holographic sculpture. '*Renounce perverted childhood,*' whispered the voice-over, '*suffer psychic meltdown, be remade in the cast of civilized morality, comply ...*'

'It doesn't matter to me if they destroy my ghost. She never gave me anything. Dahlia was trouble.'

'Trouble was her middle name.'

'No,' said Jaruwan, 'her middle name was Prudence.' She laughed.

'I remember,' I said. 'Yes, yes, I remember. But what movie was that?' Jaruwan, as if feeling a sudden draught, sat up, pulled her striped, cotton smock over her knees and hugged her calves.

'To hell with it. I went back home to try to stop any more of my people becoming like me. Why shouldn't I help the stepfathers?' She pressed her forehead between her thighs; slowly, she began to rock. 'Ah, because I hate them, that's why. They're not the answer. They're just part of the problem. The biggest part of the problem, maybe. If only we could really fly away, Flynn, if only one of your goddamned UFOs would swoop down and haul us out of this bloody mess.'

Far away, there was an explosion.

Jaruwan looked up at the window, a hand to her mouth. I rose, pulled the cot across the cell, and stood on it so that I could peep over the sill. Like my own dungeon, Jaruwan's commanded a view of the harbour. Narrowing my eyes to compensate for a slight astigmatism - quite slight really, despite my years; I have always been proud of my hawk-like vision - I spotted flames leaping from the wooden facades grouped along the boundary fence; and through the flames I saw what I at first dismissed as an optical illusion; for rising out of the sea was a black, phantasmal monolith resembling the conning tower of a submarine, a sodden flag displaying a skull and cross-bones flapping from its snorkel in doughty reproof of prohibition and arbitrary law. Jaruwan stepped up to my side, squeezing her face against the bars.

'It's the last scenes,' she whispered. 'It can't be happening, but it is. It's the last scenes from *The Kingdom of Childhood.*'

'The Army of Revolutionary Flesh,' I whispered, 'of course, of course, now I remember, yes, I remember ...'

'Yes,' said Jaruwan, 'yes, yes, yes.'

CHAPTER SEVEN

And so I begin a new chapter to my story...

Following the example of the divine Marquis I have cached my earlier manuscript in its hiding place within my cell; it is for future generations of abusers and the abused to make of it what they may. Free, now, to wander the length and breadth of the prison, I have begun this supplementary account to detail the incredible events that have succeeded the coming of the *Narrenschiff III* and its bandit crew of liberators.

We are presently under siege. It has been five days since The Army of Revolutionary Flesh stormed through the perimeters of Xanthos - my fly-blown, counterfeit, and by now almost completely razed city – to take control of the Fortress of The Slavers, that over-budget extravaganza latterly rebuilt for the reform and reclamation of delinquent children, their abettors, accomplices and *âmes damnées*. Smoke rises from mock-urban debris – a discarded pack of cards – its matchwood embers sometimes caught by the sea breeze and deposited in the prison grounds like the topsoil of Hell. But the initial battle is over and we all wait for what will come next, a capitulation to our demands or the whirlwind. The quayside is empty but for a handful of revolutionary commandos who man the ground-to-air missile launcher and the Bofors gun; the populace has been evacuated; all is quiet, an immense held breath of shivery anticipation. The enemy has set up position in the hills; keeps in contact, but refuses to concede, the special telephone line accorded us forever busy, but only with talk, more talk. Elements in The Army fear The Censors will ignore our threat of summarily executing the captured stepfathers; fire and brimstone will – they mutter – soon rain down from the batteries that cut us off from the rest of Kithira, forcing us to retreat into the sea. But Tarquin is adamant we maintain our current bargaining position. His obstinacy, I fear, will be our ruin.

This morning I sought him out, tried to convince him that we should effect our escape at once rather than have it forced upon us; the ransom we held was ineffectual, the *De Luxe* not only unwilling but unable to cede to our demands that all Town inmates be immediately released. Negotiation was out; political survival compelled them to sacrifice those stepfathers we held hostage in a no-compromise stand on subversion; the public would demand no less. Kithira, a small, insignificant link in the chain fence separating North from South, would be turned into a proving ground, a ground zero above which they would explode the secret weapon that guaranteed their power: Fear. Jaruwan accompanied me, even though each encounter with her other self precipitated, in her, an emotional crisis, that image she had thought she had left behind in Hollywood, the image she had come to hate, to run away from (and she is still running, running as she has done since she ran away from home, with scarcely a pause for breath), still able to haunt her, seemingly, after all these years; but, following the fright and disgust of learning that one of the leaders of The Army was her other self, a ghost that had somehow been refitted with strange, new flesh, curiosity, as much as self-preservation – she too knows that our only hope is to take to the open seas – had spurred her into increasingly bold intimacies with her alter ego. This morning – collecting her from her cell, where, through habit, she still retired at night, and discovering her poring through old movie mags that bore her photo on their covers – I felt, perhaps, that curiosity was rapidly changing into wonder; that something, rediscovered, flickered within; and that that something was akin to a flame of life.

Our liberators were sitting amongst the miniature cedars and black pines that decorated the roof-top restaurant, a banqueting chamber employed by the stepfathers less for the supplementation of their own austere regimen than to pamper the jaded palates of the visiting officials and dignitaries who held the Town's purse strings. Tables had been pushed together so that the restaurant resembled a boardroom, with the chairman and chairwoman's position occupied by The Army's joint leaders, Captain Tarquin and his Pirate Queen, Dahlia Chan. A single red telephone squatting in front of the melancholy, cerebrative pair commanded everybody's attention. Several of the Town's Third World veterans – no longer children, but terrorists redivivus in youthful, adult flesh – stood behind their new leaders, respectful of their every need, attendant to their every danger. Child and adult prisoners of the First World had joined them in solidarity, both those who had wanted to summarily kill their hostages and those who still entertained ambiguous feelings towards the surrogate parents who had used their authority to torment and abuse them. (I had known many a boy, or girl, to fall in love with his censor.) The young woman called Mosquito – whom Tarquin seemed to treat like some expensive if contemptible toy – stood there too, an arm draped across the back of her lord's high-backed chair, long pink fingernails playing with his golden tresses, every inch of her, if you did not know her for flesh and blood, an automaton, a mechanical doll. Many of the submarine's original crew were seated along the table's length, heads nestled amongst half-eaten food, or else, with feet ruching the tablecloth into coarse origamis, lolling back, red wine streaking ruddy cheeks, goose-pimpled flesh jittering between wakefulness and insensibility. As we entered, Tarquin looked up .

'It's the moneyman who created you, kitten,' he said. 'Say hello to the nice old monster.'

'Hello, monster,' said Dahlia, tearing her gaze from the telephone and its state of suspended animation – focus of all in the room who weren't four sheets to the wind – to address me with the surly, ironic distemper she always bestowed on her lover's senile counterpart. 'You know, Cap, that's what, in time, you would have looked like if you hadn't jettisoned your old body in Antarctica.'

'Yo,' somebody murmured, 'let's hear it for revolutionary flesh.'

'But never, never in a million years would I have ended up looking like *her*,' added Dahlia, turning her attention to my wife.

'You owe your existence to Jaruwan Visuthsri,' I said.

'Quiet, Flynn,' said Jaruwan, 'we haven't come to argue' – and she stared at the tip of Dahlia's nose like a sorceress trying to retake possession of her soul, sealed within that upturned knob of flesh as if within a roc's egg, lost to her for aeons – 'we've come to *ask*, to beg you: please, let us all leave now. The Censors are not the kind of people to do deals. They will kill us all.'

'You have the submarine,' I said, 'you have the *means* of escape. Please, listen to Jaruwan. We've spent years here. We know The Censors. What she says is true.'

'So,' said Tarquin, brushing aside Mosquito's hand and standing up. 'So, you've spent *years* here, have you?' Dahlia rested her chin between her interlaced fingers; distracted herself by counting the flies on the ceiling; I sensed that she had heard this speech before. 'So you think you know The Censors? Tell them, munchkin, tell them of what *I* know.'

'Captain Tarquin has also spent time in Boys Town. A long time. Longer than the two of you, certainly.' She took out a nail file and began sawing at a sugar-pink claw, a faithful little secretary resolutely covering for her boss. 'If anybody knows anything about the Town, it's Tarquin. Why don't you try to have a little faith? We've come a long way, Tarquin and me, and we can go farther.

Much farther. We can go all the way to the stars.'

Tarquin walked towards us, his leather thigh-boots creaking, rapier slapping against a thigh; stopped; kicked a pair of recumbent feet from the table and, brushing aside crumbs, impacted mud and half-smoked cigarettes, pulled back the soiled tablecloth; seated himself on the pinewood edge; picked up an apple and bit it in half, teeth closing with a crocodile-like snap. They may have ulterior motives,' he said, swallowing the segment with one gulp. 'Remember what the bottled brain had to say, my pet?'

'Of course. But—' Tarquin raised an objectionary finger in the air, taking over the floor with a malevolent squint from his one good eye which pierced me to the *pia mater*, boring remorselessly till it threatened to exit through the back of my head.

'You were planning to infiltrate Dahlia's site, weren't you? To erase it from the Net?' I dismissed the charge with a nervous laugh; saw that it had had no effect; tried righteous indignation.

'Rubbish. I just told them that so that I could gain access to Jaruwan.'

'It really doesn't matter,' said Dahlia. 'They can't hurt me that way any more.'

'Ah, but there are other Dahlias they can hurt. Other aspects of the AI that they can interfere with.'

'But I have new flesh. It *doesn't matter*.'

'Don't you see,' said Tarquin, turning to his girl-child, 'he's a paterfamilias – don't you see he hurt your original and for two pins he'd hurt you?'

'No,' said Jaruwan, 'he's not going to hurt anyone. You called him a monster; he's not. He's an old man, just another example of damaged goods – the same as the rest of us. But would *I* have helped the stepfathers destroy your site, Dahlia? Why shouldn't I have? You destroyed my life, Dahlia Chan. More than Flynn ever did, you took away my childhood, you left me an empty shell.'

Dahlia got up and moved to Tarquin's side. 'I'm sorry,' she said, bowing her head. 'I never knew. I didn't mean—'

'What are you saying?' said Tarquin, as she pushed her head into the crook of his arm, tears staining the white cotton of his doublet. 'You owe her nothing. You're more than she ever was. You're the myth, she was just the medium.'

'You left me nothing, Dahlia,' said Jaruwan, her voice breaking with intensity, 'that's why I went back home. I thought I might find something of myself back there. But I couldn't. Everything had changed. There's nothing of me there, now, nothing of me here, nothing, nothing *anywhere.* I had to tell our people that, Dahlia, I had to tell them not to head West, not to lose their souls like I had.'

'You were right to,' said Dahlia. 'But if you're nothing, what am I? You destroyed me as well, Jaruwan. You destroyed me by donning those masks, by giving me my script, by creating me.'

'For God's sake,' said Tarquin, wriggling free of Dahlia's arms, 'shut up – shut up *both* of you. We have more important things to worry about.' He stamped over to where I stood, casting his thin shadow over my shrunken body; bent over and whispered in my ear. 'I don't like all this mutinous talk. Understand? I think it'd be better if – while waiting for us to conclude our negotiations – you were not somewhere more comfortable.' He stepped back. 'Mosquito, take two soldiers and escort Mr Flynn and Kuhn Jaruwan to the library. And make sure they stay there.' As Mosquito came forward, Dahlia suddenly drew her progenitor into her arms, rose onto tiptoe, hands tightening about her big sister's neck, the sackcloth rags that constituted her dress lifted to reveal a pubic triangle as brown and as bald as a maculate egg.

'I'm sorry,' she said. 'I'm so sorry.' Jaruwan at first resisted and then succumbed to her image's embrace.

'It's all right,' she murmured. 'Everything will turn out all right, I'm sure.'

'We didn't know you'd be here, you know. I thought you were lost. I thought you were my enemy.'

'I thought you were my enemy, too. But no time for tears now, little girl. Just keep waiting by that telephone.' Dahlia released her grip; a soldier took Jaruwan's arm. 'But remember what we said. Don't wait too long.'

'Enough,' said Tarquin, grabbing Dahlia by the arm and pulling her aside. 'Mosquito, take them away.'

'Cap, there's no need,' said Dahlia. I was jostled forward.

'Tarquin, whatever happens,' I said, 'don't head for Zeta Reticuli. It's not as you think it is. It's just part of the emulation. Cythera isn't in this universe. You'll not find it by going to the stars.'

Tarquin turned to The Army's cofounder and raised his hands. 'He's mad. We've known he was mad ever since we arrived. What would you have had me do? You know we can't take chances.' Dahlia sighed in acquiescence.

And we were led to yet another confinement.

*

'Well,' said Mosquito, 'this is about as comfortable as it gets. You have the sofas to sleep on and, of course, there's plenty to read. Don't mind Tarquin, he's getting a little twitchy. And who can blame him? But don't worry. He's got a secret weapon. The revolutionary flesh, it—' Coy, she put a hand to her mouth. 'Whoops! But you'll find out when you see it. Don't worry, nothing The Censors have got can match those who've undergone transfiguration.' She left through the double doors, her rump, squeezed into a tiny, plastic hyperskirt, swinging extravagantly from side to side, a jocular *squeak* – like that of a mouse in a sheet-metal press – emitted each time one buttock slid, up-down, down-up, against the other. 'This place must have cost a fortune,' she said as she turned to shut us in, 'however could you have afforded it?'

'It bankrupted me,' I said. But it had been worth it; anything to further the career of the child-star with whom I had fallen in love. 'Mosquito, wait—' The sex-mech lookalike paused, her vulgarly painted face sandwiched between tall, black doors. 'You must try to talk to Tarquin. Perhaps he'll listen to you. He must understand that the Zeta Reticuli system in this universe is unreal.'

'Unreal? Sounds sexy, pops.' Mosquito was but a sliver, now, an eye, half a nose and a slice of dark red mouth.

'Think: How can we tell a real universe from a simulated one? Any computation system can in principle simulate the entire universe. Everything you see around you may be no more than an enormous string of 0's and 1's. It follows, therefore, that we ourselves may be a program – cosmic software powerful enough to create the illusion of reality – that is being run on a gigantically powerful computer. Now, the massive qualities of a neutron star would provide really *incredible* logic gates, and—'

'A toy universe?' said Mosquito. 'How simply delightful! I've always dreamed of being a toy.' The doors closed. 'You must rest, Mr Flynn. I can see that your years in solitary have stirred your imagination into hyperdrive.' I heard the key turn in the lock; and then the sound of the rodent skirt (harmonizing with an insect-chorus of perilous high-heels) receding down the stone corridor in intervals of squeaks punctuated by syncopated clicks, clacks, bangs, scrapes and whistles.

'I wonder why Dahlia isn't more jealous?' I said.

'Because, my poor, dim-witted husband, if you had been born in my part of the world you would have recognized that that was a *man*. Creatures like that can pass as automata, but they can have a hard time masquerading as women.' Mosquito was a man? A man pretending to be a woman, just like I was a princess pretending to be a prince? No, no; too much weirdness already awaited digestion; this little morsel would have to stay by the side of the plate.

I clasped my forehead; I had broken out in a sweat. I searched my pockets for my antimalarials. Galactica, Gala, Gala, Galactica, recited a manic, inner voice. A sharp chill savaged my epidermis. If everything was a pretence – the whole world a cruel masquerade – how could I, who was part of that show, be so assured of my authenticity? How, in such circumstances, could I prove to myself – to anyone – that I possessed the truth? 'Am I mad, Jaruwan? Is it possible that I'm mad? Images can kill, The Censors say. Perhaps a lifetime of images has killed my sanity. The memories I have of my father, the UFOs,

Cythera – does all of it merely exist inside my skull?' I
walked to the window. But before I could reach it, a great
silence filled the room; not a natural silence, but a silence
engendered by too much noise, a noise that had caused my
eardrums to shut down in protest. And then my stomach
seemed to displace my heart as my body was squeezed by
the unheralded pressure; it was like the sensation I would
experience when, as a boy, my father would, as I passed
close, reach out and touch me with a gentle, but familiar
gesture that to me contained the quintessence of his
violence; the same sensation of physical revulsion and
sickness, momentarily transporting me out of my
shameful, hated body. With time-crippling suddenness the
window was blown in, as if the moment of horror had
been frozen in the staccato of a flashgun, the hurricane
that swept through the library knocking me on my back;
and, in obverse, as if I was now looking through the
pinhole lens of the camera that had just recorded the
shattering of the glass, I screamed as, in a blue-white
combustion that emanated from behind my eyes and
saturated the room – my eyes like melting glass, like
superheated obsidian – I witnessed the library's doors
torn apart as if by a supernatural agent presaging a *Deus
Irae*. Books spread their wings and fluttered like stricken
birds, several tomes coming to rest over my spread legs
and wasted torso, covering me in a pall of redundant
words. Then, through a red mist, I saw Jaruwan's face a few
inches from my own.

'It's begun,' she said.

I write this aboard the *Narrenschiff III*, en route to
Antarctica.

Five of us survive: myself, Jaruwan, Dahlia, Mosquito and Cytherina.

This is what occurred, as I can remember it, or rather, relive it; for it is what is happening now, each time I close my eyes, the music of the church organ reverberating through the hull's soundboard and into my stateroom ‑ silverware and porcelain tinkling as they absorb the bass notes of the sixteen‑foot ranks ‑ Dahlia playing and replaying, I am told, the fugues and toccatas that Tarquin would practise during the voyage from the Gulf of Siam to the Ionian Sea, her tears dripping onto the manuals, sheaves torn from *The Well‑Tempered Clavier* and the *Goldberg Variations* ‑ clawed to shreds in frenzies of grief ‑ gathering about the ventilation grids as, finally, unable to continue her marathon recital, she bangs her fists on the keys; screams; it is what is happening against the soaring, infernal background noise of The Wound when it again opened —

I am staggering through the prison. Blood continues to flow from the cut in my head – a shard of glass lodged intractably in my scalp – but, despite this injury, and despite the hyperperistalsis of my heart, I am able to follow Jaruwan's lead as she negotiates a passage through the smoke‑filled corridors towards an exit. The cells are mostly empty, their doors open. I recognize my own cell, the cage in which I had been destined to end my years. I put a hand on Jaruwan's shoulder to signal a pause; detour, quickly exhume the MS containing the history of my secret life from its hermetic resting place beneath the window; again assume my position in Indian file behind Jaruwan, who, impatient, uncomprehending, glances back at me like a mother hen berating a

wayward, prematurely senile chick. We come to where the
stepfathers have been locked up by The Army; terrified,
they beat their fists upon the thick, wooden doors, calling
out Fire, fire! begging us to release them. We ignore their
pleas, feeling our way along the wall, the smoke
thickening now, turning from cigarette grey to an oily
black; and soon we are on all fours, our mouths to the
ground, sucking hungrily at what air remains. I feel
Jaruwan grab my wrist, pull me into an alcove. She has
broken the glass cover protecting an extinguisher; stands
up; wields the ancient, rusted canister above her head
and brings it down on the lock securing the emergency
doors. The doors fly open and through the smoke I see
patches of sky; Jaruwan lifts me into a half crouch and,
arm about her neck, hobbling towards the prospect of
oxygen, I suddenly find that we are outside. Before I can
signal to her to beg a moment of rest, I am pushed
forward and forced to scramble down the iron helix of the
fire escape as best as my decaying body allows. Once we
are upon the ground I realize that we are standing in the
men's exercise yard, a section of its wall completely
destroyed by an enemy shell. Through the breach I see
two stepfathers astride black horses; they leap over the
rubble and bear down upon us, mouths contorted in
silent rage, their battle cries erased by an inhuman
screech from above, a ruined soprano that is performing
a perfect mimicry of a fingernail drawn across slate.
Cytherina, her great pale wings extended in the pose of a
fabulous, crucified dove, streaks diagonally across the
courtyard, fire pulsating from her upraised palms in
great liquid gouts. The horsemen burst into flames, their
own screams – inspired larynxes no longer impotent,

enjoying a last fanatical song – joining that of the angel of death in a chorale of agony and exaltation before tapering off into glottal stops. The white lady – intemperate ghost whom Dahlia and Tarquin have given flesh – makes a sharp, vertical ascent, and then dives into the approaching shock troops of The Censors who, as Jaruwan and I make for the hole in the wall, can be seen taking up positions around the Town. Armoured vehicles lumber through the streets, regulars from the mainland here to sanction whatever measures IDSIC deems appropriate, the stepfathers obviously determined – as I knew they would be – to quell this insurrection before it spreads offshore to infect other Children's Homes. I hear desperate cries behind us. Some of the hostages, effecting a breakout, have, like us, descended into the courtyard, a few via the fire escape, but others, who roll about on the concrete hugging their ankles and shins, by leaping from those cells that have been cratered by artillery rounds. Jaruwan points, redirecting my attention to Dahlia and Tarquin, who have surfaced onto the roof of the prison. 'Make for the harbour,' Dahlia shouts as she spies us in the yard. Jaruwan runs ahead; but I cannot help lingering; for joining them on the roof, and acquiring my attention, is the pickled, mechanically enhanced brain that had urged me to assist it in its detective work. Still connected to its life-support system – but with the trolley, which had previously provided its means of locomotion, now exchanged for a quadriplegic's self-propelled chair, the De Luxe kind with the big, rubber wheels and multijointed extensors of an off-world robot – and still as vindictive, the brain moves towards the Chiefs of Staff, who, unaware of its approach, are standing on the rooftop's ledge waving us onward to safety. I try to holler a warning, but my throat is parched with smoke. The minimally corporate stepfather's metallic limbs uncoil, reach towards the unsuspecting prey. Tarquin, exasperated at our seeming obstinacy, washes his hands of us, dismissing all concern with a tired shake of his head; turns to Dahlia; upbraids her – I can just about hear his words – for wasting her time with confirmed fifth columnists. Then – I can almost sense her hackles rise – Dahlia spins about; takes an involuntary step back, her coccyx pressed against the parapet; teetering, she regains her balance, then, unable to communicate the substance of her shock to her bemused lover, raises her automatic rifle and sprays the cyberdaddy's encroaching carriage with frangibles. The life-support system disintegrates; but before Tarquin – galvanized now, the very image of a celluloid buccaneer – can level his own weapon and finish the task of sending the quasi-biological life form permanently into Earth2, a tentacle winds about him, trapping his arms against his torso. 'You had all the advantages of your back-ground,' the mechanical persecutor broadcasts over his PA, 'money, loving parents. What made you such an unreasonable little shit?' Tarquin's finger is still squeezing the trigger of his weapon and a chatter of gunfire rakes the concrete and sends up a smoke screen of white dust behind which Dahlia takes refuge, desperately trying to reload. Tarquin is saying something to her, urging her to flee. Unwilling to desert the image groupie who has followed her around, through and across worlds, it is only when Tarquin manages to free an arm, grab her by her shirt collar and send her hurtling over the balustrade like a kitten picked up by the scruff of its neck and summarily defenestrated, that she is forced into conceding a retreat, turning over in mid-air, one, two, three times to land, after a fall of some eighty feet, with a skydiver's grace, her feet together, her knees imperceptibly flexing, and with only the terrific concussion echoing about the walled enclosure and the black mist of atomized bitumen rising over her ankles to offer contradiction. She scampers over to me, screaming: 'He's going to use the secret weapon. He's going to open The Wound. Run. Get out of here before it's too late.' I notice Jaruwan has paused halfway down the slope that leads to the harbour, flattened scenery all about us, mortars and artillery rounds reducing the sacked, two-dimensional city to clouds of splinters and dust. Mosquito is by her side, having seemingly found a way out of the prison by another egress, she (or he, as Jaruwan would have it, but not fellow-travelling I), a survivor to the black roots of her bleached-blonde hair. Cytherina dives out of the sun; and we reel, skip, hobble and stumble after her as she swoops and glides, taking the part of our outrider, leading us to the sea.

Behind, I hear the hysterical cachinnation of The Army's light weapons as they make a stand against the overwhelming forces of The Censors, tittering and spitting bullets and laser light in death's gross, ugly face; and I hear Dahlia's curses as she urges us forward; Mosquito's whimpering as she mourns the fate of her adored captain, he who is locked in a death-struggle with the father-who-will-not-die. As I struggle to keep up with my youthful allies – their youths as misspent, damaged, mad, perhaps, as my own – I strain to broadcast a thought message into space, to summon assistance from the gods.

'It's been so long,' I pant, one hand over my chest, 'so long since my last abduction – surely they must suspect something is amiss? If only I could find the right frequency, the correct protocol, if only I could connect.' Jaruwan stops, allows me to catch up.

'There's been enough craziness today, Flynn. We can all do without a contribution from you. Come. Keep on moving.'

Once attaining the quayside we are soon in one of the dinghies; starting up its outboard, Dahlia points us towards the sanctuary of the submarine. Coast guard vessels have their guns trained on the Narrenschiff III but withhold fire, fearful of cracking open its nuclear reactor. I pick up the binoculars that are secured to the dinghy's side; focus on the prison, its rooftop battle zone. I see a human form wrestling with a steel octopus. And then I recognize Tarquin – his face quite clear as I make adjustments to the glass's resolution – and he seems to be looking directly at me, puncturing my eyeballs with his power-drill gaze. He raises two arms – both are free now; the mechanical stepfather has him pinched about the middle, trying to squeeze the superhuman life out of him – spreads them, and then brings his open palms together in a thunderous clap that echoes across the whole of the burning, fallen, ersatz city, across the sky, across the hills and mountains, across the rocks, sands and sea so that, for the second time that day, a fanfare of judgement compresses my tympanic membrane and threatens to deafen me, as if I were the hunchbacked ringer of the greatest, most maleficent bell in the world. A black hole has opened up in the sky; it grows larger, lightning flicking from its serrated edges to lick about the foundations and the outskirts of the prison's walls. Plasma swirls, a tornado of crackling discharge that engulfs the whole Town, a merry-go-round that veils the levelled dwellings and advancing soldiers behind a blue-green, ionized curtain. Inside the black hole – it has now swollen to cover half the sky, like the base of a cone that leads to a fuliginous, unknown rendezvous – living forms begin to manifest, black shapes thrown into relief by the greater blackness of the aerial chasm, like those cooler regions of the sun that, brilliant as they are, are perceived as the distinct objects we call sunspots. The shapes writhe, dance, become figures: a million faces grinning wickedly at the tiny, damned creatures below; a million arms beckoning, inviting those minuscule creatures to join them. The prison explodes, bodies flying into the air like fireworks, to disappear at the apex of their trajectories in starbursts of painfully bright candlepower, rainbows of blue-green acetylene arcing over the sea. Debris is sucked up into the black cataract indenting the clouds – thunderheads that are a multi-hued chaos – and, as in the mushroom of an atomic explosion, dissipate in a skirt of white vapour. The twister, snaking tendrils of electricity in its ozone slipstream, rotates like a top whipped to greater and greater velocities. The arms of the snarling figures bent over the cupola of heaven extend, fingers clenching greedily to snatch at the remains of their repast; and horses, their riders still clinging to their backs, are lifted skyward; so too the motorbikes, the cars, the armoured personnel carriers, the troops themselves; the chipboard remains of the movie set follow, along with the cobbles *that a moment before had lined the streets, and then the trees, the topsoil, everything that is, or was, Xanthos, that dream city about to rejoin the collectivity of dreams that is Earth2. As the stuff of nature and the stuff of artifice, the inanimate and the human are sucked into the sky's black maw, to be propelled along its seemingly infinite digestive tract towards a state of being, timeless, ghostly, yet coadunative with our own, the smirking gatekeepers retreat, follow their new, if unwilling, disciples back into the intelligent light of the fibresphere, The Wound closing now, its edges suturing themselves until all that is left is an intense point of black luminescence that – like a point of light on an old, unplugged TV, a point inverted, a tiny, black midnight sun – mesmerizes until it disappears amongst the azure, no evidence of catastrophe marring the slopes of the island, and only a cleared, empty lot waiting for the developers to appear and begin building a new hotel or condominium.*

Through her tears, Dahlia cries out, 'I shall make them die interesting deaths!' Mosquito too has begun crying. But it is Dahlia's wails that predominate. 'I will, Cap,' she sobs, 'I really will – I shall make them die interesting deaths!'

We are two days out to sea. Dahlia has assumed command and regales us with wild, desperate tales of how she means to get back to The Belt and fulfil her mission of setting the controls of her starship for Zeta Reticuli, of embarking on an impossible voyage that she has a notion will end in planet-fall on a world which she will terraform in the likeness of Cythera, her wild imagination's home. And she will do this, she says, even if frustrated in her proposed rape of this world; even though she is virtually penniless. Jaruwan rarely leaves her ghost's side; the two have quickly developed a singular rapport which I am at a loss to be able to fully explain.

Three weeks, now, or is it four?

I like to lie on my bunk, curled up in the foetal position, believing that I am a child, no, less than a child; believing that I am in that *super-infantile* state; that time has reversed and I have been transported back, back, beyond childhood, beyond the womb, beyond life, finding a quietus in a state of being as easily confused with death as death is with annihilation. It might almost be the anniversary of my last, final happiness: that immortal season spent in a little village in Xiengkhouang province after travelling across the globe to find Jaruwan Flynn née Visuthsri, and, oh, most *amazingest* of grace – for I had never believed I would find her; my flight was a conditioned response; the convulsive jerk of a shattered nerve – again setting up home with my child-bride on the banks of the Mekong River. I would spend the mornings printing up the leaflets she would distribute on the streets; and I would spend the hot, drowsy afternoons stretched beneath a mosquito net, her body next to mine, the high waters of the river flowing through my head and carrying me to a land where I might enjoy such sweet unrest for ever. It was only later, when we moved inland, into the hills, where Dahlia had hoped to bring her message to those who were poorest, that our beautiful reconciliation became troubled. Sick with fever, half insane, I pleaded for a return to Laos; to no avail; we followed the truculent, ragtag armies of the Rim across Burma, India and, reaching Samarkand, along the Old

Silk Road towards Europe, its closed doors hung with metaphorical placards threatening watchdogs, armed response, a long and cruel death to any who attempted to intrude upon its lands. Jaruwan was stubborn; in imploring her to turn her back on the children of the crusade, I think I only confirmed her in her self-disgust and, ultimately, the disgust she came to feel, perhaps had always felt, for me. Reliving that monotonous journey in my imagination, counting off the mules, the camels, I dozed off. A river was flowing past; I could hear it. It was the Mekong. And I knew that once more I was in our little house, all sorrows redeemed, all mistakes righted. Within that dream, I dreamed again, dreaming of the dreamer.

What I liked best, those days, was simply to lie by the river, my thoughts stilled by the wind, the wind becoming my thoughts, taking me back, back to when I had been happiest, those moments of quiet love with Jaruwan. My life had been anchored, then; lying next to her, the wind of time, perhaps, blowing my thoughts forward to now, it sometimes occurred to me, the wind gusting, paralysing all doubt, that I was lying not by the river at all; I was just the dream of an earlier self, an insubstantial presentiment of a time when I would be alone; perhaps I was lying inside my house even now, far, far away, in another time, another country; perhaps I still lay next to Jaruwan, my love quiet, certain, real; and I would imagine that, at any second, I would awake; and awake, I would find it true. Yes, that is what I liked best, those days, to dream those dreams of constancy.

I snapped into the mad, bad halogen-bright light of consciousness, lost, lost. The incessant rumble of the engines shook the walls. The air conditioning clicked on. I looked at the clock, watched its second hand pass the numerals one through twelve.

Time begins, I thought. And I knew, then – in a whizz-bang of insight – that an effective way out of my prison, maybe the only way left, was by inducing time to stop; only by masterminding time's destruction would a crack open in the invisible walls that separated me from my home; it would take but a sudden rush of horrible excitation, a brief vertigo, and I would be falling again into the vortex that connects the worlds, in that timeless moment to know freedom.

This morning Dahlia visited me.

In the bowels of the submarine, as in the Town, I find that I am supplied with a good, if less than comprehensive library; reflecting Dahlia and Tarquin's tastes (and, fortuitously, of course, my own) it is stocked with a preponderance of books on the cinema. I hadn't opened a book for years, but the boredom of the voyage is such that, on waking, I forced myself to select several large volumes, sit down in my room, and peruse them. Ignoring the text as best I could I pored over the stills, the turning of each page accompanied by a thrill of suspicion that, at any moment, I would find myself coming upon an image of Jaruwan. But a fickle world had meant that the only image left to me of my child star in her wonder years was the living, walking, talking reproduction that breezed in upon my privacy just as I had been carefully examining a full-page spread of vintage 'eighties Pia Zadora.

'I want to let you know,' she began, leaning against a bulkhead artfully disguised with unwholesome yards of black crêpe. 'I mean, why I left Tarquin the way I did.'

'You don't have to tell me anything,' I said, 'if you don't want to.'

'But I do want to. You gave me life, Mr Flynn—'

'Not me alone. It was a whole production team. A whole nexus of factors. And besides, it was you yourself – I mean Jaruwan – who did the most to bring Dahlia Chan to life. She'd make up lines as we went along. I didn't even direct. I was strictly a behind-the-scenes man.'

'He told me to keep the dream alive,' said Dahlia, ignoring my mini rite of absolution. 'He told me to seek out Cythera. What choice did I have? I had to do what he said. I had to, you see' – and her vitreous eyes narrowed; held me with desperation, as if I were her psychosexual confessor – 'I was his slave-girl.'

'I'm sorry,' I said, 'about Tarquin.' I recalled Randy McAllister, the bodybuilding champion – school of Steve Reeves – who had played Captain Tarquin in my movie. Dahlia's Tarquin had looked quite different; had spoken differently, too. In just about every way, he had been an improvement on his original. Is that why Jaruwan played love games with her own image? Because she had discovered in her a reflection that, if distorted, seemed better, happier, than the chronic reality of her own life? Was Dahlia, for Jaruwan, somehow the person she had always dreamed of being? The sweetness she had tasted but never enjoyed?

'He may find a way out, you know. He's clever. He's done it before. He came to Earth2 to rescue me. Death holds no surprises for Tarquin.'

'Tarquin isn't a ghost?'

'A word doesn't really exist to describe what Tarquin is. To describe all of us, you might say. At least, neither the term "ghost" nor "human" is sufficient. Our flesh is the stuff that you find at the junction where EarthI and Earth2 meet. This' – she held out her naked arm, its raven down glistening beneath harsh neon, and pinched the skin – 'this is the stuff Earth3 is made of. Stuff that can exist in either the land of matter or the land of intelligent light. It's like ... spiritual.'

'He reopened The Wound,' I murmured, my attention meat-hooked, refrigerated and canned by the way Dahlia squeezed her flesh into a pale brown morsel of seditious baby-fat; the gesture had recalled nights spent cradling Jaruwan within my arms, her young, taut body reprimanding my hoary caresses.

'We *are* The Wound,' said Dahlia. 'We're what The Wound was waiting to become. That's what a Cytherian is – a wound that seeks healing, a bloody gash that longs for an imaginary body that will take away its pain and make it new. The cauterization: it doesn't matter. IDSIC will learn that eventually, to its cost. This flesh you see here – it's only the beginning. It's the incarnation that allows The Wound to begin its quest. The Wound must find Cythera if it is not to fester and die. That is its one consuming ache, its remorseless need: to find the island of Cythera.'

'Yes,' I said, 'I understand.' I wasn't sure if I did; but as Dahlia had spoken I had felt the universe closing in upon me as it had on other occasions, whispering, *You are the one, you are the centre, you are God.* Everything in my stateroom became unutterably, terrifyingly meaningful. Colours deepened, intensified, until they began to sing, to form chords, vast harmonies. Energy flowed along my arms, into my chest, down my legs; it was the energy of naked Being, the power of containing all things within myself, of hearing all, seeing all, feeling all, knowing all. I closed my eyes as I felt my heart begin to flutter. 'Perhaps that is why *I* have been here all along,' I said, my throat dry, 'to provide The Wound with a body, a voice.' I reached for my medicine. Dahlia saw my discomfort; helped me pop several pink, red and blue horse pills into my mouth. I gulped down a tumbler of water from the night table. Dahlia stepped back; waited patiently for me to calm down, to become human again, a mind and body within the orbit of human language, an entity she could communicate with.

'I've come here to tell you something, Mr Flynn.' There was foreboding in her voice, a doomy register at odds with her schoolgirl lisp. 'About Jaruwan and me.'

'Jaruwan?'

'You know she's dying?' I shook my head; then nodded, confused, shocked; not by the question, but by my mute answer. It was the first time I had allowed myself to acknowledge what, in the classified strongbox of my heart, I had long known: that Jaruwan was beyond the help of treatment, no matter how expensive, ingenious, newfangled or bizarre. I nodded the more vigorously, the words still refusing to come. At last:

'I knew she was positive, but—'

'She's dying, Flynn. She's a Cytherian, too, even if she doesn't have the flesh. She's hurt bad. She needs healing. And I can save her.' Placing her hands on her hips, her nostrils twitching with distaste as she filled her lungs with recycled air, she sat down beside me; put a hand on my thigh. 'For that matter' – holding her breath, her voice tight – 'she can save me.' Exhaling, she stuck a thumb in her mouth, a crude little-girl theatrical such as I had schooled Jaruwan in; and then she began to champ, worrying the digit as if she would sever it at the joint. 'I can't live without him, Mr Flynn. This person I've been, am – she must cease. I have to remake myself; and for that I need Jaruwan. The Wound needs her. Needs her to be whole. *We* need her, Mr Flynn. We need each other.' She held out a hand, the pollex dripping blood. 'We'll be surfacing within the hour. I think it's better if you just come and join us outside.' I was about to seek clarification when Dahlia raised a sleek, plucked eyebrow, and I bit my tongue, filled with a giddy surmise. 'Seeing is all, Mr Flynn. Seeing ... is ... *all.*'

I stood on the conning tower. Icicles bedizened its hand-rails, the chill jewellery like a magian gift celebrating an immanent death, an immortal birth. Across the tumult of the sea, a vicious wind cut through my dufflecoat and penetrated my thermoware. Unfamiliar with my survival gear's mechanics I felt myself being quickly reduced to a state of glaciation as I experimented fruitlessly with the controls. At last, after nearly despairing that my techno-illiteracy would leave me frozen to the boat's icy hull – a shamanic totem from another age – a surge of ions rose from my feet and up into my withered groin, heat spreading luxuriously throughout my torso. Spindrift cast off the high waves of the South Atlantic had left me sodden, lacerating gusts infiltrating my bold defences, freezing the hairs of my poorly thatched pate and fusing my feet with my boots, my boots with the sub's gummy, steel-plated skin. What goddess, what Venus, could rise from such savagery? Below, Jaruwan and Dahlia, their attention given wholly to each other, began slowly to take off their clothes.

Mosquito stood next to me. 'So,' she murmured, 'the Captain's *Übermädchen* is going to perform her party piece.'

'You're playing the bitch - even after what happened to Tarquin?'

'Why shouldn't I be? *I can't live without him*, says the little madam. Well, I can't either. He was my last hope.' Mosquito stepped up to the guard-rail to get a better view of proceedings on the deck; and as she passed - almost unrecognizable now, swaddled in so many layers of clothing, with only a small brown face evincing that a human form, or, perhaps, a non-human simulacrum, moved beneath - I knew that I was looking into a mirror. I saw myself, the little girl who was raped and who never got to grow up; the little persecuted girl who I had become when my father had torn off his human mask and revealed to me the dark secrets of the universe.

'Do you understand then?' I said. 'Have you been abducted? Are you a Cytherian?' I moved to her side.

'I'll never be a Cytherian now. Dahlia won't allow it. She wants to keep the flesh to herself. I don't think she's much interested in The Army any more. Once the melding is complete she'll be entire. She won't want anyone else coming with her to the stars. Except Cytherina, maybe.' The angel of the blessed isle circled high above us; and then, as Jaruwan and Dahlia completed their disrobing, descended to a point low on the horizon where the sun was bursting through a bank of inky clouds, shafts of stabbing light turning her wings orange, pink, magenta, as if in preparation for public martyrdom; and there she hovered, a sainted image of benediction conferring a promise of the life to come. Jaruwan rushed into Dahlia's arms, her restructured eidolon impervious, seemingly, to the sub-zero cold in a way my wife could as yet only envy. Human, she hung about Dahlia's neck – her waif's body limp, raw – as if she embraced a meatpacker in the depths of a cold storage facility, a sister who had the power both to butcher and to resurrect, the fairy godmother of abandoned meat puppets; and in the depth of my wife's eyes shone a new heaven and a new earth, soft, grave, incorruptible. Dahlia raised her hands above her head; clapped; and there followed a clamour like that of a great steel door slamming in the planet's iron, uncaring heart. Cytherina spread her pinions; ascended, the sun's rays now breaking through the clouds, shattering them in exaltation, shards of light fracturing the bleak sky. On the deck of the *Narrenschiff III* woman and girl writhed against each other, their flesh grown pulpy, strings of steaming skin hanging from their arms and thighs. Like viscid plastic figurines – fashion dolls left too close to an electric fire – they began to meld, their moans and then their screams taking to the air, like wounded birds, to flock about Cytherina; and the aural torture that I had been subject to in the courtyard of The Children's Home once again ripped into my skull as the bird-woman, who had herself begun to scream, swooped across the prow of the submarine to land at the spot where Jaruwan and Dahlia had collapsed, their bodies joined at the head, breast and hip as if as by way of an incomplete division of the ovum. A shadowy halo seemed to surround the Siamese twins, a circle of black light that began to flicker with blue-white tongues of plasma. They seemed inside some great, sepulchral membrane, their bodies – the wild grapplings finished now, the metamorphosis having assumed an irrevocable course – a single fire-baby aglow within the tomb of the resurrection. A plasticky, black slag had congealed across rivets and metal where the afterbirth had flowed over the deck. The wind had died; and the crash of the waves had so abated that I could hear the far-off keening of gulls. 'The fake becomes real,' said Mosquito, startling me, 'the real becomes fake. So it will be for the people of Cythera.' And she turned and began to clamber down the hatch. 'But not for me,' she called out, her voice echoing through the boat's steel innards, 'not for me, no, not for little Mosquito.'

The black circle that had been scored out of space and time shrank, revealing the creature of Earth3, alone, confused, atop the shiny, wet stage on which she had performed her one-act play, this epilogue so at odds with the noisome drama that had preceded that I wondered if the melding had been successful. From where I stood I saw only a naked girl who, though untroubled by the Arctic conditions, was nevertheless plainly lost and disturbed as if struggling to remember who or what she had been, who or what she was. I swallowed a few pills; descended and gathered up her clothes; but which clothes, I thought? Jaruwan's or Dahlia's? I picked up samples of each. Coming up to her, I put out a hand, stroked her face. She looked at me curiously, pitifully, as if coming out of a thirty-year-long coma.

'Flynn?'

'Yes,' I said, 'that's right, it's Flynn. Easy, easy—' I steadied her as she took a too eager step forward, coltish legs trembling, about to buckle, fold. 'Quickly, put on some of these things.' She straightened herself; but she wasn't Jaruwan's height and neither was she Dahlia's and she had some difficulty mixing and matching garments before she could achieve a reasonable fit. 'You look good,' I said. 'I mean, you look *well*. How do you feel?'

'I feel good, Flynn. Good and well. I feel—' She circled me, swinging her arms in routine callisthenics, nonchalantly taking in the horizon. 'I know what to do,' she said, as if to herself. 'For the first time in my life, I know what to do.'

'Can I help?' She examined me closely, all of a sudden the older sibling who is about to ask her kid brother to *Say that and look me in the eye*; and then she softened, her face modulating with the compassion I had often seen her extend to the stray kitties she would adopt from the temple grounds of her local *wat*, to return them a few months later after their skittishness had precipitated a neurasthenic crisis, no LA shrink to console her back there, only the over-the-counter pills that she hoarded as if expecting the immanent collapse of the tranquillizer industry.

'No,' she said. 'It's over, Flynn, I'm not—'

'Jaruwan?'

'No, Flynn, not Jaruwan, not Dahlia. Just a person who's been given the chance to take another swing at life. Maybe that doesn't amount to much in the big, fat scheme of things. But for me ... Flynn, I never had a life. Jaruwan Visuthsri. Dahlia Chan. The world had them in its sights as soon as they were born. But' – and she pirouetted like a mad ballerina who has escaped the asylum to dance half-naked in the winter streets – 'I've been born again. And this time, well – I can't really explain it. It's good, Flynn, it's good, it's good.' She no longer owned the face of a ragamuffin, of one burdened with junkie dead flesh;

gone too was the too-perfect sweet-nothing pantomime mask of the pubescent leading lady, the artificial, lacquered cutesiness of her youth as absent from her countenance as the etiolation of the punk girl-child who was to become the international hooligan who had been imprisoned in the Town; whoever had executed this latest portraiture had revealed the human form divine, the glory beneath the skin. It was hard to ascertain her age; though not a child, neither was she grown up. But the transformation that had been wrought was only partly biological (if anything in biology even approximated that spliced body *nouveau*), the nature of her sphinx-like beauty and its power signalling that the core of her being had left the quotidian world, had travelled beyond the countries of compliance and sublimation into a land where adults and children encapsulated each other; there, before me, in the strange blood and lymph that constituted a universe of desire and its outward perfection, in the radical, perverse, obsessional, imaginative flesh which now hung from her bones and which testified to her change of citizenship, a message was sketched to be read by all as she passed by – *Here be someone*, went that document, *in whose reconstituted selfhood is embodied fanaticism of appetite and a pluralism of form, Her Cytherian Majesties thereby request and require in the name of Cythera the Blessed to allow the bearer to pass freely without let or hindrance through all the worlds of childhood, the ancient kingdoms of cruelty and love ...* 'This time, Flynn, well, it's just that I know that *this* time I won't fuck up. Don't you see it's all around you? It's everywhere. Can't you hear it calling us? Cythera, it's saying, Cythera, Cythera. I've arrived, Flynn. I've finally arrived.'

I took her in my arms. She didn't resist. But we embraced like father and daughter, not like husband and wife. She was wrong, of course. I knew well that this prison called Earth is not Cythera. Her new body was a marvellous thing, but it was terran, and however much I might fancy it sanctioned by my true father, the exiled king whom I still prayed I would help one day to reassume his throne, it remained a crossbreeding of the twenty-first century mediascape and its rabid consumers. But I couldn't bear to tell her that. She was, for so many years (all the years that I had known her) always a Cytherian *in posse*; if she had found a little happiness, however deceptive it might subsequently prove, I was glad. It would be pointless, horrible, to remind her that her true home was not to be appropriated by the naive expedient of calling on its holy name; it lay across a fathomless void. But she would learn, or rather remember, soon enough; for accompanying her *imaginative* transformation into a full-fledged subject of Cythera would be the concomitant abductions, the abuse, the agonies of the heart, too surely to follow, now, unless, as I had sworn to do in the Town, I was successful in my proposed mission of contacting the Reticulans by thought-wave, commandeering a Reticulan saucer and blasting-out of the ecliptic of this emulation, into real time, real space, real power. Only when I had somehow managed to free the other members of the royal family might I hope of raiding and defeating our gaolers in their home system. *We must hurry to Antarctica*, I thought, *we must hurry. There, amongst the ice fields, I will throw my thoughts higher than the highest star, to be caught by those who delight in our damnation.*

From behind, like a thief, her bare feet silent against

the glassy hull, Cytherina, the tall, imperious angel of Nowhere, joined our embrace, sealing this pact, this new, buoyant if unequal treaty with this sad, false world, her great, pale wings enfolding us in an eiderdown of silky feathers even as the sun stole back within the coverlet of the clouds, thin rays poking through the stark, louring sky like needles that, one after the other, were snapped into halves, quarters, eighths, the slivers disappearing into a vaulted chiaroscuro that was falling, falling, to close like a trapdoor on an oubliette of love and despair.

CHAPTER EIGHT

I have renounced penmanship. The smudged manuscripts I completed while incarcerated in the Town and while aboard the *Narrenschiff III* are tucked between my thermoware and skin, a greasy wad of surplus insulation that they will discover when performing my autopsy - or, thousands of years from now, dug up by a team of archaeologists, when I am dissected, embalmed, laid out for posterity, my remains, perhaps, transported to a local museum where school teachers will lecture children on who I was, what I did and how I came to meet my end. The insulation is effective; I am surprised that, since beginning my account, I have covered so much ground, accounted for so much paper; scribble,

scribble; graphomania, I think my stepfather-cum-psychiatrist called it. But I am again as I was in my American heyday, a vanguard-man of the postliterate, my new companion a chic little Dictaphone with a big, optical disk that I bought on the Riviera; enough memory for me to be able to recite about a billion more pages, I would think; but I will bring this narrative to a conclusion (though it will rather, I think, bring me to a conclusion) long before then. A conclusion, now, is all I have left and all I have to hope for.

Jaruwan is gone. Jaruwan-Dahlia, that is. She left our party after we had docked in the Palmer City marina. She will stay in the night-kissed Riviera awhile, she said, but means to head back to Thailand.

Let me report that I am neither devastated nor even surprised by this development; her decision to leave, once anounced, had immediately seemed inevitable and right. I would not have wanted her to embark on a futile journey to the stars with the dregs of The Army of Revolutionary Flesh; and, after long insomniacal nights of consideration and reconsideration aboard the *Narrenschiff III,* I had decided that I would not want her to accompany me beyond the confines of this prison, Earth. What I propose to do is dangerous, fabulously dangerous; whether I succeed or fail, she will be safer within the switching operations of the neutron star; too many factors – not least the problem of whether or not a body exists into which she might be downloaded – argue against her joining my uncompromising adventure beyond this known, emulated universe. *'I'm glad you're going home,'* I'd said, *'your real home, that is. Cythera is not to be found in this fake old hypersphere of ours. Leave the others to waste their lives*

amongst the wrack of dead planets and exploded stars.'
She nodded, sagely; but a deep breath and closed eyes
signalled that she wasn't entirely reassured.

*'All the bad memories about your father, all the
flying saucer stuff – remember, Flynn, remember what
I've always told you. It's horseshit. Cut loose.'*
    'Remember? Just promise this: you'll try to remember me.'
    'I'll always remember you,' she'd said, *'monster.'*
And she had given me a little peck on the cheek; laughed.
*'My Svengali, my Phantom of the Opera, my Meshulam
Riklis, my poor, poor, mad, mad monster.'* Then she turned
her back on me and disappeared into a crowded shopping
mall to buy her air ticket.
    Her handmaiden, Cytherina, the angel of the blessed
isle, accompanied her.
    For I know, now, who Jaruwan was, is and always
will be; not Dahlia Chan, no, no; she was never Dahlia
Chan; Jaruwan's true name is Cytherea.
    And I will never see her again.
    Now I am at the Pole in the deserted city of
Amundsen-Scott, its population fled ever since the bubble
burst in the mining industry. I watch the remnants of The
Army of Revolutionary Flesh prepare the *Narrenschiff IV*
for launch. (*'We wanted a spaceplane,'* one of them had
tutted. *'Too expensive. Like nuclear weapons. Had to settle
for a piece of Russian junk. Yeah, I guess money's always
been a problem. But you wait and see. We'll still get to
build our starship. Our mission: it's only just begun.'*) And
day and night tiny figures scuttle about the floodlit
gantry that lies just beyond the city limits, a salvaged
Energiya rocket with its customized *Buran* strap-on

readying for blast-off to a near-Earth asteroid, next to it,
a Long March 3 teetering from a crumbling gantry, the
Chinese firework eclipsed by the bigger rocket's inter-
mittent leaks of oxidizer, supernatural mist swirling in
melodramatic flourishes that recalls to me some of the
high points of my career: Dahlia Chan emerging from
night-time wharves to confront her enemies, dry ice
licking about her calves; Dahlia Chan in the Mad
Martinet's Maze, feeling her way along mirrored walls, the
familiar special effect offering its clichéd backdrop;
Dahlia Chan battling Dr Goldberg's Golems, recently risen
from their sleep in that old Jewish graveyard we were sued
for appropriating as a location, FlynnFlics burnt so bad I
had to sell my house, the same mist circulating amongst
tombs and undergrowth as had circulated throughout
every one of my movies, a crass transfusion of style that
had kept the beast alive long enough for a quick return.

I am going out for a drink.

And I am drinking in the *Annabel Lee*, a ghost karaoke
that restores some original meaning to the word 'ghost';
for it is deserted, ransacked, like the other ninety per cent
of Amundsen-Scott, this city – following the boom-bust
pattern of other settlements in Antarctica – haunted by
shades, tormented by echoes, racked by the too-eagerly
ingested poisons of nostalgia, the whole continent, except
for the playboy stamping ground of the Riviera, rapidly
become a ghost of its past.

Downing my Scotch, I walk behind the bar to find
out whether any of the other optics are functional;
fiddling with a few switches, the lights go up; I am pleased;
so many other establishments are devoid of power. Taking

advantage of my find, I request *The Kingdom of Childhood* on the club's teleputer and am delighted to discover that – far from destroying the Dahlia Chan site – the stepfathers have been unable to prevent it from going back on line. Cult enthusiasts of Dahlia's work must either have freed-up her old venue or created a new site with copied vids, stills and disks.

PLAY.

A cadre of beautiful Viet Cong girls – in their early teens and attired in black silk pyjama tops and matching bandanas – kneel in the mud and ashes of a burning village in the Mekong Delta casting shy glances through their long, raven manes at the two GIs who guard them. Seeing the young lieutenant approaching through the smoke of the incinerated hooches, and made sensible of his intentions by the lethal, if somewhat apologetic stare he awards, first, her face, then her cleavage and then, a painful swallow contracting his raw, seared throat, her long, bare folded legs, Dahlia Chan rises, waits, passively, while being freed from the chicken-wire binding that secures her hands behind her back, tentatively rubs her wrists to restore circulation, and then, accepting the gift of a bayonet cursorily detached from an M16, follows the lieutenant to the make-shift arena where – to satisfy the morbid appetites of bitter, weary soldiers – she will be forced to fight one of her sisters to the death.

FREEZE-FRAME.

(Ah. That scriptwriter with his thing about communism, about it being soft, yielding, superfeminine, while capitalism was hard, macho. Thought the real history of the Cold War was a secret one. Thought the Cold War was a Sexual War. He was quite the philosopher.)

FAST FORWARD.

STOP.

PLAY.

In the heavily fortified Hollywood mansion where she has been imprisoned – along with other former POWs – by a clandestine society of war veterans addicted to the replaying of games initiated in the killing grounds of Vietnam, Cambodia and Laos, Dahlia Chan presses an eye to the keyhole of one of the slavemaster's rooms. The room is bare, save for a few pieces of Italian furniture – an armchair, a sofa, a footstool – its walls draped in heavy, purple bombazine, its marble floor chequerboarded in alternate whites and blacks. The gaffer orders his crew to train their lights on a confused, squinting figure – a girl dressed in skin-tight plastic pedal pushers and a sheeny brassiere made of the same material – who, at first raising a hand to shield her eyes from the glare, by degrees relaxes, tries to ignore the camera operator, crouched over his weapon, whose pose inspires recollections of friends cut down by American machine-gun fire in the shrapnel-scarred ruins of Hue; tries to ignore the clapper boy, whose chalkboard reads Death of a Runaway Slave-Girl, Take One. *The errant gladiatorix, spurred by a whisper emanating from the director's chair – 'Improvise, improvise, let your feelings out, let everything come naturally' – fastens her attention on the man who stands a little way in front of her. The co-star – tall, dressed in loose cotton shirt, leather trousers and high, piratical boots, a knife and sword buckled to his side – is a hackneyed rendering of that cinematic stereotype 'the buccaneer'; he trains upon her a cool, indifferent gaze, waiting for her to initiate the*

proceedings. *Prompted by more suggestions from the director, the girl at last essays a line:*
'Am I really to die?'
'I must do my duty,' says the stone-faced executioner. The director slaps his thigh in encouragement.
'Yeah, that's more like it,' he says. 'Listen, baby, imagine it's the future. And every pretty girl wants to be a slave. The Earth's ruled by aliens in human form – men who require a tribute of Earth girls to serve and amuse them. And there's no shortage of volunteers. Despite the fact that, like, the masters are real cruel sons-of-bitches, cold-hearted aristocrats who rule over their harem with rods of steel, you copy? Now, you really want to submit to these guys, to wait on them, to be under their discipline, understand? Go to it. It's the future, baby, you might as well have a little fun.'
   The girl's nervous fingers fumble at her cleavage as she unhooks her brassiere and, disengaging her breasts (they seem almost to sigh in relief at being spared this officious constraint), lets the plastic lingerie slip over her shoulders, down her arms and to the floor. 'Lord Tarquin is known for his cruelty,' she says as she unfastens the thick, wide belt and slowly unzips her pedal pushers. 'The other slaves speak of it often.' She pulls aside the loosened folds of polyvinyl chloride and runs a hand down the exposed V of brown flesh, long fingernails momentarily toying with a few stray ringlets of exposed pubic hair. 'Is a girl to expect no mercy then?'
   'Mercy? Expect? It is for a girl to beg, a master to grant. But one who has attempted to flee our Brotherhood should not dream too fondly of a reprieve.'
   'A reprieve?' She walks over to him, galvanizing her

hips in imitation of the exaggerated pelvic display ritual of an automaton. The brittle music of her steel-tipped heels against the floor expires. Putting her arms about her interlocutor's neck, she stretches and, on tiptoe, attempts to meet his lips with her own. But the haughty buccaneer refuses to respond and, thus rejected, disdained, renouncing hope of contact, she draws back. 'No,' she says, piqued, her midnight eyes flashing with sparks of frustrated desire, 'certainly no reprieve. I do not set my hopes so high. I suppose I must only hope that your skill does not equal your pride, for if it does I must suffer indeed.' The two players in this film-within-a-film, this scratchy homemade snuff movie, now seem so immersed in their roles that they tremble, their breath laboured, mock-eighteenth-century dialogue drowning in an ur-babble of barely controlled lust, the little moans, whimpers and sighs that collect on the doomed actress's lips counterpointing the creak of her co-star's magisterial leather as, putting an arm about her waist, he shifts his weight so that he may unsheathe the elegant stiletto that hangs from his thigh and – unbeknownst to the foolish slave still paralysed by her executioner's impassive stare – hold its exquisite tip a fraction from the taut, girlish, umber skin a thumb's-width above the pubic bone.

FREEZE-FRAME.

(Jesus, what was that actress's name? She'd been older than Dahlia. Seventeen, if I remember right. Thai father, American mother. From the Valley. Willing to do anything to break into films. Suzanne? Bunty? Tina? Lucille? 'I must only hope that your skill does not equal your pride, for if it does I must suffer indeed ...' I should have shot that scriptwriter for the dog, the cunt-hound he was.)

PLAY.

Dahlia, one hand between her legs, watches, licking her lips, as the man she has immediately fallen in love with slips an inch of razor-sharp steel into his victim's unprotected belly. The slave-girl gasps, eyes widening, her long red nails digging into the nape of the blood-thirsty pirate's neck, her breasts thrust becomingly towards his chin; then, as he presses the blade a little further into her flesh, to skewer her uterus on its slim cold misericord, screams; begins, unhurriedly, to writhe, her pelvis describing slow, elliptical circles, as if she were again imitating the coquettishness of an automaton, these writhings increasing in speed and intensity as the remainder of the stiletto is dispassionately eased into her firm, yielding abdomen. As the hilt is pushed flush against her, she attempts, in a paroxysm of agony, to escape her killer's thick, pumped-up arms, placing her palms on his chest, clawing, pushing, wriggling; but his embrace is not to be thwarted, and as she looks down, for the first time since her wounding, to where, transfixed, her belly's gentle swell meets a gloved, intractable hand – rivulets of dark wine drenching her fleece and trickling onto the marble floor – she swoons in acknowledgement of the hopelessness of her struggle.

Dahlia feels a hand on her shoulder. A fellow slave-girl bends down. 'They say we must get to the shelter. There's been a "state of emergency" message on TV ...' She trots away, beckoning Dahlia to follow. Rising, Dahlia hears, from the locked, secret room, a cry from the dying girl that makes her once again take up her position at the keyhole, even though she knows that intercontinental ballistic missiles are even now hurtling towards the western seaboard.

STOP.

(I check my pulse. Unfortunately, I have nothing with which to check my blood pressure. Stock footage of atmospheric tests, we'd used, to signal The End Of Life As We Know It. I'd thought about substituting an alien invasion sequence as the bridge connecting the first part of the film to the last, but found I couldn't afford the SFX. Besides, it might have been interpreted by my Reticulan captors as unwarranted hubris; an abduction might have resulted; a punishment equal, or worse, to the punishment meted out to my little runaway slave.)

FAST FORWARD.

PLAY.

Dahlia walks through a devastated Paris, the twisted remains of the Eiffel Tower her only point of orientation amongst a flattened landscape of rubble, melted iron, fused glass. She is heading towards the Ionian Sea where the post-apocalyptic fighting slave championships are to be held and where she suspects she may once again meet her buccaneer ...

STOP.

(To hell with the tachycardia.)

REVERSE.

STOP.

PLAY.

'Ohhhhh! You do me too cruel, too cruel! Now I know my sisters spoke true. Master is skilful. What can a girl do but beg? Mercy, Lord Tarquin, mercy, mercy, pleeeeeze!'

FREEZE-FRAME.

(Damn that scriptwriter; damn him; it was to have been my finest film. It was to have been one girl's odyssey

through pain, humiliation and despair into a post-apocalyptic world where the twenty-first century's hidden cultural agenda of sexual domination and submission became fully realized and where, paradoxically, marvellously, transcendentally, she was to find freedom and love.)
REVERSE.
STOP.
PLAY.
' ... *Mercy, Lord Tarquin, mercy, mercy, pleeeeeze! Let me—'*
STOP.
(Damn. All those games Dahlia and I would play: Did my scriptwriter simply transcribe what he had heard while standing outside our bedroom door?)
PLAY.
Her executioner has retracted the knife and loosened his grip about her waist; legs buckling, she, nevertheless, her nails tearing at his shirt, has managed to clamber back up the sheer escarpment of his body to just such a sufficient height that she might press her punctured abdomen into his groin, to perform one last grinding, pelvic dance before collapsing onto the tiles.

There is a brilliant flash that penetrates the heavy drapes lining the room; a curtain ignites; panic breaks out amongst the film crew who, forgetting the director's injunctions to save the reel – for it is only by way of these underground pornographic shockers that the Brotherhood can finance its gladiatorial obsessions – race towards the door.

The little voyeur draws back, hurries down the hallway. Dahlia has seen the future, a future that, soon, will be all that is left of the world.

And she has seen the face of the man who will become her own obsession: Tarquin, the underground porno-star and sex murderer who, in the post-apocalyptic world, will be transformed into the cruel, refined, debonair pirate captain who will surely some day rescue her.
STOP.
FAST FORWARD.
STOP.
PLAY.

Dahlia looks out of the barred window of her cell and down onto the busy streets of Xanthos, yellow light filtering through the iron grille to cast a grid of lemon lozenges across the crude, stone floor, the silhouette of a passing gull occasionally bisecting the tessellated rhombi of tiny suns, its caws growing fainter and fainter as it wheels out to sea. The captive slave-girl's eyes focus on the masts of the pale, ghostly ship that has this morning arrived in the harbour; and as the sun sets behind its sails – turning each furled canvas into a sheet of coruscating, beaten gold – she puckers her lips, as if retreating into one last, hopeless daydream before the onset of night, when she must paint her face, robe herself in the expensive dress supplied by her gaolers, and be led to the execution chamber.
STOP.
FAST FORWARD.
STOP.
PLAY.

In the small room inside one of the turrets facing out to the sea, Dahlia submits to the touch of the executioner's assistant who unbuttons her white, cotillion

*ball gown and allows it – in a susurration of crushed
silk and satin petticoats – to fall, crumpling, to the floor,
a mouse scuttling across the flagstones into the sanctum
of the wainscot as she steps out of the encumbering
finery and bows her head.*
FREEZE-FRAME.
*Illuminated by two carbon-arc lamps the victim is
revealed wearing a scintillant, milk-white corset, the
executioner's assistant – caught in flagrante by the
camera – surreptitiously fingering the laces and whale-
bone stays under the guise of positioning the condemned
girl so that she may be the more readily served by his
master (his fingers will stray to the tops of her gartered,
white silk-stockinged thighs, her white-ribboned,
ash-blonde pageboy wig, the fluttering hands, tied
behind her back with white, silken cord); the light
refracted by the elaborate corsetry ransacks the
chamber's shadows, kaleidoscopic haloes dancing before
the assembled witnesses like the evoked spirits of cruel
admirers, malevolent suitors.*
PLAY.
*The frock-coated executioner steps forward; grasps
his victim firmly by the wrists and, placing a silk cushion
over the back of a high oaken chair, bends her over it, so
that, her rump salient, her legs splayed (strappy
high-heeled feet struggling to find purchase), she can
only look over her shoulder in helpless fascination as the
elderly man who has been mandated to inflict excruciation and death holds the tip of a thin, envenomed
blade to the gusset of her cache-sexe.*
FREEZE-FRAME.
Close-up of perineum, silk-and-lace shrouded vulva,

buttocks that clench, wiggle, contract in apprehension, the blade now, like the corset, refracting shards of blinding, argent light.

PLAY.

The executioner hesitates, lifts his head, distracted from his work by a shrill whistle that cuts through the muggy air like the overture of a nemesis.

STOP.

(In the movie theatre, the children, delighted, would be clapping their hands. Pirate Peter is about to eviscerate Namby-Pamby Hook. All my films were made for children ...)

PLAY.

A terrific concussion; and then the door falls inwards, crushing the young apprentice and knocking the older man's legs from under him. Captain Tarquin – magnificent in designer corsair apparel – plucks the delicate, but lethal stiletto from the executioner's hand and plunges it into that decrepit, octogenarian's heart. Slinging his booty over his shoulder – Dahlia squeals with joy – he races from the room, drawing his sword in preparation for battle; the unwary prison guards, however, have already been dispatched by his men who, shouting encouragement to their lord of lechery and love, clear a passage for the eloping, monstrously romantic pair.

STOP.

FAST FORWARD.

STOP.

PLAY.

Cannonballs rain down upon Xanthos. Buildings explode in ragged puffballs of red-and-black. Stunt men and women leap from concealed trampolines through a

confetti of splinters and pulp-and-chipboard hail; run,
flames streaming from their clothes, through the torched
ant's nest of the streets, screaming with bathetic displays
of angst. Horses are felled by shockwaves, throwing their
riders into pools of burning oil. And through it all sprint
Dahlia and Tarquin, dodging through the panicked
multitude, the overacting extras, the sightseers who
should have been out of shot; and above it all – against
swelling strings and lugubrious xylophones – rises the
concluding song of the film's soundtrack, sung by Dahlia
Chan herself:

> Here, you have again reached the very
> anteroom of paradise.
> All past emotions – all fears, loves, hatreds,
> desires – are in equilibrium.
> The bliss. If only you could have remained
> here. If only you had never left ...

The lovers reach the quayside and scamper aboard
the ship, the pirate commandos following. And, as the
cannonade reduces the city to atoms, as the volcano
erupts and the awakened sea-monster – my salute to
Gojiro – stirs from the Mediterranean's depths, the shout
is given to raise anchor.
Tarquin cups a hand to his mouth. 'Watch if you will,'
he shouts to his prurient crew. 'Discover how a master
services his slave.' Dahlia stands akimbo, a torn stocking
revealing a bloody gash in her right thigh, the corset stippled
with tiny red dots, as if she had been pecked by a flock of
sharp-billed birds. 'So rape me,' she says, her lip curling, 'rape
me, if you're man enough, that is.' And so with the sun

*setting behind the mist, the vaporous shroud refracting its
starburst of ultraviolet like a ghostly diamond – Tarquin
bends her over a capstan and enters her savagely, rejoicing
at her cries of no, no, no, no, no's as the ship moves to the
swell of the waves, the churn of the sea.*

STOP.

FAST FORWARD.

STOP.

PLAY.

*Captain Tarquin walks up to the camera; addresses
me from behind the screen.*

'*Well, did you like that, Mr Flynn?*'

'I always like watching *The Kingdom of Childhood*.
I think, for all its faults, it's my best movie.'

'*Sure it's your best movie. Watched it all the time
when I was a kid. It sort of, well – did things to me.*'

'But these days it hardly seems like the same film.
Who invented The Army of Revolutionary Flesh? Was it
you or me? *The Kingdom of Childhood* – is it my
compromised memory, or does the narrative change each
time I watch it? You guys over there – you're a protean
bunch of bastards, aren't you?'

'*You know, Flynn, "over here" on Earth2, we're of the
same opinion about you fellas. You seem unstable, like,
your lives run backwards and forwards, always with a
different beginning, middle and end. Truth seems to be
that both our worlds are in flux right now, sort of flowing
into an Earth3. How's Dahlia?*'

'Fine,' I lied. 'I'm sure she'll be in contact soon.'

'*It doesn't matter,*' he said. '*I mean, she's here too.
Another version of her, that is. You know, I think I might
stay here for a while ...*'

'But you were both intending to travel to Cythera.'

'*Ah, it'll be here soon enough. EarthI: it's becoming acetate. And the image-world seems to be growing more real. In the end the distinction between real and artificial, image and substance, is going to be redundant. We don't have to go to Earth3 – it's coming to us.*'

'Is that the way the film ends? With you and Dahlia sailing over the horizon and into Earth3?'

'*Maybe,*' he said. '*Maybe. Who knows? Jesus, Flynn, I really don't understand how all this will end. Never really understood how it started. Beginnings, ends – there's just this continuum now, a series of mutating scenes and dialogue. Me and Dahlia – we're mutating too. I don't think there'll ever be a finale.*'

'Promise me, Tarquin – promise me that you'll treat her well.'

'*Oh, not enough that you were Dahlia's sugar daddy, huh? You have to become my father-in-law. Don't worry, Mr Flynn of FlynnFlics Co., I'll treat her better than you ever did.*'

'Goodbye. I hope you find Cythera.'

'*So long, Flynn. Did I tell you I've been writing my memoirs? I can't just stand here talking to you. Besides which, my slave-girl's waiting and, man, she's got a thirst.*'

STOP.

All trajectories lead here. To the downtown lights of the big white polar opus, Amundsen-Scott. Past the lonely filling stations, the hostelries strung along the Cimmerian turnpikes, the mirages of the desolate transcontinental roads. Here, to the neon-lit omphalos of the world's underside. What preceded the highway's end? Where did all originate? Back, back, arteries and nerves coagulating in that vanishing point of time when I popped out of the womb of Swineville, Finktown, Disgusting City. A foot pressed the accelerator to the floor almost at once. What markers along the journey? What lows, what highs? Nothing now that does not seem part absurd, wholly marvellous. The endless plains, white, white and smooth as ground glass, lie before me at the conurbation's edge, inviting. Let the marvellous prevail. Let there be reprise of a face elfin, juvenescent, beautiful. Let there be diminuendo of dank nightmare, of domestic crime. From Wardour Street to the mansions of Beverley Hills, the compulsion to *épater* a persistent itch beneath my skin, I had been as much the whoremonger as I had been the eternal child. Violence – your violence, Daddy, if later, my violence – was always followed by restitution, chocolates, toys, money succeeding cruelties most bizarre. You taught me how to buy smiles, silence. Or so it had seemed after I could *épater* no more and I cried for forty-eight hours without respite. After therapy I put aside whoring. I put it aside now, the overcast days of the past, but for the bright trace of a fabulous girl, a dying fall, a glissando of negativity. Concentrate, this is the end time, think only of her: Liquid eyes, like black glass refracting the light off a midnight ocean, eyes unnaturally big, set between wide temples and beneath a shocked bob of spiky, unruly hair; a little upturned nose; a mouth compact yet capable of scandalization; a jaw line chiselled, delicate as fine china, accentuating the expansive forehead and those eyes, so crystalline, so huge. Too intense, the vision; my meditation evaporates. Instead: A poster half peeling off a wall advertising the scenic delights of Antarctica; dead towers overarching, like trees in a night forest, props from an illustrated book of fairy tales; men in old, malfunctioning thermoware hugging themselves in the doorways of deserted nightclubs and arcades; and children, refugees from topside, prowling the alleyways, the nimbi of street lamps spotlighting their flittering, bat-like forms as they race purposelessly through the city's maze. A Sno-Cat speeds by, showering me with atomized snow. All is nought. Zero. A zero of unparalleled chill. I wish I had had time to complete my last project before I had headed East. It was to have been an interpretation of *Oliver Twist*, its working title, *Twisted*. No one will ever know now whether Oliver escaped from Fagin, had sex with Nancy, the goblin girl from the sewer cities beneath Saffron Hill the Great, no, no one will know whether he was restored to his rightful place in the celestial home of Mr Brownlow.

Walking through the abandoned city I noticed an uncharacteristic sodium-glow issuing from a window in the top storeys of a condominium. My legendary eagle eyes did not fail me; the outline glimpsed of a bob-haired, dark-skinned girl parading across the window-frame's modest, cheaply lit proscenium, made my heart skip; it was unmistakable; unmistakable enough, at least, for me to give a little shout of Yes! But in the interval in which I stopped to gobble some pills and gather my strength recognition forced a retraction; this apparition was not Jaruwan, it was not Dahlia; it was the envious one, Mosquito. I had not seen her for some days now; indeed, The Army had repeatedly inquired after her whereabouts. I entered the building; discovered that the lift, as well as

the electricity supply, was functional; and ascended to
where the lady boy had chosen to hide herself away.

'Mosquito?' I walked into the bare, frozen lounge –
the electricity was insufficient, it seemed, to retain the
heating system – and was confronted by the sight of a
young woman in a luxurious mink coat kneeling at the
foot of an armchair; before her, reclined in death's ease,
sat the petrified remains of a man. As I drew closer, I
recognized that the man was Tarquin. His skin was glazed,
as if he had been smeared with albumen and then
refrigerated, his nose, ears and eyelashes adorned with
tiny icicles. One of his arms was cast over the side of the
chair, a small handgun dangling from the crook of an
index finger. 'What—'

'I've decided not to go with them,' said Mosquito. 'It
was a mistake coming this far. I can't be like those
revolutionary fleshers. I'm looking for something else. I
don't know what. Maybe I'll never know. But I know I
won't find it in the stars.' Lowering her head, she nuzzled
the dead man's crotch. 'He was so beautiful. So fatal. So
sweet.' She regarded me, askance, with tearful eyes. 'How
shall I get home? I so want to go home, Flynn. I'm sick of
this cold, sick of these people with their stupid ideas.' She
ran her fingers along the length of her captain's marble
thigh. 'Kito might take me back, I suppose. If I promised to
be faithful. If I promised to work hard for her. She might
even give me back my fangs.' Like a forgotten celluloid
queen straining to reward the patience of an equally
ancient admirer, she summoned up a tired smile. 'You'd
like me with fangs. They made me look *so* cute.' Her
dreamy expression suddenly changing, a look of spite
manifesting itself in her eyes, she sat up, brought a closed

fist down onto the corpse's stomach. 'These Englishmen: they've been my ruin. I mean, I follow this guy all around the fucking world, and what do I get? A mouth full of popsicle, that's what. I must be crazy. Fucking crazy.' And then she again softened, as if exhausted, drugged; sat back on her heels and replaced her forehead on the cold, austere, penitential cushion of her would-be lover's genitalia.

I backed away; breathed against the window and left a message with my finger, *I am just going outside and may be some time*. Then, closing the door with baby-sitter's nicety, I retreated, eager to suffer no further discomfiture.

I walked out into the ice fields, heading towards the monument that marks the Pole, a thin, tapering, mile-high sculpture commemorating the expeditions of Roald Amundsen and Bobby Scott. When I reached my destination – it's a slow forty-five minute walk from the city's outskirts – I lay down next to the massive granite plinth which supports the bronze-clad sky-needle and switched off my thermoware, taking care to rip off the control panel and sling it into the anonymity of the ice to pre-empt a cowardly change of heart.

CHAPTER NINE

I look across the white plain to where the *Narrenschiff IV* is being prepared for launch, the countdown echoing through the ghost-town streets of deserted purlieus, empty warehouses, abandoned tenements and the ripped, plastic biospheres of dying, wind-blown hydroponic marsh. A young boy is at the controls of the Buran – I see him before me; he has my nine-year-old face; *adios, amigo* – as the raggle-taggle Army of Revolutionary Flesh grits its teeth in anticipation of the good vibrations which will signal their departure from Planet Earth. I seem to hear voices, children's voices carrying over the hard, crystallized ground as if over a sea that extends beyond this universe's horizons. What do you want,

children? I ask. We want to go home, they say. We want to
go home to Cythera. Then leave behind your wicked
stepfathers and stepmothers, leave your families and your
treacherous friends, leave them all; seek out the place
where you were before you were born, even if it means
travelling to the stars, the countless archipelagos of the
stars, to find your dream island, your home, your Cythera.
Forget the ravings of an old, embittered man, a child
trapped within an adult's body; it is surely possible that
you may recreate my home world in the outer reaches of
this unreal prison; godspeed, then. Perhaps, some day, you
will construct enough computer power to recreate
Tarquin, to recreate Jaruwan, to recreate me. Perhaps that
is the way we will eventually defeat the Reticulans. By
engineering an emulation that will encompass and
supersede their own. I will send no messages. I forsake
telepathy. Let me die in the hope that we shall rise. Let me
die into the vision astounding.

I feel the coldness pinch; soon, it will cease to hurt
and I will at last sleep without fear. Without fear? What if
the Reticulans do as my father – that is, my stepfather,
suggested – and reverse time so that I again begin to walk
down the long road of travail that has brought me to this
cold and lonely spot? I cannot bear to let my thoughts run
so freely; let me have done with thought. I hope only for a
little rest, a brief, untroubled sleep during which I may
fear no threat of abduction.

I see something in the sky, a bright light that streaks
across the constellations, stops, inertialess, and then flies
off at a forty-five degree angle. It dips to the horizon;
approaches, low, skimming over the ice; and as it nears I
recognize its blinking nimbus of multicoloured lights, its

hubcap-like skirts that spin with a faint accompanying noise that is like that of a muffled buzz saw. The saucer lands; douses its light show; a door opens and a stepladder unfolds onto the hard bleached iron of the ice. A man is walking towards me. I put my hands over my face, knowing the worst has come, that I am about to be retaken and locked in that cruel, secret room, from which, it seems, I shall never know deliverance.

I feel a hand upon my arm. Steeling myself, I open my fingers and gaze between my frozen joints. A grey-haired, bearded man is kneeling over me. Though old, he exudes strength; and the bejewelled circlet about his head denotes authority, perhaps even kingship. He gathers my body into his arms, soothing away my uncontrollable shivers. 'The bad dream is over,' he says.

'Is it really you? Is it really—'

'Hush. You will wake up soon.' He holds up a crystal before my eyes. It is like a hollowed planetoid, a limpid stone world of rainbows and sparkling rivers, of corn-flower skies, verdant hills and lush, lush meadows, of silver forests and moon-lit shores. There, the statue of Venus rises at the opening to a wood, her marble limbs entwined with roses and eglantine. A swarm of *putti* fly above the recumbent lovers, rustling like silk. It is a world of dark palaces too, of dragon-desire, of wolves racing across glittering winter landscapes, of little boys and girls roasted on spits at the midnight banquet of the Erl King. 'Pretty child, will you come with me? My daughters shall look after you ...' All opposites are reconciled. And entranced, I hear but the drowsy wind of time and space far, far away. I know at once he is offering me a vision of Cythera.

'Dad, *please* put everything right. Can you do that?'

'Yes,' he says, holding me close, his eyes grown big and lustrous, 'I can put everything right. There, there, of course I can. Of course.' And the touch of his icy hand on my brow was not, as formerly, a clammy intimacy that promised a night terror; it comforted, it consoled. 'You know, it never really happened. None of it. The memory recovery they inflicted on you: it was wrong, wrong. Forgive me. I should have been there.'

'But, but—' My throat contracts; my chest muscles loosen. The long-awaited and now too-eagerly greeted sobs pulse through my shrivelled body, and I jiggle like a skeleton on puppet strings. 'The eggs they took from me,' I pant, in between a hiccup and a gulp, the end of my race in sight, 'the operations, the implants ...'

'There, there. It was just a dream, a dream. It is over, my darling.'

And I know as he picks me up in his strong, warrior's arms, presses my head inside his thick cloak so that, in my frightened animal's burrow of darkness, I hear and feel crisp, confident strides, my true father retracing his footsteps, *know:* I am the creator of this emulation; it has always been me, all that has existed has been by and through my consciousness; and so it falls to me, now, so simply, so unsuspectingly, to bring the walls of the prison down and allow a restitution.

We enter the saucer ...

This is it, the last take, the last reel.

For I know now that I can possess nothing; all the things that have passed through my life, all the people; it seems, finally, that I can hold on to none of them; they are all insubstantial, ghosts; I cannot even possess my own memories; I cannot even possess my own self. I am a cacophony of voices, a confusion of masks. But in my poverty lies my freedom.

I hear the rocket's engines engage with 740 tonnes of thrust, and imagine, in my blind haven of peace, a plume of fire ascend into the night sky.

Though she is not aboard the *Narrenschiff IV*, the lift-off of the big *Energiya* seems, for me, a confirmation that Jaruwan has at last escaped (I always knew she would; she is the child I never had, the child I never was); it is a firework display celebrating her release. Not for her the journey across a null and all-but-measureless void; she was navigating that nothingness all her life; *her* lift-off began the day old Flynn made his last wrap, this day today, when his own homegoing – I send out the message at the speed of light – lit her soul's afterburners to send her, wherever she might be, at Mach Love towards a new, unravished country; Jaruwan, my precious, I love you, take care, please, please, take care.

To possess nothing. To be nothing.

I am so tired of this selfhood; but the dead do not walk; and it is only in death that we become something completely other.

I snuggle into the warm arms of the true father, the king of the island of joy, the one who offers solace, who disburdens and makes free, the one who is wise and good, the one who is brimful with unconditional love, the one who will defend me.

Then, flashing through the ether, a response. Unheralded. Unhoped for. From a distant part of the world I hear Jaruwan's voice. *It doesn't matter, Flynn; it doesn't matter if you were really abused or if your abuse was delusional. It doesn't matter if your memories are false or real. The consensus is blown. All that is real is unreal, all that is unreal is real. Choose, Flynn, choose your reality.* And her voice becomes bird-like; she is singing to me. *Beware. I am the source of the river and its delta. I am the beginning of your journey and its end...* I know then that this is the moment of awakening. Am I image or corporeal? Am I mad or sane? I must take my leap of faith, I must commit myself to the Night, gracious Night and its song of transcendence. I am Tarquin, I am all that was contained in Tarquin, all his alters, all his voices, just as I am Dahlia Chan, just as I am Mosquito. I am all the voices of all the worlds. And all the voices now becoming no more that we may become disburdened of ourselves, become something blessedly other. I am over the ice, swimming in an ocean now, the current strong, too strong to turn back, the sun disappearing beneath the horizon; I am swimming through the mist, the ever-thickening mist; and it is warm, warm and dark, dark and lovely; and swimming over the edge of the world I hit the ground and run, running through the deserted aerodrome at the end of my garden, the long grass stinging my calves, urging myself forward, moaning, *free, free, free*, the wasteland giving way to hills, meadows, lakes, trees, rivers; and I am running now into a salmon-pink sunset, my hand tightly grasping Jaruwan's own, the Angelus ringing in my ear, all past emotions – all fears, loves, hatreds, desires – in equilibrium. Oh Dahlia, Dahlia, Dahlia Chan – the bliss. The bliss! From the stern I watch as the last bastion of resistance falls and the town is consumed. I turn away. Again, a film of water droplets; vapour begins to envelop us and I know it is soon, now, very soon that it will end, these prisons within prisons, these worlds within worlds, all existence annihilated in a fireball of love, and the abject loneliness gone, now, and the knowledge now and for ever, the beautiful knowledge that is truth here to stay, like the presence of my resplendent king, cradling my head upon his breast as we ascend through the clouds, through the thinning air and into eternity, the night beneficent and wonderful, now, until the end of time; the knowledge that I will at last come to Cythera.